Demon's Call
Requiem of Stone Book Two

Julie Boglisch

Published by Rogue Phoenix Press, LLP

Copyright © 2021

ISBN: 978-1-62420-558-3

Editor: Sherry Derr-Wille

Dedication

To my wonderful parents, my editor and my middle school teacher. To all of those who supported me with my first series and to you, reader. Your support means the world to me.

Chapter One

Scavenging was never fun, Alex decided as he shifted what meager supplies he had been able to obtain so they fit more comfortably in his grasp. Especially when the area he was scavenging in was all rock, like most of the Underlands, and the river was quite a distance away.

He let out a long breath as he walked down the path he'd followed much more hopefully a few hours earlier. To either side of him were Ari and Leon, slaves of his friend Milos who sent them on this little expedition to begin with when Alex had found himself too restless to stay put.

He would have argued, but...

He shifted his grip once more, massaging his still-sore throat. It was only a little over a week ago when he damaged it while trying to escape from the capital of the Underlands, Raynout.

He glanced up at the day stones miles above his head, their glow a gentle warmth so far below. It was strange to think about how only a few months ago he was still home with his mother and the Grand Duke, exploring caves and seeing the day stones up close at the opposite end of the Underlands. Now the duke had been murdered and he was searching for his mother alongside a witch who had been forced to flee her home after a young man tried to force her into marriage, and an Alertian, or Demon Hunter, who had descended into the Underlands for, well, Alex wasn't completely certain. He could still remember when the man had tried to kill him and later saved him from one of the deadly creatures of the Underlands.

Ironic, he thought, *considering I am part demon, or well, one-part water demon, one part another type of demon and one-part human.*

He had found that out the hard way when Milos had convinced him to be "captured" and brought to the Martinets, or Slavers, guild. He certainly learned quite a bit there, but it left him with just as many questions. He shivered at the memories and quickly squashed them down.

Truth be told, the other thing that was bothering him right now was that it was too quiet for his liking. He was used to the silence of the Underlands, having traveled by himself for quite some time. When traveling with others, it was uncanny not to have conversation or just other sounds besides footsteps.

Unfortunately, neither Ari, the young female slave who was a heck of a lot stronger than she looked, or Leon, the slightly older man who had lost his arm a few weeks ago, had much to say. They were true definitions of slaves, sold to Milos upon his descent from the Overlands, though they were later rescued from their original master's abode and followed Milos, Rita and Alex due to that fact.

Alex honestly didn't mind their company, but he did wish he could learn a little bit more about them. After all, if not for the Grand Duke and his mother, he could have very well ended up like them.

He almost did.

He shook his head once more. He needed to stop thinking about the what ifs or what could have happened. That wasn't going to happen, not anymore. No, he needed to focus on the next leg of their journey. Milos said his mother was to the north, the last Demon stronghold and refuge within the Underlands. The path there was nearly impassable if the stories were true.

Alex glanced up, hearing the sound of quiet conversation, though he noted with bemusement it was quickly turning into a quiet shouting match, though mostly from one side.

He crested the little outcropping and glanced down the path to see his last two traveling companions.

Rita, with her witch's hat and red hair tied into a braid down one side of her face, was leaning forward, finger pressed into Milos' chest. Milos, his darker skin indicative of an Overlander, contrasting sharply with Rita's almost see-through skin, was on the verge of rolling his eyes, hand resting on the hilt of his sword as his long blond hair trailed over his shoulder, the red of his signifier gleaming in the light of the day stones. The chainmail underneath his clothes only added to the harsh impression.

Alex shook his head with a sigh, jerking Rita out of her tirade and causing her to notice him. Milos just shook his head as if to say "you didn't notice him?"

Rita ignored him, hurrying forward up the path. The red ribbon, her signifier, trailed over her skin as her worried gaze met him. "There you are, I was wondering if you were coming back. I knew I should have argued more to..." She trailed off and shook her head. "Never mind, come on." She glanced toward Ari and Leon. "Thanks for keeping an eye on him by the way."

"Of course." Ari's voice was quiet but the barest hints of a smile crossed her face.

Leon nodded, taking the food he'd acquired and bringing it over to the little pile by the bank of a lone winding river.

The gentle water of the river sang, calming Alex's thoughts a bit as a soft melody trickled into his ears.

This river, one of the many rivers of the Underlands, sang gently to him, a constant reminder of his presence and his abilities. He wondered what else he could do now that he was no longer scared at the prospect of being a demon.

That, unfortunately, would have to wait until after he got his voice back, which couldn't be soon enough.

Rita examined her friend quietly as Milos walked up to Ari and Leon to check on them. She didn't mind; it was helpful having others around and she knew she wouldn't be able to stand the Underlands by herself. How Alex did it for over a week, she had no idea.

She walked over to Alex, watching him as he placed a pale hand into the river, fingers swirling in the cold water. The tension seemed to slip from his shoulders as he sat there, black hair framing his admittedly

3

very pretty face. She found herself staring at her friend...no, that wasn't the appropriate word. How had she still not figured out the proper word?

She pulled herself from that thought as he glanced up, spotting her. He smiled weakly before returning to watching the water.

That also confirmed her thoughts as she took a seat beside him, adjusting her skort in the process. "Still no good?"

Alex shook his head, a frustrated frown gracing his face.

"I had a feeling." Milos spoke from behind her.

Rita peered back to see he was organizing everything that was scavenged. The goods ranged from Rita's paltry supply of herbs for her potions to the fish Milos had somehow managed to catch from the river to Alex's own goods.

"It's been a week since we left the capital. I know you strained your voice and demonic powers by causing a veritable tsunami from rain alone." He peered up before continuing, "That's why I wanted those two to keep an eye on you. I understand you want to help and believe me, I understand your restlessness with the situation, but keep in mind your situation right now."

Alex clicked his tongue, clearly frustrated.

Rita snapped her fingers, leaning back on one hand. "Geez, I think he gets it." Rita couldn't hide her annoyance as she continued, "We know he strained his voice from singing for gosh knows how long to give the demons and other slaves a chance to flee the capital, but demonic powers? How could he strain that?"

"He is a half-human, half-demon hybrid, and a newly exposed one at that. It might have been too much for his newly awakened demonic side to use that much power in that short of a span of time. I'm guessing he'll regain it, but it might take a while."

"So, wait...how long?" Rita felt herself pale slightly. To be unable to speak was horrifying in her book.

"I don't know." Milos shook his head before tossing some herbs to her. She barely managed to catch them, fumbling slightly. "Anyway, let's get something to eat before we head out. The land is starting to narrow around here along with the paths. Hopefully, we'll be able to come across someone with a boat or some other means of travel that will bring us to the refuge." Milos glanced up, gaze flicking to Alex. "You still want to go, correct?"

Alex nodded sharply, blue eyes gleaming.

"I wonder what the demon refuge is like? It would be nice if it's actually somewhere safe," Rita mumbled, but stood, stuffing the herbs carefully in the satchel strapped over her shoulder. Honestly? She was glad they were moving again. She was sick of just sitting around doing nothing. That wasn't exactly her strong suit.

She paused, remembering the quiet conversation she had had with Milos before Alex returned.

"Why are you still traveling with us anyway?" she asked, turning to Milos to do something else, anything else besides sit around waiting for Alex.

"I don't have many other options at the moment." He spoke evenly, unamused. "Plus, I did promise Alex I would help find his mother."

"Yeah?" Rita tilted her head, wondering. Was that the only reason why Milos was sticking around?

"You don't believe me?"

"Well, you did try to kill Alex when you first met."

"You're not letting that go, are you?" Milos spoke, posture stiffening just the slightest bit. "I'm an Alertian, I sensed demonic energy..."

"That didn't mean you had to chase us down." She growled, not even sure why she was still blaming Milos. Maybe because she wanted someone to yell at and he was the closest target? Maybe...

"On the contrary, I did." He tilted his head just enough to be staring down at her, arrogant lout. "An Alertian's duty, as you might recall, is to track down and destroy demons. I was only doing what I thought was right."

Rita clicked her tongue. Well, admittedly, he was right and he did save their asses after he caught up with Rita and Alex, but she still wasn't going to admit that.

"Though it seems you don't agree." He smirked and she growled again. *"Don't worry, if I had a choice, after making it back to the capital*

and picking up Ari and Leon, I would have been happy going my own way. It was Alex who decided to look for his mother and you decided to deal with your ex."

"Ex..." She twitched and Milos sighed.

"My apologies, that last bit was insensitive."

Rita would have berated him, but he was right.

She pulled herself from her thoughts. It still didn't answer the question of why Milos was joining them. She knew she was following Alex because she had nowhere else to go, what with her home burned to the ground and her parents.... She shook her head. She wanted to see this through. She wanted to protect the last thing she had left but Milos? Milos was an enigma and it bothered her to no end.

She stood, brushing down her skort. Her signifier, or dual signifiers she noted as the gentle silver gleam threaded through her hair, drew her attention and reminded her just how much she had lost. Those two things and Alex were all she had left of her home. The signifiers, proof of her existence, were so...she let out a breath as they began to follow the river, their footsteps echoing loudly over the landscape. She tugged herself from her thoughts.

Of course, that only led her down another path of wondering as she pulled herself over a boulder strewn over the pseudo road.

What was Alex thinking? She wasn't sure how she would feel in his shoes. To find out he was a demon and his mother lied to him about it? Rita couldn't fathom what that must feel like, what he must be going through. To be lied to all of your life and have to struggle with the truth all on your own. She wouldn't wish such a thing on anyone, especially someone as gentle as Alex.

She still remembered when she first saw his demon form, smoke filled the air as her home burned around her and yet, she remembered his song, his gentle voice causing the fire to dwindle and die as water doused everything. The black and blue wings expanding outwards from his thin frame and the utter fear in his eyes and voice as he finally caught sight of his bloody hands.

She still remembered the way he tried to scrub the blood off until he was almost bleeding himself, on the verge of tears even though he saved her.

He was a gentle soul, put into a situation he shouldn't have to be in. It angered her, she admitted to herself: it angered her to no end. His mother never said anything. He had to find out while fending for his life on the run and yet, there wasn't anything she could do about it.

At least, not until they found the woman and asked her reasoning behind why she never said anything, as well as why she would abandon Alex to fend for himself.

Some distant sound must have caught Alex's attention, because he perked up from helping Leon and Ari pull themselves up a cliff face. She had somehow managed to scramble up while deep in thought. That would explain why her hands hurt. She shook her head, stopping her eye from twitching as she watched Milos swing himself up with ease, following behind the others. "Show-off," she muttered under her breath, catching his attention.

He raised an eyebrow but didn't respond.

Well, whatever, the lout was a strange one but she was used to that. To be honest, she was kind of glad he had decided to join them, even if she had no idea what his reasoning behind it was. Though she would never admit that to his face.

"Alex? Is that the same river?" Milos called from the back, startling Rita.

What was he talking about? When she noticed Alex shaking his head, she let out a huff crossing her arms over her chest.

"Mind explaining?"

Alex sent her a sheepish look as Milos waved it off. "We're almost there anyway." He glanced ahead. "I think we're going to be reaching the end of our walking soon."

"That would be a relief," she said, ignoring his vague words.

He was right; she had no doubt she would find out soon enough and, considering neither of them was saying anything, it probably wasn't too dangerous.

It did bother her, though, being the only one of the group who had the weakest senses. Being one step behind the other two in that regard was not a fun experience, no matter how much she tried to hide it.

7

~ * ~

Milos watched his comrade quietly. Comrade...what a strange word. The half-demon perked up slightly, tipping his head just enough to show he was listening to something. All Milos could hear was a faint thrum in the distance. Rita appeared annoyed, arms crossed, but silent after acknowledging his words. She must have realized her senses weren't strong enough. He glanced at Ari and Leon, who were staring back at him. He gestured ahead, indicating for them to continue on. If they came across something, they would warn him. He wasn't worried, and they were aware of their job, to act as scouts for the three of them.

Milos continued forward, listening while keeping half an eye on their surroundings. This rugged terrain was perfect for an attack, even if he didn't sense anything. It was ingrained. He was an Alertian, a demon hunter. If he couldn't track enemies, he would be dead within seconds when coming across a demon, or so he once thought. The young man in front of him was enough proof that quite a few of the truths he once held were wrong. He frowned. Why did things have to be so complicated? His goal, when he first came to these lands was simple: kill and take the head of Satan's child, then return back home to the Overlands. He had a demon right in front of him and yet, he found himself fond of said demon, to the point where he couldn't imagine hurting the young man or his irksome friend.

His thoughts flickered to *why* he was still here. Truth be told, there was no reason for him to be following Alex or Rita to the north, no matter what he told Rita earlier. He already told them where they needed to go, and in truth, it would only be bothersome, heading to a demon refuge as a demon hunter, especially without supplies.

He withheld the sigh that wanted to slip through his lips and instead focused back on the situation at hand. A situation caused by said demon. Only a few days before, they were in the city of Raynout, an elevator trip away from home, and yet, Alex had asked for his help in finding his mother, only to end up dealing with the Martinets' guild and Milos eventually making himself out to be siding with the demons, even if that was not his intention. He was simply at the guild to make sure Alex was safe. Alex and Rita were the ones to decide to free the demons and slaves held within.

This led to a few other problems, until they eventually shut off the only known means of reaching the Overlands, of reaching his home.

In a way, he figured, it was probably good. However, knowing *them*, they would probably find out that he helped demons instead of killing them. He could still remedy this situation. After all, they were heading to the one area his ancestors were unable to find. Finding the hidden demon refuge would be more than enough, solidifying his place amongst them. Still, truth be told, he hated lying to Alex about why he was there. He knew the boy would be hurt and angry if he actually said anything.

No, he was well aware of his position. Of his decisions. He was fond of Alex and, to some small extent, Rita, but...

The sharp sound of footsteps coming to an abrupt halt caught his attention. His gaze flicked to Alex, then toward the turn up ahead.

He mentally berated himself on not sensing the strange energy swirling around the corner, faint as it was. Thankfully, Alex seemed to notice.

Ari and Leon briefly glanced back, as if to confirm and, after Milos sent them a nod, letting them know to go ahead, they hurried around the corner, out of sight.

Rita just stared in confusion. "Hey? Why aren't we moving?"

"There's something up ahead," Milos mentioned, coming up behind Alex who was carefully peeking around the corner.

Rita joined him as the three of them peered after Ari and Leon. On the other side, dipping sharply down a steep slope, was a large stone enclosure. On the far side, Milos could just faintly see a dock with multiple boats of varying shapes and sizes bobbing in the water of what was most likely the river he'd been hearing for the past few minutes. Not that far away from the docks was a hut big enough to fit a small family of lower-class nobles, plus a few slaves.

"Who's that?"

Milos followed Rita's gaze toward a... man? Milos decided; it was a man of indiscriminate age, short and bent with a shaved head and large eyes, seen even from where they hid.

The man, probably the dock worker, walked purposefully up to Ari and Leon, already talking about something or other from his short smile and waved arms.

Milos pulled back and let out a breath. "I don't sense anything and it seems this is as far as we can go, following this route."

"Understatement," Rita mumbled, staring up at the sheer cliff just past the hut that blocked their way forward. "So, what, are we just going to walk down there and talk?"

"Not right away." Milos turned, leaning against the rocky outcropping. "Give Ari and Leon a few minutes, then we'll head over. I'm curious about something."

His thoughts flickered to the line of boats. He wasn't knowledgeable on ships, but even to his untrained eye, those ships barely looked seaworthy. The north was supposed to be filled with dangers. Having a ship that could easily break apart on impact with anything wouldn't cut it and with Alex being the only one who had a probability of escape through the use of his wings—if he ever figured out how to use them—he didn't want to judge their chances.

"Yeah, so sit and wait, huh?" Rita crossed her arms over her chest as Alex pulled away, joining in the sudden huddle.

"Do you have a better suggestion?"

Rita snapped her mouth shut as Alex rolled his eyes. They sat in silence for a few minutes, the distant sound of running water surprisingly soothing to his ears, especially after the incessant silence of this underground world.

That was the thing he wasn't sure he could ever get used to: the all-encompassing silence. As beautiful as these lands were with their clear water, extravagant landscapes and strange, almost mythical stones, the silence made it eerie, uncomfortable. He would have thought he would feel claustrophobic, however, the ceiling, so high above, made it feel like a separate world, not an underground cave.

Finally, after a few more minutes, he peered once more around the corner to see the man showing Ari and Leon the boats, still gesticulating with all his worth.

"Satisfied?"

He peered back toward Rita with a flat, "No." With that, he stepped around the corner and headed down the slope, a startled yelp sounding from the young woman. Alex, probably having realized at his expression, was only a few steps behind. Rita hurried after them, grumbling incoherently under her breath.

It was almost as if a switch was flipped as they came around the corner and down the slope. The wild gesticulations of the tiny man stilled as his gaze hovered over the three of them before settling on to Alex, shock flickering on his face.

He quickly bowed to Ari and Leon before racing over to them, almost diving toward Alex's feet, causing the boy to stumble back in shock. While Milos might have been amused to watch the following interaction, he found himself in front of Ari and Leon. "What did he speak of?"

Leon answered, gesturing toward the boats, "He's a boat salesman, stationed up in these parts for travelers."

"It's been six years since the last customer." Ari's voice was quiet, as usual, but her words were pointed.

Leon nodded. "He made mention of the waters north of here being perilous and that not far down this river is the Dregas' land."

Dregas? So more of them did exist outside of the one they met months ago. He shouldn't have been surprised.

"Good work." He turned in time to see Rita pulling the man to his feet, cackling as Alex covered his face, probably flustered from the sudden onset of attention. It was strange, how the man reacted upon seeing Alex. Though, Milos shifted, taking note of the gentle swirl of air around the trio. Alex and Rita were quite normal, if Alex's was a little constricted.

The man, however? He wafted a strange air, similar to Alex. A faint wisp of magic curled around him.

A half-demon? No, that couldn't be it.

Was he in contact with a demon?

He pushed the thought to the side, joining the group as the man brushed himself down and Rita took a step back, controlling her laughter, though just barely.

"Alex?" The man blinked before looking at said boy, Rita having probably used his name to calm the man. "Ah, I assumed..." He trailed off before shaking his head. "Let's just say, I have a sixth sense about certain things and leave it at that." He turned away, heading into the little cottage as Milos hummed in thought. A sixth sense, huh? "Anyway, will you all follow me? I'm going to need to fix a few statements I gave those two over there." He gestured toward Ari and Leon, briefly giving Milos a nervous look.

"He's fine, he's with us, after all." Rita waved it off, getting a faint nod from the man before he disappeared through the doorway.

No surprise. If what Milos sensed was true, having an Alertian in the mix would be rather problematic. Speaking of, that more or less confirmed what he thought. Alex seemed confused upon spotting the river and Milos could faintly hear a strange noise, barely heard over the waves lashing against the docks.

There was another river.

"So, he's weird."

Milos glanced toward Rita as they watched Ari, Leon and Alex step inside, them only a few paces behind, but slowing to a stop.

So, the girl noticed. "He's been without customers for years," Milos pointed out before peering ahead. "However, the main reason is probably because he is a gate-keeper."

"Huh?" Rita blinked, peering up at Milos. "What do you mean?"

Milos pursed his lips in thought before striding forward, causing her to scramble after him. "Demonic energy." He glanced toward her, causing her to stiffen. "At first, I thought it was because he came in contact with other demons quite frequently, but it's possible he might be similar to our friend."

"Wait, what? A human-demon hybrid?" Rita blinked, surprised.

"Possibly, you did state that some survived after birth, but only retained their human attributes. Is it far-fetched to assume that a few of them might have been more in tune with demonic aspects, similar to an Alertian?"

12

She opened her mouth, as if to argue before snapping it shut, comprehension dawning on her face, followed by a frown. "So, if he is able to sense demons, that would be why he noticed Alex so quickly."

"It would also explain why he is now inviting us inside instead of selling us a matchstick boat." Milos waved. "He probably is a boat salesman, true, but he's also probably here to help those like our mutual friend to get to the north."

Rita shook her head, letting out a breath. "Who would have thought? I only recently knew human-demon hybrids were a thing and now..."

Milos shrugged, heading inside. They couldn't talk outside the whole time, it was already suspicious enough, and while he trusted Ari and Leon to watch out for Alex, he would feel better if he could keep the boy in his sight around someone he didn't trust.

The inside was surprisingly warm and comfortable. A heat stone crackled to one side in a little hearth and couches and chairs were set up around it. Alex was sitting in one of the chairs, perturbed. Milos could guess why as a bowl of soup was pressed into Alex's hands by an overeager boat salesman. He heard a faint growl and glanced over to see Rita blush deeply, quickly turning her face away from him. The man, once satisfied that Alex wasn't going to move for a bit, turned to Rita and Milos. "Your two comrades informed me of your situation. You want to head north through the rivers, correct?"

"Yes. We spotted some boats outside." Milos leaned on one leg, watching the man quietly. "Those wouldn't survive more than a day on regular waters."

The man's eyes gleamed, intelligence and amusement clear on his face. He was very aware of who he was talking to, so Milos' assumption was correct. "Smart lad, aren't ya?" He frowned, glaring. "No surprise from an Alertian. What are you doing with this boy?"

"We're helping to find his mother," Rita said bluntly. "You are the first person we've seen out here since we've left the capital, not counting evading a few Martinets. I, for one, am tired of walking. Milos, here, has been helping us, much to my distaste, to get here in the first place."

"I'm glad my efforts have at least improved my status from lout to simply distaste." Milos couldn't hide his lack of amusement, or the slight twitch in his eye at her words. Alex let out a sigh, not even bothering to turn to look at them.

"Mother, eh?" The man turned away, stepping away from the hearth and through a doorway off to one side.

Strange, Milos thought, he hadn't noticed the door when first walking in. He knew he scanned the room, so how...?

His thought was promptly cut off as Rita scurried forward. "These are seer glyphs! Is this actually a seer's door? I didn't even know they still existed. That must be the potion used, it's a work of art."

Her hand darted into her satchel, her fingers tugging out a small notebook and pencil he hadn't even known the girl had on her. Within seconds, she was already flipping to the next page, almost feverishly noting down the details of the door.

Other than a faint hint of magic, Milos wouldn't have thought much of the inauspicious door. He shook his head, tapping the girl on her shoulder. She shrugged it off, continuing to mutter and write.

A faint hint of amusement thrummed through his veins. He shook his head, walking over to the bowl of stew and picking up some for himself as well as Ari and Leon. He handed them the bowls before making one more and placing it a bit away from the almost empty pot before spooning some down. Quite good actually. "I would just like to remind you that we *are* in someone else's home and that drooling over a door will get us nowhere."

"It's fine." Rita waved it off, snapping between her notebook and feeling over the wood of the door. "I'm just taking a few quick notes and, wait..."

She slowly turned her head to look toward him. "Why the heck are you eating someone else's *food* then?"

"Hm? Did you want some? I figured the door was feast enough for you." He took another spoonful as Rita darted over. It didn't take much to avoid the grasping hands.

A faint sigh echoed from where Alex sat as Milos stepped away and took the other seat, crossing one leg over the other as he took another bite of stew. Rita pursed her lips before looking down at her paper and stilling.

"There's stew on it."

"You did knock into the cauldron earlier. I'm surprised you didn't burn yourself."

"You *lout*."

Milos chuckled as Rita ripped the page out, feverishly filling the page back in before stomping over to the cauldron. She stared at it, eye twitching.

Only to spot the bowl Milos made sure to prepare for her ahead of time, figuring the girl would spill the pot otherwise.

She sighed, picked up the bowl and chowed down on it.

A faint smile trailed on Alex's face as Rita quietly said, "Thanks, I guess."

Milos shrugged. "We all need to eat. Knowing you, you would have just stayed next to that door all the way up until he came back. Couldn't have that, now could we?"

"No, I guess not," she muttered, taking another spoonful before pointing the spoon at him. "Just so you know, I'm not thanking you again, you hear?"

Milos shrugged. It wasn't his business anyway. She was irksome. Though, he supposed, he honestly didn't mind.

Chapter Two

Alex watched in amusement, the finished bowl resting in his lap. He was glad Milos got Rita to eat, though he could have done it another way.

He heard the faint sound of footsteps and glanced over at the same time as Milos to the little door Rita was noting earlier. To be honest, he saw it upon entering, but hadn't thought much of it. To think it was some strange contraption used by seers. He could only assume, from the others' surprised reaction, that it wasn't actually visible to them.

The thought was pushed off as the little man stepped through, closing the door behind him. Just like the first time, Alex heard a faint hum from below, confirming his thoughts. This was where the second river was. It relieved him to *finally* know where it was.

The man stepped over to Milos, eyeing him warily before handing him a small bundle that was draped over his arms. Taking a second, Alex realized they were cloaks like the one he was wearing that Rita bought for him. He passed them around, almost hidden under the pile of long fabric.

"What's this for?" Rita asked as she pulled the cloak on before glancing sheepishly down at her bowl. "Oh, and, uh.... Thanks for the stew?"

Alex mentally chuckled.

"It's no problem." The man handed the last cloaks to Ari and Leon, who took them gratefully, glancing at Milos who nodded, allowing them to accept, or so Alex assumed as they slipped the cloaks on. "If you were without a demon comrade, or had a demon shackled..." He smiled and Alex felt a shiver run down his spine. That was not a pleasant smile.

"We would have been given one of the boats out there to float to our demise, correct?" Milos pointed out, getting a nod from the man.

"Yes, after all, I sell boats to adventurers in search of the wild norths. Some of them are earnest while others are only in it for slaughter and gain. Very rarely, a demon such as yourself comes along, seeking refuge." He turned to Alex. "Only the last one receives proper passage. The rest, as unfortunate as it is and as your Alertian acquaintance assumed, receive one of the boats stored outside. Now, a sharp-witted traveler with experience might be able to survive the journey on that, if it was only the waters they had to worry about."

"There's other stuff out there?" Rita gulped, shifting uncomfortably where she stood. Alex pursed his lips at the thought, shivering.

"Of course." The man grinned. "The north is the last sanctuary for demons, but it's also the last sanctuary for most creatures in the Underlands that aren't human. It's very rare to see these beasts in other regions, though it does happen."

"You mean creatures such as a Drega?" Milos spoke up.

Alex twitched, remembering the large black maw, swallowing a human arm whole, the way the wings covered an entire valley, sounding loud in his ears as he and Rita barely dodged away from its sharp claws.... To think, there were more of those creatures out there, when it took both Milos and himself to beat one of them.

"That is one of them, yes." The man's expression shifted, grim. "I wish there was an easier way to help those fleeing from the Martinets, but unfortunately there isn't."

"So, how are you living out here?" Rita questioned. Curiosity sounded clearly in her tone. "There's basically nothing out here..."

The man laughed, a belly-filled laugh that wouldn't have sounded off from a giant. "Young girl, you have much to learn. Below these floors, buried beneath us, is all I need for survival. That's why I invited you inside." He hesitated, as if debating for a moment before turning toward the doorway. "Anyway, as I said, those actually fleeing to the north are given safer passage, but I do still have to make preparations ahead of time." He hesitated before gesturing. "However, this time, it didn't take nearly as long, come." With that, he headed through the doorway.

"Huh?" Rita blinked before scrambling to her feet and hurrying after him as he held open the seer's door.

Alex stood, following with the others only a few steps behind. Now usually, Alex noted, you would be advised against following a stranger through a doorway and down a set of unknown stairs. He didn't sense anything and Milos was behind, hand not even near the hilt of his sword.

Not only that, but both Ari and Leon seemed comfortable, Ari even smiling slightly.

The stairwell itself was clean and brightly lit with light stones set into the side, showcasing intricate designs pressed into the walls that looked to be different types of demons dancing and weaving like a tapestry over the stone. As they descended, their footsteps resounded back to them, up and down the staircase as they walked deeper and deeper. Finally, they reached a bend in the rock and, turning the corner, Alex almost drew to a stop.

In front of him, spread out on either side almost as large as the enclosure above, were fields of greenery. A thin path wove through the patches of what Alex could tell were different types of fruits and vegetables.

"This is my little farm. It's a decent way to eat and have a living so far away from the capital. Every so often, I'll go to the capital to sell my goods, though it has gotten much harder of late."

He walked down the walkway as Alex followed behind, staring over the fields, as the man called them. In truth, they were mostly potted plants placed close to each other to resemble what Alex could only assume was a field seen in the Overlands. Different stones covered the ceiling and sides, some water stones and a few Alex didn't recognize.

He wondered how all this was even here to begin with.

"An underground greenhouse?" Milos sounded incredibly impressed, though Alex didn't recognize the term. Upon seeing his expression, Milos clarified. "A greenhouse is a building of glass often used to house different varieties of plants. It's used in order to grow food year-round, even during the winter months."

Alex hummed in thought, trying to picture it. To think an entire building could be made of glass. It sounded strange to him, but seemed pretty neat. If you could grow fruits and vegetables inside a building, it would make sense that, with the right things, you would be able to make them down here as well.

Alex turned back to the man. To one side, in his periphery, he could see Leon tentatively checking one of the leaves, a slight expression of awe and interest on his face, rare to see from the quiet and stoic man.

Their guide chuckled. "That's basically about right. I have a few other areas for cattle, but it's much harder to maintain, so I mostly use it for dairy." He shrugged, the movement causing his whole body to shift. "This is all just a side thing. I haven't shown you the most important bit. Let's keep going." With that, he moved around another corner up ahead where the large cavern curved inward once more.

Alex hurried after him as the man continued, "As you can probably hear, there is a river up ahead. This one is much safer than the one above, though only for the first stretch of water. It will at least get you past the Dregas' home, though once you hit the open water, all bets are off." He stepped past another opening before gesturing.

Alex peered through, followed by the others as they walked out into a large cavern, twice the size of the room they were just in, the roof high above their head. In front of them was a large stone dock, water gently lapping at a set of boats tied to each. The light stones from before cast only over the dock, the water itself a liquid black once it was outside the range of the stones light.

"This is the twin river, the sister of the one above. No one knows how they split or how the two flow over each other without eroding the stone. It's a mystery I leave alone." He turned to their group. "The one above is probably safer traversing if there were no monsters, but this one is safer in avoiding some of the creatures of the north. So, what do you think? Think this will work?" The man turned to the group, spreading his arms, as if trying to show something impressive, which, in actuality, Alex did find himself awfully impressed. The faint singing of the water was joyous, where up above, it was tired. Strange. Twin rivers. He could only assume they led to one place, but were they from the same source as well?

And where was the source?

"Hey, I just thought of something." Rita tapped her foot, causing Alex to turn to her in confusion. She seemed annoyed and worried. "Do any of us know *how* to use a boat?" Rita pointed out hesitantly. All eyes turned to her.

Alex quickly shook his head. He'd read about it, sure, but he never actually saw one before.

Ari winced as Leon spoke up, voice quiet. "Neither of us have had the opportunity. Boats aren't very common down here, even with nobles."

Alex blinked, taking a moment to recognize the fact that *Leon* of all people spoke, before he turned his attention to Milos.

Milos hadn't seemed bothered by it, deep in thought. He seemed to finally take notice of their looks and grimaced. "I may be an Overlander, but that doesn't mean I know how a boat operates, especially one from the Underlands. I have no doubt that, physically, they would be quite different from the ones in the Overlands."

Alex glanced toward the little man, who was smirking, a faint hum in his voice. "I suspected as much." Everyone turned to him as he walked to a particular boat off to one side. It was long, slim and it seemed like there was someone there? A faint voice trickled to his ear and Alex narrowed his gaze, hoping to see more clearly as the little man gestured. "By the way I noticed you perked up before the others. Are you sensitive to water?"

Alex hesitantly nodded and the little man grinned. "Perfect." He turned and made a sharp gesture, a wave of the hand before bringing that same hand up to his mouth and whistling sharply.

To Alex's surprise, a gentle glow began to shine from the head of the thin ship they were walking toward. The light slowly blossomed before springing forth, piercing through the waters with enough over-glow to showcase the rest of the ship, waiting in front of them. Rita took a step back, startled as Milos' expression twisted to one of amusement. Alex grinned.

Now that they were closer, it was easier to see the details of the ship. It was made of a sturdy wood, long and thin and, as the water sang around it, indicated it was probably swift and maneuverable. Two stones sat on either side, large enough to eclipse the back sides of the boat with a gentle green glow. A faint hum echoed from the back of the ship. On the front was a powerful light stone, shearing through the blackness of the cave and over the waters as it rocked gently. He briefly wondered who turned on the light stone, but he pushed the thought away. This ship wasn't like any ship he saw in pictures. It made sense, he supposed. Ships down here couldn't exactly use wind to move. He noted the gentle green glow from the stones placed carefully into the side of the ship. What were they used for?

He heard that faint hum and jerked around, spotting something on the ship. This time, it was clearer, a figure flicking back and forth, coming closer to the railing to peer down at them. What was that thing?

Milos' expression was utterly baffled, watching the thing dancing across the deck of the ship with a narrowed and calculated gaze. Was it a demon? Alex wasn't sure.

"She is what I like to call an Aqua Wraith." The little man chuckled as Alex snapped his gaze back to the man, who was watching the creature fondly, though the sadness in his voice was quite evident as well. "An Aqua Wraith is the spirit of a deceased Nyiad or Nyx. Usually, they are malignant, but this one...I'm not sure of the specifics, but she became attached to me along with that ship after, well, I'll leave that to her to tell you if she feels it necessary." He cleared his throat. "Just keep in mind she's the remnants of a Nyx, a demon."

"That's a ghost?" Milos seemed a little uncertain. "How can it operate a ship?"

"She still holds some of the powers she wielded when she was alive. She will guide you through the waterways." He chuckled faintly. "I guess I now realize why she's been so excited for the last few days." He glanced toward Alex. "She must have realized you were coming. She's been preparing this whole time so you are all set to go as soon as you are ready. That's why it didn't take much time to make the final adjustments."

Alex blinked, staring up at the creature who peered down over the edge of the railing. That sound from earlier, followed by a faint laugh met his ears. So, she was who he heard earlier?

Alex could tell she was once quite beautiful. Long hair, constantly blending into the liquid skin. See-through, yet clearly a woman. A woman of pure water. Still, it unnerved him. A ghost recognized he was coming. He wasn't sure what he thought about that little announcement.

Milos watched him for a moment before turning to the little man. "I thank you for your hospitality. Is there a way we can repay you?"

"There is no need." He waved it off as the Aqua Wraith leaned forward over the railing, smiling softly before hurrying away. "This is part of my job, after all. I make enough money from the thrill-seekers, because those people always come by in droves, and selling of supplies. Plus..." He turned toward the ship as a loud thunk sounded near it. A wooden plank landed on the stone pier, the wood bending slightly at the impact but, surprisingly, not breaking. "I think she's looking forward to meeting you all."

Alex blinked as the Aqua Wraith stood to the side, hands grasping onto the rail as she observed the group. Ari and Leon peered at Milos. Once Milos waved them off, Ari moved up the plank while Leon bowed.

"We will check it out."

"Please do." Milos spoke up, watching as the two slaves walked up the slope.

It was a few minutes later when Ari returned, bowing. "It is safe, sir."

Rita grinned. "Good, because I want to take a look at this myself," she said, before hurrying up the steps, examining everything curiously. Alex found himself staring at the Aqua Wraith, both fascinated and admittedly nervous.

He heard movement and looked over in time to see Rita hurrying back down the plank. He yelped as she grabbed his elbow and tugged, dragging him up the steps with a grunt. "Come on, you dingbat. It's rude to stare anyway."

He heard a faint chuckle from Milos as he was pulled up onto the deck. Milos wasn't far behind, a startled sound echoing from the little man as Alex peered back. It wasn't hard to tell that Milos had bowed, his back straightening as he continued up the plank. Alex returned his attention to the Aqua Wraith. She stood there, watching in silence, her form fluctuating just like the waves gently lapping at the ship. She was a ghost. Demons, Dregas, slavery. All of that made sense to him, but ghosts? He was having a heck of a time wrapping his head around that. The woman glided forward a bit and he found himself taking a step back. He heard a sigh and felt a gentle push at his back. He did *not* let himself feel a moment of betrayal as he stumbled forward, stopping a few feet from the woman.

"Didn't know you were afraid of ghosts. She set this all up for us, least you could do is be polite." Rita's voice was amused, footsteps echoing as she walked away.

Alex would have glared back at her if his gaze wasn't stuck on the creature before him, a mix of panic and comfort rushing through him. It was a strange combination of feelings, for sure.

He briefly wondered what Milos and his slaves were doing, since the slaves did already do a quick perusal of the ship, though from the sounds of heavy footsteps, he could only assume the man was exploring the ship now as well.

He kinda wanted to be doing that right now himself.

He took a deep breath and stepped forward. There wasn't anything he could say, but it seemed the woman didn't want anything. Upon his approach, he could see the shimmering of a smile cross her face, her hands clapping together in delight. A soft song threaded through his ears before the woman spun, diving over the edge of the ship. He raced over, knowing there wasn't a problem, but worrying nonetheless. When her head popped out of the water, checking around the edge of the boat, he let out a sigh and pulled back.

That was strange, but, admittedly, he did feel a bit better. He would just have to think of her more as a demon than a ghost; that should make things a bit easier.

"See? She seems pretty nice," Rita teased, causing Alex to turn and glare at her as she smirked before opening the door to the cabin set near the middle of the ship that she must have been waiting by. "Come on, let's take a look around. We'll want to get comfortable before we get going." With that, she waved and disappeared through the doorway. Alex shook his head, noting the plank was still in place. That was a relief, in a way. It meant the Aqua Wraith was giving them some time to get accustomed. The little man was sitting near the edge of the docks, staring at the ship with that same fond and sad expression. Alex briefly wondered what that was about, but shook his head. He might as well take a look around.

The deck itself was decent-sized, easily able to hold double the amount of people currently on board with ease. The cabin was large, filling the middle of the ship with room on either side. On the back side, behind the cabin, was an area slightly heightened to see above the cabin. A strange wheel sat in the middle with a small pedestal, or maybe it was a table, set to the left of it. At the front of the boat was the large light stone that encompassed the entire front of the ship. He briefly wondered how the light stone didn't light up before, but pushed the thought away.

He stepped inside the cabin, examining the walls. The inside was dimmer, two small light stones set to either side of the doorway. Even though it was dimmer, it was still bright enough to see the corners of the room, a gentle orange glow over the large space. Maps, some aged and yellow, while others seemed more recent, still a crisp white, adorned the walls. It was amazing. This place was strange. Wood was hard to come by, but the paper? Paper like Rita's was easy to get since it wasn't tree paper, but a combination of different minerals, but this... He reached a hand up, brushing over one of the yellowed maps. This was paper he only saw in old books, true paper. This whole ship, this room by itself would have taken an entire Underlander's fortune and then some. Yet the man was just giving it to them so they could get to the north? It was strange to think about, and quite humbling as well.

He pulled away, spotting a set of chairs and a table seated in the middle of the cabin. He could see divots in the ground and guessed that was where the chairs would go in if the water became too rocky. As it was, the gentle sway was strange, but not uncomfortable. He wondered if the others felt the same.

Shaking his head, he headed toward the other doorway and opened to see a steep set of stairs curling downward, another light stone suspended above, swaying slightly with the ship. He descended the stairs, coming out at the lower deck. Rita spotted him and waved as she walked toward him from what seemed to be the front of the ship. "What do you think so far? Pretty neat, right?" She grinned, glancing up the stairs. "I was thinking of heading back upstairs."

Alex stepped to one side as Rita peered at him for a moment. "I'm guessing you still haven't seen the rest of the ship?" Alex shook his head as Rita smiled faintly. "All right, I'll see you later then." She hurried back up the stairs as Alex chuckled before deciding to head toward the front of the ship, figuring it was better just to start from the front and work his way backwards. The room at the front of the ship was decent-sized, curving with the ship. Two beds were set on either side with a wide window showing the front, faint light seeping in from the stone. Everything was very clearly bolted down.

He pulled back and continued onto the next, peeking in the doorways set to either side of the stairwell, on opposite sides of the hallway. Two of them were large storage rooms that covered a good bit of the ship, one for cold storage, as indicated by a couple ice stones, and one for dry goods where Leon seemed to be checking over inventory. Closer to the back of the ship were two more doors, one leading to what Alex assumed was a bathroom and another leading to what was definitely the kitchen. As he found out when he opened the door to see Ari standing at a stove, pulling out some pots and pans with a faint clattering sound. He had to admit, he was impressed.

Ari glanced up. "Alex." She gestured toward him. "Food will be ready in a bit."

Alex nodded, gratefully. He pulled back out of the kitchen and continued. He walked toward the end of the hallway toward the back of the ship and opened the door to peek inside. There were a few hammocks strewn about and, past that, another doorway with a faint whine echoing behind it. He stepped past the hammocks and opened the door, peeking inside. Milos stood in the room, staring at a machine Alex never saw before. He could see faint steam pulsing from what he could only guess was some sort of engine. Was it to power the ship?

"This is connected to those two stones outside." Milos' voice cut through his thoughts, proving that the man noticed he was there.

Alex wasn't surprised as he stepped inside to examine the thing more closely. Milos glanced at him before peering back at the machine. Alex followed his gaze, spotting two wire-like contraptions extending to either side, close to where the stones sat outside.

"Those two stones, I didn't recognize them, but Leon did. He said they were Wind stones, much rarer to find around here. Depending on the energy pushed through them, they can create different levels of wind. Considering how lacking in air it is down there, I can see why they would be so valuable." Milos glanced toward him.

No kidding. Alex's thoughts flickered to the giant stones embedded on either side of the ship. If those let out air, then this ship would be able to move through the water just on that and probably at pretty high speed too.

"Of course, it would take a skilled hand to know how to control the amount of air to disperse at any given time so the ship can turn or even move straight. How we can utilize it when none of us know how it works? Added to that, the only one who does is a ghost of all things is going to be an interesting dilemma to figure out. It is fascinating, though, to see the craft of Underland ships versus those from above."

Alex furrowed his brow. What did he mean? He knew he didn't see any sails or anything, but were the ships that different between the two lands?

Milos glanced over before elaborating. "I don't know how to control a ship, but I still know the general design and have seen a few in my day." He left it at that, turning back to the hammock-filled room. "Let's just hope that man knows what he's talking about regarding the Aqua Wraith, because that's our only chance. Now, I'm going to assume this room is for the men." Huh? Alex tilted his head, feeling confused as he followed Milos into the room. "I'm not in the mood to deal with cranky girls and I highly doubt they would want to sleep in hammocks on a rolling ship."

Alex pursed his lips, quickly putting what he said together. Yeah, he couldn't imagine Rita sleeping in one of those. Plus, there were only two beds in the front room and three guys. He would rather not try to figure those arrangements out. He didn't think sleeping on the floor of a rocking ship would be that comfortable.

He shook his head and followed Milos out of the room and back up the stairs onto the deck. He heard movement, a faint hum and glanced back to see the Aqua Wraith. The plank was up and it seemed that the only thing holding them to the dock was a lone rope the Aqua Wraith was carefully untying. Rita was near the wheel, checking it over with a scrutinizing gaze.

"I guess we're ready to move," Milos said as the rope trailed into the water, pulled back to the shore by the little man as he waved.

The ship bobbed in the water for a moment as the woman dived through the boards, quite literally. Alex stumbled back, slightly startled as she disappeared through the planks. Not even a moment later, a faint hum trailed from the back of the ship.

"So, we're heading out." Rita's voice hung in the air as she stepped away from the wheel, walking over to the edge of the ship. They watched as the ship began to pull forward, wind whistling behind them as the little man waved. Rita waved back, a grin on her face as Alex chuckled quietly. Guess they were off.

Before long, the light of the dock disappeared and only the light from the light stone in the front, and one placed near the wheel shone over the deck, obscuring their faces in shadow.

After some time, Rita pulled back and let out a breath. "We're really on our way." She shook her head before grinning. "So, now that we know we're not going to crash as soon as we leave, or sink for that matter, let's take a look at where we are going, shall we?"

With that, she headed back to the cabin. Alex peered into the darkness for a moment before following a few steps behind Milos. Well, at least she was cheerful and it seemed the Aqua Wraith knew what she was doing. He would have to be content with that.

To be honest, he wasn't sure whether to be excited or nervous.

Chapter Three

Rita found herself leaning against the table, hands holding down one of the many maps she found while exploring. Milos and Alex were examining the others with varying levels of attention. She huffed. "Guys, come here."

Alex blinked, glancing over to her before stepping over. Milos tilted his head slightly before turning, but left it at that. She felt her eye twitch, but didn't comment as she pointed to a thin line on the map she had been looking at, a few more maps spread around the table of varying shapes and sizes. Though this one was the only one she found that seemed to be one of the few that actually showcased the waterway they were in, in any detail.

"All right, so it seems for the first leg of the trip, there is only one route we can take." She tapped the map as Alex and Milos walked over. "This is one of the few maps that shows this underground canal. It seems to have a lot of twists and turns to it, but it goes underneath quite a few territories I'm quite glad to be avoiding."

She moved her finger up, pointing out a couple names dotting the area. Some were the Dregas' territory, like the little man mentioned, but a couple were beings Rita always believed were myth. She was glad they weren't going to have to test that theory.

"So? What happens once we leave the canal?" Milos leaned over the other side of the table. "I'm not quite sure I still fully understand how the Underlands waterways work, since I didn't think it was possible to have two separate rivers right underneath each other." He side-eyed Rita who huffed.

"If you let me *finish*, you dingbat." She turned to Alex, trying to cool her thoughts. "After we exit the canal, we are in the main waterway leading toward the north which will also bring us out of this cave. In other words, we'll be able to see the day stones again."

She pointed to what she assumed was the end of the canal. She wasn't the best when it came to maps, but it seemed she was the only one in the group who could understand them to some degree, as evidenced by how the two boys successfully got lost when by themselves.

"From what I can see, it's pretty large, with mountains ringing the edges." She pointed down at a large splotch to one side of a map she had been all but ignoring up until this point. "All we know is that this is where the waters of the north flow in and out. It doesn't have any landmarks, at least, not on the maps I've seen so far, and we don't know how dangerous it is." Rita sighed, rolling up the map. "Unfortunately, we won't be able to land anywhere that I know of until we reach the opposite coast, at least according to the maps I've found, though I haven't seen them all. The area all around are sheer cliffs and rocky crags. That's probably why it's so unexplored."

"Our guide also warned that this was only the first obstacle." Milos glanced toward the doorway leading outside. "That Aqua Wraith knows how to pilot the ship, and seems to have full control of it. With Alex around, that should help us. Of course, that means there is something other than just waters there."

"That's what I was afraid of," Rita admitted before letting out a sigh. "The worst of it? Even with all these maps, I know nothing about the size or construction of where we'll actually be going, let alone if there are any safe areas." She walked over to another map, tapping it lightly with the nail of her finger. "See this one? This shows more details on the waters themselves. As you can see, it's not one solid area of water, at least, not at the northernmost point. The final leg of the trip looks like it weaves in and out of a large expanse of stone, but it also seems to be quite a way off. Alex..." She trailed off before turning to face him. "I know you might be hesitant, but do you think you would be able to learn how to use your wings?"

Alex's confusion was palpable as he stared at her before hesitantly bringing a hand up to his shoulder. His brow furrowed, seeming deep in thought before letting out a long breath and shrugging.

"Why?" Milos asked, pulling Rita's attention away from Alex. Milos leaned against the cabin wall, arms crossed.

"Because we need someone who can scout and prove that we're not enemies." Rita pointed to a few pieces of land on her map before continuing, "I bet you've figured this out already, but they aren't just going to let normal humans in, we need to show we mean no harm and that means Alex..."

"Would need to meet up with them in order to prove and ask for safe passage." Milos nodded. "I realized, but I admit, I did not think of having him stick out in such a way. After all, that is quite dangerous for him as well, or did you not realize?"

"Why? They know demons use this for refuge." Rita pulled back, confused.

"Yes, but our guide said it's been many years since the last demon traversed through his path and yet his mother is already there. Which means?" Milos gestured and Rita furrowed her brow, trying to parse through what he said. What did he mean?

She heard a quiet hiss of realization from Alex as Milos let out a sigh and continued, "What I mean to say is this. For demons that can fly, I'm guessing there is a safer route. So why would a flyer go the dangerous waterbound route?" Milos tapped his finger on his sword. "Unless it's with a party that wishes to infiltrate and possibly attack?"

"But we aren't—"

"They don't know that. Just because they might recognize he's a demon, they might believe he's trying to escape from us. He should learn how to use his wings, definitely, but not to scout ahead. If anything, when we get close to the border, it would be better for him to stay close to the ship, for all of our sakes."

Rita pursed her lips, but realized the truth to his words. He was right, unfortunately, and she didn't want to put Alex in danger unless she absolutely had to. She let out a breath of frustration. "All right, I get it." She glanced up toward Milos, who seemed a little surprised at her words. "We'll look into it more when we get closer. For now, we should figure out what we are going to do for the first leg of the trip. After all, it's pretty straightforward and, I'm guessing, will probably be one of the few times we'll be able to rest for any length of time."

"You're probably right." Milos pushed away from the wall, hesitant before he let out a breath. "I'm going to take a moment outside. Why don't you two figure out what we are going to do about the rest of the trip?"

Rita nodded before she felt a smirk cross her face, thoughts flickering to the two rooms down below. Now to see if she could convince the boys to follow her idea.

~ * ~

Milos stepped out of the room and onto the deck proper to organize his thoughts, and get away from Rita's devilish grin. That girl could be scary when she wanted to be. The Aqua Wraith glided over the deck, flitting from bow to stern, proving how useful she was with the ship. She knew the ship thoroughly. He wasn't sure whether to be worried about that or not. Was this a trap or just paranoia? However, he did not miss the cautionary look sent his way as the ship pierced through the absolute darkness of the underground waterway.

Underground waterway...he did not miss the irony of the statement. He walked to one side, close enough to see the water reflected in the light of the stone, but far enough where he would have no fear of falling in. He had a feeling the boat wouldn't stop for anyone if they were to fall, except Alex. Milos glanced back at the cabin. To be honest, he was a bit frustrated at his lack of knowledge or more so, his lack of experience. He had been on a few ships in the Overlands—he cut off his thoughts, peering back over the water. He was somewhat surprised at how much this was reminding him of the Overlands. He missed the sunlight.

A faint hum rang beside him and he turned toward the Aqua Wraith as she slowly slid up to him, watching him with a narrowed gaze. He didn't feel any fear, but he still lightly placed his hand on the hilt of his sword. The woman barely gave it a glance, slowly gliding around him, as if observing him. He noted her feet never truly touched the ground, one hand reached up and pointed.

"Verra vetchen," her voice whispered, the tongue and words archaic, ancient. They filled the air with a bell-like chime, as if echoing off the water. Milos forced himself not to step back as she curled in front of him. Those words, they were part of the demonic language. He should have expected that from the ghost of a demon, but it still took him somewhat by surprise.

"Dost thou not understand thy ancient tongue?" She asked, pulling back. "Then, I will speak plain. Beware the water, Alertian of bygone era. Soul's requiem will send you to your death. Yet, your heart is divided. Keep to what you hold truthful, and you might yet see the light which we, below, shall not see." She swirled around him once more, hovering behind him. Milos stood still, knowing it would be best to remain silent as she whispered. "Do no harm unto those for which the waters hold dear, or they will swallow us all whole." With those parting words, she disappeared, almost flowing into the woodwork.

Milos would admit that her words unnerved him a bit. Though, he would admit, they also confused him. What did she mean by do no harm unto those the waters hold dear? Did that mean Alex? What did it mean about swallowing us all whole? Alex wouldn't hurt anyone there, so did she mean herself? He shook his head. Her words were antiquated at best, cryptic at worst. However, he understood the basics of what she was saying, which was pretty self-explanatory. Don't hurt anyone. Plain and simple.

He understood it, but he wondered why she pointed it out, what did she mean by heart divided? Didn't he already make his choice? He was a demon hunter, that was all.

He let out a breath, feeling the ship slowly turn, a hint of stone shone on the left, disappearing as the ship swung right in a gentle curve, going around the bend in the river. He had to admit, it was quite eerie to be in an area so filled with darkness. When he first descended into the Underlands, he was prepared to be in a situation of constant darkness. The Underlands, as usual, took him by surprise, showcasing how they were filled with their own beautiful light. Now? Now that he couldn't see the day and night stones, he was truly experiencing what he expected from the beginning and found he was not fond of it in the slightest.

He tapped his finger on the hilt of his sword before turning back toward the cabin. Unfortunately, there wasn't much he could do on the deck of the ship right now. The light of the two light stones was barely enough to see, spreading shadows out in areas near the edge. Thinking over his options, he passed through the map room and noted Rita and Alex were gone. Not giving it much thought, he descended the stairs. He would just check on Ari and Leon, then turn in for some sleep. He wasn't exactly thrilled at the prospect of trying to sleep in a hammock, but the options were pretty limited.

He stopped at the bottom of the stairs just in time to see Rita push Alex to the opposite end of the hallway. Milos blinked, noting that Alex was looking over his shoulder, startled as Rita moved forward, Leon a few steps behind with a resigned expression and Ari...Ari was smiling? That was strange.

"What's going on?" he decided to ask, getting it out of the way.

Rita stopped, but didn't take her hands off of Alex's back. The boy took the opportunity to step away, giving her a sharp glare.

"I was making sure these two—" she gestured to Leon and Alex, "actually get some rest. They are still recovering and the only room on this ship is the bedroom up front. I don't know *why* Alex keeps resisting, but..."

"Maybe it has something to do with the fact that there are only two beds in the front, perfect for you and Ari, and the men would have no problem with the hammocks?" Milos sighed. Of all things to be arguing over.

"No can do. The hammocks swing too much and that could jar Leon's injury. Plus, Alex needs to recover his voice. Being right next to an engine room where he might need to shout is completely contrary to that." Rita crossed her arms over her chest. "So, what that means is you boys are getting the front room, and that is final."

Milos stared at her for a moment, appraising her stance. She brought up good points and he could see, with how Ari was basically guarding the back door, that both women seemed to agree. He let out a breath and waved. "Fine."

Rita blinked, startled as Alex rounded on him, looking ready to argue.

"You would probably keep arguing about it anyway and, if necessary, I have no doubt that you would throw some of that sleep powder around before dragging us to that room. I would rather fall asleep of my own volition, thank you."

"I wasn't..." Rita glanced away, licking her lips hesitantly as her hand darted away from the satchel on her hip.

Alex just gave her a deadpan look which screamed, "Really?"

Milos shook his head before walking toward the front of the ship. "We'll figure out arrangements later and, considering how everything is bolted down, I doubt we can borrow a hammock for me." He shrugged, not fond of the idea forming in his mind. That meant he was probably going to have to sleep on the ground. That did not sound inviting, to be honest.

To the point where he couldn't help throwing a jab out to her over his shoulder. "You're sure you aren't going to come out cranky and throwing a fit? Or is that what I should perceive as normal from you?"

"Oh, aren't you funny?" Rita growled before placing her hands on her hips.

Leon walked right past, guiding an annoyed Alex with him. Considering Alex didn't argue by holding back or crossing his arms spoke volumes. "Also, that Aqua Wraith has to get to the engine room. I would feel more comfortable, and I bet she would too, if she didn't have to keep sneaking by noisy men."

"Oh, so you were worried about us, how nice," Milos decided not to hide his sarcasm this time.

"I was worried about them, not you." She huffed, rolling her eyes.

"Good to see we're on the same page." Milos shook his head, walking toward the door.

"That's..." Rita's voice was faint as he paused, hearing movement on the other side, showing Alex and Leon probably spending some time rearranging the room.

He stayed silent as quiet footsteps came up behind him before stopping.

"I also thought it would be helpful if our only fighter could rest easy as well. But there's no point in telling a lout like yourself such a thing, is there?"

Milos tilted his head slightly to see her staring at him, worry flashing on her face before she turned, waving her hand.

"Ari said she's cooking dinner. Get yourself situated and join us in a bit, got it?"

Milos didn't resist the faint smile forming on his lips as he watched her walk away, Ari already having disappeared.

He slipped into the shared bedroom. She was irksome as ever, but he still couldn't find himself able to hate her for it.

The room was spacious, Milos had to admit, it was just disadvantageous that there were only two beds. He looked over to see Alex holding Leon down by the shoulder on one bed, giving him a stern look before heading to the other. Alex spotted him.

"Good to see you're focusing on others, as usual." Milos shook his head as he glanced around the room. Other than some bolted-down dressers, the two beds, and a full-length window, there weren't many other amenities. "Maybe focus on yourself a bit?"

He could almost hear the rolling of eyes as he glanced toward where Leon lay, curling into the sheet. He must have been tired, because he was already asleep, even though he'd only just laid down. Milos almost felt bad, having to wake him once dinner was ready.

Though, maybe he wasn't asleep, as proven when he tilted his head slightly to follow Milos' movement from one side of the room to take a seat in the corner. Alex placed his hands on his hips, remarkably resembling Rita in that instance. Milos tilted his head as he took a seat on the ground, one leg bent, the other out straight. "Get some rest, dinner will be ready soon."

"I think we both agree..." Leon's voice was slightly drowsy from a need to sleep, but his words were strong as he sat up slightly to give him a sharp look. "That we won't allow you to sleep on the ground. Sir." That was definitely tacked on at the end.

Milos would feel proud that Leon was starting to speak for himself, if it wasn't so disadvantageous.

"Where else do you propose...?"

Alex just pointed at the final bed.

Milos stared for a long time, battling with himself. A bed honestly did sound a lot more comfortable, but... He could feel a yawn coming on and promptly pushed it down, shifting himself to his feet. "What about you, Alex?"

Alex paused, glancing between the two beds, confusion on his face.

Milos took a seat and began pulling off one boot before pausing. He could still hear the creak of the wood as Alex shifted back and forth, almost but not quite pacing.

"Alex, come here. You can sleep with me tonight. I'm not in the mood to deal with you knocking into Leon and having to call Rita this late at night."

Milos could practically hear Alex's hesitation as he unbuckled the sheathe of his blade, placing it upright beside the bed so he could grab it easily. The chainmail was easy to get off, habit, so he was just left with simple clothing. Usually, he wouldn't go through taking so much off down here, but while the bed wasn't exactly small, it would be easy to make someone uncomfortable.

He finally heard quiet footsteps and felt the bed dip. He glanced sidelong to see Alex smiling gratefully.

"Sir? Are you sure?" Leon spoke quietly.

Milos nodded, shifting his clothes so he could lay down. "Yes. Your wound is still relatively fresh. It might be mostly healed, but I would rather not take any chances. We have very few medical supplies and re-injuring it by accident would be detrimental. Plus, if all three of us don't sleep well, Rita will be pissed."

A snorting laugh echoed from Alex as he covered his mouth.

Milos didn't spare it much thought as he continued. "This way I can keep a closer eye on Alex."

The laughter stopped promptly followed by a long sigh. What Milos hadn't expected was the sudden thump of movement on the bed, as if Alex just fell sideways, filling up the other side of the bed. The bedding promptly disappeared as a quiet laugh from across the room caught his attention.

Milos decided not to argue, just shaking his head at the action. At this point, he had a feeling Alex was going to purposefully stay beside him for that comment. There was a phrase he remembered that said to keep your friends close and your enemies closer. Milos was just not sure which category Alex fell under at this point.

~ * ~

After grabbing some dinner, which took some convincing from Rita who didn't stop knocking on the door to catch all of their attention, they headed back to the room. Alex rubbed his stomach, finding the food delicious. He would have to thank Ari later when his voice was back. When he arrived, Leon was already asleep, curled up tightly in the blankets. He must have fallen asleep as soon as he hit the bed. Alex was glad; the man did need some rest as Rita and Milos said.

They hadn't really had a chance to do elaborate cooking when on the road or in the capital. This was the first time where they could actually sit down and have a proper meal. It was nice, though it did remind him of home a bit.

His smile dropped at that and he promptly shook the thought away. He glanced down at his clothes and sighed. He wished he had something to change into. That would be nice actually. Unfortunately, he never got a chance to get a new pair of clothes. Other than the cloak and the belts wrapped around his waist, almost everything else was worn from travel. He could see rips and tears on the cuffs of his tunic and pants. Also, his shoes were basically molded around his feet. He slipped them off along with his cloak and belts.

Then again, none of them had much in the way of spare clothes. It hadn't been a thought up until now and with all the rivers around, it hadn't been too hard to wash them. He glanced toward the only bed left. It seemed Milos had been trying to hide it as well, but he was barely struggling to stay awake, laying on one side of the bed, a single sheet around him for warmth. Alex sighed and plopped down on the bed, getting a quiet grunt from Milos.

Alex chuckled as he grabbed up a pillow, holding it tightly. What

Milos mentioned earlier was true. Part of him wondered if he could try one of the hammocks, but that thought was quickly brushed off. He didn't like the idea of ropes digging into his sides while he slept, or at all. The idea felt constricting.

To be honest, if he had to choose, he would rather sleep beside Milos. He just felt more comfortable around Milos. He let himself fall sideways onto the bed, curling into the sheets.

Maybe at one point, he would have been uncomfortable staying this close to Milos, but after the last few days...well, actually, ever since he trusted Milos in order to find out the truth of what he was, which involved a way too close encounter with the Martinet's guild, he felt comfortable around him. He wasn't worried about Milos trying to kill him, no matter what he said. After all, he'd stayed his hand when they first met and every time Alex even turned demon. Hell, the man could have left him behind at the Martinet's guild, but he hadn't.

Truth be told, Rita and Milos were probably the only people he could feel comfortable around, the only ones he felt he could be himself with. Ari and Leon were nice enough, but he still didn't know them well. Technically, the same could be said for Rita and Milos. The fact he had anyone he could trust was such an odd feeling, but one he held dear.

The bed was surprisingly soft, supporting both of their weights even as the ship rolled back and forth over the waves, gliding through the darkness. The room was chilled, but not so much he couldn't handle it. The light of the stone outside slowly dimmed until it barely shone over the water, the boat swaying to and fro in the water as they gently moved along the river.

It was calming. The water all around was a lullaby to his ears. Rita and Ari were safe, sleeping comfortably in the other room. He felt Milos shift, never fully relaxed, but that was no surprise. The man wasn't exactly known for his relaxed posture and attitude. Alex was honestly surprised how much Milos had stripped off. The chainmail and sheath were something he wore when they were traveling and resting, so to see him take them off, it made him appear less menacing and, well, kinder, gentler. It was strange. Alex mentally chuckled at the thought. He was hard pressed to imagine Milos in anything besides chainmail and certainly not sitting back and taking in the sunlight.

As he listened to the gentle sound of the waves and the murmurings of Leon as he fell into sleep, he let himself fully relax. He was safe, at least for now. It was nice to know no one was going to hurt him or use him as some weapon. He could tell Milos was still awake, but that was fine. The man wasn't going to harm him and, if anything, he was glad to know someone could protect him, though he was well aware he could protect himself. Either way, the warmth of another person against his back helped to calm his thoughts as he slowly drifted off to sleep.

Chapter Four

Rita had to admit, she didn't get much sleep that night. Oh, the hammocks were surprisingly comfy, at least, enough that she could convince herself to sleep as long as she didn't shift too much. She could hear Ari's soft snores, deep asleep.

No, what kept dragging at her mind, even as the hours ticked by, was the fear of what was to come and the Aqua Wraith. She opened her eyes, peering to her right to see the woman gliding through the room, spotting her before continuing along, only to pause and move backward to face her once more. Rita wasn't sure what the woman had to say, or even if she had to say anything, but when she said nothing and once more retreated, moving past them into the engine room, Rita let out a breath. To be honest, she understood Alex's hesitancy on the woman. As fascinating as it was, it was still eerie seeing a woman of pure water staring at you. She didn't even know ghosts could exist. It made sense. If Demons and Dregas could exist, why not ghosts?

How could a ghost exist? More specifically, how could a ghost derived from a Demon exist? It was believed that Demons held no souls, being evil incarnate. Obviously, that wasn't the case, but well, Demons held a soul, right? From what she knew, souls were the only way to create a ghost, or was there another way?

It made her head spin.

She let out a sigh, picked up the satchel she threw into the corner and headed up the stairs and onto the deck. The coolness of the underground was even more present on deck. A strange breeze ruffled her hair, caused by the fast movement of the ship through the waters. The long hiss and whine of the wind stones echoed behind her as the dim light from the light stone encased in front shone over the blackish liquid. She leaned on the railing, arms crossed over the wood as she stared out. There wasn't anything to see, but she wasn't looking for anything in particular. She heard a faint sound and glanced down to the water. She stilled, watching in fascination. Below the ship, swimming all around the bottom, were silver fish. They were longer and shone with their own light, as if speckles of light stone coated their skin. A few leapt from the water before disappearing back under, their glow fading slightly. They circled the ship for a moment before continuing on down the passage, back the direction the ship came from. For a brief moment, Rita thought she saw a strange outline in the water, but it disappeared just as quickly as she noticed it and she frowned, wondering if it was just another of those fish. Shaking her head, Rita watched them go, fascinated. She had never seen fish like that: the way they leapt from the water was almost graceful. Their light shone over the surrounding cavern enough for her to see the walls and overarching ceiling. She usually wasn't claustrophobic, it was kind of counterintuitive, but when the light finally shone enough to see, she was surprised how narrow the strip of water was, how easily their ship could accidentally turn a little right or left and crash into the stone face.

It was unnerving, but would it be any safer out on open water? She wasn't sure. She would have to trust the Aqua Wraith either way. That is, unless she learned herself.

She turned, heading back down the stairs and through the backroom. She stepped into the engine room, quickly closing the door behind her before turning to the wraith. The woman turned to her, floating in silence. She cocked her head to the side, as if waiting.

"Can you teach me? How to operate this boat?"

The woman hesitated for a moment, swirling around Rita before slowly nodding. She gestured toward the engine and Rita took a step closer. Now that she was taking a closer look, she was amazed at the intricacies of the system. She hummed in thought, fingers lightly grazing over each part. Off to one side, she spotted a brass tube with a little funnel attached near the end and furrowed her brow. Where did that connect to?

"'Tis a voice-pipe. Once used for mortals to interact between the engine room and the captain's cabin. The ship does not use such a cabin.

Tis but a map room and possible resting place." The woman's voice was strange, a vibrating tone as if sung through glass or, well, water. It was eerily beautiful. Rita nodded, lightly tapping the funnel before glancing back at the wraith. So, she could talk, but...

"Curiosity plagues you, I gather? Sadly, one such as I cannot say much of my past, for I recall nothing before my demise." The woman shook her head, voice somber.

"Oh." Rita sighed. That was too bad, fascinating, but unfortunate. Still, she glanced back at the different instruments before her. Maybe tomorrow, she could talk with the others to figure out who could do what with the ship. She felt uncomfortable just leaving it to the woman beside her. She hummed in thought, that was a situation for another day, for now.

For now, she was going to use this time to learn as much as she could.

Sleep would drag at her eventually, if she needed it.

~ * ~

Milos awoke to a warmth at his back, wondering when he fell asleep. He mentally berated himself for being unaware of his situation. It only took a moment to reorient his thoughts and remind himself that the warmth was, in fact, Alex. From the even breaths and slowly rising and falling chest, Milos assumed he was still fast asleep. He carefully sat up, making sure not to wake the other as he peered over to Leon. It seemed the man was deep in sleep as well. Milos had to admit, he was relieved. While the wound he had inflicted was mostly healed, he knew it would be some time before Leon got back full equilibrium with a missing arm. Still, better a missing arm than dead. He just hoped he wouldn't have to do it again.

He would do it, but he, unfortunately, had grown attached to everyone here. Hesitation would cost him, but he had a feeling he might still hesitate. It was not a comfortable realization, but he was glad he was aware of it. A faint light filtered in through the window, a little different from the light stone he was used to. He peered out, narrowing his gaze.

It seemed as if they were reaching the end of the cavern-like tunnel. He could see the beginning of light stones, littering the edge of the space, growing brighter as they traveled.

He heard a murmuring and felt the bed shift. He glanced back to see Alex roll over, closer to where he slept, pulling the sheets close, probably for warmth. Milos quickly got dressed, swiping up his sword and gear before heading out the door. He headed to the kitchen, grabbing some salted meat before heading up on deck. He had to admit, he was surprised to see Rita standing on deck, staring out over the water. She must have heard his footsteps, but didn't turn around.

"What are you doing up?" Milos asked, leaning on one leg as he lightly rested his arm on the sheath of his sword.

"I'm figuring out how the ship works." She turned to Milos and he noted the tiredness in her gaze, even as she grinned. "I think I have it all worked out now. I'll show you guys later." She let out a yawn before waving. "I'm hitting the hay, keep an eye on things, will ya?" She walked past and Milos stared after her, a little amused.

Figuring out the ship, huh? That wasn't a bad idea. Though, he would probably get himself confused. The ships were a bit too different between their respective lands. He shook his head. Now that the light stones shone gently around the ship, he could take full stock of everything. The ship was long and slender, good for sharp turns plus fast movement. However, he could tell it wasn't bulky in any way. A few strong hits would crack the hull and they would be sinking pretty damn quick. It was still better quality than the ones he saw earlier. Alex might be able to help them, but with his voice messed up, Milos doubted he had much control over his demonic heritage. On top of that, Milos had no doubt that Alex would only be able to carry one or maybe two of them. Considering there were four and he didn't know how to use his wings, Milos wasn't going to hold his breath.

He heard footsteps and turned to see both Ari and Leon coming up behind him, watching him quietly. "Good, you're up." He turned to them. "Rita brought up a good point that I would like you two to work on." His gaze flickered to Leon's missing arm before he continued, "If you are up to it, of course."

The two nodded, though Milos didn't miss the affronted look on Leon's face. He felt a small smirk curl his lip up and quickly pushed it away. "Speak with the Aqua Wraith and see if you can learn the ins and outs of this ship. Three people who know how to operate this thing should suffice." Milos gestured, watching them go. It wasn't that large of a ship. If it was the ones from home, he would probably need everyone. With an Aqua Wraith and three people, maybe four with Alex's help, they should be fine. He walked into the map room, staring up at the maps Rita pointed out the day before.

He could tell each was rather hastily thrown together, so the accuracy of them would probably not be optimal, but he reached up, tracing a general path through the most detailed map. Unfortunately, it looked like they wouldn't be able to straight-shot it. They were almost out of the tunnel. Once they got out, he wondered just what they would be dealing with.

After all, the man mentioned this was only the first hurdle.

At least, generally, from each of the maps, he could tell that it was a rather large body of water they were sailing into. How large, he wasn't sure, though he could guess. Most of the maps were only of the northern reaches. Shoved into the corner, he spotted a map that gave an overview of the whole Underlands, but it was much less detailed than the others.

He frowned, noting just how large the northern lands were and how much farther they reached northward than he figured. For his ancestors who fought demons, what caused them to leave the northern lands alone? He closed his eyes, for once letting his senses feel over the surrounding area. He almost cringed. With the water all around, waves hitting the ship and echoing off of the walls, it wasn't easy to pinpoint magical energies. Alex and the Aqua Wraith were both water elementals; it took all his senses just to *sense* those two on the ship.

If there was something in the water...

He opened his eyes and furrowed his brow. So, water helped dull magical energies? If that was the case, then how did his ancestors catch Nyx and Naiads? Was there another way? He couldn't recall that teaching—actually, now that he thought about it, he recalled being told to avoid any large bodies of water. He hadn't thought about it much, since there weren't that many large bodies of water in the Underlands.

Was it because Alertian senses were dulled with the water?

Alertians could still fight, and if he strained, he could still sense magical energies, so, what caused the north to be so unreachable?

He pursed his lips, his thoughts swirling, but never truly giving him an answer. That worried him, more than he would like to admit. He shook his head as the sound of shuffling reached his ears. He glanced over to the doorway leading downstairs to see Alex coming up, ruffling his hair as he awoke. Alex noticed him and sighed in relief before glancing up at the maps, quizzical expression on his face.

"I'm figuring out what we might be facing and what I have at my disposal," Milos admitted before fully turning to face him. "Did you sleep well?"

A sharp nod and a bright smile was his response and Milos felt a small smile tug at his lips. "If you are wondering, Ari and Leon are working with the Aqua Wraith to learn more about this ship. It might do you some good to..."

The boy shivered, promptly shaking his head and rubbing his arm.

Milos observed him quietly as realization dawned on him. "You really are nervous around her."

A slight squeak.

Milos chuckled. "I'm guessing you are not much of a fan of the idea of ghosts. Who knew?" Milos turned away, causing Alex to scramble around his side and stand in front of him, arms crossed and glaring. Milos shook his head, amused. "There's nothing wrong with that, but you still might want to think of her more as a demon and less as a ghost. After all, considering where we are going, she will probably be with us for a while."

Alex shuddered, indecision clear on his face before he sighed, slumping.

It didn't take much to realize that Milos won the pseudo-argument and gestured downstairs. "If you're still that nervous, grab something to eat and drink, then go work with her."

He nodded before frowning, he placed a finger to his lip, deep in thought before turning and giving Milos a sharp look, pointing.

"Me?" Milos blinked as Alex nodded. "I know more about Overland ships. The likelihood of me mixing up the two is highly..." To his surprise, he was cut off by Alex's unamused expression and suddenly tight grip on his upper arm. With a sharp pull, Alex tugged him toward the stairwell. Milos was, admittedly, surprised at the boy's strength. Was his demonic side coming back now that they were on open water? Milos shut his eyes, quickly zeroing in on the boy before him. To his surprise, and slight relief, he mildly noted, he could see the rather dismal energy that felt constricted before had actually increased. The latent water, so teeming with untainted magic, seemed to be flowing toward the boy.

"Hm... seems you'll be recovering soon," Milos admitted softly, letting himself be dragged down the stairs.

The waters here, unlike in other areas of the Underlands, really were rich with magic. For most demons, except fire, this would be a great area to replenish strength. For a water demon... Milos eyed Alex quietly. For a water demon, including one like Alex with demon-human blood and only a small portion being water, it would still have a profound effect. Milos wondered how long it would take, under these conditions, for Alex to not only be able to use his powers again, but to also be able to speak again.

While it was usually easy to read the boy and figure out his cues, it was difficult to work with him and Milos knew full well that Alex was beyond frustrated with his inability to speak.

However, if his analysis was right, that meant Alex's voice was completely connected to his demonic ability. Was that truly the case? Or was it a mix of straining his throat and powers that caused all of this? Thinking about it, his throat would be just starting to heal from the strain put on it. Maybe the two were intertwined?

So lost in thought, Milos found himself standing in front of the engine with Alex and the Aqua Wraith. She was watching him in silent contemplation and, if he was honestly seeing things right, a hint of amusement.

Milos sighed. Guess he wasn't getting out of learning how this ship worked, and he'd been so close too.

~ * ~

Alex had to admit, it was actually quite fun to learn how to control the ship. He wasn't sure, but he could almost feel the way the ship slid through the water, the easy way it turned and changed speed. It all felt smooth and almost reliable. It was weird, feeling like he was sensing something he couldn't see. Milos had figured it was just because of his demonic side being more attuned to water. Alex wasn't sure, but he would take what he could get.

Once the teaching was done, the group gathered for lunch before returning to the map room. The Aqua Wraith mentioned they would be leaving the tunnel soon and they would need to prepare. Alex wasn't sure what to prepare though. What were they going to face?

He stared up at the maps in contemplation. Almost all the ones that actually held details of the north showed a rather large body of water. But he was going to be frank, he couldn't imagine it would be that large.

He shook his head, deciding to let Milos and Rita talk it over. He stepped out the door, hearing their faint bickering in the background as he massaged his throat. For some reason, his throat hurt more lately and he had no idea why. Shouldn't it be healing? After all, it was a while ago when he lost his voice. Maybe Milos was right. He had been doing a fairly good job ignoring it, but the last day especially brought the annoyance to the forefront. While traveling, it wasn't much of an issue, but when trying to discuss where everyone would be and what everyone was going to do, well, it left him more than a little frustrated. He let out a quiet hiss as the boat gently swayed back and forth, the light was getting brighter as they descended through the passage. Actually...

Alex glanced to either side before kneeling down on the boat, closing his eyes. Now that he was paying attention, it did feel like they were descending downward. It wasn't incredibly noticeable, but enough to show that they were dropping down. Why down? Shouldn't they be going up? After all, if this river and the water above are twin rivers, then shouldn't they meet up?

Alex heard a faint gargling sound, causing a shiver to run down his spine as the water seemed to quaver. Its voice, which was at the back of his mind, suddenly shrilled. He let out a yelp, backpedaling before realizing he was on his knees and falling onto his back with a jolt. Rita and the others must have heard the sound because Rita darted out the door.

"Alex. What happened?"

Alex sat up, massaging his throat in hopes of saying something. What could he say though? That he sensed something in the water? He opened his mouth, just as the Aqua Wraith came out and said, "This ship 'tis almost out. Be careful." She wavered. The water was almost vibrating as she swirled around. "Danger's afoot. We are in need of evasive action." Her words were spoken in a light tone, but the words themselves were enough to alarm everyone.

In no time, Alex found himself helping direct Milos while the rest rushed to the engine room as the pitch and speed of the river suddenly accelerated. The water began to flow more fiercely, crashing against the walls as the descent went from gentle to very much noticeable. Milos gripped the wheel. Alex wished he could shout instructions, but...

He gritted his teeth, hearing the water suddenly screech before it disappeared.

Why did that sound like it was dis...?

Not good, not good!

"Milos."

The word, faint, wispy, but very much there, rang over the water, causing Milos to snap up and stare at Alex in surprise. Alex's hands darted to his throat, but he quickly shook it off. Pain flared up, but he ignored it. He might not be able to speak loud, but by *gosh*, was it a joy to be able to speak again.

He raced over, leaning up into Milos' ear. "Something is up ahead." It really hurt to speak; his voice was weak at best and very faint, but he had to thank Milos' acute senses, since the man seemed to be able to hear anyway. "Almost sounds like it's swallowing the water."

"Swallowing the water?" Milos thought for a moment before a few curse words that completely startled Alex slipped from the man's mouth.

Alex didn't even *know* the man could swear like that. He certainly never saw it before from the stoic man. Which definitely confirmed the terror welling in his spine.

"Where is it? Can you sense water around it?"

Alex blinked before covering his eyes, trying to listen. It was faint, but... "Yes."

"Good. We might be able to avoid it then."

Milos pursed his lips. He turned to the pipe, which Alex knew was connected to the engine room, and flipped it up. "Be ready for a sharp turn. As soon as we exit the waterway, we are going to be needing all the speed we can get, understood?" He snapped it closed, not waiting for a response as he glanced over to Alex. "I'm glad you have your voice back, but you won't have much time to celebrate."

"I didn't think so," Alex muttered, grimacing. He had a feeling it was going to hurt to talk for a bit, but he wasn't going to worry about that right now. The river suddenly leveled out, but the flow only grew worse, tugging at the ship as a gargling sound filled the air.

A gargling sound that even Milos could hear, it seemed. Alex didn't miss the way Milos snapped his eyes closed for a second before suddenly wrenching the pipe up. "Belay that last order. Full reverse. On the double!"

"What, why?" Rita's voice was faint, but Alex could hear her and the Aqua Wraith responding. He had no doubt that the woman could sense it the same as him and Milos.

That wasn't a natural occurrence, whatever was ahead.

Before he could think any more, the ship suddenly slowed, air streaming past and over the deck as the wind stones worked double time to slow them down. Alex braced himself against the cabin as Milos widened his stance, tightly gripping the wheel with grim determination. Oh, that's definitely a pleasant thought, Alex pushed the worry away and peered ahead as the tunnel suddenly opened up.

If he still had his full voice, his next reaction would have, no doubt, been a very unmanly scream as he noticed the swirling water and the *teeth*. As it was, he let out a high-pitched squeak that Milos summarily agreed with, followed by another slew of curses. Milos sharply turned the wheel to dodge one of the *way too big teeth*. Alex could only guess at the size of the creature underneath the water if its teeth were that big. Though it wasn't too hard to imagine with the curtains of water plummeting down into a crevice of black. Through the waterfalls, Alex could just see pink flesh, stained with rot and algae. Alex was glad Milos thought to slow the ship, because they would have been tossed right into that giant hole. The gaping maw, because that was all it could be, almost pulsed as if swallowing the water and air. The gargling seemed to come from far below, the streams of water doing nothing to hide the gruesome flesh and teeth that could shred a Drega whole. Thankfully, the wind stones were on their side. Milos turned the wheel, flipping up the pipe before shouting, "Full speed! Forward."

Alex braced himself once more as the ship sharply turned, the water still swirling, sucking them closer to those teeth, closer to the sudden and deadly drop only feet away from the wood of their ship. A moment later, right as Alex could almost touch the grime of the teeth, the ship shot forward, wind howling behind them as they peeled away. Alex jerked back, watching as the teeth suddenly snapped shut. For a brief moment, a large eel-shaped creature lurched into the air before plunging back under the water. It was only thanks to a swift turn of the boat from Milos that they didn't capsize as the ensuing wave slammed into their ship. Alex stumbled, barely holding onto the wall of the cabin. Within moments the shadow of the creature, vaguely seen through the sheen of the water, disappeared below, leaving the surrounding water still and placid, as if it was never there to begin with.

Milos didn't stop. Not for a good couple minutes before the wind stones slowly died down, his grip loosening only slightly as Alex let out a breath of relief. His legs shook as he crumbled to the deck, pulling in sharp breaths. "What the heck was that?"

He let out a choking cough, but thankfully, Milos seemed to hear, because the man responded, voice surprisingly hoarse. "One of the monsters of the deeps, I would presume." Milos let out a breath, pulling away from the wheel before peering out over the water. "The water here must be deep for it to completely disappear lik..." He suddenly grew quiet, catching Alex's attention.

Alex massaged his throat once more before following his gaze and freezing. Before them, stretched out for as far as the eye could see, was water.

Logically, Alex knew there was an end to it, but as he scanned the horizon, waves beating gently against their ship, he had a hard time reconciling the notion.

"To think something like this could be in the Underlands." Milos' voice was filled with respect and admiration. "It would explain how something like that could disappear into the depths."

Alex stared. Was this what a sea looked like? Maybe an ocean? He wasn't sure. He could see the day stones gleaming high above, reflecting gently off the lapping water, but he couldn't see any other stone except the mountainous crags behind them. He peered back, spotting the large opening they came through quite a way away and another river that wove down, landing only a few feet away from it.

Both would have gone right into that creature's jaw. Whatever that creature was. Alex shivered as footsteps sounded up the stairs.

"What was that?" Rita suddenly barged out before stilling. Ari and Leon weren't far behind her as she let out a breathy, "Whoa..."

Alex didn't blame her. The way the water sparkled was beyond fascinating and the casting of the day stones made it shine brilliantly, creating a warm and bright glow around the area.

"To answer your question." Milos walked over, causing Rita to turn. "We encountered a creature at the end of the waterway. It was set up to catch any prey that might be going down the river."

"So that's why the fish were fleeing the other way," Rita muttered, causing Alex to blink.

What fish was she talking about? Seeing their confused expression, she shook her head and glanced out over the water. "It's amazing. How could something like this exist in the Underlands? How did we not know about it?" She paused for a moment, deep in thought before she turned and asked, "Did we?"

"I have no clue," Milos admitted before turning to Alex, sending him a questioning look.

Alex stared, unsure why Milos was watching him before Milos

let out a sigh. "Alex, how are you feeling?"

Alex paused, realizing what he meant and reached to his throat once more. While it was still sore from earlier, it was already starting to feel better. "Okay." His voice was a whisper.

He suddenly found Rita beside him, checking him over, causing Alex to squeak in surprise. Rita examined him, stunned. "You got your voice back! Are you okay? Does it hurt?"

She paused, almost smacking her head before digging into her satchel. "Stupid, of course it probably hurts. Here, I made this earlier while we were traveling for when you got your voice back." She pulled out a stoppered bottle and shoved it into Alex's hands. Alex withheld a yelp as he caught the bottle. He stared down at it, debating before sighing.

Rita was the only one of the group who knew anything about medicine, and his throat was killing him after the last few minutes. He unstopped it and, with only a bit of hesitation, he downed the whole thing. It took all he had not to toss it back up, the bitter flavor sticking to his tongue like a vice. Rita swiped the bottle from him as he wiped his mouth, trying not to cough.

"That works." Milos watched with amusement before his smile dropped. "It seems that the waters and scare were enough for him to get most of his demonic power back, which seems to have unblocked his vocal cords. He's still going to be hoarse, I assume, but he should be able to speak from now on."

"That's a relief." Rita sighed as she stuffed the bottle away.

Alex glared, but didn't comment, deciding to massage his throat instead as Rita scanned the tunnel that they'd left so far behind them. "So, we almost got swallowed by a monster. Are we actually ready to go through this, well, underground sea?"

"Don't know." Milos walked back to the wheel. "We do need to move. Rita, which direction?"

"Huh? Oh. Uh...por—I mean starboard," She trailed off, hurrying into the map room. After a moment, she poked her head out. "Hey, Alex, can you come here? I'm going to need your help. If Milos is right, you can sense the waters, right? I'm going to need you to help me figure out where we are."

"Sure?" Alex muttered, hurrying over.

This was weird. Now that his voice was back, he could feel the voice of his demonic side. It was calling, a feeling he was so scared of before. It was actually comforting to hear it again after a week of silence. He could practically feel energy gently flow from the water. It was warming, soothing. He had a feeling it would be a bit longer until he could talk normally, but he was fine with it.

He followed after Rita as she stood over one of the maps. Ari and Leon had already disappeared and, he suspected, that they went down to the kitchen to maybe make something to eat. He had no clue where the Aqua Wraith could be.

Frankly, he wasn't too worried about it. Rita tapped at the map. "So, we know we're somewhere south of this point, but I'm not sure how far east or west we are. Our frantic escape from the tunnel definitely didn't help my sense of direction."

Alex pursed his lips, scanning the area before shrugging. "I don't know," he trailed off. "I can't exactly..." He stopped as Rita glanced up. She stared at him for a moment and sighed.

"Yeah, sorry. You're still trying to figure that all out. Hm... can you get a general viewpoint? You were outside when we veered away from whatever was after us."

Alex nodded and glanced down at the map. She pointed out what was probably the tunnel and he hummed before pointing a little to the right—or was it starboard? It was hard to remember everything the Aqua Wraith mentioned—already a little north from where they were before. Rita nodded, glancing it over before rolling up the entire map. As she did so, her hand moved over the wood of the table and she paused, blinking. Alex leaned forward, curious as Rita placed the map down and slowly felt over the wood with her fingers.

After a moment, she let out an "Ah-ha" and tapped on a part of the wood that looked exactly the same as the rest. Alex saw the wood press in slightly, as if there was a button there, before a space in the middle suddenly slid to the side, disappearing into the surrounding wood to expose an entire interior compartment. There were a couple items in there, but before he could get a good look, Rita's hand darted in, pulling out a compass. It was gold with a simple white inlay. It looked quite sturdy. Alex heard a sound and glanced back down to see the piece was back in place.

He would have asked how that happened, considering he didn't see Rita press anything, but he decided not to bother. From his brief glimpse, he didn't really see anything besides more papers. Rita lifted the compass up, the glass glinting in the light.

Glass. Alex couldn't help but whistle as Rita tapped it. Even Alex could tell it was of high-quality.

"Perfect." Rita grinned, feeling it over. "I was worried, but with this, we should be fine. Tell that lout to turn the wheel toward port a little, so we can go back to heading north instead of northeast."

"He's not a lout, you know," Alex muttered, coughing slightly.

Rita grimaced, bringing the compass down. "Right, sorry. Until you get your voice back, I'll try to be more careful."

"Only until then?" Alex couldn't hide the deadpan expression on his face.

Rita shrugged. "Even then, I make no promises."

Alex sighed, that was about the best he was going to get out of her, no doubt.

He shook his head, watching as she reopened the map and peered over it, making some marks using the compass. Alex turned and headed back out. Milos was leaning against the cabin, half an eye on the horizon, half on the wheel. He spotted Alex and pushed away from the wall.

"You heard?"

Milos nodded, heading over to the wheel. "She keeps forgetting I have sharp hearing. She's not exactly quiet either."

Alex chuckled at that. No, she wasn't. Though, she wouldn't be herself if she was. Alex felt the ship drift to the left a bit before they were once more going along. In the distance, all Alex could see was water, and what he guessed was the roof of the Underlands. He didn't even see mountains, except for behind them, which were already disappearing as their ship parted the waves.

"How are you?" Milos spared him a glance.

Alex walked over to the edge of the ship, peering out over the water as he thought over his answer. After a moment, he responded, voice soft. "Okay, though I'm not sure how much Rita's medicine helped or if it was something else. It's strange." He pushed away, turning to Milos as he nodded, seeming to understand. "I am more energized, but..."

"Well, even with all the magic in these waters, it's going to take some time for your body to transform it in a way that works with you."

"Hm... did you learn that in training?" Alex coughed. His throat did hurt, but he hadn't talked in ages and it wasn't as bad as earlier. He would have to thank Rita later. Especially since he couldn't seem to convince himself to stop talking.

Milos stared at him for a bit before returning his attention straight ahead. "It was one of the things I learned in training." He hesitated for a moment before continuing. "Truth be told, I don't know much about water demons. No one does."

"Even Alertians?"

"Even Alertians," Milos repeated, smirking slightly. "Remember, we aren't infallible."

"Could have fooled me."

Milos could barely hold back a snort, which caused Alex to chuckle. Silence descended over them as Alex stared out over the waters, deep in thought.

They stayed in silence until Rita stepped out, peering up at the sky before observing both of them. "I'll keep watch up here. You two, get something to eat."

Alex went to argue, only for his stomach to growl. He blushed before shrugging. Yeah, that would probably be a good idea.

Rita stared at him for a moment before smiling softly. "I'm glad you got your voice back, by the way."

"Me too." Alex smiled in response.

Milos shook his head, walking past with an amused smirk.

Rita sent him a quick glare as Alex followed after him, deciding that, yes, he was *very* hungry right now. Almost hungrier than when they left.

He wondered if it was because of the sudden influx of magic. Maybe, maybe not. He wouldn't worry about it for now.

Chapter Five

Rita stared out over the water, finally letting her mind rest. Up until now, she was worrying about the tunnel, about where they were going, what they were going to do...everything. To be honest, it was a huge relief and a weight off her shoulders when Alex spoke. It gave her a chance to think of something else.

That something else ended up being her parents. To be honest, she'd been trying not to think about them, but now that she knew that Alex was recovering, and they were all safely on their way, she couldn't help but think about her parents.

How many weeks—was it really weeks?—had it been since she saw them alive? When they were still with her, all of them were so stressed, and for what?

Her mouth felt dry, her chest aching as the memories surged forward, catching her somewhat off guard. She didn't realize, as she stood there, staring out over the open water, just how much she missed them. Mom with her soft smile and Dad with his encouraging words. Their dead gaze haunted her this whole time, never fully letting her rest. Her anger hadn't helped that much.

Now that she had the time to think...

She bit her lip harshly, trying to rein in the emotions. Divon was no longer in her life. He was no longer after her, she was finally free of him. So, why? Why did she have to lose her parents? There was no reason for the Martinets to kill them, not like that. She could still remember the way Father jerked as he was shot, over and over and over again. She could still hear the thud of his body hitting the floor, the blood soaking her hands as her mother gently told her to run, to get away. She still remembered the heartbroken smile on her mother's face as she stood and charged the man. The way her footsteps faltered with each shattering bang.

Rita didn't realize she was crying until she felt the tears drip onto her arms, crossed tightly over her chest as she shivered. "Mom. Dad. I'm...I'm sorry," she said, finally realizing.

She didn't ever say sorry to them, she never actually got a chance to mourn or grieve. She just kept pushing ahead, aiming for the next goal, dealing with the next worry. She found herself slumping to the deck, shaking as she no longer held in the gasps. She wasn't worried about the others seeing her. They would be downstairs anyway.

"I'm so sorry." She felt herself crack. "I'm finally free. I'm free, just like you wanted," she whispered, pulling her arms away to wipe at her face, not doing much as fresh tears dripped down. So, now that she was free, why did it *hurt* so much? It hurt so damn much.

What would her parents say to this situation? What would anybody she knew say?

Her parents were gone, her home practically burned to the ground, her teacher missing and probably dead and her only means of support being a demon and a demon hunter.

"What is up with my life?" She weakly chuckled. She didn't expect to end up in this situation. She just wanted to be a seer, like her role model. She wanted her parents to be proud of her, she wanted them to have a good life.

Now she would never have that opportunity. She couldn't go home, not anymore.

She hated it, hated this feeling. It was strange, how a small boat with so many people could feel so lonely. As she cried, she struggled to remember the happier times, the moments of genuine warmth and joy. It was so hard, so hard when those moments were tossed aside to be replaced with the empty gazes and blood-stained corpses.

A soft sound met her ears, almost like a gentle singing. She ignored it, wiping her eyes a few more times in futility as she realized her sleeves were soaked through. Words, words in an ancient tongue, slid over the deck. She blinked blearily. She spotted the Aqua Wraith at the other end of the ship, staring out over the water as she sat on the railing.

It didn't take much for Rita to realize she was the one singing.

It was a calming song, something she heard from her mother...from herself...from Alex. It was the same lullaby she taught Alex when she first met him all those weeks ago.

She couldn't help but let out another sob, very much grateful for the soft tune as it covered her loud crying.

At this point, she honestly didn't care anymore. Let them see her. She had held this in for so long, she didn't realize until the emotions poured out of her. As much as it hurt, she could already feel the weight lifting off her shoulders, the ache in her heart, just that little bit lighter.

She would mourn now. So she could protect those who were still alive later.

Someday, she would give her parents a proper farewell, but for today, this was enough.

~ * ~

Milos listened to the soft wails from above deck with a solemn silence. There were times he wished his hearing wasn't so sharp. Though, to his relief, Alex seemed to hear it too. At first, the boy wanted to charge back upstairs, but Milos laid a hand on his shoulder. It seemed to be enough to dissuade Alex from doing anything reckless.

After all, as much as Milos might bicker with Rita, he also knew she needed this more than she would care to admit. It hurt, losing a loved one. As much as he bickered with her, he couldn't help but respect her strength in pressing forward.

Alex sat back down, appearing agitated, but understanding. That was enough for Milos.

Milos sipped at the tea, staring out the window of their shared room. To be honest, the silence as they slid through the underground ocean's waters, which he still found himself reeling at, reminded him of home. A home that, at one point not that long ago, he wanted to go back to. A home where...he shook himself from the thought, he knew where it was heading, and it would do him no good. At this point, no matter what he did, he would be seen as a traitor. His goal. His dream. It was forfeit the night he helped Alex. At least, part of it was.

There was still a chance he could obtain his dream. All he would have to do is find a way to capture the demons of the north and present them to his father. The other option was to lead them to him. He'd thought about this earlier, briefly. Now the thought swirled in his mind, solidifying itself. He held no special regard for the demons; the only one he truly held any respect for was Alex.

Alex's mother...for a mother to do what she did.

Though he was helping Alex, he had no such hesitation on that demon. No mother would abandon her child. Not unless they had no other option. Not a real mother at least.

A demon...a powerful demon, such as the one he sensed through Alex, would have many options.

He clenched his fists, feeling his gaze sharpen on the outside. It made him a bit angry. He acknowledged. He shook his head, loosening his grip. He would have to wait and see. There were still opportunities in the future.

"Milos?"

Alex's voice caught his attention and he turned to face the half-demon. He was glad the boy was able to speak. Though it was soft, he could hear the lilting tone he recognized, the surge of power as he spoke, beckoning, calling. Was it more powerful? It would make sense that, to deal with the injury, Alex would have been absorbing as much energy as he could.

Milos briefly wondered if the excess energy expanded his demonic reservoir or if it simply opened up the already extensive one he possibly held in his lithe frame. It was an interesting question. One Milos did not have an answer to. "Yes?"

"Did you sense that creature? The thing under the water?" Alex watched him in worry.

Milos shook his head. "No. Our line may be good at sensing demons, but our powers don't necessarily extend into the water. Water often absorbs magic and reflects it back. To us, it's the same as trying to look through multiple layers of stone while something is covering our ears. We may know something's there, but it might also be just a fluctuation in the current, thus the magic. Plus, from what we saw at the end, I doubt that was a demon, or a normal animal for that matter."

"Ah..."

"I would presume you sensed it?"

"Sort of," Alex admitted, seeming sheepish. "I could feel the way the water was screeching before it suddenly disappeared."

"So, you felt its surroundings, not so much the thing itself."

Milos hummed, intrigued. That would make sense, and would be an interesting way to sense things. Actually, with the way water intermingled with magic, it might be the *only* way to sense things, similar to a sonar.

He would have to keep that in mind, going forward. "Would you mind keeping an ear out for more of those disturbances?"

"Yeah, I can do that." Alex smiled, seeming happy to be helping. Milos couldn't blame him on his enthusiasm. "Still, I'm not sure I want to imagine seeing more of those things." Alex shivered and Milos simply nodded.

He wouldn't deny he was shaken at the idea of plunging into that gaping maw, seeing the rotting flesh and remains of creatures he would rather *not* recognize. If that was something at the very beginning of this journey, he wasn't sure he wanted to imagine the other horrors that awaited them. "That's for another day." Milos stood, noting that it was now surprisingly quiet upstairs. Alex perked up, peering up the stairs before jumping to his feet and racing out.

Milos followed at a more sedate pace, noting a quiet thumping from the storage room which indicated Leon's position as he moved up the stairs. Outside, it was peaceful, the day stones shifting slowly to their night-time counterparts. Had it really been a whole day? Had their timetable been thrown off by being surrounded in darkness for so long? He tried to recall what they were like when they first left the tunnel, but to be honest, the stones barely differed unless it was late into the evening. He would have to ask the residents how they were able to tell the passing of time. Still, he was going to have to get used to that. He turned to see Alex kneeling beside Rita, whose head was in her arms. It seemed the crying caused her to fall asleep.

Milos shook his head, chuckling faintly. For once, he wasn't going to berate her. He watched as Alex tried to pick her up and failed. Milos shook his head and walked over. Alex spotted him, pausing in trying to bring one arm around his shoulder.

"Will you be able to carry her down the stairs?"

Alex paused for a moment at Milos' question, peering at her quietly before nodding. "Yeah. I'm just trying not to wake her, but she feels light to me."

Milos could only wonder what Rita would think about that statement, but brushed it off. "Let me help you get her on your back. It might be easier to carry her like I did for you."

"I remember that. Thanks, by the way. I never got a chance to thank you, what with the lack of voice and all." He kept his voice down, but a soft smile crossed his face as he knelt down.

Milos withheld the chuckle as he lifted Rita carefully from her armpits, letting her arms and head rest on Alex's back. Alex carefully wound his hands around her thighs and stood, carrying her piggyback. He stumbled for a moment when standing, hearing a quiet murmuring from Rita.

Milos peered over to her, noting the way she seemed to curl her arms around Alex's neck in her sleep.

Alex just shook his head, a slight blush on his face. "Thanks."

Milos nodded as Alex turned and headed toward the doorway. Milos waited, standing with his arms crossed as Alex paused before peering back over his shoulder. "Hey, can you open the door, please? That would help, you know."

"I was wondering if you would notice."

"Really? Milos, you could have just opened it you know." He frowned before shaking his head. "Right, Rita. She would be yelling at you at this point for that."

"I know."

Alex snorted softly, chuckling quietly as Milos opened the door for him. "Anyway, do you want me to tell Ari or Leon anything since I'm heading down there anyway?"

"Just tell Ari to keep an eye on her and for Leon to continue doing what he's doing."

"All right...I'll be back later." With that he descended down the stairs as Milos closed the door. Well, at least he got a bit of a break from staring out over the water.

Milos' internal clock was thrown off. It was strange to think it was already night. He was surprised Rita was able to stay up so long, after all. He peered up at the now slowly brightening night stones.

Of course, he had no qualms about staying up. Night was usually when things were most dangerous. He leaned against the cabin, keeping half his attention on the wheel and the other half on the water. He jerked up, noting a hint of light in the distance, coming closer. It was low in the water, like a wave. He hurried over the wheel, gripping it tightly. He held no doubt that at least the Aqua Wraith was in the engine room. He waited, watching as the light approached. It was hard to tell, the way it shimmered under the water.

A silver fish leapt out of the water, before splashing down. Milos loosened his grip slightly, examining the silver fish that glistened in the night stones' light. Milos had to admit, they were beautiful creatures.

However, he couldn't help but feel nervous at their presence, a strange feeling of urgency sang through his mind as he pursed his lips. They were swimming quickly, but not ridiculously so. Were they running from something, or simply migrating?

He hoped it was the latter, but he had a feeling it was the former.

He watched them pass by and under the ship, leaping out of the water before disappearing back into the dark depths. The night stones weren't doing nearly enough to calm his nerves. The water fluctuated between a gentle shine and an inky blackness as soon as the fish left, disappearing back the way the ship came. He watched them go before staring out over the water. Another wave crested, glimmering a faint bluish silver in the dim light of the night stone and the lone light stone at the stern.

Rita mentioned fish earlier, and those were the only ones he saw so far. Were they the same as what she saw? He followed the trajectory of where they came from, slightly to port, and shifted the wheel so it was angled more toward starboard.

Hopefully, whatever was causing those fish to move about, whether fleeing or through migration, wouldn't come and find their ship as a snack.

He kept his attention on the water as the night passed on. A few hours into his vigil, Alex came up onto the deck, spotting him. He walked over and gave him an unamused poke. "You're going to keel over." He was frank and to the point.

Milos couldn't argue. He was still tired and, though it wasn't necessarily a long day, staring at the same thing for hours on end without moving could be surprisingly draining. "I'll take over for now." Alex would have probably said more if he hadn't started coughing, reaching a hand up to his throat in agitation.

Milos watched him for a bit before nodding. He could feel a yawn coming on and quickly suppressed it. "I'll leave it to you." He tilted his head before following Alex's advice. He stopped for a second before glancing back. "Oh, and I changed our trajectory slightly. It shouldn't throw us off too much, but it should, hopefully, avoid any more of those creatures."

Milos withheld a yawn before heading inside, just barely noting as Alex nodded toward him, a faint smile on his lips.

Hopefully, Alex would be a bit more attentive than Rita was.

Alex took a seat by the wheel, staring up at the night stones. He lightly juggled his light stone from hand to hand, letting his thoughts wander. He had already made sure Rita was asleep, noting the calm smile on her face as she curled into the hammock, murmuring soft words he couldn't make out.

It was kind of cute.

He shook his head and stood, noting the direction they were going. Milos mentioned that he changed their direction. Could he have sensed something? No, Milos wasn't able to sense anything within water. It must have been something else. He closed his eyes, letting himself listen to the water. Its calm waves slapped against the side of the boat as they gently pushed ahead, keeping the engines low for now.

To the left, at a strange angle, he could sense something large. The water morphed around it in a serpentine fashion. He shivered.

Yeah, that was probably the reason. Good thing Milos was paying attention. Still...even with the change of course, that thing was a little too close for comfort.

Alex flipped up the pipe before hesitating. Would whoever was down there hear him?

"Speak."

Alex jumped, letting out a squeak of surprise. "Uh...we need a bit more speed."

"So, 'twas noticed. I wondered on why the ship changed its course."

Alex nodded before realizing the stupidity and, blushing, said, "Yeah. Milos noticed."

"Hm... the Alertian. I will profess, I'm surprised. However, I guess I should not be, as he has shown to be quite astute."

Alex blinked, trying to decipher what she meant before giving up. The Aqua Wraith's dialogue was always so archaic. It made his head spin, just trying to figure it out. He felt a slight shift and found their ship to be moving faster than before. He felt relieved when he realized they would be able to just get out of the creature's way.

How something that big could exist in the Underlands? And to have more than *one*? Why, oh *why* were there creatures like that? At least it was near the surface and he was able to detect it.

He kept his gaze on the horizon, occasionally spotting something like a tail break through the water, easily the size of half of their ship, before plunging back in. Thankfully, the creature didn't seem to notice and the ship slipped by without catching its attention.

Alex let out a sigh of relief before returning his attention to the horizon.

He was suddenly grateful he came upstairs. Milos was falling asleep on his feet and they needed someone to keep watch.

For once, he wasn't going to complain about the lack of sleep. He could deal with it for tonight.

Chapter Six

The rising of the day stones was a relief to Alex's tired eyes. The water, which constantly shifted between inky black and dark blue, was finally glistening its gentle hues like the day before. The surroundings held a more peaceful air, unlike the constant stress of the night.

To be honest, he wasn't sure which was worse: to be out in the empty lands or the open waters. Both were equally as terrifying at times.

He shook his head. It was probably a bit easier for him. At least, he could rest and listen to the waves to calm his nerves. The others would have to actually keep watch.

That would be fun to figure out. Alex shook his head, letting out a yawn as he glanced down at the compass he grabbed earlier. The ship kept seeming to want to turn slightly northeast, so he kept having to make minor adjustments so it continued to go straight north. It wasn't anything major, but it was noticeable enough to cause them to cut a little time. His stomach growled as footsteps rang in his ears. He glanced over in time to see Rita poke her head out the door. She seemed much better, a calmness in her posture he didn't remember seeing in, ever. She spotted him and hurried over. "Were you up all night?"

Alex nodded, covering his mouth as another yawn slipped through. Rita's expression was downright unamused, hands on her hips. "Grab something to eat and go to bed."

Alex raised an eyebrow. "Really?"

"It was one time." Rita frowned, annoyed. "I slept, so I can keep watch better than your mostly asleep arse can."

Ah, there were her made-up swears. It had been a while. Alex shook his head, realizing what he was thinking. Yeah, sleep sounded good.

So, taking her advice and handing over the compass, he headed downstairs. He could smell something wafting from the kitchen and snuck over to take a peek inside. He could see that Leon, to his surprise, was at the stove, the fire stone's warm light emanating from within as something cooked.

His stomach growled and he blushed before slipping inside to take a seat. Leon peered over. For a brief moment, Alex thought he saw a faint smile on the man's lips before it was wiped away. Leon opened the stove and pulled out what appeared to be fresh bread. But, when he cut it, Alex could see stuff mixed in.

It looked good.

It didn't take long for him to down the food, the bread acting like a sort of bowl. Sometime while he was eating, Milos came in to check on them and grab something for himself.

Alex didn't mind, he hadn't realized how ravenous he was.

Eventually, he had his fill and let out another yawn.

Okay, okay. Sleep it was. For a brief moment, he hesitated, wondering if they would be all right.

"Get some rest. Keep in mind, the Aqua Wraith can warn us of anything dangerous as well, and you'll miss stuff in this state," Milos said, affirming Alex's thoughts.

Alex blinked before letting out a breath. Leave it to Milos to realize what he was worrying about. He smiled. "All right.... Thanks."

Milos waved it off, a surprisingly warm smile flitting on his face for a mere moment.

It was enough for Alex as he hummed to himself, heading to the bedroom. Sleep did sound good right now.

~ * ~

Rita didn't realize just how boring it would be to drift over the waves for hours on end. When her shift was up and Milos, of all people, took over, she found herself with nothing to do except to stare out over the water, contemplating what they were going to do next.

Not the most exciting thought process, she deduced. She let her elbow lean against the railing as she pushed her cheek into her hand. At least when they were traveling over the land, they were doing something. Sure, her legs hurt a lot afterward, but it was something she could focus on. Now she didn't even have that comfort.

She let out a groan, before pushing away from the railing and heading toward the map room, cabin, whatever they were calling it now. As she stepped in, she noticed Alex scanning over the table, curious.

He jumped upon her entrance and grinned sheepishly. "Oh, hey, Rita."

"What are you doing?" She raised an eyebrow and he glanced down at the table once more.

"I was looking for that compartment you found the compass in. I thought I saw a couple books in there."

"You like to read?" She had probably asked that before, but she couldn't remember.

"Yeah. I just haven't gotten a chance to in a while." He turned to Rita. "So, how did you open it last time?"

Rita walked over, stepping on the other side. She glanced at the wood before reaching toward one side of the table. A little gnarl of wood, barely visible unless you saw it before, or felt it like she did when picking up the map, stuck up slightly from table's surface. She lightly pressed it, feeling the mechanism snap into place as a slight, almost familiar, pulse slid through her fingers. In the middle of the table, the wood slid sideways, revealing the compartment. She kept her hand there, remembering how quickly it closed when she released it last time, and let Alex browse. Other than the compass, there were some documents and a small leather-bound book. Alex picked up the book, jostling something inside the compartment. They exchanged looks before Alex placed the book to one side, reached down and, to both of their surprise, picked up a vial. At first, Rita thought it was empty, but after a moment, she noticed a faint smoke whirling in the vial, constantly in motion. They both stared at it wordlessly.

"Do you think," Alex cut off, coughing into his other hand as he held the vial away from him. Once he could speak again, he continued, "Do you think Milos would know what's in this? What about the Aqua

Wraith?"

"Considering I don't, I'm not sure." Rita shrugged. "The Aqua Wraith might, but she's not really that talkative, I've noticed." Her mind flipped to the few times she saw the Wraith. Almost every time, she was either humming, or flitting between duties, never really staying in one place.

Alex chuckled, seeming to agree before he placed the vial carefully back down. "I'll have to ask her later."

Rita briefly wondered if it was all right to put it unprotected in the compartment, but from the way the dust resettled, she guessed it had been there a while. "Well, at least you got your book, right?"

Alex nodded, opening the pages before pursing his lips. "Except..." He flipped through, brows furrowing in confusion. "These are journal entries, but the handwriting is different on each page, as if different people wrote in this."

Rita blinked, startled as she let go of the button and stepped around the table, peering over Alex's shoulder. He was right.

As he flipped through the pages, she noticed the writing go from an elegant cursive, to a scrawling print, to a cursive that made her squint at how anyone could be that messy. What was the point of a journal if multiple people wrote in it?

"Are you going to read this?" Rita asked incredulously. Honestly, it was already giving her a headache to try to jump between the different scripts and she was used to the hard-to-read witch's books. Those things needed a freaking translator.

Alex nodded, flipping back to the first page, intrigue clear on his face.

"Well, let me know whatever it is you read. Got it?"

Alex peered up before a soft smile trailed on his face. "You are curious."

"Curious, yes, but bored enough to try to translate that? Not quite. Though, I am getting pretty close."

Alex snorted, amused, before placing it under his arm. "That's fair." He glanced toward the doorway outside before shrugging. With one last wave, he descended the stairs, leaving Rita in boredom once more.

She wasn't sure how long she sat there, perusing the maps before finally throwing her hands up.

Great. She still didn't know what she was supposed to be doing and wasted the past hour on nothing. Maybe she could find the Aqua Wraith and ask her about the vial? Deciding there weren't that many other options and, getting sick of staring at maps, she stood. She guessed the Wraith would be in the engine room. She descended the stairs, listening as probably Leon, though she wasn't certain, worked in the kitchen. She briefly wondered how Alex was doing with deciphering the book, but promptly put it off, heading toward the back room. She passed Ari, who squeezed past her, heading toward the stairway with a yawn. She smiled toward the slave, startling the girl before Ari nodded shyly.

Rita really wasn't sure what to make of the two slaves. Though she was getting used to them. She moved past the hammocks and slipped into the engine room. As she guessed, the Aqua Wraith was inside. She turned back toward Rita and pulled away from the controls. She hovered over before pulling to a stop. "You had a question." Her words were soft, but not at all phrased as a question. Rita wondered if she was psychic, and then mentally laughed. It was a ghost she was talking to. They didn't have to make sense.

"Yeah, I did." She walked over, facing the woman as the door closed behind her. "We found a compartment in the table upstairs. I hadn't thought much of it yesterday but we found some interesting things in there."

The Aqua Wraith swirled around her, stopping just to her right. "What has thee curious?"

Rita shifted to better face her, hand on her hip. "A vial." She noted the woman tilt her head slightly in acknowledgement as she continued, "A vial containing what appeared to be a strange gaseous substance. Considering you probably have a good amount of knowledge on this ship, I figured you would know what it is."

"You are not wrong." The woman swirled around once more before pulling back, legs extended forward as if she was leaning back in the air, though the rest of her posture was straight. "Tis a substance from former travelers." She spoke quietly. "Tis dangerous, thus I sealed it. You are a witch, are you not? You should recognize the signs."

The signs...Rita frowned, her thoughts flicking back to the table. She recalled how Alex could never see it and her eyes widened. Of course, it was just like the door back at the gatekeeper's home. "It's a seer's contraption. How did..."

"Thy sight was obscured due to my presence." The Aqua Wraith leaned forward. "A double-layered enchantment. I felt it fine to let you see within."

"So that's why..." Rita mumbled. She remembered a faint tingling, similar to the feeling she received from the seer's door. For a brief moment, she remembered seeing a flash of an image, but she ignored it the previous times, as if just her imagination. "Still, it doesn't answer..."

"Tis something too dangerous for one such as yourself to know..." The Aqua Wraith trailed off before diving through the floorboards, startling Rita, as her last words drifted to Rita's ears. "For it has to do with a promise. A promise I desire strongly to keep."

Rita glanced toward where the Aqua Wraith disappeared. Her thoughts whirling a mile a minute. A promise? What sort of promise? What could she mean?

She let out a breath, almost wishing she hadn't come down here. Now she had *more* questions than before. Why obscure something so vital behind a seer's lock? You would have to be extremely lucky, or extremely talented to find such a thing. Were the things within that dangerous?

What about the journal? She groaned and headed back upstairs, deciding to return to the maps, at least they made more sense.

Climbing back upstairs, she found Ari pulling a couple maps out of a compartment off to one side. The girl glanced over before continuing what she was doing.

Rita decided to join her, organizing the maps as best as she could. After all, they were going to probably be out at sea for a while. None of them knew a thing about the sea, or this type of travel in general.

They would have to stop sometime. If she could keep track of their progress and places to land, then it would probably help so they didn't get completely lost. She calculated in her head for a moment how much food they had and frowned. Actually, Alex had been eating a lot more lately, so their food count was probably lower than usual. They would have to find someplace to stop to collect more food. Sure, they could go fishing, but other than the silver fish, she hadn't seen much of anything. She honestly didn't want to hurt the beautiful things, or eat them, for that matter, if she could help it. She hadn't seen the bigger creatures Milos or Alex saw, but from what Alex mentioned, they would be too big to try to capture, nonetheless eat.

She glanced at her map, tracing a northward line from where Alex pointed earlier. Though they already encountered a few detours, she at least had something to work with that she assumed was the best she would be able to get for figuring out the closest landing spot.

She forwent most of the maps, grabbing only the ones that seemed to detail the waters. Ari took the rest to continue organizing them into piles and rolls. Most were hurriedly drawn in representations or just spattered words, but it would have to do. She glanced them over, laying them over each other to get a general representation. It seemed they already missed one island to the west a few hours ago, but that would have been too much of a detour. After another moment, she took note of an island a few hours away, only slightly northeast of their current travel path. It seemed fairly big, but there were scrawls that she couldn't figure out written beside it, along with an x. She wasn't sure what that meant, maybe it didn't exist anymore? No, that probably wasn't it. She glanced at the words, startled to realize that they were written in the ancient demonic tongue.

The only ones here who might be able to read it were the Aqua Wraith and possibly Milos. She didn't think Alex would be able to read it. Yes, he could speak the language, but reading was a whole different matter.

She decided it was best to not worry about it. It hadn't been that long since her previous interaction with the Wraith and she was not in the mood for more questions. Milos was out of the question. She stepped outside, noting Ari left at some point during her map scouring. She glanced over to the wheel to see Ari exchanging with Milos. Ari turned to focus on the water with her normal stoic gaze. She glanced as Rita borrowed the compass, lifting it up enough to see in the day stones' light before returning her attention to the map. "Can you turn us a little starboard? There's an island up ahead we should check out."

Ari nodded, turning the wheel slightly. Rita felt the ship gently turn in the waters before they were off once more. Milos observed her for a moment before heading to the edge of the ship, taking a seat near the cabin while staring out over the water. Rita barely gave him a moment of her attention as she glanced at the compass before nodding and handing it back to Ari. She placed it in her pocket so it wouldn't be lost. Well, that was all Rita could really do now.

She was still bored though.

~ * ~

Alex leaned back against the headboard of the bed, using one of the pillows to prop up the aged book as he carefully leafed through the pages. Some of the pages were definitely yellowed with age, while some appeared newer. He flipped through the beginning pages, annoyed to find he couldn't read them. Not because of the scraggly lettering, but simply because he didn't recognize the language, which irked him. Finally, he came across some more recent entries, the script turning into something more recognizable, but still somewhat archaic. He noticed dates and peered closely at them. It seemed these were from around sixty years ago. He glanced over the lettering, slowly piecing together the words.

It was the entry of a male demon who escaped from his owners before he was to be executed for a crime he didn't commit. As Alex read through, he noticed mention of an Alertian having been chosen to do the deed and gulped, reaching to his throat before shivering and continuing on. The demon met the same little man and found his way onto this boat with a few others who escaped. Alex frowned. How *old* was that man? He shook it off and continued, deciding not to bother worrying about it.

According to the file, the first few days were peaceful, if a little strained. It wasn't long before things began to get weird.

This ocean is a strange locale. Currents as strong as vipers and creatures the size of mountain ranges. My companions and I are running low on food, but no place is safe to stop. We lost a member on the last island and I don't want a repeat of that.

Unfortunately, that leads me to wonder if we are just drifting to our death. I hear a call outside, that of that treacherous creature whose been following us for the last few hours, winging above us.

I did not believe such a creature existed before this, but the wind slashing at the ship and rattling booms say otherwise. The only one willing to go outside is a young woman we met on an island before the last. I'm not sure how she does not fear death, for even one that is dead fears the creature, hidden from our sight.

Where this creature comes from, how it constantly disappears from the very air itself, leaves me to wonder how we can escape from it, or if we ever can. It's a terrifying thought and one that's cemented itself in my head since we began this ill-gotten journey.

I hope at least one of us makes it to the refuge, but I daren't hold out hope.

More scribblings followed, but they were written in such a hasty scrawl Alex found himself unable to continue, rubbing his eyes tiredly. A creature that could live in the air and disappeared over the open ocean? What sort of thing was that? Did it dive into the water? No. The writer would have made mention of that. Instead, he mentioned how it just vanished, but how would that be possible?

He pushed away from the book, peering out the window as day stones flickered above. It was so hard to keep track of time on the water, no matter how much he was used to the day stones' cycle. He never had that problem when walking, but now, as they swayed back and forth over the water, he couldn't quite track the strength of the stones. He let out a sigh, closing the book before placing it carefully on the side table, making sure it wouldn't drop to the floor if they had to make a sudden turn like yesterday. His stomach growled. He hurried to the eating area, or galley, as the Aqua Wraith called it. He could see Leon cooking while Milos glanced up from where he was eating. He gave a nod as Alex walked over to Leon to see if he could help. Before he could ask, a plate was shoved into his hand, already filled with breads, cheeses and a little bit of fruit. "Thanks?" Alex backed off and took a seat. Yeah, he obviously was not needed. He peered over, smelling something delicious wafting through the air and could only assume it would be for dinner or something. He could live with that.

He munched down at the food, somewhat worried to find he was still hungry after finishing it off.

It was frustrating, how hungry he was lately. Especially since he was able to go days with barely any food when he first left home. He let out a huff, stomach growling once more. A hint of amusement flitted across Milos' face, but he didn't say anything. They sat in silence, not sure what to say to each other; at least, Alex didn't. What could he ask the Alertian that he hadn't already? Sure, he could talk about the Overlands more, but he knew, though Milos never admitted it, that the man was missing his home.

Considering it was more than partially his fault, he couldn't help but feel bad about the situation. Unfortunately, that didn't leave many options for conversation topics.

He didn't want to go back to trying to decipher the book, nor did he want to sit here. After some thought, actually a lot of thought, he decided to head up on deck.

There was one thing he wanted to try. Though wanted was not exactly the term he was searching for. He stepped out on deck, passing by Rita as she muttered over the maps, and listened as the water swelled against the ship and wind gently blew from the stones. He headed toward the front of the ship. He hesitated for a moment. Did he actually want to do this?

No, but now would be as good a time as any to see what he could do. With even breaths, he thought about the last time he transformed. Milos told him the transformation was not out of fear of his own safety, but fear of others. That was partially correct, he noticed as he thought about the times where Rita and Milos were both in danger. He listened to the water, hearing its encouraging song. A familiar feeling settled over him, not so much painful as a tingling sensation that pulsed through his veins. A faint sound echoed behind him as his wings expanded outward, curling around his frame. Something sat on his head, heavy but not cumbersome and he felt another strange thing shift behind him, like an extra phantom appendage. He brought his hands up. Hardened claws coated where his fingers had been, vicious and curved. He shivered, remembering the damage they did in the past, and quickly moved on.

He reached up. With the hard claws, he could still feel the smoothness of a pair of horns, gently curling on either side of his head. The tips seemed sharp and pointed. He briefly wondered what they looked like. His wings spread out to either side, somewhat twitching before curling around him. He felt surprisingly calm as he gently fingered over the thin membrane. It was similar to the Dregas' wings from all that time ago. He would have to be careful not to damage them. He paused, trying to remember how to fold them before concentrating harder than he would like to admit. Thankfully, they settled against his back quickly enough. Finally, he turned his attention behind him. Something long and thin curled around, curving into sight and, on instinct, he grabbed at it, catching it between his claws.

With that, he realized he wasn't imagining things. He did actually have a tail. Part of him wondered if it was to help with flight and balance, another part was just shocked at the leathery feel of it. He wasn't sure how to describe it. It wasn't exactly whip-like, but it was long and thin. It was mostly black with streaks of blue trailing through it at uneven intervals. He slowly let it go, watching as it swerved back behind him. In a way, it reminded him of pictures he observed in the library books from home, of a creature native to the Overlands called a cat. Though, from what he remembered, those held a fluffier appearance to them and he knew they didn't thin out as they went, so maybe it was just his imagination.

He shook his head. Okay, he was done checking himself over. He reached a claw over his shoulder, feeling the bony mass that was his wings. Now he had to figure out how to use these... hopefully.

He groaned at the thought. This was going to take a while.

Chapter Seven

He wasn't wrong. He stumbled forward as his wings snapped outward, throwing him off balance for the umpteenth time. At some point, Milos came up the stairs and watched from a distance, hints of amusement showing on his face. Rita didn't seem amused, but he could tell she had no idea how to help, having stopped her map perusal at some point. Alex didn't blame her, but it was still frustrating.

At least he hadn't toppled into the water yet.

Catching his balance, he hissed. His wings refused to listen to him beyond a simple fluttering. He took another deep breath, only for a sigh to echo from behind him.

He blinked, peering over his shoulder with surprise as Milos stood up and walked over. Alex went to turn, only for Milos to raise his hand. "Stand still, I want to try something."

Alex hesitated, but did so, watching quietly over his shoulder as Milos stepped to Alex's left side. He reached toward the wing and it was all Alex could do not to flinch. Milos seemed to realize, but he didn't respond, just simply placed his hand on the bone. Alex waited, feeling an urge to twitch...or well, smack him away.

"You can feel my hand, correct?" Milos' voice caught him off guard.

"Yeah. Why?" Alex couldn't help but ask.

"All right, you can feel them. What does it feel like?"

Alex blinked, confused for a moment before it occurred to him what Milos was talking about. He could feel it, but he hadn't really thought of where or why. In some ways, he associated it with his arm, but that wasn't the case.

Now, as he was paying attention to where Milos gripped his wing, he found himself noting the differences. Milos moved his hand down, gripping closer to the base of the wing, closer to his spine, and he actually did flinch this time.

He briefly sent an apology to the Drega he helped kill all that time ago. If he knew how sensitive wings were, he might have been a bit more hesitant to damage them. He shook the thought away as he returned his focus to the task at hand.

Rita seemed to get the hint of what they were doing and stepped up to his other side, moving mostly in sync with Milos. Alex couldn't help but feel grateful, though it did feel incredibly awkward and more than a little uncomfortable.

Why did it feel intimate? He would have to ask another demon that question. Shivering slightly, he felt both of them place their hands to the wing tips and stilled. For some reason, he hadn't realized just how far the wingspan was. Sure, he could observe them, but to actually feel the distance...

So that's why. He tentatively pulled away from their touch, focusing on not moving any other part of his body. To his surprise and excitement, the wings did what he asked, carefully curling away from their fingers.

"Did that work?" Rita asked curiously as Alex focused and slowly expanded the wings back into Milos' and Rita's hands.

To his delight, the wing tips landed softly in their open palms.

He could feel the beaming smile on his face as he realized. The next thing he knew, Milos and Rita were quickly backing off as Alex flexed the wings, focusing on the bones and joints, the feel of a breeze at the tips of his wings, the weight curling over his back. It all felt so real and almost calming, if he wasn't so happy about the fact that he could actually control the wings. Of course, he wasn't going to attempt flying, but this was good enough for him. He hummed in delight as the wings expanded outward before curling around him. They sat around him for a moment before pulling back and curving against his back, like putting his arms at his side. It seemed strange, now that he was doing this, that it was so difficult to control in the first place.

He could only assume it was because of his fear of the things and his desire not to have anything to do with them that made it so difficult. It would make sense, he supposed. He let his wings spread out, going as wide as he could. At their longest, they covered the view of the front of the ship completely, their length probably three-quarters of his height.

He pulled them close, letting them settle easily against his back. Now that he was also paying attention, he could feel his tail slowly sway back and forth, curling through the air. It really was all...it was pretty neat, he had to admit, now that he wasn't completely terrified.

Of course, he was still left with many questions, but he was no longer fearful of the transformation and changes, at least, not nearly as much.

He turned to thank Milos and Rita, only to realize that Milos already walked away, taking a seat near the cabin, one leg up, while Rita was staring at his wings, a pink flush on her face.

"Rita?"

She jerked before focusing on Alex. "You got them working."

"Mostly, yeah." He grinned. "What do you think? I remember you saying my wings were, what was the term, pretty?" He found his tone lightly teasing, having remembered the short conversation. Though, it did make him feel better at the thought.

"Well, yes." Rita shifted, seemingly more than a little embarrassed. "I did say that, didn't I?"

"What? You don't think—"

"No. It's not that." She quieted down, so much so that Alex couldn't hear what she was saying.

"Huh?"

"It's nothing. Anyway, are you going to try to figure out how to fly now?"

"No way." Alex shook his head. "I've finally figured out how they work. I'm not sure I can imagine..."

"Well, try it." Rita suggested, grinning toothily as she leaned on one leg, arms crossed. "We're in the middle of nowhere with water all around, your natural element, so what's the harm?"

Alex let out a sigh. He resigned himself to the fact he was making a fool of himself, but, conceding to Rita's words, he turned back to the tip of the ship. Before him was open water with day stones gleaming brilliantly up above. Actually, not as brilliantly, it seemed like it was getting closer to nightfall.

It would explain why he was getting hungry again. He had never stopped since he last ate.

Shaking off the thought, he expanded his wings out once more and flapped them like he noticed the Drega do. It honestly felt silly and he immediately noticed it also felt wrong. Quickly stopping, he frowned. With a slight twist of the joints, he had them pointing more downward than forward and, very carefully, he flapped down.

He yelped, tumbling head over heels as air surged under him and his wings caught a non-existent breeze. He groaned, his wings tangled around him, hard wood on his back and legs hanging over the side of the ship. He reached a hand up to his head, wondering what the hell just happened.

Laughter reached his ears and he glared over to Rita, who was covering her mouth and holding her stomach, as she hurried up to him and knelt at his side. Milos was equally as amused, a surprisingly wide smile on his face. Even Ari was hiding her mouth, a faint smile slipping through the gaps. Alex huffed, rolling onto his front so his wings were no longer jammed under him. He took Rita's hand and was quickly pulled upright.

"You okay?" she asked between chuckles as he brushed himself down.

"Yeah. Fine," he mumbled, though his back definitely smarted now.

"It seemed your wings generated their own air." Milos' voice surprised him as he glanced over to where the man was sitting. His smile was mostly gone and his eyes were narrowed, calculated. "When you angled your wings downward, there was a shift in the surrounding magic. I think you're on the right track with that last attempt."

"Though it was hilarious," Rita said, smiling sheepishly. "You even let out a squawk of surprise."

"No, I didn't." Alex frowned, not recalling doing anything like that. Sure, he yelped, but...

Rita rolled her eyes, lightly patting between his wings. "Anyway, take two."

"Right now?"

"Yes, right now. Hop to it."

Alex groaned, suddenly regretting deciding to practice with his wings. This was going to hurt.

Thankfully, for his sanity and his aching back, the day stones finally decided to descend and be taken over by the night stones. He rubbed his shoulders, knowing there was definitely a large bruise forming there. Milos took over the wheel, staring at the compass as he adjusted their course. Hadn't he just been on it? Alex wasn't going to question who was doing what at this point. Meanwhile, Rita was leaning against the railing, watching him as he folded his wings back once more.

He blinked, frowning in thought.

How was he supposed to change back?

A moment of panic washed through him, but he quickly pushed the fear down. Okay, he could do this. He let out a breath, closing his eyes to concentrate. How did he feel when the demonic side disappeared? Mostly tired, to be truthful. Every single time, he knocked himself out.

He partially wondered if that would happen this time or not. He had a feeling it wouldn't be as bad since he had carefully pulled the demonic energy out instead of it being wrenched out of him.

His wings twitched, unsure what to do. He turned his focus away from them, which was harder to do now that he was fully aware of them, and listened to the calming sound of the water. He wasn't sure how it happened, but felt as a slow pulsing ran through his veins. A moment later, it almost seemed like everything was folding in on itself. He stumbled, head pounding. He darted a hand up to his temple, his body trembling. He groaned quietly, wondering why it was so hard. Though, it was pretty hard to become a demon too, so...

He shook his head and pulled back, noting his fingers were back to their usual pale white. His clothes settled back around him normally.

"How are you feeling?" Rita was right there, like she was ready to catch him. Made sense.

"All right." He pursed his lips, mentally checking himself over.

To his surprise, his body seemed to agree. He didn't feel tired or sore. At least, not as sore, and his mind was clear and sound. What a strange feeling.

He nodded, before a loud rumbling sounded from his stomach and his hands darted down.

Rita let out a laugh before gesturing toward the map room.

Alex glanced over to Milos as his attention drifted from the compass. He nodded in their direction. "Rita, when you're done eating, you're taking over. It should be Alex, but..."

"Yeah, no." Rita rolled her eyes. "I'll deal. I didn't do it for too long earlier and I want to figure out where we are again." Rita waved.

Milos frowned slightly, before returning to observing the surrounding waters.

"Oh, Milos?" Alex drew to a halt, catching the man's attention. "Thanks for your help earlier."

"No need," Milos said. "Remember, it's good for me to learn more about demons as well."

Alex stared at Milos for a minute before chuckling quietly. He noticed the slightly softened smile on Milos' face as he turned away, and knew that, while the words were probably partially true, there was a bit more to it. He glanced toward Rita, who was glaring at Milos in distaste. "Oh, and thanks. Though, did you really have to laugh?"

"Yes. It was hilarious," Rita spoke up bluntly, grinning. "Now let's eat. I'm hungry." Alex shook his head, descending the stairwell. He couldn't exactly argue with that.

Chapter Eight

Rita let out a yawn as she spun the wheel slightly to return onto the main course. In the distance, she spotted an island just barely visible from the glow of the night stones. She probably would have only spotted a dark outline if not for the night stones being at their brightest. Still, it seemed like it would take about an hour or so to get to it since it was nothing more than a pinprick glowing faintly in the night light in this stupidly vast ocean. She thought back over the day and chuckled. She admittedly felt bad for Alex, but she found the whole situation amusing as heck.

Though...she felt her cheeks heat up. When she felt the tip of his wing lightly touch into her palm and saw the beaming expression on his face as realization dawned on him, she couldn't help to note how nice he appeared. His smile was brilliant, his blue gray eyes sparkling in delight. Plus, his wings...she expected them to feel strange and bony. Instead, they felt smooth, almost powerful, and they were beautiful, a kaleidoscope of different shades of blue with tinges of silver and black.

She shook her head violently as she realized what she was thinking. *Yep, nope, not thinking of this*, she thought, focusing back on the task at hand. Yet, she couldn't seem to get the smile off of her face at his delight. She chuckled once more at the image of him upside down, staring up at her with his wings tangled around him. It was surprisingly cute.

Shut up, brain, she admonished as she forced herself to focus on the compass in her hand, then back at the island up ahead. As they approached, she nodded to herself, recognizing the general shape as what she recognized from the map. It wasn't really large, but it was big enough for them to land and be able to stretch their feet for a bit. She wasn't sure if they would find anything, since it seemed pretty rocky, the stones a pale blue in the night light. In the middle of the island was a slightly raised hill. She hummed in thought at that, but pushed it off as she flipped open the speaker. "There's land up ahead." She paused, taking a moment before continuing, "How do we go about landing?" Her words were sheepish.

The Aqua Wraith chuckled from the other end. "Dost thou plan to journey alone?"

"No, I figured we would all like a rest."

The Aqua Wraith said nothing for a moment before a sound that startled Rita came through the speakers, a low hum.

After a moment, the Aqua Wraith spoke once more, sounding off. "I dare say that thou may wish to avoid said land."

"Why?"

The Aqua Wraith didn't respond and Rita sighed, watching as they approached the island. She hadn't noticed anything on the island and it didn't seem dangerous. Actually, she didn't see any movement at all.

She thought for a few minutes before groaning. "Can you wake everyone up? We might as well decide as a group what we should do."

The only acknowledgement she received was the quiet hum of the engine turning to a neutral state and the faint sound of a door. Wait, the Wraith could move through wood. Ah, it wasn't her business.

She closed the tube, staring out over the water as they approached at a slightly slower pace. The island grew bigger and bigger as footsteps sounded up the stairs. The door opened as the rest of the group came up, followed by the flowing form of the Aqua Wraith. Alex let out a yawn, rubbing his eyes as Milos simply stared at the distant island.

Ari and Leon were as difficult to read as ever, but they seemed a little surprised.

"Is that an island?" Alex blinked, following Milos' line of sight.

"Yep. It was on one of the maps and I figured we need a chance to get off this boat for a bit and check if we can find anything," Rita admitted as Alex hurried to the edge of the boat, leaning over the rails.

The Aqua Wraith stared at the island. Rita wasn't sure, but she thought she noticed hesitation on the being's face, followed by a frown.

"Hm...do we know if it's safe?" Milos finally turned away, hand resting on his sword. "It seems pretty open, but..."

"It should be fine." Rita shrugged, only hesitating for a split second. Sure, the Aqua Wraith's words sounded ominous, but she also didn't know the creature very well. "Though I haven't seen anything move while we've been approaching."

"Nothing moved?" Alex blinked, glancing back at her. "What do you mean? There's no life on the island?"

When he said it like that, a shiver ran down Rita's spine, her thoughts once more flickering to the Aqua Wraith's words. "That..."

"That island." The Aqua Wraith's voice caught them all off guard as she glanced at Alex. "Doth thou not sense it?" The words sounded almost pleading, as if desperate to say more to the point that Rita couldn't deny that maybe the Aqua Wraith might have a point.

Alex furrowed his brow as Milos closed his eyes.

Rita tilted the wheel, not so much to go toward the island, but more to draw to a stop near the island. The island was closer now, directly in front of them. It didn't appear strange to her, no matter how ominous it sounded. She spotted stones dotting the land and, now that they were closer, a few scraggly roots curling over the ground. The hill she noticed earlier seemed like a pile of rocks, they glowed an eerie color in the night stones, an eerie silvery...white...

Footsteps jerked her away from her thoughts as Milos practically sprung to her side, wrenching the wheel from her grip and turning it almost ninety degrees as he shouted, "All hands, evasive maneuvers. We need to get away from that island."

As Rita stumbled back, she noticed Ari and Leon were already disappearing into the map room, though Leon promptly returned with a weapon grasped firmly in his good hand.

The Aqua Wraith disappeared with a swirl of water, shooting down through the wood.

Alex paled, slowly taking jerky steps back. "What...what the hell?"

The swear surprised Rita almost as much as Milos' shout and the sudden blast of the wind stones and the engine. The boat turned, slower than it seemed like both Alex and Milos liked. Rita, not sure what was going on, just reached over, toward the wheel as she noticed Milos struggle. She gripped on and pulled, stunned as it only slightly shifted with both of their weights.

A sound, a whispering, clattering sound reached her ears. Rita peered over toward the island and felt all warmth leave her body. That silvery white hill wasn't a hill.

A head slowly rose from the pile, vines curling around the skull and clinging to the earth. A thwack sounded on the boat as Rita and Milos finally succeeded in twisting the wheel. The sudden twist and shoving of the boat caused Rita to stumble away from the wheel.

Stillness fell over the ship for a split second as nothing moved. A faint crack echoed from below as the ship jerked to a halt.

Milos cursed. "Take the wheel." He pushed Rita into place before darting to the back of the ship, sword flashing from the sheath. The next moment, Rita saw a thick vine surge out of the water as a howling wind like a roar echoed from the center of the island, filled with bones of various sizes and shapes. Some appeared fishlike while others held more humanoid appearances. It grew, vines tangled around the bones to create a distorted monstrous shape. The night stones did nothing to hide the empty eyes and writhing vines, only adding an eerie blue glow over the mass.

The vines lashed out, curling around the bones and toward the ship as Milos hacked at the vines with his sword, slicing cleanly through root after root as the wind stones howled, pushed to their max. Alex must have shifted slightly to his demonic form in his panic, water splashing up as his wings whipped, blocking some of the vines. Leon seemed to be doing the same, protecting the other side of the ship, as the vines thrashed, slamming into his injured side, causing him to stumble and miss a slash. Rita ducked as one tried to pierce through where she stood before it fell, shriveled and dead to the deck. She peered back toward Milos standing to her left, sword already moving in an arc to stop another vine from wrapping around the tail end of the ship. She heard him curse. She peered back and paled as the creature shifted toward the edge of the island, long claw-like appendages reached out toward their ship, vines swirling out from around its fingers like writhing tentacles. Horror was the only thing she felt as she tightly gripped the wheel, doing all she could to hold it steady as she noticed Milos sprint headlong to the back of the ship. He practically leaped over the side as his non-sword hand gripped the railing. He swung, sword slicing cleanly through whatever was there.

One minute the ship was still. The next it jerked, tilting back slightly before it shot forward, almost skipping over the water as the creature roared behind them. A clang echoed from the side of the ship as Milos swung himself back around, pulling one leg over the railing as the sword clattered to the ground. Alex hurried over with Leon a few steps behind as Rita peered back, watching as the vines writhed, reaching upward like a dark silhouette, already disappearing in the distance. With the last tendrils of fear dissipating, she watched as the creature slowly descended back down, the island still once more.

She shivered, just as Alex let out a worried, "You're hurt."

Rita peered back as Milos quickly moved his arm away from Alex's hands, reaching into his pocket for what she could only assume was the vial from before.

Leon sat off to one side, watching worriedly, weapon resting over his lap. A strange yellow liquid dripped from the wood, similar to Milos' sword and Alex's claws.

"Alex, don't touch him." Rita hurried over, causing Alex to freeze. She dug into her satchel, pulling out a vial and a cleaning cloth. She grabbed Alex's wrist, startling the poor boy, before watching as some of the yellow liquid dripped into the vial. She pulled it back, carefully giving it a sniff. "Good thing you haven't changed back yet." She tossed a rag to Alex. "Clean that stuff off and throw that rag away." Alex blinked, startled, but did as he was told as Rita's gaze snapped to Milos, who stilled in his movements, probably having realized the same thing she did.

"Paralysis," Milos muttered, peering down at the wound in slight disgust.

Rita nodded, digging into her satchel once more after carefully capping the vial. It wasn't long before she pulled out some potions she had left over from home. Thank the heavens she hadn't had a need to use them. She was definitely going to need to make more soon, she noted, as her bag was feeling a bit light. She was only grateful for her teacher's gift. She still remembered when Alex gave it to her after receiving it from her teacher. It was a simple little bag with seer's runes sketched in that allowed it to change into a metal cauldron she was more familiar with. It was probably one of the best things she could have out here.

She squatted in front of him, examining the wound carefully. It was a thin graze, but it definitely dug in quite a bit. It would heal fine, but...she unstopped the potion before handing it to him. He took it, hesitant. "Drink, it won't kill you, unlike that thing."

Milos obviously wasn't amused at her words, but followed her directions anyway. As she cleaned the wound, noting the grimace that crossed Milos' face, she found herself relieved. She figured this was the only damage that occurred during that strange attack. She heard footsteps and spared a moment of attention as Alex returned, once more back in human form and cleaned of the venom.

"What was that?" Alex sat down, glancing back the way they came. "The island, it came alive."

"Not quite," Milos muttered, causing Rita to return to focusing on him. He winced as she tipped another vial over the wound, watching as the liquid within splashed over the already reddening skin. "The island itself was just an island, but that parasitic lifeform must have taken residence of the place. My guess is it's a good resting point for creatures or people trying to travel through these lands. There would be plenty of food from unwary travelers and, if those bones are any indication, it's been feeding for a while."

"How did you sense it?" Rita finally asked as she wrapped up the wound and dug into her bag once more, pulling out a few herbs and her mortar and pestle.

"The rotten smell, right?" Alex ventured hesitantly. "I didn't notice until we got closer, because I think the vines were letting out a coating scent to hide it. That, and I noticed a strange pulsing around the island."

Milos nodded as he watched Rita work. "That's about right. Though I do wonder why it keeps the bones above land." He trailed off.

"They wouldn't get bleached from sunlight and deteriorate. No, no point in wondering."

"I hope other islands aren't like that," Alex muttered quietly as Rita finished up, feeling a little uncomfortable. She remembered spotting the X on the map, but at the time she had thought nothing of it. Not only that, but she practically ignored her own instinct as well as the Aqua Wraith's warnings, which could have been deadly.

"If we hadn't turned when we did," Rita muttered, still remembering how they just managed to wrench it into place right before the ship froze.

"The ship would have been tangled in the vines more than it already was and we all would be dead right now. That thing's food." Milos nodded as Alex winced.

Rita grimaced opening and closing her mouth before letting out a long breath. "You're right, if you hadn't reacted like you did," she trailed off, finding her gaze drifting to the floor, hands stilling in the process of applying the salve. "Thanks, Milos."

Silence filled the air, causing Rita to turn her gaze back up. Alex was staring at her with a mix of shock and curiosity and Milos—she snapped a mental note of his startled expression, filing it away for later—she had never seen such an expression on his face before. He schooled his expression quickly, quirking an eyebrow. Rita, realizing the conversation wasn't going anywhere fast, rolled her eyes and crossed her arms over her chest. "Hey, no need to stare, I know when a thank you is necessary."

Alex chuckled as Milos shook his head before frowning, glancing down at his arm.

Rita unclasped her arms and returned to her work. "Thankfully, we were able to get off most of the paralyzing agent. With the size of those bones, I'm guessing it was pretty potent. You feeling any different?" She glanced up to Milos, who grimaced.

"It's still numb."

"Hm... that was a quick-acting potion I used. Hopefully, this one will be able to flush out the rest of the venom." She splashed a little water from her water skin into the bowl before handing it over. Milos hesitated this time as he stared at the murky green brown mush.

"It's disgusting, isn't it?" Alex said sheepishly.

Milos didn't respond, just tipped the whole thing back, almost swallowing in one gulp.

His lips pursed into a thin line and, Rita had to admit, she was impressed that he didn't react any more. Alex watched with what appeared to be sympathy.

"As foul as the previous one." Milos stood up just as Leon returned, causing Rita to blink. Wait, when did the man leave? She couldn't recall, now that she thought about it, but in his hand was Milos' sword, cleaned of the yellow liquid. His own weapon was nowhere in sight. Milos nodded, as if in thanks before he awkwardly managed to slip it back into its sheath.

"So, what now?" Alex stood up as Rita groaned.

"We keep moving. Hopefully, we'll find an island soon that isn't crawling with giant vine-like parasites."

"You don't hear that every day," Alex said, before shaking his head. "Either way, I'm awake now. Do you want me to take over?"

Rita hesitated before nodding. She had just taken over from Milos, but her mind was racing. She needed to look at the maps, just to make sure something like this didn't happen again.

~ * ~

Milos gritted his teeth as pain surged up his previously numb arm. He should have been more careful. How could he let something like this catch him off guard? That was such an amateur mistake. He hissed to himself as he moved his arm, feeling the bandage tighten. At least it was a decent quality bandage. If nothing else, Rita did know how to take care of basic wounds.

He turned his focus to outside the window, hearing faint pounding. It sounded like Leon was busy fixing a few gashes made into the wood of the ship. At least only the back end was damaged, but still, they were lucky the thing hadn't attacked the engine or wind stones. That was the only saving grace of the incident. His thoughts flickered to the attack and he frowned. To be honest, their response was not very coordinated. It was lucky they didn't get hurt worse than they already had.

He stretched his arm out, flexing his fingers a bit. The potions she gave him did the trick, no matter how foul the concoction was. Though, as the pain thrashed up his arm, he wasn't sure if he was happy about that or not.

He heard a knock on the door and glanced over. When nothing happened, he called out. "It's open."

He was only slightly surprised to note as Ari walked in, carrying a small bowl and some bread. It was the food from earlier, just warmed up again. She placed the food down beside him and pulled back, gaze locked on his arm.

"Ari?"

Her gaze whipped up to him and a strange hesitation filled her posture. It wasn't so much her normal fidgeting, her fingers curling into her clothes. This time it seemed more like a tension Milos wasn't used to sensing from the normally stoic girl.

"You got hurt."

Milos blinked before nodding. "I was a little careless. It's nothing to worry about."

He took the stew, placing it in his lap as Ari furrowed her brow. She didn't respond, but she did take a seat on the other bed, as if watching him.

Milos wasn't sure how to respond to that, so instead just took a sip of the broth. At least it washed the taste of Rita's fowl concoction from his senses.

They sat in silence for a little while as Milos finished off his meal and set it aside. He wasn't surprised when Ari stayed put, gaze flickering to the empty bowl for only a moment before returning back to him.

"There's obviously another reason why you came." Milos leaned forward, letting himself relax.

Ari hesitated for the longest time, which Milos didn't mind, the girl was quiet to begin with. This was a new approach for her, and probably something she was convincing herself to do. He wasn't going to try to push too hard.

It was obviously the right decision as she schooled her expression, placed her hands firmly in her lap and stared at him with more determination than he had ever seen from the girl. "Can you show me how to fight?"

Milos stilled. To be honest, part of his mind already acknowledged that sort of request was inevitable, but another part wasn't sure how to respond.

Ari, probably guessing his hesitation meant something else, leaned forward, bowing her head low, hair falling in waves around her slender shoulders. "Please, I do not like when you are hurt. You or anyone else here. Please, I beg of you. Give me a chance to learn to fight."

Milos paused, thinking over his answer as the girl stayed firmly in place, only a slight shaking in her taut knuckles any indication of her fear, the fear of saying something out of line. He finally let out a long breath. "If this is what you want, I don't mind showing you a few things."

Ari tilted her head up, shock playing over her face, before a small, but brilliant smile flashed onto her lips. "Thank you, Master Milos."

Before he could say anything, she stood up, gathered the material and headed toward the door. "Please, let me know when you can meet with me to show me." She bowed low once more before hurrying out, as if afraid that if she stayed, he might rescind his offer.

He stared after her, frowning slightly. Master. He had never heard either Ari or Leon use that term before for him. He shook his head, maybe he was tired and happened to notice this time.

He pushed the thought aside and stood, pulling his sword from the sheath. He gripped the hilt, peering at it in the faint light of the night stones, gleaming through the windows.

He wondered if anyone was getting sleep tonight. Leon was busy outside, being helped by Alex. Ari was obviously on cooking duty and he doubted she would sleep after the conversation they just had, while Rita was busy in the map room, charting their course.

He slid the sword back into its sheath, letting his mind calm. It would do no good if all of them were dead on their feet, come morning. Deep breaths in, slow breaths out. Slowly, his body relaxed from the tension, letting it seep away into the floorboards below his crossed legs. Soon enough, he felt his mind finally calm and stood, moving over to the bed. He took a seat, pulling his hair over his shoulder as he peered at the length quietly. The hair had grown long over the years, yet it still wasn't quite as long as his father's, or...he gritted his teeth in frustration. What a disgrace. He'd been so caught up in keeping track of Alex and, to some extent, Rita, that he'd let himself go lax on his training. Ari only reminded him of that fact as he realized he wasn't quite sure how to teach something when he was so out of practice. He grasped the hair tightly, his hand shaking slightly. As an Alertian, he couldn't let that stand. His signifier clinked, the red glow shining as it trailed slightly over his shoulder, curling around the long strands of hair. Right, he would be fine. He just needed to get himself back on course and he would be all set. He let the hair swing back behind him, almost relieved to no longer behold the pseudo-signifier.

After all, he was an Alertian. He didn't need *that* to prove it.

He let himself relax into the bed. In the morning, he would have to restart some training regime for himself and create a new one for everyone else.

For now, though, he should let his mind and body rest.

Alex rubbed his eyes as the night stones slowly shifted into their daytime counterparts. He'd been up all night. Leon finished up sometime a few hours ago and headed downstairs to help Ari in the kitchen. The ship was quiet, almost nothing moving in the still air. He let out a yawn before a gentle sound echoed up through the boards. He jerked slightly as the Aqua Wraith slid through the planks and onto the deck. She observed him quietly before heading to the edge of the boat, sitting on the railing as she stared at him.

Was there a reason? Probably, but he wasn't sure he had the mental capacity for anything right now. He frowned. Actually, that wasn't quite right. "Why did you warn us?"

No, that didn't come out right either.

"Doth thou wish I didn't?"

"No, that's not what I meant." Alex shook his head, tired. "I meant, why were you so vague? You warned us, but..."

She only hesitated for a moment, figuring out what his addled brain was saying as she stared out over the water. "I cannot say." She lifted herself off, swirling around him. "It is a promise, an oath I cannot break. I mean you and your companions no harm."

Alex watched her circle around and let out a sigh. "I know." His words dragged her to a halt, startled as he continued, "If you truly meant harm, we would be dead already. I was wondering, that's all." He let out another yawn, feeling incredibly sleepy all of a sudden.

The Aqua Wraith hovered beside him. Her arms were extended before freezing. He stared at her, blinking blearily as she slowly pulled her arms away, crossing them so tightly, it almost looked like they melded into the watery skin of her chest. For a brief moment, she appeared vulnerable, though it could have been just Alex's tired thoughts. She smiled toward him and moved away. "Rest well, young one." With that, she dived below the deckboards.

Alex shook his head, feeling it sink slightly where he stood. He quickly jerked, trying to keep himself awake and failing miserably, he noted as his head tilted down once more.

He wasn't sure how much time passed. Footsteps sounded from the cabin before the door opened.

Alex glanced over to Milos as the man moved right up to him, unimpressed. "You stayed up all night."

It wasn't a question and Alex nodded. "No one took over."

Milos rubbed the bridge of his nose. Alex thought it looked funny on him, that sort of exasperation, and chuckled. "Get downstairs and check on Rita, I'll take over."

Alex let out a yawn and pulled away from the wheel. Why was he so tired anyway?

"Because you became a demon twice yesterday. It probably drained most of your energy and you haven't eaten much at all, even though your body has been demanding more sustenance to keep up."

"I asked?" Alex blinked.

"Yes." Milos glanced toward him, gaze narrowed. "Though I probably would have told you anyway, since you are more than dead on your feet." He scanned Alex's posture before shaking his head. "Get yourself to bed."

"But..."

"Alex," Milos interjected, voice stern. "You are useless in this state. Get some sleep."

Alex tilted his head slightly, trying to parse through the words, before he nodded. How did he get up here so fast anyway?

Milos stared at him before briefly checking their heading. A moment later, he walked over and, to Alex's surprise, swung one of Alex's arms over his shoulder. "The ship will be fine for a few minutes, let's get you downstairs. You're not thinking straight."

Alex hummed, but didn't argue as he was practically dragged into the cabin and took the stairs carefully. The ship was silent, the others probably having fallen asleep.

"Are you all right?" he slurred, feeling himself list slightly.

"I'm fine. I figured this would happen and slept. The Aqua Wraith woke me."

Ah, so that's why he was upstairs.

"The others should be waking soon, but you need to rest. Once you're awake, we'll begin working more on your demon side. As I've realized with that last attack, all of us are in desperate need of defensive training."

"I'm a demon," Alex muttered, Huh, he really was tired.

"Yes, but you are also a human. You need to know how to defend yourself either way," Milos pointed out as he helped Alex into bed.

Alex looked around. He hadn't realized they made it back to the room.

"Okay," he finally decided before grinning. "I'll trust you."

The man shook his head. "You're delusional. Get some rest."

With that, Milos swept out of the room as Alex watched him go.

He wasn't sure why the man always was so...eh, not his problem. He fell sideways and found sleep taking over before he even fully hit the pillow.

Chapter Nine

Milos watched the waters, the day stones brilliantly shining up above. His analysis was right: no one had slept at all. He shook his head, briefly recalling the cold splash of water on his face as the Aqua Wraith brushed by. She simply pointed upward before disappearing back under the deckboards. Leon was fast asleep. From the way he lay, it was obvious he'd just gone to bed. Milos peeked into the girls' room long enough to notice that the other two were sleeping soundly, curled up in the hammocks. He mentally reminded himself to mention to the girls that they might want to lock their door. He doubted anyone would do anything, but prudence was better than negligence.

To think he would find Alex almost draped over the steering wheel. He shook his head. He was going to have to set up a schedule for work and sleep.

He mentally categorized where everyone would be best. Rita set herself up to be their navigator, which, contrary to Milos' attrition, he didn't particularly mind. God forbid he tried to navigate open waters without sunlight or moonlight to guide him.

It was a miracle he ever ended up in a town his first month in the Underlands.

Shaking himself from that thought, he continued on. The Aqua Wraith was aware of the danger, but she would have no reason to talk with him. He hadn't missed the way she avoided him, compared to the others, and he was fine by that.

That left merely himself and Alex to keep watch. Leon was still struggling to deal with the imbalance of losing an arm. He was fine in regular travel, but not in battle, as Milos noticed last night. Ari—his thoughts stopped short as he remembered the way she bowed, the beaming smile when he said he would teach her and he let out a sigh. Ari was smart, but she was also still young with absolutely no fighting experience. Yet, the determination he noticed in her...he laid his hand on his sword, debating.

He wished he had at least a wooden practice knife or something like he used when he was younger. Leon had a wooden sword that had looked crudely fashioned, but he had a feeling it would be too heavy for Ari. After a few moments of thought and weighing his options, he let out a breath. He didn't have any choice in the matter. He flipped open a rarely used pouch, held close to his side much like the salve he kept in case of emergency. He slipped his hand in, fingers resting on the pommel of a thin knife. He rarely used it, having no need over the past few months. He wasn't an assassin. Knives weren't his strong suit, but he had it with him anyway, just in case. With a tentative ease, he pulled it out, noting the light glint off the blade. It was a gift, right before he had descended into the Underlands and, to be honest, he had almost completely forgotten about it until now. His sword suited his purposes much better than a flimsy knife, but he supposed it wasn't a bad thing. He flipped the knife, feeling the pommel land in his hand with a firm thump before letting his fingers grasp around the hilt.

Giving a weapon to a slave was practically unheard of. Did that really matter though? He was throwing away most of the rules his family had taught him at this point. After all, he was working with a demon and a witch while giving a knife to a slave to train her for fighting.

He honestly had no idea how things had ended up like this and if he was truly okay with it. While it made sense to have more protection at the same time, it completely fought with what he once valued...

His thoughts slammed to a halt at that. Things he *once* valued? Did that mean he didn't value being an Alertian anymore? No, that wasn't it, it was something else. He gritted his teeth, deciding that now wasn't the time to figure out the mess his mind plodded into. No, his main focus was to figure out how to keep everyone alive. He would figure out the other things later.

He peered up at the day stones as he slipped the knife back into his pouch. He would give it to her later when he set up the practice schedule. He would need to ask the Underlanders how best to keep track of time, but it should be easy to set up shifts so this didn't happen again.

The water lapped at the boat as they sailed forward, barely any change from the past day. To be honest, it would be easy to assume it would have been a peaceful journey. These waters didn't have storms or weather abnormalities to deal with. He had yet to sense any currents, or feel their tug. It was oddly tranquil.

Yet, he couldn't let himself relax, or more, he didn't want to. This ocean had already shown just how dangerous it was, no matter how beautiful it appeared. He groaned, massaging the bridge of his nose. How big was this ocean anyway? He knew the Underlands were massive, but to think there would be an ocean this size under here. It would certainly explain why no one was able to attack the north.

A splash caught his ear and he jerked. His gaze narrowed. Nothing moved in the water and there were none of those silver fish that often swam by as warning. He kept his ears open as he focused. The energy of the water wrapped around the ship, so powerfully he could almost hear it humming. He wondered, briefly, how Alex heard it. Considering he was sleeping, it must not really affect him.

The boat creaked as it swayed back and forth, pushing through the waves.

Nothing. He couldn't sense anything. There were fluctuations in the water, but he had no way of knowing whether that was normal or not. He mentally cursed, wishing he checked before they left. Not much he could do about it now.

He spotted the Aqua Wraith drifting around. She was obviously inspecting the boat, a curious expression on her face. Milos decided to leave her alone. She probably heard the splash too, and she was better attuned to the surroundings anyway.

He returned his attention forward. Now to wait for the others to wake up.

~ * ~

A few hours later, and with a couple groans, everyone except

Alex was awake and upstairs, called up by Milos.

"What is it?" Rita muttered, adjusting her witch's hat before it slipped sideways again. She gave up with a huff, crossing her arms over her chest.

Milos resisted the urge to chuckle and instead turned to the rest of the crew, leaving the Aqua Wraith to manage the ship for now. "I was thinking, we need to set up shifts for the rest of this journey. We can't have another incident like last night."

"It was an honest mistake," Rita snapped, her words brimming with annoyance, and Milos just tilted his head.

"I wasn't talking about the creature, that's for another discussion." Her posture was flustered for a moment as he continued, "I'm talking about what happened after. There was no plan. As we've all probably noticed, these waters are dangerous, it would be best to make sure we are adequately prepared for them."

Rita let out a groan of resignation. "Fine, I can understand that. So how are we splitting the shifts?"

Milos nodded, mentally grateful that she was conceding so quickly. It didn't take long to lay out the plan and, to his surprise, he noted Rita was actually taking notes. When he asked, she just waved it off, mentioning it became habit with her witch's training. He just shrugged it off and continued. When he mentioned Ari's training, giving her the knife, she was both startled and giddy with excitement, something he never thought he would attribute to the young girl.

"There, that should do it." Rita wrote in the final schedule and glanced up at the day stones. "We're about halfway through the day and Alex is still asleep, but we should be able to get started. As much as I might be loath to admit it, this is a pretty good set-up."

"Thanks for the generous compliment," Milos deadpanned.

She rolled her eyes before hesitating. "You mentioned training? I didn't want to interrupt, so I'll ask now. What sort of training? You mentioned for each of us?"

Milos nodded, leaning against the side of the cabin as he turned his gaze to the water. "I was made painfully aware last night of just how..." He chose his next words carefully, earning a shock of surprise from the others. Rita stiffened. "...inept most of us are when it comes to combat."

"When you say it like that," Rita muttered as Milos turned toward her.

"As painful as it is for me to admit it, that statement includes myself." The shock was back and more prevalent this time. "That is why all of us will be training, not just you. It'll be basic weapons and dodging training, though for Alex, I can assume none of you mind helping with his demonic side, correct?"

Rita promptly shook her head while Ari and Leon were a little more hesitant. Finally, they agreed. Though, while most of Ari's focus seemed to be on the knife, Milos noted Leon had a small frown on his face, brow furrowed in what must have been agitation. He mentally noted he would have to check with Leon later about it.

Milos pushed away from the cabin, gliding past the Aqua Wraith. He nodded, and she briefly smiled back before drifting away. He took the wheel and glanced back toward the group, noting they were still in place. "Well? Get to it."

Rita stiffened, but soon after, followed his instructions. Ari was already gone, but Leon...

Leon hesitated, standing in place for a long while, hand curling and uncurling in a fist. After a moment, he stepped forward. "Sir." The one word was filled with hesitance and, to Milos' sharp ears, fear.

"What's wrong?"

He pulled away from the wheel for a moment to fully face the man. One glance made it easy to tell that the man before him was terrified of what he was going to say. Actually, his posture was quite reminiscent of Ari's own from the night before. Milos briefly wondered why that was.

"I'm...you made mention of training."

Milos tilted his head slightly in thought. "Yes. Ari came to me last night in regards to training and I agreed to help her, however we need someone to help maintain the ship and I figured you..."

"I'm aware of that sir. I just meant that my job is also to protect you, much like Ari probably said. Sir." The last bit was definitely tacked on, though for a different reason this time around.

"There is no reason—" Milos found his words cut off as Leon stiffened and promptly shook his head.

"Milos, sir, I can fight."

For a brief moment, his hand darted up to his injured arm and Milos didn't miss the hint of terror before Leon seemed to force himself to calm. He tilted his head up, staring at Milos for a brief moment. "I can fight. I promise, I will protect you as you have us." His words trailed off as his signifier clanked and he stiffened. "I don't mean that with any offense, I'm just—"

"Leon." Milos cut in, both surprised and a bit happy. "It's fine, don't worry about it. There is no need to be nervous around me."

Leon's mouth jammed shut as he watched Milos in surprise as Milos continued, "I understand your concern. I'll admit, I'm a bit startled that both you and Ari have come up to me regarding this matter." He let a faint smile onto his lips, the movement startling Leon. "I won't lie, while it is odd to hear someone desiring to protect me, I'm not totally opposed to it."

"Does that mean?" Leon's voice cracked slightly as he spoke in nothing more than a whisper.

"That is up to you. After all..." Milos' gaze flicked to the damaged arm, still tightly bound and clearly missing. "...I am the reason that..."

"Milos, Sir, with all due respect." Leon said, only slightly surprising Milos. "You saved me back there. If it wasn't for your swift action, more than my arm would have been lost to me that day." He hesitated for the briefest of moments before continuing, voice strong. "...I lost my arm that day, but you did not get rid of me like so many would." He bowed his head. "I will not let such a grievous injury happen again to you or anyone else. As Ari probably mentioned, we want to protect you and everyone else here. I won't deny that I am fearful at the thought of a weapon, but at the same time, I am more fearful of what would happen if someone here is hurt."

Milos stared at him for a long time before shaking his head. "I don't understand." The words came out in a faint whisper as he stared at Leon. "What reason do you and Ari have to hold me in such high regard?"

Leon tilted his head up and, where Milos expected uncertainty, there was instead a fierce fire and determination. "Why wouldn't we?"

The three words threw Milos more than he would like to admit. They were such simple words, and yet...Milos let out a long breath. "If that is what you want." He noticed Leon's expression shift to surprise as he continued, "Then, yes, I will teach you as well. I guess it's only fitting considering I already told Ari the same last night."

He peered out over the water, unable to look at Leon for a moment as he spoke his next words. "However, at this stage, your help is needed more in maintaining this ship. God only knows Rita, Alex and myself would be unable to do it." His gaze flicked to the cut-off arm. "You've acclimated admirably to the change, I will admit. Much better than I was expecting."

He felt Leon's gaze on his skull as he moved over to the wheel. "I'll adjust the schedule when I am no longer at the wheel and inform you of the changes, will that suffice?" He corrected their course, having noticed the way the boat drifted slightly north-west during their conversation.

"Thank you." The words caught Milos' attention as he turned to Leon, who was bowing low, lower than he'd ever noticed the man bow. Leon was shaking, though Milos wasn't quite sure why. "Thank you for giving us this chance, Master Milos."

Master. That word again.

"Leon?"

Leon hesitated for only a moment before lifting his head up. "Master?"

"That word. Why are you and Ari using that word now? I thought you always used sir?" Milos couldn't hide the confusion this time around as he stared at Leon.

Leon pulled himself upright, faint smile on his face, as if realizing why Milos was so confused. "Ah, so Ari used it as well." He chuckled faintly. "She would use it first without explaining." He placed his hand to his chest, standing tall. "To answer your question, Master. It was our own little way to fight against our owners. Ari and I were both taught from previous slaves of the duke to use the term sir instead of master.

I'm not sure what other slaves learned of the practice. Some of the young ones are too frightened to follow it and if they demanded from us, we would say it, but otherwise, we would always use sir or ma'am. Most people don't really notice the difference."

"So now you find the need to use master?" Milos' eyes narrowed, fists clenching over the wheel for a moment. Was he being mocked? He hadn't demanded for them to use the term. So why—

"No. We *want* to use the term." Leon bowed once more, causing Milos to still, his mind grounding to a halt for a brief moment. "You have been good to us, and you have listened to both Ari and myself and were willing to work with us when no one else has. This is our way of saying thank you and repaying you back for everything." With that, he stood once more. "Well, as you instructed, I shall be going to check the engine room." With that he turned and practically fled, as if embarrassed about what he said.

Milos mulled over the words, finding himself amused and a little happy, to be honest. Acceptance. What a strange and foreign thing it was.

~ * ~

Rita found herself in the map room once more, scrutinizing the upcoming islands for any other clues on which ones to watch out for. She automatically crossed out any that had an X on them, but wasn't sure what to do about the others. Some held writing she didn't recognize, some just had a general drawing, but nothing specific. It didn't leave her many options. She peered over the papers, wishing she had a second compass to work with. Right now, Milos was outside with the compass. Leon passed her a while ago, a faint smile to his face, something she so rarely saw on the man. From the sounds echoing from below, he was probably in the kitchen now. Ari was working in the engine room. Speaking of, Ari didn't *need* to be in the engine room, right? The Aqua Wraith could do the job too, so...she shook her head. Knowing that man, there was probably a reason. Maybe to swap people out easily for training?

She didn't mind the idea, but what could they even use to defend themselves? Punching the vines wouldn't have done any good, that was for sure. She groaned, pushing away from the table to peer over the walls. For now, she would just have to plot out their course with the new information she had.

Milos was right, though. They had been lucky so far. Coming up with a plan of action would definitely help to make sure nothing else happened. It wouldn't end well if they were caught off guard again.

She let out a sigh, realizing she was getting nothing done. She stepped out, catching Milos' attention. He didn't comment, just waited as she came over, glancing at the compass as she stepped to his side. They were still heading north. She picked it up before hesitating and glancing up to Milos. "You don't mind me being navigator?" Her words were terse, but she was curious on his response.

He simply shrugged, sparing her a glance. "Should I?"

She snorted and shook her head.

"If it's about that island, don't bother." He pulled away from the wheel, twisting slightly to face her. "I've seen the maps, the fact that you found the island at all is impressive."

She blinked, finding herself surprised at his honesty. She leaned forward, peering up at him with a slight frown. "Are you complimenting me?"

"I don't know." He tilted his head slightly. "Is it a compliment that you managed to get somewhere in your homeland? When you are the only one of our group who has traveled by will?"

She clicked her tongue, pulling back. "You annoy me, you know that?"

"Huh, we agree on something." Rita could definitely spot a hint of a smirk now.

Yep, something cheered him up, though she wasn't sure what.

"Oh, you're quite funny, aren't you?" She huffed, walking away. "What about the high and mighty Alertian? Getting injured on the first day?"

There was only a beat of hesitation before he responded, "Interesting, coming from the witch who can't do much more than brew potions."

She felt her fingers twitch as she whirled around. She opened her mouth to argue, then snapped it shut as she realized, unfortunately, he had a point. Milos briefly flashed a confident smirk before returning to a neutral expression. "Unfortunately, while your medical abilities are especially important, you need more than that for survival."

"I never expected to be surviving like this in the first place." She crossed her arms over her chest as Milos shook his head.

"Who does?"

The question threw her and she blinked, unsure how to respond. He didn't say anything, just turned the wheel slightly as if to stay on course.

Finally, she threw her hands into the air, letting resignation sing through her veins. "It's hard to deal with you sometimes." She let her arms drop to her side. "I hate to ask, but what do you propose we do? Only a few of us can actually fight. I know you mentioned training earlier, and all of us caught when you gave that knife to Ari, but..."

Milos nodded, attention returning to her once more. "We'll figure that out during the training sessions. Speaking of..."

Footsteps sounded from the other room before a door opened, revealing Leon standing in the doorway. He held two wooden bowls on a platter that he must have found in one of the storage rooms. He extended the tray out to each of them. Rita took hers gratefully as Milos did the same with a short nod. Leon disappeared back inside before returning and taking over for Milos at the wheel.

As he did so, the two ate in silence, downing the food at a rate that would have surprised Rita if she didn't find herself so gosh-darn hungry.

"I thought you said you had no knowledge of how time worked down here?" She finally spoke up as she finished off the last of the food.

Milos scoffed and, placing his food down next to Leon, returned to Rita's side. "I don't. I just pay attention."

Oh, she wanted to slug this guy. Huh, maybe training would pay off. It would be great if it was hand to hand so she could punch the living daylights out of that smug way too annoying face.

Unfortunately, or fortunately, she acknowledged later, he started with the basics of dodging. "Good offense is good defense," he mentioned as he had her try to hit him. The way he fluidly dodged her attacks only pissed her off more before her fist finally ended up in his hand, though not from any of her doing. "It does no good if the enemy can't hit you, so that's what we're going to focus on. Your..." he hesitated for a moment before continuing, "slender build will help in that."

"You're not exactly buff yourself," Rita growled.

Milos twitched slightly, but didn't comment as he proceeded, much to her surprise, to show her how it was done. It was mostly about awareness. Being a seer, it should help since she was used to scrutinizing different things and getting exact amounts. He must have realized that and, Rita was annoyed to realize, she gave him credit where it was due. He knew what he was doing.

Time passed as he pointed out ways someone might move that would convey a punch or a kick and also how to best avoid different attacks, whether it was to duck down, side step or simply jump backward.

To her surprise, it was actually rather enjoyable to learn, even if she was frustrated at the fact that he had no qualms about hitting her if she didn't dodge in time.

Oh, she had no doubt this was an easy way for him to deal with her frustrating attitude toward him, but she made sure to make it so she wasn't an easy target. In some ways, it became a game. So, when time was up, she found herself exhausted, but grinning wildly. Milos was amused, waving her off.

She hummed, hurrying back to the map room. She felt calmer now and, as such, it was time to tackle that all-important demon called navigation.

~ * ~

Milos wiped his brow and leaned against the rail, thinking over the quick training session. He was much more out of practice than he realized. It was not easy holding back on Rita, which made dodging his attacks much easier for her. That was fine since she was still in the amateur stage, but to let himself get that uncoordinated was abysmal.

Unfortunately, there was no one he could fight with that would help him keep up to the ability he needed to be. It was a frustrating realization.

He would have to just make sure to get as much training as possible for himself through training the others. It would be a good test.

He stared out over the waters, frowning slightly as he noticed the weakening of the day stones, a few fading into their night-time counterparts. He guessed that meant it was afternoon. He hadn't typically watched them when journeying through the Underlands, but out in the open water, there wasn't much else to do. It was fascinating to him, how so much light could be shed from those stones. How could they produce so much light?

Same with the night stones, actually. It was fascinating how much you could see during the night and day. He shook his head and walked into the map room, spotting Rita poring over one of the maps. She barely gave him a glance. "What?"

"Do you have an idea of where we're going next?"

Rita paused for a bit before peering up toward him. "I think I have our next island. It's a little to the northwest though."

"Think about it." Milos continued down the stairs, hearing a huff from above.

"Don't have to tell me twice."

Her voice followed him down the stairs as he chuckled lightly. It wasn't long before he was in what had evidently become the men's room. Alex continued to sleep, curled up in the sheets. Milos took a seat on the other bed, pulling his sword from its sheath. In the light from the few remaining day stones, he could tell it still held the same shine. He held it straight out, feeling the weight of it.

"What are you doing?" Alex mumbled as Milos tilted his head slightly.

"Just testing something." Milos slid the blade back in. He would have to clean it later, but for now, he should check on Alex. "Are you up already?"

Alex sat up, rubbing his face tiredly. "Yeah." He shook his head. "Seriously, though, what are you doing? Shouldn't you be upstairs or something?"

"I figured you would be waking soon," Milos said, turning to face him. "I need to talk to you for a moment."

"Sure?" Alex said, voice pitching up in confusion.

Milos found himself analyzing Alex for a bit before turning his focus to the window. He hesitated only for a brief moment, realizing how ludicrous he was about to sound. "When you're ready, we're going to work on your demonic powers."

Alex shifted, startled. "Huh? I mean, I worked on them yester—"

"You shifted to your demonic form during the attack, correct?" Milos interrupted, turning back to him. Alex winced and nodded. "Yet it took you how long when you were just practicing?"

Milos kept his gaze even, giving Alex time to think over the last few days. Noticing the dawning realization on the boy's face, he continued, "Loathe as I am to admit it, Leon is unable to fight, though he has expressed desire to remedy that, and Ari is by no means capable at this time of fighting though she is just as opposed to the notion. Both have expressed their desire to learn."

Milos thought back to when he first got the two slaves compared to just a little while ago, up on deck and in this very room. They improved immensely from their broken and malnourished state, but they were still weak and unsteady at times and he had a feeling, though Ari hid it well, that the girl had a mild case of seasickness. It wasn't uncommon. "As for Rita..."

"I don't want Rita fighting," Alex admitted, causing Milos to shift his attention back to the boy. Alex fidgeted slightly before continuing, "I mean. Not if I can help it?" That was definitely more of a question and Milos found himself slightly amused at Alex's words. "She *is* the only person on board who knows anything about medicine." Milos watched as Alex pursed his lips and let out a sigh. "I'm not helping much, am I?"

"Don't worry. I was thinking the same thing." Milos waved it off.

Alex blinked up at him, startled. "Really?"

"There is no reason to tell her that, though," Milos said as Alex chuckled and shrugged.

"I wasn't planning on it." He crossed his legs before letting his smile drop. "So, what do you want me to do? I can't pull out my demonic side at will like that." He snapped his fingers, the sound echoing slightly in the room. "Who's going to teach me?"

Milos stared at him for a bit, pushing any arguing thoughts to the back of his mind.

Alex tilted his head for a moment before his expression drew blank. "You're an Alertian. Why would you want to help teach a demon? *How* would you be able to teach a demon?"

"For two reasons." Milos glanced down at his sword. "As I stated earlier, we need more fighters, so if that means one of the fighters is a demon, so be it. Two, as you are probably aware, I hold no hatred nor violence against you. Nor would I dare allow myself or another to hurt anyone on this ship." He paused at those last words, wondering how much he himself influenced Leon and Ari, considering what they said.

"That includes Rita?"

Milos did not miss the mischievous grin on Alex's face and decided he needed to have a talk with the girl in question. Her annoying traits were rubbing off on Alex. "Contrary to how things might appear, yes, that includes Rita." At Alex's nod, Milos continued, "As for *how* I would teach you?" Milos pulled out his sword, pointing it at Alex, who stiffened. "Through the way I was taught."

"Let me guess." Alex tilted his head back a bit, almost cross-eyed as he watched the tip of the blade. "I'm not going to enjoy this."

"Probably not." Milos admitted, smirking slightly as Alex groaned. He pulled the sword back, letting it slide back into its sheath. "You've just woken up, there is no need to start right now."

Alex let out a breath, only to blink and stare back at him. "So, when?"

Milos tilted his head slightly. "Speak with Rita about that. I already gave everyone their schedule while you were sleeping."

"You can't just tell me?" Alex asked and Milos shrugged, earning a sigh from Alex. "I swear." He shook his head. "How are you feeling? The paralysis gone?"

"You remembered," Milos said.

"Of course." Alex appeared offended by his comment. "I was

tired, not completely out of it."

"Which is impressive since you did shift into your demonic form during the attack."

"Yeah." He grinned. "It was nice that I didn't faint this time upon reverting back. Do you know how much of a pain that is?"

"I can imagine." Milos shook his head, realizing what he said. He could understand a demon. Something really was wrong. "Get yourself something to eat. We'll train in a little while."

"Already?" Alex sounded more than a little disgruntled. He let out a sigh. "Fine."

Milos stood and walked out of the room. He reached a hand up, staring at it in the faint flickering of the light stones that glowed in the hallway, the door firmly shut behind him and no one around. His hair drifted over his shoulder as he curled his fingers into a fist. He was an Alertian. He always had been an Alertian. He was only doing this in order to survive.

He was a demon hunter, not a demon helper. He grimaced as a thought sliced through his mind and he quickly pushed it away. There was no reason to think of anything from home right now. Not when he was so far away from it.

He still needed the head of a demon, the head of Satan's child. He glanced briefly over his shoulder, eyes narrowed. He knew it would hurt Alex, but he had a feeling he knew of a way to accomplish it.

He felt a crooked smile flash onto his lips. He did not miss the irony of training someone like Alex. It was ridiculous in so many ways and went against everything he knew.

So why was he so willing to do it? Just simply for survival?

"Demons are the enemy. They will manipulate you, twist your heart and soul without a care," Milos muttered, the words flashing through his mind.

He clicked his tongue. He couldn't deny that. He hadn't thought much of *his* words recently, but it seemed he couldn't avoid it forever. He slammed his fist into the wall, shaking slightly. Damn it. It was his choice to help Alex because he was *human*. He had demonic traits. He was part demon, but he also was very much human.

So why was he so conflicted? It was rational to teach Alex what Milos knew. It was logical to make sure the boy could defend himself. So why was he suddenly hesitating? He let out a long breath, slowly unclenching his fist.

Deep breaths, he reminded himself.

He would figure it out later. For now, he was going to get himself something to eat and calm his thoughts. They were getting him nowhere, after all.

Chapter Ten

Alex winced as a sharp thwack sounded from the hallway. He leaned against the door, staring at the window. Now that he thought about it, this whole thing must have been hard on Milos. He reached his hand up to his cheek. He still remembered how Milos attacked him when they first met, almost as if on instinct. So how much of his Alertian side was he pushing away?

Alex chuckled weakly. Was Milos in the same shoes as himself or something? He shook his head. Milos was always a strange one. Kind in his own ways, but strange nonetheless. Was it an Alertian thing? An Overlander thing? He wasn't sure. Speaking of the Overlands... Alex tilted his head slightly. The man must be missing home. Alex knew he did. No matter the fact that he technically had no home to go back to.

He pushed away from the door, crossing over to the bed and scooping up his cloak and light stone. The warmth from the stone pulsed between his fingers and he felt a faint smile trail on his lips.

As he thought all that, he wasn't worried. He trusted Milos and Rita as well as Ari and Leon in their own ways. He knew Milos was struggling; he understood it was probably difficult for the man to agree to teach a demon, but he did it anyway. Alex was grateful for the help. He wanted to know more about himself and if Milos could help him with that, he would take it.

He slipped the light stone into his pocket and headed into the kitchen, noticing Ari was working on what was probably a pot of stew, seemingly getting ready for dinner. Alex could see some dishes drying off to the side. He supposed they had been used for lunch. Milos was sitting at the table, sipping some sort of drink as Alex walked in. The man didn't even spare him a glance. Just placed the cup down, stood, and walked out the door.

Alex watched him go before turning to Ari. He found himself unsurprised at the girl's stoic expression as she stared at him.

"Did you do something to Master Milos?" Her voice was monotone.

Alex shook his head, pausing only briefly at her words. Had Milos demanded them to say that? No, he didn't recall that ever happening. He frowned in thought. Up until this point, he never heard them use the term. He recalled hearing about the practice when at home and once asked Mother about it. She only chuckled and, ruffling his hair, said he wouldn't have to worry about it. Alex sighed, deciding he didn't want to know why they suddenly changed terms.

"Is that so?" Her words pulled him from his thoughts, having almost forgotten he answered her question as she scooped up some of the stew, placing it in one of the bowls they used over the past few days. She handed it over.

Alex took it, watching her quietly. He never talked with the slaves much. Ari and Leon were both quiet, almost to a fault, following Milos' every word down to the letter. Alex could understand why. Unlike himself, they didn't escape slavery unscathed. He could still see the traces of what once must have been a chain collar around Ari's neck, signaling that she was a certain type of slave. He shivered, recalling the Martinets attempting to put the same collar around his neck all those months ago. It hadn't ended well for anyone involved.

"Milos trusts you." Ari's voice caught Alex off-guard, pulling him out of his thoughts. She watched him quietly. "You know that." It wasn't a question, but Alex nodded anyway. "Support him for now and keep an eye on him. I have promised to do the same, however..."

Huh? Alex stared at the girl as she turned her attention back to the stew, stirring it quietly. "What do you mean?"

"He's struggling with something. He won't tell us." The normally quiet girl was tense, a hint of frustration slipping into her voice before she seemed to realize and she reverted back to neutral tone once more. "I suspect I know and I suspect you do as well."

Alex took a bite of stew, mulling over her words before he

shrugged. "I can do that." She glanced back at him. "He's my friend."

"Right."

The barest hint of a smile trailed onto her face before it was wiped away. Alex grinned, spooning up another bit of the stew.

"Besides," he continued. "Rita wouldn't leave him alone."

Ari let out a quiet chuckle, quickly stifling it.

Still, it made Alex feel a little better that Ari and Leon were beginning to show emotions. He shivered at how they could have ended up in that state and found himself immensely grateful for the Duke's protection once more. He wasn't going to berate her for hiding it. She would open up at her own pace. He continued to eat, thinking over their conversations.

Eventually, he drifted upstairs. Milos was on the deck, sword in hand, with Leon standing in front of him, breathing heavily as he held onto a wooden sword. Alex briefly recalled the weapon to be the same as what he saw the day before when they were trying to escape the tentacles. Where did Leon get that anyway? Was it somewhere on the ship?

Alex decided not to think about it, instead focusing on the training.

Milos' stance was fluid as he blocked and wove, occasionally pointing out something in Leon's stance or occasionally lightly hitting the slave on an open side. Surprisingly, it was usually where his sword arm was.

Alex found himself watching, fascinated.

"They've been doing this since Milos got upstairs. I'm kind of grateful I just did dodging practice now," Rita said, catching Alex's attention.

Alex had to agree as Milos deftly dodged out of the way, placing the blade lightly to Leon's throat.

He pulled it back as Leon put his hand to his knee, almost heaving in gasps of air. Milos knelt on one knee, hand on his shoulder and saying something to Leon in a quiet whisper. Whatever he said seemed to perk the slave up, a faint smile on his face as he nodded. Milos stood as Leon slid his wooden sword into a belt and hurried away into the map room. Alex watched him go before glancing over to Milos, who was casually waiting, sword back in his sheath and gaze firmly on Alex.

"Well, might as well get started, right?" Rita chuckled, gently prodding him forward. "I'm curious what he has planned."

Alex wasn't sure how curious he was, but he decided to just go with it, heading over to Milos.

Milos watched him for a moment before walking over. "Alex, what do you think would be important for you to practice?"

"Me?" Alex blinked, pointing at himself. He figured Milos would tell him, not the other way around. Milos just quirked an eyebrow, but didn't say anything, affirming Alex's thoughts. "Uh...maybe knowing how to change back and forth from my human to demon form and stuff?"

Milos nodded. "That will suffice. I was thinking of working on your water abilities, but maybe you are correct, it wouldn't do to have you faint every time you turn back into your human form." He smirked slightly. "You usually wouldn't have much time to transform into your demon form, if attacked." He shifted his stance down slightly, hand hovering over his blade. "We'll practice in a controlled environment. Since you already know how, we're going to practice you switching back and forth while in a combat environment."

Alex gulped, immediately regretting coming upstairs. Milos chuckled faintly, shifting his stance up slightly. "Don't worry, I don't plan to hurt you." He pulled his hand away from the blade, lifting his hands. "I only used my blade with Leon because he wished to fight sword to sword. I am not interested in doing the same to you."

"That's a relief." Alex said before pausing. "What are you planning to..." His words were cut off as he barely dodged out of the way of a palm strike to his side. "Right. Noted," he yelped as a short laugh echoed from Rita near the wheel. Alex dodged out of the way as Milos turned, sending out a kick to his side.

"Focus, Alex. You need to be able to transform in situations like this. You already know how it works, so concentrate."

"R-right," Alex managed to stammer out, wincing as he barely brought his arm up in time to stop a roundhouse kick to his shoulder. That was leaving a bruise. He dodged once more, desperately trying to remember how to shift. To his relief, it was actually easier than he was expecting, a faint song trembling through his ears as he felt the tell-tale weights forming over his skin and curling around his back.

He glanced up, just in time to lurch back as a fist sailed through where he'd stood. Milos' lips quirked up. "Do you think an enemy will stop just because you transform? Keep your eyes open when you do that, so you don't get knocked to the ground."

"He did hesitate a minute though," Rita called, causing Milos to glare over to the girl, who simply stuck her tongue out.

Alex pulled in a deep breath. Right, Milos was right. He couldn't close his eyes every time he changed. He dodged out of the way as Milos swung a fist almost lazily. No. It was Alex who saw it clearer than before. His sight was sharper in this form. He ducked.

"Now, try to change back."

Alex gulped. Yeah...this whole training thing was going to suck.

A shriek pierced his ears and he yelped, feeling something smack into his side. His hands slammed against his ears as he noticed Milos spin away, one hand on the deck, knees bent. Milos seemed to notice Alex's sudden change. He paused for a moment before his attention snapped toward the surrounding waters.

Alex found himself on the ground, one arm supporting him as another shriek met his ears, barely being blocked by his other hand. His side smarted from where Milos hit him, but he quickly ignored it.

"Alex? Milos?" Rita called, curiosity and concern clear in her voice.

Alex stood and opened his mouth to respond, mildly noting he was back in human form, when another screech filled the air just as the ship jerked sideways.

Alex yelped, barely stopping himself from falling over as Rita let out a cry of surprise. Milos' gaze snapped toward the suddenly violent water. Alex followed his gaze as a wave slammed into the side of the ship, causing it to tilt precariously the other direction. Alex stumbled forward, unable to catch himself this time. Thankfully, Milos seemed to have been prepared, grabbing him around the waist with one hand while the other clung to the railing.

"What's going on?" Rita shouted, tugging desperately on the

wheel, either that or using the wheel to stay standing, Alex wasn't sure.

He heard movement as the Aqua Wraith appeared. Milos helped him over to the map room so he could clutch the doorway before hurrying toward Rita, stumbling slightly as another wave slammed into the ship. Alex watched them as the Aqua Wraith glided to his side, a hint of worry and fear in her expression.

"Thou can sense the water's warning, correct?"

Alex nodded, "What...?"

"I cannot answer, only say that thou must focus. Calm the waters."

"That's great and all," Rita shouted, probably having heard the conversation. "But unless you can randomly pull some convoluted mess from your demonic half, which—why the heck did you return to your human form anyway? Whatever, hold on."

Before Alex could respond, the wheel jerked again and Alex quickly grabbed the cabin wall, staring out over the water. The Aqua Wraith was already gone, disappearing into the floors below.

Alex wondered that himself, wondering why he was back in human form, but ignored it. These waves, where did they come from? The ocean had been peaceful up until now, only disturbed by those giant creatures, so what was this?

"Listen to the water." Milos' voice caught his attention, causing him to look over to the man. "Water demons are automatically in tune with the waters around them, similar to breathing for humans. Remember when you saved us when the tunnels near the capital collapsed? Think of that."

Alex nodded, closing his eyes and focusing. It was hard, listening as the ship was tossed back and forth over the rolling waves. It was disconcerting.

A song echoed in his mind, a faint hum of fear trailing through his ears. The water was running from something, pushing and battering at the ship.

"You said there's an island near here, right?" Alex asked quickly, opening his eyes in time to see Rita nod. "Get us there as quick as you can. Something's coming."

"Don't have to tell me twice." She spun the wheel with Milos' help and shouted in the tube to go full speed ahead. They slid through the waves, rolling slightly whenever a particularly vicious one reached for them. Alex listened intently, humming quietly to himself whenever he could. At times, the waves calmed and he wondered if he managed to do it.

Soon enough, an island appeared in the distance, rapidly coming closer. It was in a slight u-shape, similar to the crescent moon Alex heard about from the books in his grandfather's library. White shone near the water, causing fear to spike through him for a second before he noted the trees covering part of the island.

It wasn't long before the wind stones shut off and they drifted to a halt in the middle of what Alex could only assume was a bay or lagoon, anchor plunging into the water as everyone peered out toward the sea proper.

Alex stared in surprise, awe, and fear as the water itself twisted, shifting and quavering for a few more minutes before forming serpents, water serpents. One leapt from the water, its spiraling and shimmering form almost dragging the ocean along with it before it splashed down with a mighty crash, others soon following in its wake, crisscrossing over and under each other as if in an elaborate web or dance. He briefly wondered if they were related in some way to the Aqua Wraith, but pushed the idea off.

As beautiful as they were, crisscrossing over the ocean waves before splashing down, he was glad they got out of there when they did. The sea churned as the serpents flung themselves through the sky, water raining down before exploding up in plumes as they crashed down into the waves. He was grateful the island was blocked on three sides, because it certainly helped calm the waters. He stared for a while, the humming resonating in his ears.

"It's going to be like that for a while, isn't it?" he muttered, staring at the spectacle before letting out a sigh. Well, no point worrying about it now.

Alex pulled his attention away from the serpents to peer at the island, feeling anxious. Nothing looked dangerous, upon first critical inspection, but after the last island, he wasn't sure what he expected. It seemed he wasn't the only one. Milos had a hand on the hilt of his sword and Rita was holding her satchel tightly.

They stared at the island for a moment, breath caught in their throats before the Aqua Wraith swirled before them, a gentle smile on her face.

It was enough indication for Alex that he let out his breath in a whoosh. He smiled at the Aqua Wraith before hurrying over to the edge of the boat and actually taking a good look at the island. In the bright warmth of the day stones, he could tell it was a beautiful little island. White sparkled over the ground like shifting dirt. Sand, his mind reminded him. He'd only heard about it in books.

They were in the middle, not far from the shore, but still a couple minutes out from being able to disembark.

He wanted to dive in.

It was a strange feeling, wanting to just dive under the water. He spotted the Aqua Wraith beside him, her watery hair blowing as she actually jumped, a broad smile on her face.

Alex heard a gasp behind him and a quiet curse.

However, if the Aqua Wraith was okay with this...he grinned and, before he could think over what he was doing, he swung himself over the railing and dropped into the water.

The cold shock caught him off guard at first and it took him a moment of panicking before he realized that he was heading back to the surface, the water itself practically pushing him upward. It was crystal clear below, a shimmering blue and green coating his sight as he stared at strange tendrils of what he assumed must have been seaweed. To the right, where he knew the island was, was a large rocky cliff face cutting sharply down into the water, a gentle slope at the top being the only indication of where the shore was. He moved toward it with ease, quickly reaching the sloping area, fingers gently trailing over the sand as it billowed in the water.

He shot upward breaking the surface. He took a deep breath, water dripping into his eyes as he observed his surroundings around in wonder. After the initial shock, the water felt inviting as he settled onto the sandy piece of land, water lapping at his waist.

"You idiot. You daft dingbat. What do you think you're doing?" Rita's shouts echoed from above as he tilted his head up enough to spot them.

"It's fine," he called over. "The water's nice and the Aqua Wraith had no problem with it."

At the edge of the boat, practically falling over it, was Rita, her expression showing her discontent as much as Milos' crossed arms showed his own annoyance. "That...she jumped in the water when we first got on the boat too. Would you have called it safe then?"

Alex sighed. While she did have a point, back then, the water hadn't been tumultuous and he hadn't sensed anything in the water, so...

Still, even as he stood there feeling the water lap at his skin as the sand trailed around his shoes, he felt positively refreshed. Of course, he figured it had something to do with his demonic heritage, but at the same time, the water here was calm, serene, as if separated from the twisting sea serpents just outside the island. "Come on, that's another thing entirely. Besides, the water's safe."

Rita placed her head in her hands with a groan as Milos closed his eyes. Alex stepped toward the island, pulling himself from the water as he scanned the surroundings in awe. The sand shifted under his feet as waves lapped against his ankles. His clothes were soaked through and dragging at his body, but he didn't particularly care right now. The island was bigger up close, much bigger. Trees, scraggly as they were, twisted and curved over the ground. There seemed to be some sort of greenery coating the ground as well.

There was a splash behind him, causing him to jump. He whipped around to see Milos swimming with a surprising grace before seeming to stumble for a second where Alex knew the cliff was. He pulled himself up out of the water, wringing out his hair and clothes as he eyed the island. "A tropical island? Down here?" His words were soft, but Alex caught them anyway.

"You joined me," Alex pointed out, feeling happy, as he glanced back at the ship, wondering if Rita would as well. He briefly noted her harried expression, her gaze darting between the water and him, before she pulled away from the railing, more annoyed than anything. Alex turned his attention to Milos.

Milos sent him an exasperated expression. "Do you think it was really that wise to jump over the edge of a ship into unknown territory just because the Aqua Wraith did? Rita was right for once."

Alex pursed his lips, but decided not to argue anymore. After all, all of this reminded him a little too much of what he knew about the Overlands. For a split second, he had been able to imagine being there.

He let out a breath as Milos shook his head and, tossing all of his clothes except the thin tunic and trousers over his shoulder, he started walking a bit away from the water. "I assume we are going to forgo the rest of your training. For now, we might as well explore what we can as we wait for the others."

Alex watched as he grabbed one of the broad leaves of a nearby tree and sliced through it with his sword, setting it on the ground before placing his clothes onto it. "Take off your cloak, it's just going to drag you down for now."

Alex hurried over, slipping the cloak from around his shoulders and feeling grateful for the release of weight. It was heavier than he thought. "Is Rita staying on the ship?" he found himself asking as Milos laid out the clothes, stood and nodded.

He pulled his long hair over his shoulder before squeezing some of the water out. His hair dripped and, for a moment, Alex wondered why the man kept his hair so long. He hadn't really thought much about it in the past because it just seemed a part of Milos, but as it draped over his shoulder, tangled as it was, he couldn't help but wonder. "I'm not sure on the specifics," Milos said as he glanced up. "I can assume it has to do with wanting to avoid the water."

Made sense. Speaking of... "Wait, you can swim?" Alex wasn't sure where the question came from considering he just saw the man swim over, but the reaction he got was a blank expression from Milos.

"Yes," he finally said after a moment before turning right to head around the sandy part of the island.

Alex briefly glanced back to the ship, noting Rita was leaning against the railing, chin in her hand. A small pout was on her face as she leaned against the railing. He could see Ari patting her shoulder with a neutral expression, for the most part. Alex shook his head, returning his attention back to Milos. "Are you okay? With exploring the island?"

"Not much else to do until those serpents leave and, as Rita has mentioned, procuring food is essential." Milos stopped, peering up at one of the trees.

Alex found himself curious about what Milos noticed, considering the only thing he observed since getting on the island were the broad leaves clinging to the trees, similar to what Milos used to place their clothes down. Milos simply shrugged it off and kept moving. "This island seems to have a thriving ecosystem, so hopefully, we'll be able to obtain some items such as fresh fruits and meat. Though a little more wariness next time might be helpful." Milos' voice was cold as Alex glanced away.

Okay, okay, he got it, Milos didn't have to keep mentioning it. It wasn't like he was ignoring the possible dangers. He saw, well enough, what the Underlands were capable of. He also knew that living in fear all the time wasn't going to help anyone. He knew that all too well.

His thoughts flickered to when he was running away. How long ago had that been? How long ago was it since he last saw his mother? Had she actually abandoned him? Alex brought up his shaking hands, observing them quietly as the fingers slowly curved into fists. He was going to find Mother, he reminded himself. This was just a momentary pause to gather his thoughts. He knew everyone needed a moment to breathe and, to be honest, he trusted the Aqua Wraith. He wasn't sure why, maybe it was a demonic thing, but he felt no malice from the being. His thoughts flashed to the other night, when the Aqua Wraith talked with him alone. She mentioned an oath, or promise, as she also said. What sort of oath was it? Did it have to do with protecting the ship? Something else? Whatever it was, she could still show emotion and, considering she did warn them every previous time, he felt it right to believe her here.

"We'll have to stay near the coast, but this island should be safe enough to stay for the time being." Milos 'words snapped Alex out of his thoughts.

Huh? he thought, turning to face Milos, who seemed to be watching the tree line quietly.

An echoing crack and crash caused Alex to jump, a flash dazzling his eyes as he turned, followed by another crack.

"Lightning? Here?" Milos questioned, his voice sounding more than a little perturbed. Milos shifted, as if ready to race back toward the ship, only to stop.

Alex shielded his eyes as lightning, as Milos called it, crashed into the tree they stood beside. Flame erupted as Milos stumbled away. A strange warbling cry filled the air, a screeching sound before one more flash filled the sky. Alex's gaze darted to the sky in time to spot long wings disappear over the trees, silence filling the air once more.

"What...what was that?" Alex barely found his voice, staring up at the sky. Well, that contradicted what Milos just said spectacularly.

"Something that doesn't want us here." Milos spoke stiffly.

Alex found himself sending Milos a blank expression. "Would you like to phrase that better?" Milos didn't even glance his way as he hurried back in the direction of the ship, keeping half an eye on the sky.

Alex quickly raced after him, deciding that, no, those words definitely sufficed.

Chapter Eleven

Rita groaned, peering down at the water. As stupid as it was for someone who hadn't been in anything deeper than a stream, she wanted to jump in. It honestly seemed refreshing and she needed a good bath right now anyway. Most of them did. They could only do so much with the water produced from the meager water stone they found for drinking. She stared out, watching the boys disappear into the tree line. Ari stepped away, moving to the other side of the ship. Rita could feel the wheel shift slightly as they drifted closer to the shore.

Of course, at least from here, she got a good view.

Shaking her head, she pushed away from the railing, spotting as the Aqua Wraith swirled back on the ship, seeming content.

"Was that necessary?" Rita frowned, as the Aqua Wraith swirled around her.

"Is it not necessary to calm one's mind? There is no harm in resting from one's trials."

"We don't know if this place is safe," Rita protested.

The Aqua Wraith smiled and went to speak before her entire being seemed to freeze.

Rita never saw the Aqua Wraith move so quickly, the water swirling in a panicked momentum that momentarily lost shape as she turned to face the island, just as light smashed into the ground, almost blinding Rita. Dots speckled her sight as she rubbed at her eyes, her ears ringing as a shout of surprise echoed behind her. Whether that was her own voice or someone else's, she couldn't tell.

"What is such a creature doing here?" The Aqua Wraith's words cut through her thoughts as Rita finally managed to pull herself together, hands gripping the railing as another lightning strike flashed in the distance where the boys went.

Alex.

She wanted to jump, to make sure he was all right, but she knew that would be utterly stupid. So, she waited, breath caught in her throat, as a loud warbling cry filled the air. She glanced up to the sky, surprised she hadn't thought to look up, only managing to catch the bare traces of plumage as wings curved around a body, plunging into the tree line and disappearing from sight.

"That is not what I call safe," Rita growled, rounding on the Aqua Wraith, only to still as she noticed the being frozen, the water shaking, but the posture as stiff as, well, water could be.

"Tis a bad omen." The Aqua Wraith's words were whispered as she stared over the tree line. "It seems the creature has traveled again without my knowledge, and yet we are trapped on these shores until the ocean subsides."

Rita glanced behind her, reminded of the sea serpents. She clicked her tongue. They couldn't leave the island, but she could tell staying wasn't safe either.

What could they do in this situation?

She shook her head and turned to Ari, who managed to move them a little closer. Leon stepped over, startling her, when did the man get back up here? "Are we close enough to get to the island safely?"

"We should be." Ari called as Leon nodded, already heading over to the gangplank.

The Aqua Wraith nodded and wisped away to help. Rita turned back to the coast, staring down as she heard a thump on the sand. "Knowing those two, they are probably fine, but we're out in open water." She trailed off, now realizing she wasn't sure what to say.

The ship wasn't safe, but if all of them got off, the ship could be destroyed and they could end up stranded, but even if they left someone there, then...there weren't many options.

"I'll stay."

Ari's voice caused Rita to jerk. She glanced toward the girl, who only gave them a faint smile. "You two should check on Master Milos and Master Alex."

Rita blinked, startled, before nodding. "Thanks, Ari." With that, she darted over toward the gangplank, Leon already descending down, wooden sword clutched in his grasp. Rita was only a few steps behind them as they stepped onto the sand, heading toward where the boys disappeared.

"Rita, are you guys okay?" Alex's voice echoed from the beach.

Rita turned, spotting him waving his hand as they came closer. He seemed to relax slightly when she waved back.

"We're fine."

Milos was standing a little back, his attention on the ocean behind her. A frown curled over his face as he seemed to realize the same thing she already did.

"That thing didn't hurt you, right?" Milos asked as he stepped over, examining the ship.

"No, it didn't." Rita shook her head, noting how neither boy seemed injured.

"Was it just warning us?" Alex tilted his head up, a strange expression on his face. Rita stilled, glancing at Alex as he leaned on one leg, shrugging. "If it was simply warning us, as long as we stay out of its way and leave as soon as the sea is clear, we should be fine, right?"

"You're being very optimistic." Rita snorted before letting out a sigh. Unfortunately, he was also right. It was the only thing they could really do at this point.

"Better optimistic than thinking we're going to die because we pissed off something dangerous," Alex admitted, though the way his words trailed off indicated that it was exactly what he was thinking.

Rita smiled, feeling the sand dip as she took another step forward. Speaking of, how was there sand and tropical islands in the Underlands? She hummed in thought. She was aware the sand was probably just the minerals from the surrounding oceans getting caught by the shape of the island, as well as progressive erosion, but that didn't explain the plant life. There were some things here she never even saw before. Of course, from a cursory glance, she could tell there were quite a few things that could be both helpful and deadly if they weren't careful.

She shook her head. It was probably just her imagination. She finally caught up to Alex, smiling beatifically. She noted as Milos took a step to one side. Alex blinked, confused.

She promptly slapped Alex in the back of the head, or attempted to, considering he quickly yelped, dodging backward with a, "Hey, what's that for?"

"For being a dingbat and jumping into the water without actually letting us know first." She pulled back, hand on her hip, even as an amused grin crossed her face.

He huffed, but didn't argue, peering into the undergrowth. "So, what now? That creature is still out there, we are stranded here until the water calms and we do need to restock on food."

"We restock." Milos spoke up, staring up at a few trees. "If there are signs of that creature, we hide, simple as that."

"That's pretty vague, coming from an Alertian." Rita raised an eyebrow, arms crossed.

"I'm an Alertian, not an animal hunter," Milos deadpanned.

"You sure it's not a demon? Maybe you're just losing your touch." Rita grinned as Milos' finger twitched slightly, the only indication of his irritation. It was victory enough for her.

"A witch such as you should be able to foresee this." His retort was clipped. "Did you screw up another of your witch brews?"

"That was once," Rita snapped, causing Milos' lips to twitch up in slight victory.

"Guys..." Alex's voice cut off their conversation as he stepped between them, then pointed over toward Leon. "Come on, can't we just help Leon? He's already started to collect some herbs and berries to take back to the ship."

True to his word, Rita noticed Leon had managed to already acquire a good handful of said items, placing them neatly in a bag he had brought with him. Smart.

She would have to stick with her satchel, though it was already almost full. She shook her head and turned to the group. "Ari will remain on the ship with the Aqua Wraith. Since we're already split, we'll go our separate ways. We'll meet back here in an hour, got it?"

"I'll assume Alex knows how to tell time then." Milos turned and

Alex only shrugged helplessly before hurrying after him.

Rita watched them go, glad that they were all right, before turning toward Leon. The man watched her quietly before nodding and continuing what he was doing. She walked over, deciding to help. It would be faster that way.

~ * ~

Milos shifted, peering into the tree line and occasionally glancing toward the sky. He wasn't sure why, but he had felt disconcerted for a little while now. It had been over half an hour since they separated once more from Rita and Leon. He could still see bits of the ship in sight, but none of the people that were supposed to be on it. Alex was a little ahead, peering around the underbrush.

Milos, in order to rationalize the possibility of tropical plant life in the Underlands, decided to attribute it to the strange nature of the Underlands and the wells of power that fluctuated around these seas. It was easier than trying to rationally figure out how this much plant life could grow without the sun in this much diversity.

The other thing that was unsettling him was a feeling he didn't think he would experience in this stretch of oceans.

Being watched.

He glanced toward the water, spotting the ship as it drifted in the waves, just barely within view, past the towering walls of the crescent-shaped island. A serpent leapt high enough to gleam in the day stones' light, piercing over the higher cliffs that surrounded the island before disappearing.

Alex didn't seem to mind, not that the boy would notice. Milos would be remiss to see the excitement the boy held for this little adventure. To Alex, this was the closest he was going to get to the Overlands. While Milos felt strange to admit it, this little stretch of beach, if he kept his gaze glued to the trees and ignored the staleness of the air, could be part of the Overlands. He couldn't help but feel a hint of a smile at that, before quickly wiping it away.

It didn't help that the feeling of being watched would not go away.

At least, not for any long periods of time.

However, nothing happened as they collected what they assumed was food, and returned to meet with Rita and Leon. Thankfully, as he presumed, the island was rich with different ingredients. He wondered if there was any hunting that could be done. Just because he wasn't an animal killer didn't mean he avoided knowledge regarding regular hunting. It just wasn't his forte.

He would have to think about it, however, when they came back to find all they had was a few berries. The rest were poisonous or held no nutritional value, according to Rita. Unfortunately, the day stones were starting to disappear. Milos sighed and walked over to where he left their clothes, only to freeze.

The leaf was still there, certainly...

"Rita? Did you grab my cloak?" Alex asked, peeking over Milos' shoulder.

"No?" Rita piped up, almost questioningly. "I haven't touched any of your clothes." Rita walked over in a huff as Milos' mind raced.

He peered into the forest, gaze sharp. Even in the growing gloom, he could see traces of footprints. He couldn't quite make out what they were. A small child's? A young adult's? He closed his eyes, noting a strange shift in the air. He wasn't sure what it was, but considering the way the air swirled, as if hesitant, around where the clothes once lay...

"Where is it?" Alex's voice pitched up. "Why would anyone have a reason to take them?"

"You sure Ari or Leon didn't just bring them onto the ship?" Rita guessed, pointing out what would probably be obvious. Milos stood, having knelt to inspect the area.

"You would assume." He peered into the darkness. "But that's not completely accurate."

"Wait, is there something in there beside that giant bird creature thing?" Rita yelped before glaring at Alex, who quickly waved his arms defensively.

"Possibly. For now, let's get back to the ship. It's dangerous to move at night." Milos interjected.

"But—" Alex cut himself off as Milos shot him a look.

Alex sighed and nodded, peering into the darkness before pulling his tunic close. The kid was probably cold, now that Milos thought about it.

Plus, if he recalled correctly, he heard the cloak was once a gift from Rita. While the girl grated on his nerves, it was plain to see Rita and Alex held each other in high regard. Admittedly, it was something that fascinated Milos as he watched them. It was strange to watch just how close they were.

He shook his head and walked back to the ship, Rita a few steps ahead and Alex meandering a few steps behind.

That feeling. It was still there, as they climbed onto the ship and pulled up the plank.

He wondered if he would be feeling it until they left the island.

Hopefully, come morning, the sea would have calmed enough for them to do just that.

~ * ~

Rita stared out over the water, leaning against the railing once more. She kept her ears open for any sign of the creature, but didn't hear a thing. Though, that didn't necessarily mean much, considering she hadn't noticed it until lightning was flung down at them, but still...the sea serpents' glimmering sheen glowed under the dawning day stones' light, leaping from the water with ease. As beautiful as they were, the churning of the sea just enforced the idea that they weren't leaving. She let out a sigh, slumping slightly. She figured as much when she awoke the next day to take over for Leon, but still...

She glanced toward the island, feeling the ship shift gently back and forth. It seemed the creature from the day before had left them alone. She wondered if it was because they weren't on the island. Was it protecting the island?

She sighed. Part of her wanted to go onto the island. She saw a lot of herbs that she could use for medicine and, admittedly, poisons that she wasn't able to carry back with her. She briefly thought back to her assumption yesterday. She hadn't put it into words, believing she was imagining things, but the environment of this island was almost like a witch's haven. The plants were all, or almost all, things she could use for brews and spells. Why? What reason was there for the island to be that way?

Still, as much as she wanted to explore the island, she was also not so dumb as to think she would be fine, going alone. She had berated Alex about that yesterday.

She pushed away from the railing, startled as footsteps sounded from the doorway. The door opened, revealing Milos.

Rita grunted, acknowledging him. He just sent her an unamused look.

"What are you doing up so early?" Rita crossed her arms.

Milos turned toward the island for a moment before responding, "Is it that early?" He shrugged, gaze drifting to the day stones. "It's hard to tell down here."

"Even now?" Rita was curious, admittedly.

She was so used to the way the day stones shifted, strengthening and weakening as the hours progressed. Maybe it wasn't noticeable to an Overlander? Milos had been down here for over a month. Wouldn't he have adjusted by now?

He watched her, giving her enough answer by itself. She rolled her eyes as he finally turned away, staring up at the ceiling. After a moment, he headed to the other end of the ship, drawing his sword as he walked. Rita watched him quietly as he came to a halt and, letting out a long breath, shifted his stance, placing the sword level. His movements were slow, calculated as he brought the sword around him, slashing through the air as he moved through what were obviously practiced movements. He just decided to start training. It made sense, she supposed, there wasn't much else to do at the moment and neither one was keen to go back onto the island. She took a seat next to the cabin, leaning against the wood as she, admittedly, watched in fascination.

His movements, as time passed, became quicker, more precise and calculated, almost graceful, Rita admitted to herself. The hints of chainmail glinted in the light, probably a spare; a tunic she never saw before hung over his frame loosely. Where he found it, or if he had it to begin with and just miscalculated on size, she wasn't sure. Finally, as the day stones grew bright enough to wash the whole island in light, he drew to a stop, sword sliding back into the sheath as he let out a long breath, sweat brimming on his brow.

The others were probably going to be up soon and, no, she was not going to admit she was glad to have gotten something nice to watch during her shift. As much as she might find Milos annoying, at least he was *very* pleasing to look at.

Rita shook her head as Milos walked back over, eyebrow raised and a slight smirk on his face. She had no doubt on what the smirk was for, his words only cementing it. "It's not nice to stare."

"Why would I be staring at you?" she asked, keeping her voice carefully unexpressive. He tilted his head up slightly, amused before frowning, his gaze snapping to the island. Rita watched him quietly as he peered toward the tree line. The hand that had been pushing back his bangs stilled. Rita followed his gaze. For a split second, and maybe it was her imagination, she thought she saw something move.

Faster than she expected, Milos darted to the railing, flinging himself over, sword drawn. A quiet splash reached her ears. Rita raced over, as Milos landed in the sand, water slapping against his boots. He raced toward the tree line. She mentally cursed, staring down at the steep drop, before trying to remember how the Aqua Wraith...

As if the Aqua Wraith was aware, Rita heard a clang and glanced over just as the plank slipped out and onto the ground.

Rita swore the woman was psychic, but ignored it, shouting a quick, "Thanks," before charging after the rapidly disappearing figure of Milos. Her satchel shoved into her side, but she ignored it, darting into the tree line.

For a split second, she thought she had lost him, only to slam into him, causing her to stumble backward and for him to let out a quiet grunt. She shook her head as Milos quietly clicked his tongue, sword drawn and gaze focused.

Rita took a step forward, causing Milos to glance her direction. "Who's there?" she called, glaring into the darkness as her hand sat near her bottles.

Silence filled the air except for their harsh breaths, or mostly hers, actually. Milos was incredibly quiet and it was eerie just how focused he was.

She only briefly saw him in his hunting state when he was after Alex. She watched him move through the trees, occasionally peering skyward. His steps silent, especially compared to hers as leaves crackled under her shoes.

What was it she spotted? From a quick glance, and she could have just been imagining things, it looked like a person.

Still, no one answered her call and she couldn't find it in herself to ask again.

"Let's go back." Milos' voice was quiet, a whisper of a breeze, if one existed.

Rita wasn't sure she liked that idea. She didn't like the idea of something she didn't know watching them, but...

She relaxed slightly, as Milos turned to face her, only to see him tense before his sword whizzed through the air. Rita yelped, stiffening as she noticed the blade resting on her shoulder, inches away from her neck.

What startled her even more was the panicked yelp that echoed behind her.

She threw herself away from the blade, turning in the process.

Behind her, hand reaching toward where her satchel was, was a child, probably a girl. Unruly long brown hair trailed down to a thin waist. The girl was covered in dirt and she was more than a little malnourished, freckles covering her nose as she peered at them with wide brown, almost gold, eyes.

Eyes that were staring at the sword placed very carefully in front of her nose, causing her to freeze.

"Who are you?" Milos' voice was cold, his sword not budging an inch.

The girl stared at him, not speaking for a moment, only tilting her head slightly in confusion.

Milos pursed his lips, watching quietly as Rita observed the girl in front of her. She seemed young, but at the same time it was hard to tell just how young with the dirt, ragged plant-like clothing and occasional burns she saw marring the girl's skin. Rita winced as she saw one burn mark on the inside of her arm. The girl observed her for a moment before turning back to Milos.

Before either of them could respond, she jumped away, racing into the tree line. Milos started, only waiting a split second to chase after her.

"Milos," Rita yelped, stumbling after the two for a second before quickly catching up. "What the heck, you dingbat."

"Why is there a young child on an island in the middle of nowhere?" Milos questioned, sending her a look. "No one has traveled these parts in years."

Rita slammed her mouth shut, unable to respond. The child disappeared into the brush, but that didn't seem to stop Milos. He darted around a tree, telling Rita to stay close.

Rita didn't have to be told twice, following after him as he slid down a sharp embankment. She couldn't see anything. Milos seemed to be just fine tracking whatever, or whoever that was.

A strange warbling echoed over the surrounding area before a sharp cry rang above the trees, causing Milos to slide to a halt. Rita mentally cursed as she jerked her head skyward.

Lightning flashed as wings, glimmering a bright gold in the day stones light, flared up before them, arching over their heads. A burning smell filled her nose before another crash of lightning slammed inches from where she stopped.

That cry sounded again, the creature circling high above before drifting away, toward where the girl disappeared to. Lightning flared once more, slamming into a tree.

It took Rita way too long to realize what was going on. "That thing. It's attacking where that girl disappeared."

"How convenient," Milos muttered quietly as another warbling cry rang out.

Rita stared back up at the sky, finally getting a chance to actually observe the creature. It could only be described as a strange bird. A pair of wings spread over a large form similar to a fox. A long flowing tail twisted and curved in the sky, curling around the creature as its large wings swung it through the air. The creature let out another cry before the wings folded around itself like Alex did. The two stared as it purposefully tilted its body downward, plunging through the sky. Its fur flickered for a moment, as if resembling flame, before a large flash slammed into her eyes, causing spots to appear as a mighty crash followed suit. She felt herself land on her butt, hands covering her eyes as pain lashed through her head. That freaking hurt. Her ears rang even though she knew the sound was long past. The only thing that seemed to be working was her sense of smell, which caught a burning wafting over the trees.

A faint sound of a thud echoed beside her as the ringing in her ears slowly faded.

She could feel a tingling along the ground, shocks zapping at her legs and fingers. To feel the static, even at the distance they were was incredible and a little bit nerve-wracking.

She was incredibly glad they weren't any closer when the lightning went off. The flames didn't seem to have spread. The flicker of flame she saw wasn't incredibly strong, more similar to a spark. So why did she see that? What about the little girl? Flashes of the burns decorating the girl's arms pushed her to open her eyes.

All she could see were splotches at best, but slowly, she was able to make out the form of Milos. He'd used his sword, pierced into the ground, to keep himself steady, though he did manage to fall onto one knee.

He was already getting to his feet, wobbling slightly. She carefully pulled herself up, her body shaking. Thankfully, once she was on her feet, it seemed she could mostly see again, her ears no longer ringing.

The creature was gone, a wisp of smoke permeating the tree line.

Rita caught her breath, worry suddenly spiking. The little girl went that way. Was she safe?

She turned to see Milos closing his eyes, teeth gritted in concentration. Before long, he let out a breath. "I think that thing is gone for now. Whatever it did, it dispersed whatever magic is around, so it's hard to tell."

"What about that girl?" Rita wondered.

Milos frowned, not responding before letting out a sigh. "These Underlands really are strange."

"Yeah," Rita agreed hesitantly. "I've never seen anything like that before."

"Really?" Milos slid the blade out of the earth, before carefully wiping some of the clinging dirt off of it. "Figured something like that would be your sort of thing."

Rita felt her eye twitch, but didn't respond as she started to head down the slope. Milos clicked his tongue, but followed after her.

Admittedly, like with Alex, her curiosity was getting the better of her. She hurried through the trees, heading in the direction she last saw the girl. Thankfully, it was fairly easy to dodge where the creature disappeared. The smoke filling the air in one specific area was indication enough.

Before long, she heard the sound of scrambling and drew to a halt, exchanging startled expressions with Milos. Milos had obviously been letting her lead, not saying a word, but she figured he would have said something if she got off track.

She wasn't sure if that was a comfort or not.

She shook her head, peeking through the underbrush in time to spot the little girl pulling herself into a small cave Rita would never have spotted. It was buried slightly beneath the earth, covered in thin underbrush. This island was so strange.

Not even a moment later, the little girl scampered back out and Rita didn't miss the way she winced, a burn curling around her neck as she disappeared into the trees.

"Satisfied?" Milos spoke, voice low.

Rita didn't say a word, only watching for a minute longer before darting to the opening. She heard a frustrated sigh behind her, but ignored it as she peeked inside. The cave was surprisingly big and cozy on the inside. It was obvious it was dug out, but she couldn't figure out by what. Different things lined the walls and ground from gold and knickknacks to clothes and furs.

Off to one side, draped neatly over what was probably supposed to resemble a chair, was...

"So that's where it went." Milos' voice startled her. She hated to admit to herself that she let out a high-pitched "meep" at his voice.

Milos' slight grin indicated he wasn't going to let her forget that either. The stupid lout.

She slipped inside, having to duck. She hurried over, swiping up Alex's cloak as Milos grabbed his own things, peering them over carefully.

"Why would she steal it if she already has a lot?" Rita muttered quietly, scanning the surrounding area. You could almost mistake the place as a home, but the distinct lack of furniture or anything resembling a bed made that less likely.

Milos didn't respond, just hurried back out the entrance, his lean frame helping him slip through. Rita wanted to stick around a little longer, trying to figure out what to do.

Finally, she let out a sigh and followed after him, scrambling out of the little opening. She was no closer to figuring out who that girl was, or the creature that seemed to be after her.

She grunted in annoyance as she stood up and froze.

Standing before Milos, watching with wide eyes, was a young man. A young man dressed similarly to the little girl from before.

His gaze darted to what they held in their hands before returning his attention back toward them with a deep frown. "What are you doing?"

Chapter Twelve

Milos narrowed his eyes at the boy before him, noting the choppy haircut and burns crisscrossing his arms and neck, the boy's words slipping through his mind. He was slender, almost malnourished, with brownish gold eyes. Was he possibly related to that girl? Milos pursed his lips as he watched the boy, who seemed to be eyeing them just as warily, hands curling around a stick at his side.

Milos mentally noted that he didn't seem to hold it in a good grip, fingers too tightly clasped and placed too close to the end of the wood to be of any use.

"We're getting our stuff back." Rita spoke up, voice pointed and annoyed. "Seriously, though, why was it here to begin with? What's the point of stealing it?"

The boy glanced at her, sizing her up quietly. "Reasons." He slightly loosened the grip on the stick. "My...sister must have caused you trouble then."

The words were stilted and it was obvious, as Milos watched, that the boy wasn't used to this sort of conversation. Though the hesitation on "sister" was interesting. "I apologize. We meant no harm. Most of the clothes you see within no longer fit us, or never fit us to begin with. I'm guessing my sister was looking for something for me."

Milos noted as he shifted, the clothes on his person affirmed his words. They were completely tattered, barely held together with plantlike rope.

"Well, whatever, we got our stuff back." Rita shrugged, hefting Alex's cloak over her shoulder. "Don't worry, we didn't take anything else."

The boy watched her quietly to the point where Milos could

almost see Rita fidget and, deciding to give her some reprieve, spoke. "How are there humans here? How did you and your sister..." the little girl, Milos presumed, "...end up on an island like this? I was led to believe that no one has traversed these waters for a while."

"Not from the south, no." The boy shook his head, finally placing the stick through a loop on his cloth belt. It sagged slightly, but held. "At least not since we ended up here."

"The north. Of course," Rita muttered as Milos observed the sky for a second. "Wait, not since you ended up here? How long have you *been* here?"

The boy glanced at her before looking away. "Approximately six years, give or take a few days."

Six years, huh? Milos noted the shock flicker over Rita's face. He felt a moment of sympathy for the boy before pushing it off.

Of course, that led him to wonder what he meant when he mentioned people not coming from the south. Were there humans to the north? He believed it was only demons, but it was probably possible that human slaves fled there as well. "What about that creature, the one who seemed to be chasing your sister?"

"We mostly stay out of its way. As long as we don't trespass on its territory, it usually leaves us alone." The boy hesitated before stepping away from the tree line, coming closer. "Are there more of you?"

"Huh?" Rita's eloquent response caused a quiet snort from Milos, amused.

"Yes, there are a few more," Milos spoke up, but left it at that, clasping his fingers over the hilt in an obvious sign. The boy stilled, tensing.

"Geez, you don't have to scare him. He and that little girl probably haven't seen other humans for six years." Rita rolled her eyes before smiling. "Right, we never got your name. Mine's Rita, Rita Trillian. This lout is...-"

"Milos," Milos cut in curtly, shooting Rita a glare.

She just stuck out her tongue before turning back to the boy. He seemed confused, but he responded anyway, "Suzuhah...my name is Suzuhah."

"Isn't that a girl's name?" Rita chuckled, hiding her grin behind her hand while Milos sighed.

The boy stiffened, as if stung. "It's Suzuhah with an H, not an A. It's a perfectly fine name, thank you."

That was the most emotion Milos had seen from the boy so far. It was quite interesting to watch his flustered expression before he quickly corrected himself. "Er...well, yeah." He coughed. "I haven't spoken with others in ages. Can I meet the others?"

Rita blinked as Milos stiffened. It was one thing to introduce themselves, it was another to march this stranger back to their ship.

"What of your sister?"

Milos tilted his head slightly, letting his signifier shine for a moment. When the boy didn't respond, either unsure how to, or not recognizing his status, Milos shifted, shoulders tensing.

"Suzuhah?" Rita prompted, hefting Alex's cloak over her shoulder to better grasp it.

"Oh, right." Suzuhah grinned sheepishly, rubbing the back of his neck before wincing. "Well, you see, she's not really good with strangers. Whenever we meet travelers, I'm the one who usually does the talking." His gaze narrowed into slits and, for a split second, Milos could have sworn the boy's eyes gleamed a bright gold. "Please let me be able to trust you guys, for my sister's sake, at least."

Rita grunted before letting out a sigh. "All right. Alex and the others are probably worried sick by now."

"Thanks."

The boy smiled warmly, hurrying up to Rita with a beaming grin. Milos stayed a few steps behind, keeping a close eye on the boy. To be honest, he felt unnerved by him. He could almost feel something rolling off him, but he couldn't tell what it was. Was it just because he was in close proximity to that creature? Milos pursed his lips. He didn't have an answer.

He would have to keep an eye on the boy and his sister. He glanced briefly toward the cave, the sky, then the forest. He couldn't feel a thing.

He didn't think he would ever feel unnerved by the idea of no one watching them.

~ * ~

Alex glanced around, shading his eyes so he could better see the coastline. The thump of the plank against the sand woke him up. Having quickly dressed and hurried up the stairs, he found Milos and Rita gone. The Aqua Wraith stood to one side, staring out over the railing. Leon and Ari weren't far behind, coming up on deck in equal parts curiosity and confusion.

Considering Milos and Rita weren't up there as well, Alex assumed they went onto the island.

"They'll be fine." Ari spoke up, as if sensing his worries, voice monotone before turning to Alex. "I'll prepare breakfast, keep a lookout for them."

Alex nodded as Ari disappeared below. He turned to Leon, who stared out over the landscape before noticing Alex's attention. He bowed his head and, without saying a word, disappeared below deck. Those two were so strange. Ari's words of warning rang in his head.

Lightning seared into the sky and he stiffened as a loud crash echoed clear over the island, rattling the wood and waves. He gripped tightly, panic flaring through his veins. Were they okay? Was that the creature?

He wanted to just jump over and run out there, but he knew that wouldn't do anyone any good. He growled in frustration, wishing he knew how to use his wings. Being able to scope out the area from above would be incredibly helpful. He shook his head, taking in calming breaths. They would be all right. It was Rita and Milos, of all people.

Hell, he almost felt sorry for the creature with those two out there, as long as they weren't arguing.

He chuckled at the thought. They did like to argue. As frustrating as it was, at this point, he had a feeling it was more out of habit than any actual animosity, though both would say otherwise. He let out a breath, pulling himself away from the railing. Right, they would be fine. He had to remind himself of that. He shook his head and stepped to the other side of the boat, scanning the water past the little island they found sanctuary in. The water serpents leapt from the water, drawing his gaze as they arched over the sea. How was it they were still going? Were they just in an area where it would occur? He leaned his chin in his hands, watching quietly. The sea hummed around him, the cove a soothing melody. However, on the edge of his hearing, he could just catch the faint cries of wild waves. They weren't as loud as they were the day before. Hopefully, that meant that they were weakening. Maybe they would be able to leave by tomorrow? It would be nice.

While it was neat, taking a look at this island, it just reminded him of what he was supposed to be doing. Finding his mother. What would he even say to her though? How would he react? Would he be able to see her?

He knew nothing of the northern refugee camp. It was filled with demons, beings he held no knowledge of. Milos knew a heck of a lot more than he did, but even then, Alex knew that Milos' knowledge was attuned to killing, not learning.

He clicked his tongue, realizing his thoughts were going in circles, this was not getting him anywhere. He peered down at the water, and stilled. For a split second, he thought he saw something flit away, a fin disappearing under the boat. He leaned forward, but didn't see anything else, the water barely even leaving a ripple as the boat swayed with the waves. He was probably just imagining things.

Though it did stop his desire to just jump in the water again. If there was something down there, he didn't want to come face to face with it. He shivered at the few creatures he had seen so far out on these waters.

Was there anything that wasn't going to kill them?

He sighed as he realized what he just asked. That was a stupid question and he knew it.

He wasn't sure how long he stood there, staring out over the water, before he heard movement. He glanced back to see the Aqua Wraith hovering near the plank, staring out at the island. He couldn't see her expression, but her posture was tense. He walked over, curious to see what was going on. He didn't get a chance. She stiffened, just like she had previously whenever that winged creature appeared before diving into the deckboards without a word. He watched her go, stunned and more than a little worried.

Was she sensing something? He closed his eyes, trying to listen. He wasn't quite as used to using his senses, compared to the Aqua Wraith or Milos, but he was starting to pick up on things here and there.

Even so, he couldn't feel anything strange. Though he did hear the snapping of branches.

He opened his eyes and headed toward the edge of the plank just as Rita broke through the underbrush, patting down her skort. She spotted him, as he noticed the cloak slung over her shoulder. A few steps behind her was a boy Alex never saw before. Strange, he thought the Aqua Wraith disappeared because that creature was back, but he didn't see the winged being anywhere. Almost instantly, he felt the boy's eyes land on him, scrutinizing and almost hard. For a brief moment, Alex wondered if the Aqua Wraith sensed that boy, but he pushed the thought off. Alex pursed his lips, but a second later, the boy's expression shifted to one of curiosity. Had he just seen things?

Behind the strange boy was Milos, who seemed to be on guard, his posture stiff and sword held at his side. At least they somehow got their clothes back.

"Alex, you're up." Rita grinned, hurrying up the plank. She handed the cloak over. "Here."

He took it from her, more than a little grateful as he slung it over his shoulders, once more relishing in the warmth. He chuckled before turning back toward her. "Why do you have to sound so surprised about me being up?" Alex sent her a quick smile before glancing toward the boy who followed Rita.

Rita seemed to notice and gestured between the two. "Alex, this is Suzuhah, Suzuhah, this is Alex, a... friend of mine." Rita stuttered slightly at the words, catching Alex's attention.

He frowned, curious, but quickly pushed it off as the boy hesitantly walked up the ramp, still watching him with that same scrutinizing gaze. It wasn't hostile or anything, but it did make him feel a bit uncomfortable.

After a moment, the boy smiled and extended a hand. "It's nice to meet you, Alex. Rita talked about you on the way back."

"Oh?" Alex glanced over to Milos, who smirked, and Rita, who blushed brightly.

"I did *not*. I only mentioned who was on the ship." Rita crossed her arms over her chest and huffed.

Alex shook his head before noting that the boy still hadn't let go of his hand. He very carefully pulled it back. For a split second, the fingers tightened before promptly loosening.

This guy was weird.

"Oh, and before you ask, it's Suzuhah with an h, okay?" His voice was dispassionate as he spoke, causing Alex to chuckle.

"I wasn't going to bring it up."

The boy blinked, startled. The movement made Alex note the burn marks. They marred small patches of skin, slightly pink compared to the paleness he was used to seeing down here.

"What...?" Alex paused and shook his head. "It's good to see that everyone's okay. I saw lightning earlier..."

"Yeah, that creature was back. I never saw anything like it." Rita turned to Alex. "It knocked Milos and me for a loop when it dive-bombed the nearby trees."

"It's a Vulfulas." All eyes turned to Suzuhah as he spoke. "I remember hearing about it from one of the seamen I traveled with to get here. Unfortunately, said seamen didn't make it past the water serpents, misjudging the timing, so I couldn't find out anything else. Not that I particularly care since they left me and my sister, but..."

"A Vulfulas?" Rita's voice pitched up slightly, startled.

Wait, did she recognize the name? Not only that but was no one going to ask about the whole abandoning thing?

"Care to share your sudden epiphany?" Milos must have joined them at some point, since he was leaning against the railing, arms crossed.

Rita dug into her bag, riffling through it before pulling out the notebook she used earlier with the seer door.

As she flipped through it, Alex turned to Suzuhah. "They just outright abandoned you here? Why?" Alex asked, feeling a tinge of empathy. It sounded way too familiar.

"Don't know." Suzuhah turned to him, seeming confused. "My sister and I haven't really thought of it much lately. After all, at least we are still alive. Considering they plunged to their deaths, it was probably a blessing in disguise. Though we suspected the real reason was because, well..." Suzuhah shrugged.

Alex went to ask what he meant when a breathy, "No way," sounded from Rita.

Suzuhah jerked, glancing over to Rita. This time, he seemed to spot her notebook, or whatever was inside. "Wait, are you a witch?" Suzuhah's eyes gleamed in wonder. If Alex wasn't imagining things, he could have sworn there were stars in the boy's eyes, hope clear on his face.

Why hope?

He shook it off, focusing on Rita as, startled from Suzuhah's sudden enthusiasm, she almost dropped the book. Juggling it for a moment, she caught the pages. "Well, yeah. What did you think I was?"

"Do you really want us to answer that?" Milos jested, grinning.

"Oh, shut it."

Alex shook his head as Suzuhah seemed to reel himself in, clearing his throat harshly. "Well, that's...that's good to know. I'll...I'll make sure to tell my sister."

Did the boy stutter that much before? Alex couldn't recall. He shook his head. "So, what's a Vulfulas?"

"Ah, right." Rita flipped the page over, showing scrawled notes plastered all over the page in tiny script and, to one side, what could only be a quick sketch of a winged creature. "It was one of the creatures I learned about in my studies. Predominantly used by seers, a Vulfulas is a type of familiar that is known to cause lightning storms. It is said that they can take on the form their seer most desires, however, their base form is always this." She pointed out the winged foxlike creature. "Considering the base form is the only one we've seen, I'm going to guess that there are no seers on the island. Forgive me if I'm wrong."

She gestured to Suzuhah who quickly waved his hands. "I've never seen anyone else, and my sister and I don't know much about witches, nonetheless seers."

"Makes sense. The Vulfulas was probably here for a while." She turned back to Milos and Alex as she continued, "I'll be honest, I don't know what happens to a Vulfulas after their seer passes. Not much is known after all. I've only ever heard of them since they are rarer than even Drega."

"Why would a seer want something like that?" Milos asked, brow furrowed.

"How is it different from a demon?" Alex couldn't help but ask, peering out toward the horizon where he'd previously seen the creature.

"Um...my notes don't really say, just that a Vulfulas takes the form their seer most desires," Rita apologized sheepishly as she closed the book. "For Milos' question, I could only assume it's to make sure there's a spark when creating potions. Often times, potions need a catalyst, but if you send a charge through it, then it raises the effectiveness, sometimes even nullifying the use of a catalyst."

"You're quite well informed, aren't you?" Suzuhah spoke up, admiration practically exuding from him in waves.

Rita grinned, seeming excited to be talking about seer's brews with someone who seemed just as interested.

Alex felt a pang of annoyance at that, but brushed it off. It wasn't that he hated when she got into her seer mode or whatever he would call it; it was just sometimes hard to keep up. Milos seemed to not care in the slightest.

"Why did you ask about demons?" Suzuhah turned to Alex, arms crossed.

"Well, we are heading to a demon's refuge, so I, well, just assumed?"

Suzuhah pursed his lips, but didn't comment, instead turning back to Rita.

Alex watched them delve back into conversation about different potions, catalysts and seer-witch aspects that Alex found mind-boggling. The intricacies of a simple health potion were ridiculous.

"What do you think?" Milos' footsteps were all the warning he got before the whispered words met his ear.

Alex pursed his lips, watching the exchange. "I don't know. He seems friendly enough."

Milos just stayed silent, staring away from Alex.

Alex paused, thinking over the conversation. "He mentioned a sister?"

Milos turned, nodding.

"Where is she?"

Milos opened his mouth, before snapping it shut, frustration curling his lips downward. That answered that question. The man honestly didn't know.

Alex focused back on the conversation. He wasn't sure what to make of Suzuhah. While he was distracted, it seemed that Ari and Leon came upstairs, introducing themselves. Suzuhah, while meeting everyone, held a gentle smile on his face and seemed to stick close to Rita. Whether from admiration, curiosity, or something else, Alex couldn't tell. It bugged him, but he wasn't sure why.

About halfway through the tour, Rita's stomach growled and she grinned sheepishly. "Right, I haven't eaten practically all day."

Milos shook his head as they decided the kitchen was the next place they were going. Suzuhah seemed curious, exploring every nook and cranny in interest.

Alex noted, however, that he had yet to see the Aqua Wraith. Where could she be? Why was she still hidden? Why did she have such an adverse reaction to the Vulfulas? There was obviously something Alex was not getting and it bothered him.

He shook the thought off as he realized Leon was at the stove, cooking. He had to admit, Ari and Leon were *really* good cooks. So, he didn't mind when they did the cooking, most of the time. They took a seat around the table, Ari joining them to help Leon set the plates and food. It was a simple meal of berries from the island, some salted fish and a slice of bread each. While Rita and Suzuhah chowed down, Alex and the others ate much slower. Well, not much, Alex noted, glancing toward Milos who was discreetly speeding up his cuts, and they were not getting any smaller.

He chuckled at the idea before turning to Suzuhah. "So, what are you going to do now? You can't stay on that island with a—what was it—Vulfulas?"

Suzuhah paused in his eating, placing the fish down and carefully wiping his hand on a nearby towel, not necessarily facing anyone. "I'm not sure. If my sister and I could...could we join you?"

A heavy silence filled the room as everyone stopped in their eating. After a moment, Rita let out a sigh and shrugged. "Sure."

"Rita." Milos seemed resigned, as if he already realized.

Alex smiled. Yeah, that was just like her. Then again, he probably would have said it as well. No one deserved to be abandoned.

Ari and Leon didn't seem to have a problem with it. Both seemed to have taken a shine to Suzuhah rather quickly.

Suzuhah, however, appeared utterly stunned, staring at Rita in shock. "Wait. Really? I don't have to beg or anything?"

"Why the heck would you have to do that?" Rita seemed outright scandalized by the idea. "Why should anyone be forced to stay on an island like this by themselves? Or be abandoned on one, for that matter? Sure, it's full of herbs, which makes sense now that we know there is a Vulfulas here, and probably once a seer, but still."

"I think he gets it," Milos pointed out before returning back to his food.

Rita shot him a glare.

Suzuhah, however, seemed unsure how to respond, fidgeting in the chair, emotions flickering across his face faster than Alex could pick them out.

"If...if we can." A broad and incredibly sunny smile bloomed on his face. "We'd really appreciate it."

Rita blushed before shoving some food in her mouth.

"I think she wants to say, no problem." Milos didn't even divert his attention from his food, just taking another bite.

Rita let out a choking noise, slamming her fist to her chest before swallowing harshly.

"Hey. I can speak just fine. You don't need to translate anymore."

"Oh? You sure seemed to be struggling to say it yourself."

"You stupid jerkish lout."

"Funny, coming from our choking witch."

Alex sighed. Okay, maybe the arguing was getting on his nerves. He hoped one day, they could just have a civil conversation, but that was about as likely as him being crowned prince of the Overlands.

So... never.

"I'll go get my sister." Suzuhah stood up, hands on the table. His plate was empty, wiped clean.

Alex glanced at him before exchanging looks with Milos and Rita. Rita was patting her stomach, having probably eaten too quickly, and Milos set his things down. "Alone?"

"Hm?" Suzuhah turned to Milos as he shifted. "Well, yeah, I don't want to be a bother to you guys too much, since you did feed me and are bringing us with you and all."

Alex shook his head, chuckling slightly as Milos sighed.

"What about the Vulfulas?" Milos prompted, causing the boy to stiffen.

"Er...well, that's...I should be fine." He shifted before heading toward the doorway.

Alex watched him go before pushing away from the table.

"Where are *you* going?" Rita cut him off, expression stern.

"Going after him." Alex tapped the table lightly. "Something bothers me, all right?"

Milos stared at Alex for a moment before nodding. Rita let out a quiet groan, massaging her temples. "Fine. Just be careful?"

"You were the one willing to let them on our ship without a thought." Alex grinned, heading out the door as Rita growled, flustered.

"You would have too," she called after him and he chuckled, not fully denying it as he headed up the stairs.

He glanced around, hoping to see the Aqua Wraith, but her calming form was still missing. He couldn't even sense it. How strange.

He shook his head and walked to the deck. As he opened the door, Suzuhah whipped around, letting out a startled squawk.

"What are you doing?" Suzuhah's voice was pitched up in surprise as Alex closed the door behind him and walked over.

"Well, you're coming with us, right?" Alex shrugged, keeping half an eye on the boy. "I haven't met your sister, so I figured I would come with you."

Suzuhah seemed to debate for a moment, glancing between Alex and the forest. "What about the creature? It's not exactly safe and I do know my way around and all."

Alex wasn't sure how to respond to that and shrugged. "Isn't it just as dangerous going alone? Two is still better than one..."

"No, no. It's fine." He waved, his expression puzzled. "How about this? I need to collect some things, but I want to make sure my sister gets back safely. Can you keep an eye out for her while I head back? It shouldn't be too long and I would prefer if someone could watch out for her."

Alex opened his mouth to argue, then snapped it shut as he thought over the request, the boy watching him with a strange, worried expression. He eventually let out a huff. "Sure, I can keep an eye out for her."

Suzuhah appeared more than a little startled at that but his lips twitched up in amusement before he nodded. "Thank you. I best be going." Suzuhah's expression shifted for a moment into a wary and almost scrutinizing gaze before he turned and hurried away, down the plank. As he disappeared into the tree line, Alex frowned. He was strange.

A little while later, as a strange sound echoed over the tree line, the faint sound of water echoed in his ears and he turned to see the Aqua Wraith slip through the decking.

"Tis...tis the end." The woman seemed resigned as she turned to him.

"What do you mean?"

"Once met, death is all that awaits. Such a creature shall not let us go." The Aqua Wraith bent her head forward, hands clasped to her chest. "The forgotten one. I did not know it was on this island."

"What do you mean?" Alex asked, leaning forward. "The Vulfulas? It doesn't seem to be attacking us. Well, not right now, at least." Alex smiled sheepishly, causing the woman to waver slightly before slowly relaxing.

His thoughts flickered to Suzuhah and he frowned. Could she be talking about him? He didn't seem dangerous and Milos wasn't doing anything, so he wasn't a demon. Still, even as he stood there, the thought wouldn't leave his mind.

"Tis accurate." She paused, staring out over the water. "I shalt pray that this voyage does not end with thine death." She hovered around him, curling around in a gentle wave. "My oath binds my words, but still...I wish to tell of the past." She stilled, hair falling, quite literally, in waves over her shoulders. "Thou art not the first to meet the creature." She sighed and trailed around him once more. "I curse this oath, but I shan't go against it, for I still wish to traverse these oceans. I may not be able to come forth from now on, my presence being dangerous even now." The woman leaned forward, placing a hand to Alex's cheek, startling him greatly. It was surprisingly warm, and it didn't feel wet, how strange. "It must sense thee as well, since thou are similar to I. It does not like our kind."

Does not like our kind? Is she talking about their affinity to water? Or specifically demons? "All right. I'll be careful." Alex nodded as the woman pulled away.

She smiled before stiffening. A moment later, she dived below as a cry echoed through the sky. Alex jerked, glancing up as the Vulfulas winged overhead. He hadn't realized the size of the creature, but now, watching as its shadow covered the ship, he could understand the Aqua Wraith's warnings. No way was she talking about anything *but* that thing up there. He hurried into the cabin, peeking out through the door as lightning slammed into the water, waves jerking at the anchor and trying their best to tip the boat. He held on tightly as another warbling cry rang out and then, silence.

What was that all about?

He slowly opened the door and glanced out toward the beach. He didn't see anything there. The creature was gone. The Aqua Wraith. She sensed it before Alex could sense it. How? Alex wanted to ponder, but his thoughts were caught off guard as a figure came bursting out of the tree line, glancing over her shoulder wildly. Who?

It was a little girl, what must have been the sister, because she appeared remarkably similar, down to the freckles decorating her nose as she scrambled up the plank, glancing around wildly. Almost instantly, she spotted him and hurried over. "Are you Alex?"

"Uh," Alex blinked before nodding. "Yeah, Yeah, sorry. I'm guessing you are Suzuhah's sister?"

"Yep." She chirped, clapping her hands. "My name is Suzuha. Suzuha with an A. My brother mentioned you were one of the people he met and you would keep an eye on me? He told me you would probably be waiting on the ship. He's gone to pick up some things from home."

Suzuha? The same name? That was unimaginative. Who would give their children the same name? Alex shook his head and pulled back. "It's nice to meet you, Suzuha." He smiled. "Have you eaten?" His gaze flickered to the sky, but there was no sign of the creature.

"Yeah. Though I guess I am still a little hungry." She smiled sheepishly.

Alex watched her as she hurried down the stairs, confused. Didn't Rita say the girl they met was shy? Was that Suzuhah who said it?

By gosh, having two people with the same name was going to be a nightmare.

He pushed the thought away as he descended back downstairs, just in time to see Suzuha introducing herself to the others. Milos and Rita seemed just as startled by her cheerful demeanor and, when they asked, she simply responded, "Well, Brother said you're all right. So, you're all right in my book."

Alex wasn't sure how to respond to that, and it seemed no one else did either.

Eventually, she let out a yawn, rubbing her eyes tiredly. "Um...so, can I sleep here tonight? Brother should be coming back soon."

"Oh. Sure." Rita, who had been reading through her notes, probably to see if she could find out more about Vulfulas, nodded. "The girls' room is in the back, with the hammocks."

"Not beds?" She blinked, tilting her head slightly.

"Nah, we gave them to the boys. They need them after all, right?" Rita grinned, elbowing Milos before placing her arm on Alex's shoulder.

Milos twitched, seemingly ready to respond, but Alex quickly cut him off.

"Yeah, we do." He grinned, matching Rita's expression. "After all, we sleep much more soundly with only two beds when we could *definitely* use three hammocks? Like what you guys have?"

Milos covered a burgeoning smile as Rita huffed, lightly swatting at Alex's head. Ari chuckled quietly and Leon just shook his head, the two actually seeming to warm up to the little girl surprisingly quickly.

"Yes, sharing a bed is oh so comfortable." Milos took a sip of soup as Rita frowned, arms over her chest.

"Geez, it's not like you're doing anything, right? Plus, our shifts make it so that never happens."

Alex blinked as Milos choked, placing his bowl down with a quiet crack. Rita's grin was almost catlike as she cackled. Alex decided to brush off the strangeness and glanced back toward Suzuha, who seemed to be watching with an odd expression.

It disappeared as soon as she noticed him watching. "They are a funny bunch, aren't they?" She chuckled. "Thanks for having us." She let out another yawn. "Is it okay if I turn in? It's been a long day."

"Oh, Sure." Rita stood up, only to be stopped, and startled, by Ari gently pulling the girl up.

"I'll lead her." Her voice was quiet, but warm.

Rita hesitated before nodding and sitting back down. Ari's expression shifted, surprisingly soft, before she placed her hand on the girl's back and they walked out.

Silence filled the room before Milos let out a sigh, standing up. "Well, we are not getting anything done. Let's send one more group out to the island to gather anything else, then get ready to leave. Hopefully, the sea should be calm by morning."

"Sounds like a plan." Rita grinned.

"Yes, so who's going out and who's staying on the ship?" Alex leaned on the table, palm pressing into his cheek. "Especially since I saw the Vulfulas again and I doubt you all missed the cry."

No one responded. After a few moments, Rita let out a sigh, stretching. "To be honest, I'm quite tired myself."

"Done traipsing through the wildlife, finding strays?"

"Why, yes, yes, I am." Rita sent Milos a sharp glare, earning a shrug from him.

Alex pinched the bridge of his nose in frustration.

"Master Milos, why don't you stay here to rest as well?" Leon, of all people, spoke up, startling Alex.

Milos merely tilted his head to appraise the slave for a moment before nodding. "I think I'll do that. Go and see if you can procure some more supplies."

"I'll go with you. It's probably dangerous for only one of us to go out there." Alex stood, feeling uncomfortable sending Leon out by himself, even if he didn't know the man well.

"That would be much appreciated." Milos bowed his head before standing up. "I'll see you two later."

Alex noted the way his jaw twitched and wondered if he was suppressing a yawn as well.

Alex chuckled and headed out the door, followed by Leon who held a bag over his shoulder for supplies. Alex quickly grabbed his own and they were on their way.

Chapter Thirteen

Rita groaned, heading back to her room. She heard quiet humming inside and peeked in to see Ari leaning against the wall, gently rocking one of the hammocks where Suzuha was curled up, close to being sound asleep. She was all the way in the corner, on the farthest hammock from the others. Rita briefly wondered why before she mentally rolled her eyes. Why was she asking? The little girl was probably still a little wary of them, it would make sense she would put some distance between them when she slept.

Ari glanced up, stopping her humming.

"You can continue," Rita spoke softly, walking over to her own hammock. After a few moments of hesitation, the girl resumed in both rocking and humming.

Rita watched her for a while, a soft smile on her lips. "I didn't know you liked children."

Ari nodded, but didn't stop humming.

After a few more notes, she slowly stopped and pulled away, turning to Rita. "I often took care of the younger slaves." Her voice was soft, as usual, a depressed tone echoing in the words. "Most would be about her age, before..."

Rita winced, sitting up in the hammock. It wasn't an easy feat, but she'd gotten used to it, crossing her legs under her to even the weight. "What was it like?" Rita found herself asking, not sure why she was asking in the first place. It was rude, in her opinion, but she couldn't help it, curious to find out more about her companion.

Silence filled the room for a long time until Ari's soft footsteps rang over the wood. She took a seat in the hammock beside Rita, using it like a swing.

"Hell." Ari finally spoke up, shivering visibly, her fingers twitched, as if she wanted to curl into herself. Instead, she gripped the hammock tightly, the rope practically digging into her skin. "I'm never really sure if I'm out of it or not."

Rita widened her eyes, shocked. "But Milos doesn't treat you like that." Rita leaned forward, trying to keep her voice low even as she found herself defending the man she usually argued with. "He's defended you two and rescued you guys when he didn't have to. He may be a lout, but I have no doubt he does care about you two, so..."

"Yes, Master Milos does care." Ari tilted her head up, glaring at Rita, causing the girl to stiffen. "I am not besmirching the kindness he has given to us, nor the freedom." She glanced away. "I am merely stating a fact. You asked, I answered."

"That's..." Rita breathed. "Even then you still feel like you're in that hell?"

"You never truly escape it." Ari's words were mumbled, faint.

Her fingers trailed up to her neck, trembling as Rita noted the scars. She saw them before, but never really thought too much about them. Now that she recalled, those with neck chains were slaves specifically for what some might call "pleasure." It was disgusting, but there was also not a thing Rita could really do about it.

"Who...?"

"How many, is the better term." Ari seemed to realize what she was asking, not really looking at her, just placing her hand on her neck, trembling. "I... the faces muddle together." She shifted, as if she wasn't sure what to do with herself, where to put herself. Rita hopped down from the hammock and walked over, standing in front of her. Ari glanced up and winced.

Rita grimaced, hand on her hip. "Look, I'm not good at trying to be emotional support," she admitted, thinking back to the time she'd gotten Alex to outright yell at her. "I'm not even going to pretend I comprehend what you or Leon have had to go through, but..." She shifted slightly, wanting to do something with her hands besides having them lay at her sides. She shifted a few more times as Ari watched her, quietly and curiously. Rita finally groaned, adjusting her hat. "All I'm saying is that, if not Milos, because I know he would do all he could to protect those around him, the rest of us will definitely make sure that doesn't happen again. I know I don't know you that well, but that doesn't mean I don't, well..." She clicked her tongue, only to stop as a soft giggle met her ears.

She glanced up to see a warm smile curling over Ari's face. "Thanks."

Rita grinned, shrugging. "Sure, I didn't really say anything amazing, but..."

"It's not that." Ari shook her head, startling Rita. "Thanks for just being willing to talk. I was nervous to speak up to anyone." Once more, she reached her hand up to her throat.

"Right. I'm going to assume Milos was the first one you ever really talked to?"

Ari nodded, a gentle expression on her face. "He's a kind master, if a little..." She trailed off, as if lost in thought.

Rita could easily fill in the blanks, but held her tongue.

"He gave you a chance, right?" Rita knew the words sounded cheesy as they rolled off her tongue, but Ari didn't laugh at her for it. Instead, she just simply nodded. "I'm guessing Leon feels the same way?"

"Very much so."

Rita chuckled. "Well, I'm glad you're willing to open up. I was worried for a while that we would never get to know you."

Ari bent her head down, but didn't respond. Rita's expression softened. "Let's get some sleep. Unless you would rather stay up?"

Ari thought for a moment before pushing herself from the hammock. "I'll stay up to keep watch." With that, she walked out the door, leaving in a rush.

Rita watched her go before letting out another yawn. Yeah, sleep, it sounded great right now.

~ * ~

Alex jumped as the crackling of branches sounded behind him.

To be honest, he kept thinking he would see Suzuhah, coming up behind out of nowhere. But the boy never showed up and Alex was left wondering where he was. He heard a quiet grunt and let out a breath as he realized it was Leon. While the man could certainly be quiet at times, at others, it was hard to miss him. Alex found himself with nothing to talk about, however, with the man. They searched through the trees, picking up herbs and other items that might come in handy. There were very few small animals, but occasionally, Leon would pick up a rock and throw it up into the trees. His aim was strangely impeccable though, when asked, he mentioned he'd been practicing since losing his arm.

"How are you?" Alex asked, hefting the bag he was carrying which was already starting to fill with berries as Leon picked up the bird he'd knocked out of the tree. Alex didn't recognize the species, but it was pudgy, like it didn't do much flying.

"I am fine." He spoke curtly, flinging the bird over his shoulder so it lay on top of the bag already there, wrapped around his side, its legs bound together by rope.

"I mean..." Alex trailed off, unsure where he was going with the questions before letting out a sigh. "I'll be blunt, what about your arm? Don't you ever feel upset with Milos about that?" To be honest, he'd been meaning to ask the question for a while now, but never could figure out a time to ask it. He wasn't sure now was that great, but he finally had enough of waiting.

"No." Leon's words were immediate, startling Alex. "He saved me and kept me on even after I lost my worth." Leon spoke, words weakening by the end.

Alex nodded, briefly recalling a conversation he caught when drifting off to sleep the other day. Milos kept his voice down as he spoke with Leon about training and schedules, listening whenever the slave talked and answering with a warmth he rarely ever showed.

"Yeah, sorry."

"It's fine. I can understand why you are asking." Leon pushed through another bit of forest as Alex caught up to him. "He has since quelled any fear or hatred I might have held." Leon brought his good arm up, staring at the fingers tightly curled around the rope of the bags and bird. "I would gladly do it all again for all the chances I've had now."

He turned and, for the first time, Alex actually saw a genuine smile cross the man's face. It was weak and barely there, but nonetheless visible.

Alex returned the expression. "He's a good man."

"The best," Leon admitted. "He's allowed us our own freedom, but still gives us opportunities and ways we can help."

"Hm..." Alex swayed back and forth, partially realizing what he meant. He wasn't in the same exact boat as Ari and Leon, but he knew the general gist of their plight and saw it himself. Sometimes too much freedom could be just as dangerous as no freedom.

Those thoughts made him hesitate. Did that apply to that girl? Ame? Was she all right? Alex lightly bit his lip, remembering the last time he saw her, sold off to another random stranger in the capital. He gritted his teeth and returned to collecting the nearby herbs and throwing them in his bag. He pushed his thought back onto their conversation, curiosity thrumming through his veins. "How have you been coping?"

"It's taken some time to get used to the balance," Leon admitted after a long time of thought.

Alex could understand that. Though, in his case, it had more to do with adding things than taking away. But the demonic changes still almost always managed to throw him off balance, so it made sense losing them would do the same.

Leon seemed to be handling it fine as he joined Alex in scrounging for more herbs, the bird and bag at his side. With a practiced ease, he tightened the bag and once more tossed it over his shoulder as he stood and turned to Alex. "We should return to the ship. It is getting late."

"Yeah." Alex stood, wiping his hands down, glad to finally have his cloak back.

He hefted the bag, wincing slightly at the weight. On the way back, the day stones were already starting to disappear, shifting to their night stone counterparts.

Alex peered at the ship, watching it sway back and forth. Past the ship, he noticed the water serpents had died down. He spotted one or two leaping from the water, but the ocean was no longer the frothing roiling mess it was the day before. Hopefully, that was a good sign.

They walked up the plank and onto the ship.

Ari, who was curled up next to the cabin, watching the water, turned her head slightly before promptly standing up, a subtle flinch in her movements. Alex noted as Leon stilled at his side, pulling back slightly.

Ari grasped at her shirt, knuckles white. A faint ripping sound lingered in the air as she watched both of them with a startled, fearful gaze. He went to take a step forward, only to feel a hand on his shoulder. Leon pulled him back gently, shaking his head as Ari stiffened, eyes wild and body shaking.

After a few moments she slowly started to relax, grip loosening on her blouse. Breathing in and out in long drags, as if to gather her thoughts.

"H-hey, Ari." Alex finally spoke up when Leon let go of his shoulder, causing the girl to slowly tilt her head up to him, obviously exhausted.

"Hello, Alex." Her words were soft, to the point of being almost imperceptible.

"Are you all right?" Alex cautiously took a step forward.

Ari spared Leon a glance, over Alex's shoulder before turning back to him. "I'm fine now. I apologize for worrying you."

Alex shook his head, smiling hesitantly. "It's fine. We didn't mean to startle you."

Alex briefly wondered what she had been thinking, but as he noted her hand lingering by her neck, he didn't have far to guess. He only saw it happen once or twice when at home with his own mother. That momentary lapse in what was real and what was the past. He figured it was the remnants of what slavery did to her, and Ari seemed to be in the same boat. He mentally berated himself for not noticing, grateful Leon stopped him.

It was somewhat dangerous to approach someone in that state. Often times, the person couldn't tell friend from foe in their fear.

Ari stood, bowing her head slightly. Leon nodded before slipping by and down the stairs. Alex watched him go before turning back to Ari. "Are you on watch now? I thought Rita..."

"I couldn't sleep. So, I took over her shift." Ari tipped her head up, glancing at him curiously.

"I see..." Alex trailed off, unsure what to say." I should probably head back down and get some sleep myself. Don't hesitate to wake us, all right?"

Ari nodded as Alex walked past, glancing back once he was at the doorway to see her staring out over the water, once more, deep in thought. He shook his head, not much he could do for her at this point, just like there hadn't been much he could do when Mother ended up in that same state of mind. It frustrated him, but he was also aware it was a matter Ari had to come to terms with herself, just like Mother eventually did, right?

Alex headed to the storage room, storing the food before going into the kitchen to grab something quick to eat. Once done, he hurried to the men's room, peeking inside. Suzuhah still wasn't back yet. He forgot to check on the young Suzuha in the girl's room, but he found himself too tired. He figured Rita was a light enough sleeper to notice if anything happened to her. He let himself fall into bed, pulling his shoes off in the process. Milos shifted in his sleep, but didn't do much else, so Alex ignored it, dropping tiredly into sleep beside him.

~ * ~

Milos woke to movement, and this time, it had nothing to do with Alex's and Leon's return. A creak of floorboards echoed through the ship and he stood, hand grasping his sword, gently laid against the side of the bed. He didn't recognize the footsteps.

Carefully, he got up and wrapped the sword to his waist. Alex and Leon stayed fast asleep.

Milos walked over to the doorway, peeking out. The hallway was dim, only one faint light stone casting warmth over the hallway. Near the stairwell, frozen in step, was a slight figure. Milos shifted, recognizing the form, but not relaxing as it turned. "Suzuhah."

"Ah...Milos?" The boy descended the last of the stairs, grimacing as he touched down. He wasn't holding anything and seemed a bit disheveled. "Did I wake you?"

Milos shifted, pulling his hand away slightly, but still keeping it up and ready. "I'm a light sleeper," he explained stiffly.

Suzuhah stiffened, his eyes glowing gold in the light from the stone. "Noted." He walked over, sizing him up. "It seems the water serpents have calmed, but I'm not sure how long that would last. Should we not set sail?"

"At this time of night?" Milos didn't need to glance outside to be able to tell it was the dead of night.

"Isn't this the best time to leave?" Suzuhah asked curiously.

Milos eyed him before shaking his head. "We'll leave as soon as the day stones start to light up."

Suzuhah pursed his lips, but didn't respond, glancing up and down the hallway until he shifted in realization. "Um, where am I sleeping?"

Milos thought for a moment before sighing and gesturing for him to follow. He couldn't ask the boy to stay up for watch. For one, he didn't trust him that much, and for two, there was no point on throwing someone new into a position they probably never did before, or at least, haven't done in quite some time. Suzuhah hesitated. Milos opened the door, stepping back into the men's room.

Suzuhah followed after, glancing around. He spotted the two beds and his gaze drifted to Alex, eyes narrowing to slits.

Milos walked over, taking a seat, not removing his sword. "You can sleep in here." His voice stayed low. He could see Leon shift, and had a feeling the slave was awake as well. Alex, however, was still out of it.

"Where?" Suzuhah asked, glancing between the two beds with a wary gaze. "No offense, but I'm..."

"You have two options." Milos cut in, tired and just wanting to get some rest, no matter how fleeting it might be now. "One, you can sleep next to Leon, or two, you can find someplace yourself. It's not my job."

"You're pleasant."

"So Rita has told me."

Suzuhah blinked before a faint chuckle slipped from his lips. "Okay, fair." He glanced toward Leon's bed, as if sizing it up for a moment, before he shook his head, moved to the far wall and plopped down on the hardwood floor, curling up on his side.

Milos watched for a moment, noting the way the boy curled himself into a ball, as if trying to suppress a chill.

Made sense considering how lacking his clothing was. Didn't he grab something else for himself?

Milos shook his head, that was something he would worry about in the morning. He grabbed his pillow as he shifted to the floor, leaning against the bed. Suzuhah cracked one eye open, only to yelp as the pillow went flying, slamming right into his face.

"Ow." He winced, before glancing down at what actually hit him. "A pillow?"

"Unfortunately, we do not have spare sheets." Milos shrugged, draping one arm over his bent knee as he leaned his head back against the side. He was probably going to regret this in the morning, but he was still wary of the boy.

"You know, I'm not going to do anything." Suzuhah's arms curled around the pillow, hugging it tightly to his chest.

"I'm aware," Milos lied. "However, you are new to us and your sister did steal from us. Is it so wrong to hold up our guard?"

"No, I suppose not." Suzuhah stared for a moment before flopping onto his side, still curled around the pillow. "I guess you're not too bad." He paused. "I still don't trust you though."

"I would be surprised if you did." Milos whispered. Suzuhah cracked one eye open for a long moment before shifting to get comfortable once more. Not long after that, proving just how tired the boy must have been, Milos could hear the sound of the quiet breaths of sleep.

Milos shook his head, realizing he wasn't getting a decent sleep tonight. He might as well rest as best as he could.

~ * ~

Alex awoke, feeling surprisingly cold as the day stones flickered through the window. It took way too long for his groggy mind to spot the tuft of hair, leaning against the bed to one side. Instantly, he wanted to slap Milos before he noticed the other figure in the room.

Suzuhah stared back at him, brownish gold eyes almost glowing as he observed Alex, arms and legs somehow curled around a familiar pillow.

It was eerie. Alex shook his head and sat up as Milos shifted.

"You're awake." It wasn't a question.

"Morning to you too." Alex held back a yawn, glancing at Suzuhah. "When did you get in?"

"Late last night." Suzuhah stood, patting his clothes down. "Oh, and thanks for the pillow."

Milos shrugged as Suzuhah tossed it back to him, catching it with ease. Alex's gaze snapped over as Milos tossed something at Suzuhah that appeared to be a tunic and trousers. Suzuhah fumbled, trying and somewhat failing to grab it all.

"You like throwing things at me, don't you?" Suzuhah yelped before he actually appeared to take in what Milos gave him.

Alex chuckled quietly. That was a very Milos thing to do, he noted, as Suzuhah's mouth snapped shut and he stared at it. "Wait are you...?"

"Get changed already. Your clothes are barely staying together and I believe the girls would rather avoid any indecent exposure."

Suzuhah's face burned red as he quickly turned away, mumbling something under his breath as he quickly pulled the clothes on, the rest of their group giving him the privacy needed for such an action. Alex shook his head and pulled himself out of bed, this time unable to suppress the yawn. He tilted his head, listening quietly to the water as it lapped against the ship. It was calm. All of it.

"The sea died down. We should be able to go." Alex grinned, turning to Milos. "As interesting as this place is, I really think we should get going."

Milos was already on his feet, retying up his long hair that seemed to have fallen loose during his rest. "Yes, I am not keen on meeting up with a Vulfulas again."

He walked toward the doorway, not sparing the others a glance. Suzuhah, now dressed in clothes that appeared somewhat long for him, hurried after him, with Alex a few steps behind. He briefly glanced back to Leon, who rolled over, curling into the sheets. Deciding to let the man rest, he slipped out of the room.

The hallways were quiet as they walked upstairs and onto the deck. This time, Rita was up there, having taken over for Ari. She spotted them and smirked. "So, the sleepyheads are finally up?" She spotted Suzuhah and blinked, as if confused.

"Morning, Rita." He smiled widely, hurrying up to her. "Were you able to finish that brew you were mentioning yesterday?"

"No?" It wasn't hard to tell she seemed utterly thrown off by his words as she peered at his clothes.

Milos shook his head. "So, do you know where we're going next?"

"Ah, Right." Rita pulled herself away and turned to Milos. "Once we leave this cove, it's due north for a bit, then we'll head toward the east in about..." She seemed to mentally calculate it for a moment, staring up at the day stones before continuing, "To be honest, it'll probably be a while. Once we turn east, it'll take approximately three hours, I think. That should be sufficient to get us to the next island." She let out a breath. "Hopefully, it's the last one we'll need to stop on," she muttered, garnering Alex's attention.

"Why are we stopping again anyway?" Alex found himself asking. "I mean, we got the food we need here. Shouldn't we be able to go straight north from here?

Rita shook her head. "As much as I wish to, no. You see, just north of here on almost every map, there are long stretches of water, with x's placed all along one side. The only way through seems to be close to the island. So, since we have to go close by anyway to avoid those areas, we might as well stop to recollect ourselves for the last section of the ocean."

Alex pursed his lips, but didn't bring it up again. What she said made sense, and he trusted her when it came to the navigation. She had helped keep them alive so far.

Plus, being on a ship this whole time was probably not that interesting for the others at a bare minimum. He'd already seen how it was just causing more aggravation between some of their friends. Personally, he had no problem with traveling by boat. In some ways, this felt normal.

He paused, thinking over the schedule Milos made up, including his demon training, kind of hard to do with two people on board who, well, had no knowledge of him being a demon. Truth be told, he wanted to keep it that way. He glanced toward Milos. "Ah, what about training?"

Milos seemed to realize what he meant. His eyes narrowed. "We'll have to make do." His gaze flickered to Suzuhah, who was once more talking animatedly to Rita, who had a faint smile on her face, occasionally yawning from sleepiness.

Alex frowned. Making do didn't sound like the best plan of action, but it was also probably the only plan they had in order to keep Suzuhah from finding out. Both Suzuhas. Alex sighed. He was going to punch whoever decided to name their kids the same name.

He glanced over the water, helping to pull the anchor up before they could head out. Listening carefully, he noted there was still a gentle hum over the ocean. In the distance, quite a way away, a quiet screech echoed over the waves. He winced.

"Er...we might want to hurry out of here," he mentioned as Rita took the wheel, spinning it so they were facing out as a faint roar of engines met his ears.

"Already on it, dingbat," she replied without any heat.

Suzuhah disappeared and it seemed the Vulfulas was nowhere to be seen, along with the Aqua Wraith. He wondered if she was okay, but quickly pushed it aside as they passed out of the cove and turned sharply to the left. The wind stones, now able to use more power away from the rocky walls, sang to life and they shot forward, away from the island. He peered back at the island, quickly disappearing out of sight, leaning carefully over the railing. It was such a strange island, and, in a way, he was almost going to miss it. He pursed his lips and pulled back, letting out a sigh. There wasn't much he could do about it now. It would have been nice to just be able to relax on the sand, but with the Vulfulas there, along with both Suzuhahs, well, he had a feeling it would have been a lot more stressful than relaxing.

Speaking of, where did Suzuhah go? Back downstairs?

That guy was weird.

"You might not be able to change form, but we can practice your senses." Milos' voice jerked Alex out of his thoughts, causing him to turn to Milos. An amused expression danced on his lips as he gestured out to the water. "You can try to see what you can do in your human form without switching over. I do not believe you've attempted that before, correct?"

"No, not really," Alex admitted sheepishly. It was a good idea and he mentally berated himself on not thinking about it.

He turned to the water, trusting Milos would keep half an eye out for him. He closed his eyes, listening to the beating of the waves against the ship.

"Keep your eyes open."

"Huh?" Alex blinked.

"Having your eyes closed in battle is suicide." Milos leaned against the railing, watching him carefully. "The opponent will not give you time to sense your surroundings or center yourself. I told you this before when we were practicing your shifting. If we practice with you closing your eyes to hone your senses, you might end up reliant on such a thing in battle, or in other instances."

Alex pursed his lips, feeling a hint of frustration well up. It made sense, but...he turned back to the water, listening to it while also noting the way Milos was tapping his finger against the hilt of the sword, the creak of the wood of the ship, Rita's faint footsteps as she stepped away from the wheel for a moment.

Right, he always did tend to listen more to the water. He guessed in most cases, it was better to practice honing in on one thing, but he'd been doing that so long...

He lightly chuckled in realization as Milos shifted, seeming amused. "So, you noticed?"

"That I'm always *too* focused on the water?" Alex turned to him and nodded. "Yeah, I mean, it makes sense and all, but who could imagine being too focused on something?"

Milos 'expression flashed to a harsh one for a moment before disappearing. Alex wondered if he actually saw it, or just imagined. Shaking the thought away, he stared back out over the water, this time listening to it while also keeping half an ear to his surroundings. It wasn't easy, trying to keep track of the humming song of the waves and everything else, but...

He wasn't sure how long he stood there before he let out a gentle hum. The water sang back as the shifting of clothes indicated Milos pushed away from the railing.

He watched as a wave gently hit the side of the ship before hanging, suspended, near the edge. It stretched, almost like a tendril, following the ship before he hummed once more and it collapsed back into the water. So, he did have some control over water.

He wondered about that. He felt a faint smile cross his lips as the gentle coaxing of his demonic half sang to him. He could feel it relishing in his practice. It was both soothing and heartening, knowing that it wasn't trying to take him over like before, that it was there, but as a presence, not as a force. The grin widened slightly as he hummed again, watching the water flow alongside the ship, hovering in the air. It was exhilarating, though also surprisingly draining.

"Good, now keep doing that until you can bring the water to your hands."

"Erk." Alex winced, feeling his enthusiasm draining. He was already regretting the idea of this training. This was going to be a long day.

Chapter Fourteen

Rita chuckled as she watched Alex collapse to his knees, somewhat yelling at Milos. Milos only held a little grin on his face, arms crossed. It was pretty funny, admittedly, to see Alex concentrating so hard. She couldn't see exactly what they were doing, but she could get the gist of it from snippets of conversation and a few splashes of water.

Speaking of—it took all her energy not to burst out laughing as some water splashed into Milos' face, drenching his hair and shirt. He just stared at Alex before pointing.

Alex almost scrambled to get back to practicing.

Man, that was amusing. That momentary shock on Milos' face was picture perfect. Too bad she couldn't draw. She would have loved to immortalize it.

Shaking her head, she frowned, glancing up at the day stones. Shouldn't Leon be taking over for her now? She stepped away from the wheel, catching Milos' attention as Alex let out a groan and slumped over the railing.

"Be right back." She waved before heading inside. Walking down the stairs, she heard a soft sound and stilled. It was, a moan?

She stiffened and slowly turned toward her shared room. Ari was asleep, right?

She walked over, steps light before knocking on the door. A quiet yelp and a thump sounded through the doorway, followed by a groan.

Rita wasn't sure whether she wanted to open the door or not. She shook her head and slammed it open, arms crossed, before pausing.

On the floor, rubbing her butt, was Suzuha. The young girl was grimacing, wiping drool from her lips as she tilted her head up. "Huh? Rita?"

It looked like she fell out of one of the hammocks. Ari was just waking up, grimacing before her hand darted to her shoulder. A moment of confusion flashed on her face before she shook her head. "Miss Rita?"

"Ari? Suzuha? Are you two okay?" She walked over, helping the little girl up. Ari nodded, pulling her hand away from her shoulder in puzzlement. Suzuha brushed herself down before smiling up to her.

"Yeah, I'm fine. Your knock startled me and I'm not used to hammocks yet."

Rita chuckled. "I know what you mean, those are a pain to deal with." She frowned, glancing around. "Hey, where's your brother? I saw him go downstairs and I thought he was going to wake you."

"Nope." Suzuha shook her head. "Haven't seen him. He's probably in the men's room or storage room."

"Why the storage room?"

"Why else?" Suzuha tilted her head, confused. "That's where all our stuff is."

"Oh? So, your brother did grab it?" Rita couldn't remember ever seeing Suzuha, either one, bringing anything on board. Though, she could just be mistaken. The only thing she could recall clearly was that Milos seemed to have lent Suzuhah his clothes for the day.

"Well, yeah." Suzuha peered up at her, confused, before shaking her head. "Anyway, what brings you down here?"

"Oh, Right." Rita smiled sheepishly. "Sorry, didn't mean to wake you two. I thought...never mind." She turned and hurried away, feeling embarrassed. Her mind was not helping her at all. She found Leon, fast asleep. She knocked on the doorframe, causing him to jerk up. She blinked, noting he had circles under his eyes, though she knew he was asleep the whole time. Did he not sleep well?

He turned to her and blinked a few times before sighing and pushing himself out of bed. "My apologies," he muttered, hiding a grimace.

"Are you all right?" Rita found herself stepping closer, worry taking over her exasperation.

"I feel a little dizzy is all." He shook his head and straightened. "Did you need something?"

"No," Rita decided, shaking her head. She walked over, startling the man as she laid a hand on his forehead. His skin felt only slightly hot to the touch, but she wasn't going to take any chances. "Do you mind if I take a look at you? We don't need anyone getting sick."

Leon hesitated for the longest time until finally giving her a nod and laying back down.

She checked him over, noting, as she thought, that he was a bit warmer to the touch than she would have liked. His pulse pounded under her fingers, heightened somehow. She frowned, unsure what the cause might be before digging into her satchel.

"Here, drink this and get some rest, it looks like you haven't fully recovered."

She handed him a bottle she'd brewed the other day. A sleeping agent that she figured would help his body heal properly. She had a feeling she would be keeping tabs on him for any changes, but this should be enough for now.

"Yeah. Thanks."

The fact he didn't argue only partially alarmed Rita. She knew the slave wouldn't argue in general, but how quickly he accepted it worried her a little more than her general examination.

The bottle was drained and she made a mental note to prepare a few extra, before Leon lay back down. She walked over, watching as he rolled onto his left side, grimacing before promptly flipping onto his back. She frowned, leaning forward. The medicine quickly took effect, putting him back to sleep. She touched his shoulder, wondering at what could have caused the pain. She hadn't noticed anything earlier during her initial examination. Why would his good arm...why would he grimace lying on his good arm?

She didn't want to pry, so backed off, frowning.

"Rita?"

She jumped and glanced over her shoulder to see the older Suzuhah. The young man stared at her in confusion. She shook her head and straightened. "Where were you? I thought you came downstairs to wake your sister." She frowned and he glanced away, shrugging.

"I was busy?" He chuckled before glancing back at her. "I wanted to try making one of those potions that you mentioned, but uh...I kind of failed?"

"Huh?" Rita paused, wondering before she shook her head. "Where did you get the ingredients anyway? You didn't use mine, did you?" She placed her hands on her hips with a glare.

The boy shook his head, promptly. "No. Nothing of the sort." He smiled sheepishly, rubbing his neck. "I just grabbed some on the way back that appeared to be the ones you used and tried to copy you, that's all."

What potion could he have attempted to make? She had been talking about a lot of different things with Suzuhah, so maybe she mentioned a simple one? "So where is it?"

"I tossed it out." He shrugged and Rita groaned. Of course, well, it made sense. A lot of potions, when failed, actually let out toxic fumes the longer they sat. She couldn't berate him for that.

"Did you at least see your sister?"

"I did, she and Ari were sleeping last time I checked."

Huh? They both must have still been tired. Or did he see them earlier? Rita shrugged. Not her business. "So, what brings you here?"

"I saw the door open and took a peek and noticed you were inside. Though aren't you checking the wrong bed?"

Rita blinked before blushing brightly. So, the boy had...wait...when?

"You, Milos and Alex seem really close." A fond smile flitted on his face. "It's good to see after so many years."

"Right." She almost forgot the Suzuhahs were stranded on that island for the last six years. It was hard to imagine, surviving that long with a rogue Vulfulas on their tails. "We're not that close." She huffed.

"Hm? Is that so?" He smiled strangely, as if he was aware of something she wasn't.

The smug look immediately annoyed her. Thankfully, for him, he seemed to notice and quickly brushed it away, coughing into his fist. "Anyway, could you maybe teach me?" He watched her hopefully. "I really would like to learn more about witches, please?"

She hesitated, feeling the annoyance dwindle a little, she smirked.

Giving Leon one more cursory glance to make sure he was all right, she slipped out the door. Suzuhah followed at her side, talking animatedly about some of the few things he knew about witches, how timing needed to be perfect and how some could use spells without potions as long as they knew what items were supposed to be in the potion and had a strong enough knowledge of the end result. Those were usually seers, however. "Oh, can you see the future? I know some witches and seers and even some prophets can, so..."

Rita hesitated before nodding as they stepped into the map room, taking a seat around the table. It was probably the easiest place to work on witch's brews and incantations, compared to the rest of the ship. Made sense, now that she thought about it. It did have a seer's sigil on it, so potions and such would be somewhat enhanced just by proximity. Thank gosh seer potions and spells didn't cancel each other out. She would just have to hope the boys were keeping an eye on things. She paused at the thought and sighed. Thank the heavens she wasn't that much in a hurry.

After a moment of thought regarding how best to answer Suzuhah's question, she responded, "Sort of..." She noticed him stop and turn to her, confused. "I don't know what triggers it, or what it is going to show me. I don't even know if it's showing something that will happen right away or in a few minutes or even a few days." She shrugged. "So, I guess it counts?"

He stared at her, a strangeness about his gaze, as if contemplating her words, before he turned away. "Gotcha. Thanks for telling me." The words were almost monotone and sounded a little strange, coming from the surprisingly cheerful boy's mouth. However, when he turned back to her, he was once more grinning. "Now about those lessons..."

She rolled her eyes, yet smiled fondly. As exasperating as the idea was, it was great to be able to show her skill off once in a while. She appreciated the others, but they just did not understand why she loved this so much. She paused in thought, and slight realization. In the past, she would have mentioned she was doing all this for freedom and her desire to meet Killah, but now, she really did enjoy it. She felt her lips twitch into a wide smile at the thought.

It's amazing how things could change so quickly.

~ * ~

Milos watched as Alex cheered, eyes lighting up in joy as he brought the small bubble of water over, letting it hover above his hands to show him. Milos would have almost associated the expression to one of a little kid's, if not for Alex's beaming smile and words. "See? Geez, you could have let me relax a little."

"If I had, you never would have gotten it before the day stones died."

Alex rolled his eyes, as he lightly tossed the water from hand to hand. The pride in his eyes at the nonchalant movement was quite telling. "True, but..." He shook his head. "Still, thanks for the help. It's still strange that you're helping me with this at all."

Milos pursed his lips and glanced up toward the day stones, watching their light strain all the way down to them. He didn't have a response to Alex's words. He was still trying to figure out the whys himself.

"Milos?"

"Right, sorry." Milos shook his head and redirected his thoughts back to Alex, who was watching him worriedly, water suspended between his hands. "I'm surprised you haven't thrown that at me yet."

"That's Rita, not me," Alex deadpanned, causing Milos to raise an eyebrow, amused. He sighed and turned, letting it dribble out of his hand and over the edge of the railing. He watched for a moment before turning back, arms crossed. "See?"

Milos shrugged, heading back over to the wheel. Since Rita's departure, he'd made sure to keep half an eye on their trajectory. Thankfully, the wind stones did a pretty good job of keeping them straight, even with the waves pushing at them. The island had completely disappeared by this point and there were no sounds of the Vulfulas, so they must have left the creature behind. However, considering it didn't seem native to the island, which he construed from a few things he heard from Alex, he had no doubt they would probably see it again.

It was just their luck, after all.

He would worry about it later. Hopefully, when they got to the next island, he could figure things out. Spreading out his senses, he noticed Rita and Suzuhah in the cabin. It was hard to tell below, with the water in the way, but on deck it was a bit easier. Speaking of...

"Alex." He turned, startling the boy as he kept his voice low. "When we get to the next island, you are going to practice with your wings, got it?"

Alex grimaced before letting out a sigh, slumping. "Yeah, sure." He paused before glancing up, curious. "So, what now?"

Milos shrugged. "Since it seems that Rita allowed Leon to sleep and Ari isn't up yet, I'll stay here. Mind checking on them and grabbing some food? I bet you're tired."

Alex hesitated, looking ready to agree before pausing. "Hey, Milos?"

"Hm?"

"Suzuhah. What do you make of him?"

Milos glanced over toward Alex, who was staring quietly at the doorway to the cabin. The faint sound of conversation filtered through the aged wood, a familiar and not so familiar voice chatting back and forth with a surprising amount of enthusiasm. "I do not know them, and I'm somewhat surprised you're not asking about his sister as well."

Alex turned to him, hesitant before laughing sheepishly. "Right, it's weird how they have the same name and all. It confuses me sometimes, I guess."

"You're not wrong." Milos turned the wheel slightly, feeling the ship gently curve through the water. "There's nothing wrong with being wary, and there's nothing wrong with being friendly either." He hesitated, mentally wondering at his own words. Of course, there was a problem with being too friendly, especially to strangers. He shook his head, noting Alex was still listening, curious. "If you really feel uncomfortable, let him know. If you feel threatened..." Milos smirked, feeling an edge to his smile that he usually held in reserve. Alex stiffened. "Well, I don't think we have to worry too much about that, right?"

"I'm not killing anyone." Alex gritted his teeth and Milos sighed.

"I'm not saying you have to," he pointed out, quickly checking the compass once more before stepping away from the wheel. "I've gathered from working with you what I need to know."

Milos didn't think he needed to add how the boy was sometimes too gentle of a soul. He knew Alex was well aware of that fact. Unlike Milos...though Milos felt his kills were quite justified and he managed to stay his hand when necessary, usually. His thoughts flickered to his first meeting with Alex and he shook his head. Part of him wondered what his first instinct would be upon meeting the demons to the north, if he tried to skewer Alex upon their first meeting when he was still in human form...

He wasn't sure how he would react, period. He had helped demons escape, though not by his own hand and more by his lack of stopping Alex. Now he was training a demon to use his powers. Should he despise what he was doing? Or should he feel something else?

"You listening?" Alex's face was much closer than when Milos last noticed and he mentally backpedaled to figure out what Alex said. The boy pulled away, smiling faintly. "Guess I caught you zoning out, quite rare. Rita would have a field day with that, you know," he pointed out, grinning childishly.

"Good thing you're not Rita." Milos stepped away, getting an amused grunt from Alex. "One Rita is more than enough."

"She is something, isn't she?"

The fondness in his voice was quite obvious to Milos' ears as he shook his head. He never asked about the specifics regarding how the two met, and he found no reason to, but he was curious about how the two became so close over the span of what was only, at most, a month or so. Though he didn't exactly have a right to speak, considering he was traveling with them as a comrade himself.

There was that word again. It really did sound odd in his head, but he did kind of like it, more than he wanted to admit. Comrade...it had a nice ring to it. "So now that you're done being jealous of Suzuhah—"

"Jealous?" Alex stiffened and shook his head before hesitating. "I guess I am. She's my friend, after all."

"Hm... that's true." Milos peered toward the doorway. "The two of them are strange, but if they really meant harm..." He turned to Alex with a pointed glare. "A few of us would probably be dead by now."

"Huh? Why?"

"No one here keeps a complete eye on them all the time, we can't, not even on such a small ship. They've been alone with a few people at this point, but things seem fine. Don't you agree?"

Alex blinked as Milos peered back at the doorway. Yes, he could tell there was something strange about Suzuhah, but he didn't feel anything dangerous, no change in the flow of air, no distortions, not even the fluctuation of magic except when Alex used it earlier. There was a faint sound from the cabin and quiet murmuring from inside. A moment later, the door opened to reveal Ari. She was awake. Yawning, but awake. She spotted them and gave a quick bow before walking over. "I'm sorry for my tardiness."

"It's fine." Milos waved it off, getting a nod from the girl, who took over at the controls, confirming his belief. Suzuha, the little girl, would have been alone with her, yet Ari seemed perfectly fine.

He spotted Alex relaxing, a little more at ease with Milos' words and Ari's tired, but normal condition.

Milos, himself, however felt a little uneasy. With everything that happened recently, it seemed strange nothing was happening in this part of the ocean. They'd traveled for quite a few hours already. He hoped it was just lingering paranoia, but he had a feeling it wasn't.

He heard a loud growl and glanced over to Alex, who was mumbling something under his breath, holding his stomach awkwardly. "I guess I'm hungrier than I thought?" The end lifted up into a question as he laughed nervously.

Milos sighed, right, Alex had used up a lot of energy with trying to manipulate the water. Maybe he should have let him rest first. Though, Alex should have said something himself. Milos had, after all, mentioned the boy should grab something to eat first. "All right, let's check on Leon and get some food started."

"Do you even know how to cook? I don't remember seeing your name on cooking duty."

Milos hesitated.

"No, he doesn't." Ari's voice was faint, but still heard loud and clear.

Milos felt his eye twitch, but didn't respond to her cheeky words. Though he did spot the faint grin on her lips as she watched him.

"Really?" Alex seemed amused. "My mom was a pretty bad cook as well, always setting the temperature and time wrong and causing havoc for the others..." Alex trailed off, thoughts probably flickering to the woman who all but abandoned him. "I wonder if she's gotten any better." He shook his head. "Let's get something to eat already. I've made a few things myself, so it shouldn't be too hard with two of us."

Milos watched as he hurried into the cabin and right down the stairs. Milos followed, seeing Rita smiling faintly, staring at the stairwell as Suzuhah watched her with a contemplative expression. Upon seeing Milos, he gave a respectful nod before turning his attention back to a set of notes, placed on the table.

"Oh, hey, Milos, what has Alex in such a hurry?"

"Hm?" Milos glanced toward Suzuhah, who was leaning forward just a bit to peer at the notes and as such, was almost on top of Rita. "Well, Alex decided he needed something to eat and it's getting late."

"Oh, right." Rita pulled away, turning the chair she sat in enough to face him. "Leon wasn't feeling too well, so I let him rest. That means we don't have a cook at the moment."

Milos narrowed his eyes. He wasn't feeling well? He seemed to be fine earlier when Milos left this morning. He would have to double-check. "Thanks for letting me know."

Rita blinked before pointing at herself. "Wait, you of all people are thanking me?"

Milos felt his eye twitch again, he really needed to fix that. "I know when to share proper thanks, unlike a certain lousy prophetess."

"I'm a witch. I preferred it when you used my actual title."

"Could have fooled me." Milos waved as Rita fumed. The girl was fun to rile up, even if he was aware his reactions were not much better. "Hm? Did you say something? A pseudo witch? Is that what you wanted me to call you?"

"Ergh...you're annoying." She paused. "You know, I thanked you earlier with the whole vine-like island thing, so..." she cut off as Milos tried and failed to hide his smirk.

"I'll take that as a compliment, considering I was trying to be polite in the first place."

Rita bit her lip, seeming to not want to respond and give him more fuel. Milos let it go, noting the way Suzuhah was watching them with an odd expression, as if he were analyzing their exchange. Upon noticing Milos spotted him, he smiled hesitantly. "You two, you like to argue a lot. Do you like each other or something?"

Milos wasn't sure if he found the statement offensive or amusing. Rita just seemed flabbergasted, unable to even respond.

Suzuhah let out a laugh, pointing at Rita's expression. "Oh man. I'm sorry, but I've been waiting to say that since I met you two. You argue all the time, yet you are all so close. I couldn't resist. I do apologize." He clapped his hands together, smiling sheepishly. "Don't mind my little joke."

"It wasn't funny," Rita muttered, finally seeming to get her voice back.

"Hm... I see where the amusement is in it though," Milos pointed out, barely holding back a grin. "Though to be associated with one such as yourself..."

"Save it, dingbat."

Milos shook his head, letting the conversation die. "Still, Suzuhah, I would probably watch your words from now on. Both of us were able to tell quickly that it was a harmless prank, however, that might not always be the case." He let his expression shift, cold to the point, he noticed even Rita scoot away slightly.

Suzuhah barely batted an eye, nodding solemnly. "Yes, my apologies. I'll be more careful."

With that, Milos turned, waving before heading downstairs. He faintly heard Rita mutter, "He could have at least argued."

He knew full well that arguing or bursting out in that sort of situation would only lead to unnecessary misunderstandings. He saw it happen enough with others who he knew. He shook his head. Sometimes it was better to follow along than to try to cut off the flow of conversation.

He turned, heading toward Leon's room. When he stepped inside, he noticed the man sleeping calmly, clearly under the effects of a potion if the residual magic swirling around him was any indication. Rita's medicine was as powerful as ever, it seemed. He stepped closer, glancing over him before frowning. He was laying on his back, wincing whenever he went to roll onto his side. Knowing how the man slept, Milos knew that he was probably uncomfortable. So why?

He reached over, carefully checking his neck and arm. There didn't seem to be anything. He knew Rita would have spotted anything obvious, but she didn't seem concerned. After another moment, he pulled away and shook his head. Leon was fine.

Milos paused and frowned, glancing over his shoulder. Now that he thought about it, where was the little girl? The younger Suzuha? Her brother was clearly upstairs, but he couldn't remember seeing the little girl in a while. Thinking of that, his mind flitted to the male Suzuhah. Maybe it was just his nature, but he didn't trust Suzuhah, and, though the boy appeared quite comfortable around Rita, he still seemed wary and almost a little odd in his observance of the rest of them.

He shook his head. While those two held an odd air about them, and now that he thought about it, he couldn't recall seeing them together, he wasn't sure what that meant. He clicked his tongue and turned, closing the door to the men's room behind him. There wasn't really anything he could do about it now. He would just have to keep an eye on things and see what happened.

Either way, he needed to stop procrastinating on going to the kitchen. He let out a quiet groan. He would let Alex take care of it, but he said he would help the boy.

Chopping up some vegetables should be good enough. Right?

Chapter Fifteen

Alex turned as the door to the kitchen opened to reveal Milos standing there, hand stiffly holding the handle. If he didn't know the man, he would have completely missed the tension in his shoulders, or the slightly nervous expression on his face. To a normal viewer, he just seemed his normal stoic self. It was a strange and somewhat amusing contrast.

Alex returned to the salted meat he'd grabbed earlier. Salted meat was good and all, but he could really use a change of pace, maybe a sauce and some sautéed veggies? They had retrieved some fruit when on the island, so, instead of the dried stuff, he could use something fresher to sprinkle over the meat. His thoughts whirled as he heard the fire hiss. While he wasn't as good of a chef as Ari and Leon, he felt he was decent enough.

He heard footsteps stop to his right and he glanced over to see Milos scanning the kitchen.

Alex hummed before grinning, Okay, maybe he was starting to take after Rita a bit. "Wash your hands, and don't forget to put on an apron." He gestured to his own blue one that Leon often wore when cooking. He hadn't really thought of it, or noticed it in the past, but it made sense with how much the ship rolled and how easy it was to splash stew or something on you from a large bowl. Plus, he only had one set of clothes.

Once again, he really needed to fix that.

Milos was unamused, but followed suit, grabbing a plain white one out of a side cupboard before tying his hair up in a way where it wouldn't land over his shoulder. Within no time, he was standing in front of the veggies, a little lost.

Alex sighed, pulling away from the meat, turning down the heat in the process, and walked over. "Have you never cooked before?"

"Once. It was when I first arrived in the Underlands. Ari and Leon took over about half-way through," Milos said before facing him. "Other times, I didn't need to."

Translation, Alex surmised, he had slaves to take care of it for him. "Well then, let's start simple. You know how to wield a sword, so cutting shouldn't be too difficult." Alex picked up a knife from its container and laid a carrot on the table. It was still fine, but in a day or two, it would probably be too bad to eat. He would have to talk with Ari and Leon to see if they could cook up the other vegetables and store them before they rotted. After Leon woke up and Ari finished her shift upstairs. Shaking the thought off, he curled his fingers. "To avoid cutting your fingers off, you curl your fingers inward and use part of your knuckle to hold the vegetable in place." He sliced through it with ease, cutting a few more times before handing the bulk to Milos. "Go ahead and try." He swept up the pieces he made, throwing the stem to one side.

He watched as Milos followed his example, his gaze sharpened and he started cutting. A little too fast.

"Gah." Alex pulled away. "You're not trying to kill it."

Milos glanced up before looking down at the pureed carrot. Alex glanced at the mess in front of him. Okay, he was probably over-exaggerating a little. Still, he didn't know it was *possible* to cut a vegetable into that many tiny pieces. He glanced up in time to see Milos wince.

Alex sighed, before chuckling. "Okay, let's try that again, just a little slower this time?" He scooped up the pieces, throwing the whole thing in with the meat. No point in wasting it.

Milos nodded and returned to it, this time a little slower. So, the afternoon progressed with Alex pointing out adjustments the man could make, when it was best to stir in the vegetables so they weren't so soft as to be mush and, once he was done with the vegetables, how to cook the meat so that it was cooked evenly. Milos stayed stoic the whole time, but Alex noticed the curious expression that flitted over his face every now and then, well-hidden as it was. He also didn't miss the slight tilt to his lips, indicating a barely there smile when he finished off some of the cooking.

Alex found himself having a bit of fun. Who knew he would ever have *fun* cooking, nonetheless with Milos of all people? It was strange, seeing that side of the man. It was funny, to be honest.

Made even funnier with the apron wrapped around his waist as he picked up the small salad they made and placed it on the counter, right as Leon walked in.

Leon took one look at the salad, before noting Milos' frozen expression. He turned to Alex. He gave Alex a sharp nod of appreciation, before turning and heading out the door.

"Oh, Leon," Alex called, causing the man to stop. Alex glanced toward Milos, who straightened, adjusting his expression back to neutral. "How are you feeling?"

"Better. Thank you." He bowed his head before once more taking in Milos. He seemed to be barely able to suppress a smile before disappearing.

Alex chuckled as Milos pulled away, untying the apron. "I guess that means he's getting the others. Glad to know he's feeling better." If Alex didn't know any better, he would have thought Milos was flustered. "Thanks, Alex."

Alex shrugged, smiling warmly. "Hey, you've been teaching all of us a lot as it was, at least I can teach you something in return." He brought the food over, taking a seat and pulling his own apron off as the sound of footsteps rang on the stairs. Rita rushed in, before pouting.

"Ah...I wanted to see you in aprons. Leon said you were wearing an apron."

Alex raised an eyebrow. Why would Leon mention that, of all things? Milos' eye twitched in a way that screamed annoyance. Rita took a seat and, soon enough, everyone else piled into the room. Everyone except Ari, who said she would stay above to keep watch until someone took over.

"Suzuhah said he was going to wake his sister and take a nap. He must be exhausted after the last few days." Rita took a seat as Leon sat beside her.

Alex nodded, placing some of the salad into his bowl, just as the door swung open.

Standing in the doorway was little Suzuha. The young girl glanced around before almost bouncing into the last seat, staring at the food in wonder. "This looks good."

"Our resident demon hunter and Alex made it." Rita waved.

The girl perked up, glancing over to Milos and Alex. "Really? Well, thank you." She bowed her head before scooping up a good portion of food and shoving it onto her plate.

Rita grinned before taking a bite to eat. "Huh, not bad." She swallowed, before taking another bite.

Leon just carefully cut his meat up before chewing slowly.

Alex smiled before glancing at Suzuha, who was stuffing the food down faster than Alex could blink. Geez, and he thought he was hungry. "Hey, Suzuha?"

The girl perked up, cheeks stuffed to bursting. She swallowed before placing her fork down. "Hm?"

"I was just wondering, what are you going to do now? I mean, you were fleeing the south a long time ago, so..." He trailed off, feeling awkward.

Her expression dimmed slightly as she placed her fingers onto the table, curling into the fabric. "Suzuhah didn't tell you?"

"Your brother? No." Rita shook her head, before taking another bite to eat.

"Oh..." Her voice was faint before she glanced up. "Well, I was really young, so I don't remember much and I know my brother doesn't like talking about it." She shrugged. "I mean, I know what I want to do *now*, but I'm not sure why we fled to begin with." She hesitated, her expression shifting slightly, faster than Alex thought possible. Huh... "As for what we want to do now, well, I'm not sure about my brother, but I know I just want to be somewhere with people. Lots and lots of people. I want to talk with them, eat with them, like we're doing now and just, be somewhere where I'll be safe, I guess."

Alex nodded, taking a bite to eat to give him time to mull over his thoughts.

"You don't believe the Vulfulas will follow you?" Milos interjected. His gaze narrowed. "After all, it did seem keen on attacking you."

The girl hesitated before looking down. "I don't know." She shrugged. "I mean, I always thought it was just territorial." She glanced up. "I think my brother once mentioned that it was our fault, we were abandoned. We were abandoned because the Vulfulas was actually after us." She paused, fingers tightening on the wood. "I didn't want to believe that, I would rather be abandoned because of an accident or something. To be abandoned because a creature we didn't know was after us? I asked my brother what he meant, but he never explained, so..."

Alex stopped in his eating, anger surging through him for a brief moment before the emotion subsided into a dull ache in his chest as he wondered if Suzuhah mentioned it. He couldn't quite remember if he did. Milos just seemed peeved, though Alex wasn't sure why *he* of all people was.

"You didn't think to mention this to us earlier?" Milos placed his utensils down, hands in his lap as he scrutinized Suzuha, to Alex's surprise. "It would have been beneficial for us to *know* the beast is after you two, even if it was only speculation from your brother."

"That's..."

"Oh, leave off." Rita huffed, sending Milos a look. "Would it have made a difference? Sure, I'm a little upset about that, but it doesn't necessarily matter at this point and do you think any of us would abandon them there?"

Milos shook his head. "I know, quite well, neither of you would abandon someone. I'm just saying, a word of caution would have been prudent."

"Well, we know now, right?" Alex interrupted, trying to assuage the situation a little. This wasn't Rita's or Milos' normal argument. "It's awful how they were abandoned to begin with, so it makes sense that they wouldn't say anything right away."

Alex let out a breath as he caught both of their attention, resting his hands on the table. "Maybe we could have prepared, but how? Honestly, would it have made any major difference knowing now versus knowing when we were still on the island?" Alex glanced toward Milos for the last bit.

The man stared at him for a moment before returning to his eating, not saying a word. Alex let out a breath, feeling a faint smile trail over his lips. Seems that answered that.

"Still..." Rita trailed off, peering from person to person. "Who abandons kids, little kids at that, to the mercy of some creature? I mean, sure, it's a Vulfulas and they are said to represent seers." She sighed. "There was an opposing guild on the ship, wasn't there?"

"Opposing guild?" Alex blinked, finding himself confused.

Though he was grateful for a change in conversation. Was there an opposition between guilds? He thought they all just kind of did their own thing.

"You didn't know?" Rita glanced toward him. "Actually, it makes sense if you didn't. Basically, it's when competition arises between two guilds. An easy example is the Blacksmithing and Engineering guilds. They can work together just fine, but neither side will bow to the other, always competing with each other for clients and innovations. Most guilds are like that, but there are a few that almost never see eye to eye." Rita leaned back in her chair. Her arms were crossed over her chest. "One such set is the Seers guild and the Psychics guild. At one point, the two were one guild, but due to differing interests, the two split. Most guild members will be uneasy around the other guild, but they will at least talk if necessary. However, some more extreme members will banish or even kill those who show any sign of working with or for the other guild. It's not as common on the seers' side, but it does happen." Rita sighed, glancing away. "It's not something I like talking about, no one does."

"She's right." Milos gestured briefly, gaze hard. "It happens in the Overlands as well, usually between the warrior guilds. It's not as dangerous as the gap between the psychic and seer's guild, but it's there."

"Okay. So, what...?" Alex found himself cut off by a sharp look from Rita.

"As I was saying..." She glanced back toward Suzuha, who was watching quietly, plate already cleared of food. "My guess is that the group you were traveling with consisted mostly of psychics. As soon as the Vulfulas, a seers' creation, took interest in you two, they wanted nothing to do with you. It's cruel, but it's happened before."

Alex gritted his teeth. Weren't there enough problems in the Underlands? He thought the guilds were fairly safe from that, but it seemed it wasn't the case.

"It's unfortunate," Milos sighed, "that your crewmates, or even just one of the crew, was extreme in their views. Just one person can sway a crowd against someone else for stupid reasons." Milos took a bite as Alex watched him, curious. It almost sounded like Milos knew what he was talking about. Alex hoped Milos didn't have to deal with that in the past, but he didn't know much about his friend, so he couldn't tell.

Suzuha seemed to be deep in thought before she reached forward, grabbing more from the table before stuffing it in her mouth. "I don't want to talk anymore," she mumbled once she swallowed. "Can we just eat?"

Alex exchanged looks before shrugging and digging back in. He got the answers he was searching for, though it did open up a whole other can of worms he would rather not have known about.

~ * ~

Rita groaned, laying on the hammock as she stared up at the ceiling in thought. It was a few hours after dinner, the night stones firmly in place and most of the people probably sound asleep. Opposing guilds, huh? She hadn't thought much on it, since it hadn't affected her when at home, or looking for a seer. Now that she thought about it, the psychic class had become more prominent during the last few months and didn't Milos mention something? Was she just remembering wrong? It was hard to tell sometimes. Still, if the psychics were becoming more active, it would explain why she was having trouble finding a seer to teach her.

If that was the case, then what did it mean?

She rolled onto her side. It was one thing to hear about it, it was another thing to see the results of it. She sighed, glancing over to see the hammocks empty. Ari was probably having dinner, now that Leon took over for her and Rita had no clue where Alex and Milos were. She noted the absence of Suzuha, but figured the little girl was probably with her brother at the moment. Who knew, since both of them should probably be sleeping like she was supposed to be doing. She sighed before flinging herself out of bed and heading toward the engine room, just to get her mind off of things for a moment.

So, she was startled when she heard a faint sound and glanced over to see the Aqua Wraith. The woman was wavy at best, shimmering in the faint light as she swirled around Rita before heading back toward the machine, nervous.

Rita frowned, checking that the door was firmly closed before walking up to the woman. She wasn't sure why she did that, but she felt it was right. "Are you all right?" After she said it, she wanted to slap herself. No, the Aqua Wraith wasn't all right, she was dead. She mentally berated herself on her stupidity, only to freeze when she noticed a hand extend to her cheek before pulling back.

The woman smiled faintly before responding, "Do not worry. I thank thee for asking." She peered up to the ceiling, water wavering around her form, making it hard to tell leg from waist from just a makeshift tail. "Tis still dangerous for me to appear." She spoke softly, turning back to face Rita. "Please be wary," she whispered, looking frustrated. "I wish I could tell more, say more, but my..."

"Your oath or promise?" Rita shook her head, closing her eyes.

Her thoughts flickered to the little vial, remembering the swirl of energy. Now that she thought about it, it felt very similar to the Aqua Wraith herself. She paused at that, why did she think of the vial in the first place? She felt a strange shudder trail through her mind, but shook it off as she stared back at the Wraith. "Still, it's good to see you. I thought we lost you back at the island."

"This ship and I are entwined. Thou wilt not lose me at such a junction." The woman peered toward the door before swirling forward. "Watch your comrades, for even as I feel you will not be harmed, I do not feel the same with your friends. The others...watch them." The woman pulled back before diving under the floorboards, out of sight. Rita watched her go, frowning.

What did she mean? Was there still something dangerous around?

Her thoughts flickered to the brother and sister, but quickly shook her head. There was no way. They were kind and thoughtful, and the little girl was sweet. She paused, thoughts flickering between them. Though, it was kind of strange how she never saw them together. After her parents' death, she stuck to Alex with a fervor, though he was only a stranger. Those two were siblings, but she couldn't recall ever seeing them side by side. Maybe it was her imagination? That was probably it. She shook her head. She was just paranoid. Did they bring something back from the island that could cause problems? Something she hadn't noticed? Alex and Leon did go hunting after she went to sleep. Could they have returned with something?

It would make sense, with her witch's training, she would be immune to most things that were on that island, but that was probably not the case for the others.

She glanced up toward the ceiling, thoughts flickering. She wasn't too worried about Milos. The man was probably already aware of any problems on the ship and he could take care of himself—not that she would ever admit that to him. She could probably tell Leon and Ari to keep an eye on things, but they seemed tired lately and she wasn't sure how aware they would be. As for Alex...

She paused at the thought, debating with herself. Should she really worry him, when she had no idea what to watch out for? After all, he was still worried about his mother and stressed since they were still trying to get through this way to big ocean.

She let out a yawn. She frowned slightly before shrugging and returning to her hammock. She would worry about it in the morning. The conversation with the Aqua Wraith had drained her for some reason.

She would deal with it in the morning.

~ * ~

A little before noon the next day, Rita found herself staring into the storage room, her original idea of grabbing food for lunch rapidly disappearing. She felt lost, confused and more than a little nervous.

She clearly remembered the conversation with Suzuha last night.

The girl mentioned her brother was either in the men's room or the storage room. When Rita asked why, she mentioned that all their stuff was in there and that her brother was probably organizing it.

Yet, peering around the room, Rita didn't find a single thing out of place, other than a bag which she recognized as the bags Alex and Leon took with them to go out scavenging. So where was it? All the clothes and other items those two stored back at the island? Why couldn't she find hide nor hair of it, if Suzuhah supposedly brought it with him?

It made her skin crawl, and she wasn't sure why.

She heard movement and jerked, glancing back to see Suzuhah peek in. He spotted her, startled. "What are you doing in here?" he asked, voice hesitant.

He seemed ruffled, a little annoyed and frazzled. She turned to him.

"I was checking something."

He tilted his head, confused, before pulling the door open. "You might want to check where we are. You are the navigator, after all. Right?"

Rita hesitated before walking past. She noted Suzuhah briefly glance into the room before closing the door and following after her. Her thoughts flickered to the Aqua Wraith's words from her restless night. She shook her head. She already decided not to worry about it. After all, it made no sense.

She stepped into the map room, observing it. She couldn't do much from here, so she moved outside to take a look at where they were. The day stones hung high above, their light shining brilliantly, showing it was probably just past noon.

She walked over, catching Alex's attention. Leon was manning the wheel, barely sparing them a glance as he peered ahead. Dark circles sat under his eyes and she grimaced, realizing she was supposed to take a shift last night. She quickly apologized to the man, who waved it off, before she turned to Alex.

"Oh, hey, Rita. Suzuhah." Alex's gaze skipped to Suzuhah's, a flicker of emotion flashing through his eyes before disappearing, having been watching from a distance as she apologized to Leon before joining him. "I see you're together again." The words were only half-joking. "I keep hea..."

She noted the way he stopped, peering at Suzuhah. He probably felt uncomfortable talking around the boy.

Rita sighed and turned to Suzuhah. "Can you go take a look at some of the maps? Grab the compass from Leon, I'll be there in a second."

Suzuhah's gaze snapped between them, expression odd before he nodded and hurried over to Leon.

Rita turned back to Alex, who was watching the boy warily. "Okay, enough with the jealousy, what's wrong?"

Alex jerked, pursing his lips in thought before he turned to her. "Don't you find him odd? He's always staring at me, I mean, I get he and his sister have had it rough, I won't deny that, but, well, the way he freaks out around you, almost like you might if you met Killah, is just..."

"Is that so strange?" she wondered out loud, staring at him. "Both of them haven't talked with people in years."

Alex sighed. "Yeah, like I said, I know. Sorry." He smiled weakly before turning toward the railing once more. "Anyway, something seems really weird about these waters."

"How so?" Rita walked over, leaning on the railing beside him.

She could see him struggling to put words together before he pointed to a wave as it splashed against the side of the boat. She watched, confused, before she frowned.

The waves...she knew the ship was moving forward, but it almost seemed like the waves only hit the ship once every few minutes, not like the constant bobbing they were doing up until now.

She glanced around, unnerved as she noted a strange silence. All around them, the ocean seemed still. Once she first saw the size of the water, she expected most of the ocean to be like this, but that hadn't been the case. Not until now.

"It isn't humming like usual," Alex admitted quietly. "It feels like it's struggling. It keeps flipping between shrieking in warning, and falling silent."

Rita wondered what he meant, what exactly was he hearing? She knew he was in tune with the water, but this was the first time he spoke of what that meant.

She just wished his words didn't have to sound so foreboding.

"All right, I'm going to see where we are. Stay nearby and let me know if anything changes." Rita got a nod from Alex before hurrying back into the map room.

Suzuhah glanced up from perusing over one of the maps, handing the compass over to her. "You might want to take a look at that."

Rita picked it up, twisting it so it shone in the light of the light stone. She froze.

The needle that had so faithfully been facing north up until then was swinging violently left and right, flicking back and forth over the north as if someone was shaking it. "What the heck?" she yelped, checking it over as Alex's words met her ears. She darted over to one of the maps, peering over it before stilling.

After a moment, she raced outside and over to Leon. "Leon."

The man jumped, turning to her as she held the compass out to him. "How long has it been doing this?"

Leon glanced at it, startled. "Only a moment or two ago. I was just about to notify someone when Suzuhah asked for it."

Rita glanced around them, noticing as Alex stiffened, fingers tightening around the railing.

"Leon, turn this boat around right now." Rita's voice pitched up as a strange sound echoed over the water. She could see Alex slam his hands to his ears just as Leon wrenched the wheel almost one hundred and eighty degrees. She grasped onto the cabin, the ship almost tilting sidewise at the sudden movement. She noticed Suzuhah stumble, holding onto the doorway.

"Get us out of here!" Alex's scream caught her off guard, pain flickering in his voice.

She heard a hum followed by a blast of air from the wind stones as they surged through the water. Water rushed past them, though only partially from the wind stones' help, as if some was being sucked backward. She glanced back, horror shearing through her veins as she noticed a fin pierce out from below, a few more following in its wake.

The sea frothed as teeth pierced inches from where the boat was only a moment before. The teeth slammed shut, plunging back into the water as their ship rocketed forward. Leon spun the wheel, their ship weaving and dodging as more teeth erupted out of the water, gaping maws, pure black, inches away from their boat. She heard pounding footsteps as Milos darted on board. Ari must have been in the engine room.

He took one look at the creatures and cursed. "I didn't think *this* many of those things would be in one place." He ran over to the wheel, taking it from Leon. "Strap the items downstairs in the storage. Suzuhah, help him and keep an eye on your sister." The two nodded, darting down as he wrestled with the wheel, spearing them through the water. "Rita, point me where we need to go to get out of this mess, Alex, focus on trying to calm the water enough for us to get through."

Alex nodded, hands still to his ears. He stumbled to the middle of the ship as Rita peered down at the wildly swinging compass, if only... She grimaced and peered up at the day stones as they started to slip to their night time counterparts. If they were still in this area when the day stones died, she wasn't too optimistic on their outcomes. She felt the boat move faster and noticed the way Alex was swaying as she peered down at the compass once more. "Go to starboard forty-five degrees then straight."

Milos followed suit, barely dodging as another set of teeth pierced up from the frothing ocean, water surging down the thing's gullet before it disappeared. They were moving faster, the water around them almost splitting to give them passage. She was shouting directions, flipping between the occasionally still compass and day stones.

Finally, after what felt like a frantic hour of travel that was probably closer to a few minutes, they came to a halt, the sea once more quiet and serene, waves lapping normally against the hull as Rita collapsed to the ground, shaken. She wasn't sure, her mind still riddled with panic, but it seemed as if things quieted down slowly as they fled. If she gazed into the distance, she could see the churning of waves and a few fins disappearing back into the waters, but it seemed that none of the creatures chased them. It wasn't necessarily a clear-cut line of where those things were and where they weren't. That was probably because they hadn't stopped, even when they got out of the mess.

Alex was on all fours, gulping down air as if he ran a marathon. It wouldn't be far-fetched to assume that's actually what it felt like.

Milos let go of the wheel, checking the compass once more before walking over to Rita. "Explain."

Rita took in another breath as she stared up at him. "I should have realized sooner. Remember that area I told you about that we needed to avoid? Well, we should have turned to port, now starboard, about two hours ago. I was hoping to avoid that area. Though, I didn't expect..." She stilled before glancing over to Alex, who finally managed to catch his breath. "Hey, Alex, how did you not sense those things?"

Alex shook his head and sat up with a grimace, pushing himself to his feet. "There were so many, it just felt like the water was shallow, the ground maybe rippling a little. That's why it kept going back and forth. The creatures were probably opening their mouths to eat, which caused the screeching before it became still again. I didn't..."

"We're out of there. That's what matters." Milos turned to Rita. "Though I certainly didn't expect to find a whole area of them living together. Up until now, those things have only hunted individually."

"Maybe this is a mating ground?" Suzuhah's voice startled Rita, making her jump and, glance over to Suzuhah, who was back upstairs, wiping sweat from his brow. Leon was a few steps behind him. Suzuhah turned toward Rita. "I've heard about those things before, but I only occasionally saw them in my travels. I think they are called Kimora? Something like that." He frowned, finger to his lip in thought. "Maybe it was Kamoray?" He shrugged. "That's about all I know of them though."

"That's more than we know." Milos pointed out, watching the boy closely.

"So, you think it was mating season?" Rita frowned, attention once more on the slowly quieting horizon. "That would be our luck," Rita grunted, frustrated as she peered back, the ship once more moving along at a sedate pace.

Suzuhah shrugged. "Could be worse. Usually, they would all be out hunting these waters. I mean, they are not always in this region. That was some impressive evasion. I could hear how close we were from the storage room." He glanced toward Milos, an expression on his face a mix of confused and grateful. "By the way, thank you of thinking of my sister during all of that. She's fine. She was hiding in the girl's room. It sounded like your other friend—Ari, I believe? —was in the engine room. She seemed fine, from what I could tell."

Milos nodded as Rita let out a relieved breath before she peered at the compass. It was pointing northward. "I would just like to know why the compass was acting up."

"I can probably answer that." Milos spoke up, nodding to Leon as he took back over, turning their ship toward starboard. "It happens sometimes in the Overlands. There is probably an underground volcano in the area, or even a chain. Something like that would keep the waters warm, good for mating, but would also cause magnetic rock, such as iron, to form at the bottom of the ocean. With it constantly being pulled up by the creatures, it probably mixed in heavily with the water, thus coating even the surface with the magnetic field."

Rita nodded, the words allowing her to connect the last few dots. It made sense. It would explain why the waters were calm, laden down as they were and with barely any water to begin with, due to the bulky creatures' stagnant forms. Add that with volcanic activity and, geez, even without the creatures, that area was dangerous. She sighed, handing the compass back to Leon before once more plopping herself back down on the ground.

"Let's not do that again anytime soon, or ever, thank you."

"Couldn't agree more," Milos said, startling her as Alex nodded, taking a seat beside her.

Suzuhah walked over to the railing, leaning against it with a cheeky grin. "I don't know. I had fun."

Rita huffed, but didn't respond.

"Are you a thrill seeker or something?" Alex asked, leaning forward slightly.

Suzuhah shrugged. "Call it whatever you will. Probably why I survived so long with that thing around."

Rita couldn't deny that. Terror would root someone in place, adrenaline would allow them to move and evade when necessary while usually thinking a bit more clearly, especially if they enjoyed it. She shook her head. Suzuhah was so strange.

Speaking of, she would have to thank Ari for getting those wind stones running so quickly and constantly. Talk about impressive.

For now, though, she was just going to get her breath back and rest up.

Sleep sounded like a good idea.

And it was only midday. This was going to be a long day.

Chapter Sixteen

Milos wondered why it took almost a whole day to end up in trouble with the ocean. They must have used a lot of luck to get that far without a problem.

Though, he supposed it did rebound quite a bit as they dodged around teeth almost triple his height and width. He could only be grateful that Alex was a water demon, to some extent, because they would have been dead multiple times over if not. No wonder so few survived these lands. Just a few moments of carelessness could get you killed. He didn't blame Leon or Rita. They were both doing their best to keep an eye on things, and Leon even admitted that the compass just started acting up when the whole mess began. It was the same with the water serpents and the first island. They barely received any warning before mayhem erupted around them.

Alex and Rita found their way downstairs and Ari was still working in the engine room, which he wouldn't be surprised was probably a little worse for wear after that. Suzuhah... he wasn't sure where he was, or his sister, for that matter.

He frowned, heading into the map room. He noticed Suzuhah staring at the table, a deep frown on his face and finger to his lips. He jerked up upon Milos' entrance and then let out a breath. "Sorry, you startled me."

"It's fine." Milos headed past, deciding not to ask where Suzuhah's sibling was. He had a feeling he wasn't going to get a straight answer anyway. He reached the doorway, only to stop as a small sound echoed around the room.

"Thank you for keeping tabs on us." Suzuhah glanced up as Milos narrowed his eyes. "I know it's just because you think we're up to something, but she's still my sister, so I'm grateful she has someone watching out for her when I can't."

The words sounded off to Milos. The gentle smile on Suzuhah's lips made him sigh and shelve that thought for later. "Since you are already aware of why I'm watching you two, there is no reason to thank me. Plus, I believe the others would be upset if anything were to happen."

"True." Suzuhah chuckled. "There are...good people on this ship." The hesitation in Suzuhah's voice was strange, but the boy simply shook his head and continued, once more staring down at the wood. "You are a demon slayer, correct?"

Milos fully turned, pulling away from the stairwell to watch Suzuhah warily. He didn't respond, and it seemed Suzuhah didn't need a response.

"It's not hard to gather. The only reason for people to come this way is if they are fleeing something, if they are a demon, or if they are hunting demons." Suzuhah peered up at Milos with a strange look. "I have a question for you, demon hunter. Are there demons that you find yourself unable to kill?" Milos stilled at the words as Suzuhah glanced away. "To continue that train of thought, are there demons you would kill without mercy? With relish?"

Milos let out a breath, tilting his head slightly so his hair drifted gently over his shoulder. It took him a moment to respond. "My job is simply to hunt demons. I don't relish the task, but I am also aware that showing mercy can get you killed." He watched the boy quietly. "However, sometimes there are moments..." He paused in his thoughts, trying to organize what he was going to say, not knowing himself. "Sometimes things turn out different than you think. Something you once thought was hardened fact, could very well have its exceptions."

Suzuhah didn't say anything to that, just continued to stare at the wall before finally pulling his attention toward Milos once more, a heavy sadness and anger in his expression. "I'm not sure I can agree with that." One hand curled into his clothing. The same clothes Milos lent to him. "The truth is the truth." He paused. "Did you know...?" He seemed to debate with himself for a long time, and Milos let him. It seemed Suzuhah was grateful for the moment, because he continued, letting out a slow breath. "You all are so strange," he muttered before peering up toward Milos. "Would you help me if I told you there was a demon I absolutely have to kill?"

Milos nodded, no hesitation in his movement, startling Suzuhah. "Even..."

"I'm guessing this demon hurt you in some way, correct?" Milos interrupted, thoughts flickering to things he would rather forget before settling on Alex.

There was no way Suzuhah could be speaking of him. Alex was a bit too kind-hearted to hurt someone so much that the other would want to kill him. However, Alex wasn't like most demons, right?

"Like I stated, there are exceptions, but a demon such as that is not one of them. My job is to hunt and kill those demons. So, I have no reason to oppose helping you."

Suzuhah opened and closed his mouth, seemingly unsure on how to respond to that, grip slowly loosening on his shirt. "I didn't think you would agree so readily," he whispered, a moment of hope shining on his face before he shook it off. "Especially since..."

Milos felt a sense of unease as Suzuhah briefly glanced toward the doorway, as if lost in thought, before turning back to him. "Well, if you're certain. There was a demon who..." Suzuhah trailed off, as if unsure how to continue before letting out a long breath. "You know what? Don't worry about it. I'll mention it if we ever come across that demon. After all, that demon is long gone from these waters by now."

Milos watched the boy for a few minutes, finding himself somewhat relieved he was correct in his earlier assumptions, before he turned to the stairwell. "I won't ask any more questions on that subject. Just keep in mind what I said." He continued toward the stairwell and this time, Suzuhah didn't stop him as he descended downstairs.

He peered up the stairwell, listening before heading toward the girls' room. He briefly went into the engine room, where Ari was busily running around, steam filling the room, just like Suzuhah mentioned. He vaguely sensed the Aqua Wraith flitting from place to place, only forming for split seconds. It seemed that the steam was thinning and it was mostly under control. Ari wiped her brow before acknowledging

Milos, confirming his thoughts.

He waved before heading back into the girls' room. He noted it was empty except for Rita, who was seated to one side, brewing up some potions, from what he could tell. She gave him a tired nod, barely diverting her attention away. He let her be, continuing on, still keeping half an ear on the surroundings. No footsteps echoed from the stairwell, so he could only assume Suzuhah was *still* upstairs. His movements, careful as they were to make as little sound as possible, progressed him down the hall. Checking room after room left him once more wondering. Finally, he arrived in the men's room, noting that Alex was fast asleep, buried under the covers. The day stones lightly lit the room, casting shadows over the wall. The boy must have been exhausted from however he controlled the water, having collapsed right on top of the sheets. Milos didn't doubt he needed at least a quick nap to recover his energy.

The only problem was, that there were no signs of the little Suzuha.

"Wh...?" Alex's voice came out groggy, as he blinked and Milos winced. Guess the boy wasn't quite as out of it as he thought.

"Didn't mean to wake you," Milos noted, heading toward the doorway. "Go ahead and go back to sleep."

Alex shook his head. "No, it's fine. I shouldn't be napping. I just felt..." he trailed off.

Milos leaned against the wall, relaxed. "Don't worry about it, Alex. I could feel the magic you were using clear as day. In your human form, it took quite a toll on you. I'm surprised you are still awake."

"Oh." Alex let out another yawn. "Well, I mean, it's not too bad. Anyway, are you looking for something?"

Milos couldn't hide the amusement. Well, Alex wasn't necessarily wrong. "I'm looking for Suzuha." At his confusion, Milos elaborated. "The little girl."

He let out a quiet, "ah" in realization before swinging himself out of bed.

Milos rolled his eyes, walking back over. "I told you so you would know, not so you would join me to look for her. You're drained as it is." He didn't even have to check to see the water's magic desperately whipping toward Alex, his body shaking as it was. "You're not used to controlling water to that degree in your human form. You should be unconscious, as I said not even a minute ago."

Alex frowned, but eventually complied with a groan and sigh. "Fine." This time, he buried himself under the covers, tiredness fluttering across his face. "Just tell me when you find them, please?"

"They bother you as well?"

Alex only nodded, letting out another yawn before curling into the bed. Milos watched the light dance through the room as the boy's breaths evened out into the signs of a deep sleep.

Satisfied that Alex was actually taking his advice, Milos turned and left, closing the door carefully behind him.

The hallway was quiet, only the faint sounds of movement from above and the lapping of waves met his ears.

No footsteps sounded from the stairwell the whole time he was downstairs, and he knew that for a fact.

That, unfortunately, only heightened his unease. The little girl was small, easy to miss, but he was thorough. So, where was she?

He quickly peeked into the rooms once more, noting how quiet they were before heading upstairs.

Halfway up the stairs, he heard faint footsteps before someone came flying down. He flipped out of the way, catching the young girl's arm as she leapt past. She hung, letting out a pout as he set her down. Suzuha peered up at him.

"I thought you were going to catch me."

"I did." Milos tilted his head, knowing what the girl was talking about, but leaving it at that, hiding his moment of surprise behind a thin veneer of stoicism.

"Not like that." She huffed, arms crossed and chin down before she let out a sigh. "So, sorry I wasn't able to help earlier. It was scary, wherever we were, and I thought we were going to drown."

Milos shrugged, turning to face her. "It's fine to be scared." He was tempted to ask where her brother was, to see what she would say. He didn't ask the older Suzuhah earlier, but he decided to ask a two-fold question. "What about your brother?"

The girl hummed slightly before shrugging. "I think he's somewhere on deck? Don't know."

Milos frowned and noted he didn't hear anyone in the map room. He let out a breath. Suzuha's sudden appearance distracted him, it seemed.

"Plus, he puts on a brave face, but I think whatever that was frightened him as well." She smiled, a moment of calm overriding her demeanor before it promptly disappeared.

"Is that so?" Milos furrowed his brow, unsure of what to make of her response.

Those two were strange. The conversations he had with both of them cemented the fact. It was almost like they knew how the other was feeling, even though he was certain they never interacted with each other. Unfortunately, he wasn't sure what that meant or how it would help him. She perked up, peering up at him curiously.

"So, what are you doing? Eating? I'm quite hungry myself."

Milos nodded, unsure what to say to that. "Well then, the kitchen..."

"I can't reach it though." Suzuha walked down the steps. "With how the food is secured, it's too high for me."

Milos let out a sigh, following after the little girl. It was an obvious distraction ploy. Yet, he felt he probably wasn't going to be able to avoid it either way, so he didn't bother.

Heading into the storage room, he grabbed some vegetables and some dried meat, handing them over to Suzuha, who grinned, scooping them up before downing some. Well, guess he was going to have to keep an eye on her for a while.

The girl seemed to know that, taking her sweet time chowing down on her stick of dried beef as she gazed up at him curiously. "What were you doing?" She took another bite. "Brother said you were downstairs for a while."

Milos leaned against the door, his arms crossed. He thought carefully over his next words, keeping his senses open. There wasn't anything in the air, just the typical swirling of water and flickers of other things he couldn't quite name. Unfortunately, they were momentary at best. "I was searching for you." He decided to be blunt. He wasn't sure where or when his suspicions arose, but now that they were there, he couldn't ignore them.

The girl stopped eating and tilted her head upward. For a split second, her expression shifted to resemble her older brother's, eyes gleaming a bright gold as her lips shifted into a thin line, but it was gone as soon as it appeared. "For me?"

Milos withheld a frown, knowing for a fact he saw the expression. "Yes, since your brother was upstairs, after all."

Suzuha hummed, chowing down on another bite. "Are you sure you didn't miss me? I did sneak upstairs not that long ago." She hummed, a faint smile on her lips. "Sneaking around is fun, almost like playing hide and seek."

"Maybe I could have." Milos stepped away from the doorway, noting the way the girl watched him as she chewed at a carrot before breaking right through it.

"So, were you looking for me to play? I am getting quite bored."

Her words sounded strange to Milos' ears. For a split second, the voice was a little more neutral, less child-like.

He narrowed his eyes, confirming his suspicions. There was something up with this little girl, and he had yet to hear a thing from upstairs, no sign of her older brother.

Yet, they hadn't done anything.

"That's fine. Just stay close by to someone, we don't need anyone falling overboard."

"Are you worried about me?" She blinked, hands stilling, a started expression on her face. "Brother mentioned it earlier, but..."

"Not so much me, but the others would be," Milos admitted.

A flicker of annoyance was all he caught as the girl straightened, a faint smile forming on her lips. "That's fine. I'm going to take a nap now, is that all right?"

"It's still fairly earl—"

"But I'm tired," she whined, letting out a yawn that was too wide to be real. "Everyone else is either busy or sleeping themselves."

Milos hesitated for a moment before letting out a sigh. She wasn't necessarily wrong on that one.

He shrugged, keeping an eye on her as he led her back to the girls' room and watched, alongside a yawning Rita, as the girl crawled into her hammock and curled up on her side, facing them. Still as wary as the day before.

Rita glanced between them before she waved. "I'll keep an eye on her. That's what you were going to ask, right?"

Milos let out a quiet chuckle before nodding and turning.

That just left one thing.

Where was the older Suzuhah?

Chapter Seventeen

A faint humming reached Alex's ears as he struggled out of his sleep-induced haze. The boat rocked to and fro, as the weight of the blanket wrapped around him. He curled into the warmth, not sure if he wanted to wake up or not.

He felt a shift in movement and heard the faint sound of footsteps. He furrowed his brow before slowly opening his eyes, feeling a strong need to wake up. He jerked upward when gold eyes met his gaze from across the room. Male Suzuhah—he needed a better way to distinguish the two siblings—was seated on the floor, gaze on him before turning his attention toward the window. "So, you are up."

Alex blinked a few times, sitting up as the sheets pooled around him, rubbing one eye tiredly. "Suzuhah? What are you doing?"

Suzuhah hummed thoughtfully, but didn't respond for the longest time. Finally, he turned back to Alex with a faint smile. "Just wanted to check something, that's all. I didn't mean to wake you."

"Oh." Alex wasn't sure what to say to that. He swung his legs out of bed, still a little tired, but feeling like he'd been sleeping long enough at this point. "Is everything all right now? Do you need some help?" He couldn't suppress the yawn from escaping and quickly covered it as Suzuhah's head jerked in his direction.

"Ah, yeah, everything's fine." Suzuhah stared at him for a while, confusion and a hint of— was that frustration? —played over his face. He stood, pushing against the wall and walking over to the doorway, brushing past Alex. He paused at the doorway, staring at it for a while. Alex stretched and pushed himself to his feet, feeling his stomach growl. He winced and grinned sheepishly. "Hey, have you eaten?"

"Aren't you suspicious of me?"

The stark change in topic startled Alex, causing him to still. Suzuhah turned to him, the frustration now clear on his face. "I know your friend is, Milos, and I know the way you look at me and my sister. So why...?"

Alex paused, thinking over his response carefully before letting out a breath. "Well, to be honest, of course I'm suspicious of you." Suzuhah stiffened, yet Alex continued, "That doesn't mean I won't still try to be friendly with you or your sister. Milos has the suspicions covered, and I know you wouldn't hurt Rita." Alex couldn't help the smile from stretching over his face as Suzuhah shifted, seeming somewhat uncomfortable. "Basically, I can be suspicious, but still want to try to be your friend, right?"

"Not really." Suzuhah stared at him blankly and Alex shook his head.

"That's fair. I guess it's just me who thinks that. Maybe I'm just overly optimistic." He shrugged. "But to be honest, I would rather be optimistic, wouldn't you?"

Suzuhah opened and closed his mouth for a moment, lost, before he snapped it shut and turned to the doorway, opening it sharply. "Why can't you all just make sense?" He spoke harshly, but Alex noticed the faint fondness that trickled into his voice.

He chuckled. "It's more fun that way, to be honest." He followed after, keeping his attention on Suzuhah, but humming as he moved. Suzuhah quieted, glancing back at him with a narrowed gaze as Alex continued to hum, heading toward the kitchen. "Anyway, aren't you hungry? You've probably been up for a while, right?"

Suzuhah pursed his lips, before quietly taking a seat at the table. Alex didn't mind, he could feel Suzuhah staring at him, watching him.

Sure, he was a little uncomfortable, but when he turned to walk over to Suzuhah with two plates, one for each of them, he didn't miss the way Suzuhah gnawed on his bottom lip, fingers wrapping tightly around the spoon Alex handed to him.

"It would be easier if..." Suzuhah's voice, as faint as it was, trickled to Alex's ear, causing Alex to glance over. Suzuhah turned away, but ate the food, a grateful, "thanks," slipping from his lips.

Alex chuckled and dug into his food. He briefly wondered how the others were doing. What about Milos and Rita? Were Ari and Leon resting?

"The humming." Suzuhah stared at him in bewilderment for a brief moment before continuing, "No. Never mind." He turned his attention down toward his food, indecision flaring over his face. "It just reminded me of something, that's all."

Alex glanced over, spoon in his mouth as the soup sat on his tongue before he promptly swallowed. Alex frowned, unsure how to respond, before shrugging and digging back into his food. If Suzuhah wanted to talk, then he would, for now, he was just going to enjoy the quiet moment while it lasted. It felt like he rarely got any these days.

Suzuhah suddenly stood up, attention on everything but Alex. "I need to check on my sister."

Alex, startled, dropped his spoon with a clatter into the soup, some of the broth splattering over the table as Suzuhah, out of nowhere, rushed away.

Alex could have sworn he saw frustration and uncertainty on Suzuhah's face, but maybe it was just his imagination.

Alex let out a breath. As Suzuhah said, a lot of the people he knew were weird, he really should get used to it. Sure, he was a little jealous when Suzuhah first arrived, but he wasn't necessarily one to hold onto those feelings. Plus, the two hadn't really done anything and Suzuhah himself just seemed like he wanted to talk. Alex finished up eating and stood, putting the dishes away before going to check on the others.

He found Ari and Suzuha, the little girl, sleeping soundly in the hammocks. He wondered briefly if Suzuhah just said that as an excuse to get away. Considering how anxious he was, he probably would have woken his sister. Alex peered over the little girl, who was curled up tightly in the hammock and frowned as he noticed tears tracing down her cheek.

He hurried over, checking her, before realizing she was sound asleep, whatever caused her to cry seemed to be over, since she was sleeping peacefully. He frowned at the thought, but decided to let her rest.

He walked over to the engine room, opening the door enough to peek inside.

Rita sat there, letting out a long yawn as she twisted a control lever, the stones humming a little louder as a result.

"Oh, morning, Alex." She turned to him as she rubbed her face, as if still waking up. "Didn't realize you were up. Have you seen Milos this morning? I kind of just came right in here after grabbing breakfast, since Ari was fast asleep already when I woke."

Alex shook his head, finding himself a little worried. Milos had been staying up a lot the last few nights and, while Alex knew it was probably because of Suzuhah, he felt a little worried for Milos. "I'll go check on him."

"Please do." Rita let out another yawn, before stiffening. "Oh, and forget I said that."

Alex let out a quiet laugh as he closed the door. "I'll make sure to tell him," he called, hearing an angered growl from Rita as he moved away, chuckling as he went.

Well, guess he wasn't the only one worried about Milos. Passing through the quiet girls' room, he headed up the stairs. He passed a half-asleep Leon, who walked past with a heavy yawn. Alex watched him head toward the men's room, swaying slightly. He really did appear incredibly tired. Did he stay up all night? He doubted it. Milos wouldn't have allowed that.

Alex shook his head, before continuing his trek upstairs. The map room was empty, the only thing a little odd was the pile of maps covering one portion of the desk, around where he recalled the compartment was. The one Rita found. He shook it off, heading outside. The night stones were just starting to fade, trickling into day stones. Milos was at the wheel, checking the direction.

"You're awake."

"Yeah, not sure why. Anyway, how are you feeling?" Alex asked, examining Milos quietly. "You've been staying up a lot lately. Are you sure you're not pushing yourself?"

Milos' gaze flickered to Alex, narrowing just the slightest bit before he shook his head. "I will feel more comfortable once we're on land, or at least someplace safe."

Alex peered out over the water and decided he at least understood that much. While the ocean was calming for him, for the others, especially Milos who seemed to be almost overwhelmed, this place was nerve-racking.

As Alex listened to the waves, he noted the way Milos shifted, uneasy. Yeah, that matched with what he suspected.

"How far are we from the island?" Alex decided to ask.

Milos' gaze flickered to him as he stepped away from the wheel to the railing beside Alex, a comfortable distance between them. "Should only be a few more hours."

"I guess that's good. Maybe," Alex hesitated, he wanted to ask if he could practice with his wings, but...

"That would probably be a good place for you to train." Milos pushed away from the railing. "You are still weak with your wings. If the island provides any cover, it will be helpful."

"True," Alex trailed off, staring out over the water for a moment before turning to Milos. "Will you be helping?"

"I had intentions to, yes." He focused on Alex, confused. "I'm not sure why you are asking, though, we already discussed that."

"Well, yeah, but I know you've been going non-stop. Shouldn't you rest a bit once we get there?" Alex pointed out, leaning against the railing as well.

Milos paused, examining him quietly before shaking his head. "I'll be fine. Once we get to the island, we can restock and reorganize. I do want to get back to training everyone and keeping to a schedule. I'll have to change it, now that Suzuhah and his sister are here, but..." Milos paused before continuing, "Nothing for you to worry about."

Alex huffed, but didn't argue. "Do you want me to take over for you? I mean, I know you just took over for Leon, but..."

"For Leon?" Milos frowned. "I took over for Leon a couple hours ago, he should have been in bed already."

Alex stilled, thoughts flickering as he recalled Leon's tired form stumbling down the stairs. "I just saw Leon go downstairs. I passed him on the way up."

Milos' expression shifted, before settling on concerned. "I thought he headed downstairs." He pursed his lips, worry flashing over his face. "Could it...he wouldn't have collapsed in the map room because I would have heard it."

Right, that could have happened. Alex shook his head. He walked over to the front of the ship, sitting down. He was still tired, but for some reason, he felt safer up on deck with Milos than in the bedroom. He knew he should probably check on Leon to make sure he was fine, as well as maybe Suzuhah, but...

He also wanted to observe Milos to make sure the man didn't overexert himself.

Alex wouldn't be surprised if he did.

Milos noticed the concerned expression on Alex's face as he settled against the headpiece of the ship. Milos walked back to the wheel, checking the compass once more as his thoughts flickered. Alex's words confused him more than he cared to admit, and worried him.

He had sent Leon to bed a few hours ago and he was positive he heard him head downstairs. Though he could be wrong. The wind stones strengthened for a moment, pushing them faster through the water, distracting him. Still, there wasn't anything he could do about that.

He frowned, thinking through what he knew. He had yet to spot anyone else besides Alex. He should probably check on the others.

"Status report," Milos said as he flipped up the communication tube that connected to the engine room. In the distance, seen a little clearer now that the day stones were out, was the beginning form of an island, the shape indistinct at their distance, but steadily coming closer.

"Everything's normal. Good to hear you are actually doing your job. Was wondering about that."

Rita? What was she doing in there? Milos thought before saying, "What happened to Ari?"

"She was already asleep when I woke up. I kind of just came in here when I realized there was no one operating it."

Milos stilled. Already asleep? How? "Rita, is Suzuha in the room with Ari right now?"

"Uh, yeah? Why?"

"Can you check on them both, please?" Milos heard a sharp intake of breath as he tried to connect what he knew. Alex stated that Leon just went downstairs and Rita was in the engine room which meant that no one was paying attention to either Suzuhah. To be honest, that unnerved him, more than he would like to admit as a name flashed through his mind, but it just as quickly disappeared. He growled in frustration. He heard about this before.

"Milos?" Alex watched him curiously, that concern still on his face as the young man observed him quietly, once more back on his feet. "Is everything all right?"

Milos' gaze flicked to Alex, but his attention was pulled away when Rita responded, "Huh...Ari's here, but Suzuha is gone. I wonder where she went."

Rita's voice caused Milos to stiffen as his thoughts slammed to a jerking halt.

"Do you mean that no one on this ship has seen either Suzuha?"

The way Alex stiffened behind him caused Milos to stare at the boy.

"Suzuha was in the room with Ari before I came upstairs and I was talking with her brother not long before that."

Milos frowned. "You didn't see them together, correct?"

Silence invaded the air from both sides as Alex frowned in contemplation.

"So, you noticed too. I guess I'm not surprised." Rita's voice echoed through the pipes as Alex said, "Now that you mention it..." at the same time.

Milos wondered what that meant when none of them could recall seeing the two siblings at the same time.

"Rita, can you keep watch on Ari for me? I'm going to go downstairs to check on a few things. Alex, do you mind staying up here and keeping watch?"

Alex blinked, startled at the sudden change in Milos. He nodded.

"Don't worry, I can take care of everything up here."

Milos hesitated for the briefest moments before shooting a small, but grateful smile toward Alex and, making sure the pipe was closed, raced to the map room, spreading his senses out wide.

He needed to find those siblings quickly. They weren't far from the island now, maybe only an hour or two away at best. Considering how both siblings were missing, he felt something bad was going to happen, and quite soon. He needed to figure out what was actually going on and what exactly it was.

He was positive he wasn't going to like it.

Pushing the thought away, he slunk down the stairs, hand on the hilt of his sword. Senses pushed as much as possible. It hurt. The magic of the surrounding water pushed at him, battering at his thoughts, but he ignored it, focusing only on those on the ship.

The wood creaked under his feet as he listened quietly. Once downstairs, he headed toward the men's room. His breath was shallow, soundless as he moved forward, his footsteps lost to the creaking of the ship.

He stopped by the door, placing his ear carefully near the edge, listening. For a brief moment, he had a flash of déjà vu. He did this when chasing Alex almost a month ago. Trying to discover something that eluded him. This time, however, he didn't think he would hesitate to kill if need be.

Last time, he stayed his hand. He wasn't sure he could do that now, even if he tried.

He waited, noting how no sound slipped from the room. He shook his head and opened the door, quickly taking in the room.

Curled up on the floor, was Suzuhah, his head on the pillow Milos tossed him the other day. On the other side was Leon, his clothes somewhat ruffled as he lay on his back. Milos stepped in. As he did, his gaze narrowed.

He thought Suzuha would be in here, but it seemed that the little girl was not, but at least he found Suzuhah, the older brother. Unfortunately, it didn't relieve his wariness.

Milos walked over to Suzuhah, squatting next to him. No matter how he stared at the person before him, he could not figure out what his mind was trying to tell him. Suzuhah, the one laying before him, he was involved in what was going on with the ship, yet how?

He hovered a hand over Suzuhah's side, letting himself feel the air around them. He appeared to be asleep, but Milos knew that couldn't be true. Yet the air was relaxed, confirming his thoughts. This wasn't a demon.

"I don't know what you and your sister are up to, but don't think to try anything before or when we get to the island." Milos stared down, noting that Suzuhah didn't twitch at all during his words. "I hold no desire to hurt or kill unless necessary. As long as you and your sister don't try anything, I'll stay silent and let you continue to stay on this ship." He stood and walked over to Leon, keeping half an ear out for a response to his words.

Contrary to his earlier thoughts, he felt his words were true. There was no reason for him to kill anyone, especially a little girl. He wasn't going to jump to conclusions like he did with Alex.

When he didn't hear anything, he checked over Leon. Nothing appeared outwardly wrong with him, but Milos noticed the lack of energy falling off of him, the magic seeming almost dry and brittle.

What? He was perfectly fine earlier. Milos couldn't spot any injuries beside the obvious and nothing seemed to have changed. Yet, he was in more of a state of unconsciousness than sleep. It made no sense to him. He figured it was just Rita's medicine or something, but he still felt unnerved. He gave the room a cursory once-over again, noting Suzuhah's prone position before heading to the doorway. He would be back in a second, but he wanted to check on Ari.

He hurried over to the girls' room and peeked inside. He could see Ari off to one side, shuffling back and forth in the hammock with a grimace on her face. He stepped over, keeping some distance as he examined her. Like Leon, she was without injury, but also like Leon, the magic around her was brittle, frail. He almost didn't want to disturb it.

Something had happened to both of them.

He gritted his teeth and slipped out, examining each room as he went.

Reaching the end of the hall once more, he peered inside the men's room. Nothing changed. Suzuhah and Leon were both still fast asleep. Milos closed the door before leaning against the wall, thoughts going haywire.

The ship wasn't that big and yet...

Suzuha—the little girl—was nowhere in sight.

~ * ~

Rita's attention snapped up from perusing the engine, noting that the Aqua Wraith hadn't made an appearance this time. She frowned in thought as she flipped another switch, hearing the drone of the wind stones outside as she moved.

She peered into the girls' room, noting that Ari was curled up in the hammock, appearing almost worse for wear. That made no sense, considering the girl was finally getting a much-deserved rest. Rita did a quick once over of the machine to make sure it was running smoothly before walking over. She leaned over the hammock, taking in the girl's visage. She felt Ari stiffen slightly under her touch, but pressed on. That, more than anything, spiked her curiosity to downright worry, mentally remembering Leon's reaction was similar when she checked him the other day. There was nothing, no wounds, no fever, nothing. Yet, Rita could tell something was wrong, there was something missing. It didn't help that the girl barely reacted to her touch. This wasn't sleep. Something or somehow, she was knocked unconscious, and the why of it...

It bothered her to no end.

She let out a huffing breath. As much as it irked her, knowing there was something wrong, she also knew there was nothing she could do. She didn't recognize the symptoms or the condition she was in. It wasn't anything she knew about and she had a feeling she was missing something important. Something that would explain things to her. She heard a sound from the open door leading to the engine room and paused.

Right. She couldn't just stay here and watch Ari, no matter how much she might loathe the idea of moving away from her when she was like this, but...she turned and hurried over to the pipes.

"Rita?" Alex's voice filtered through the pipe, as sonorous as usual.

"I'm here," she called as she closed the door behind her, feeling unnerved at the idea of keeping it open. Whatever did that to Ari was probably still around. Until she knew what it was, she needed to make sure no one else caught it, she was going to be careful. "Need something?"

"Yeah, we're approaching the island pretty fast, can you cut the speed a bit and maybe wake the others?"

Rita paused, thoughts flickering. "I can't do much about the second part," she admitted as she worked to slow the wind stones, hearing their whine die down to a faint whisper. "Ari isn't..." She paused before letting out a breath. "She won't be able to do much right now and I'm not sure where the Suzuhahs are."

"Oh." Alex's voice sounded conflicted, a faint hum trailing down through the pipe. "All right, I'll let you know when we arrive, and tell you if we need to keep moving instead."

"Right." Rita grimaced. She was not in the mood for a repeat performance of the first island.

She was so lost in thought, the opening of the engine room door caused her to jump a good foot into the air. She whipped around before letting out a relieved breath, though she wasn't going to admit it. "Don't do that, you lout, you startled me."

Milos huffed. "I shouldn't have, I came in earlier. You just weren't paying attention, it seems." He stepped through the doorway, keeping it open. Rita noted that with a slight frown before glancing back at him.

"Fair. Anyway, Alex just mentioned we're almost at the island. We'll stop there for a short rest, then keep going, sound good?"

Milos nodded. His brow furrowed before he spoke. "That's fine." The pause caused Rita to stiffen uncertainly. "Be careful," he finally said, surprising Rita.

"You're warning me?" Rita leaned forward. "This must be serious if you of all people are warning me of something coming. Though you're being as vague as the Aqua Wraith right now."

Milos huffed, almost as if in agreement. "I have a feeling you wouldn't believe me if I mentioned my ideas. So, I'll just say, watch everyone. Ari and Leon are both unconscious from something and I can't find Suzuha."

"Really?" Rita questioned slowly, fear piling slowly into her veins as ideas clicked into place. "Both Ari and Leon?"

Milos nodded as Rita peered through the doorway, now understanding why Milos kept the door open.

It was to keep half an eye on Ari, like she *should* have been doing. "I'm guessing you're paying attention to the rest of the ship?"

"On this floor, at least." Milos nodded, as his gaze flicked to the engine. "Though I don't know what the goal is. The engine wasn't damaged and nothing else is out of place."

Rita gulped, not liking the sound of things. She shook her head, hurrying past him. "Well, let's go upstairs. I want to check on Alex and we are almost at the island."

Milos nodded as he followed her. She was fine with that, almost grateful to have him at her back. She noted as he glanced toward the men's room before they both hurried up the stairs.

If she guessed, Leon was in the same boat as Ari, which meant the only ones functioning right now were her, Milos, Alex and the Suzuhahs.

That was barely enough to help if the ship got in trouble at the new island.

Sure, she should probably stay in the engine room, but for some reason, an intense worry was pumping through her veins.

She had no idea why.

Chapter Eighteen

Alex raised his hand to his eyes. The island was becoming more distinct as they approached and, truth be told, he couldn't believe what he was seeing. The other islands were interesting, but usually nothing too big. This, however, was a piece of land that almost seemed to have been wrenched out of the southern parts of the Underlands and tossed into the sea with some vegetation. He couldn't see where the water even began to circle around and, he briefly wondered, if this was an island or the actual camp they were trying to get to. However, he trusted Rita, so this must have been just another place along the way.

He observed what parts of the coast were visible, the early morning light casting shadows over the rapidly distinguishing land. Scraggly trees and undergrowth dotted what was visible of the island, intermingled with chutes of rock. Thankfully, for his mind, he couldn't sense anything from the island that appeared to be out of place. In a way, it reminded him of the last island, at least in feel, if not size. It was rocky with almost no sand and there was a legit mountain in the center of the island, seemingly splitting it in two. He heard movement and glanced over as the door opened.

"Suzuhah?" Alex turned, curious as Suzuhah stared past him, peering at the island with a strange expression, his lips turning upward slightly. Alex's thoughts flickered to Rita's words. The older brother was here, but where was the younger sister? Speaking of him, there was a strange calm about the way he moved, as if he had come to some sort of decision. Alex frowned slightly as he watched Suzuhah.

"Oh, Alex, you're up here. Perfect," Suzuhah spoke, glancing over to Alex before walking over. "Thank you for the food by the way." Alex watched him warily as Suzuhah stopped right next to the railing, head tilted slightly. "You know, I haven't been to a new island in a while."

"Makes sense." Alex pushed away from the railing. "You were stuck on the previous one for a long time." He felt nervous as Suzuhah turned to him, curious. "Along with your sister. Where is she? Weren't you going to check on her?"

Suzuhah hummed, gold gaze piercing in the light of the day stones. "I did and she's here." He leaned back, still gripping the railing as he peered up at the day stones. "Speaking of, I have a question for you." With a sharp movement, he turned, catching Alex off guard. He took a step forward, almost looming. "Are you a demon?"

Alex froze, trying desperately to hide the shock. Suzuhah smirked and pulled back, arms crossed. Alex gulped, straightening himself to center his thoughts. "What are you talking about?" he cut in, a weak and thoroughly fake smile crossing his face. He never was one for lying and it was now biting him in the butt. "Why would you even think that?"

"I told Milos this a while ago." Suzuhah stepped away from the railing, circling behind him, causing him to stiffen. "There are certain demons...a certain demon, I suppose, that I want to see dead. I guess that feeling extends to that demon's kind as well."

Alex watched warily as Suzuhah circled him. Where were Rita and Milos? What the heck was going on with Suzuhah? "Okay? And? Why are you mentioning this now? That's something I think we all should know."

Suzuhah came to a halt in front of him, smiling serenely, almost as if he was ignoring Alex's words. "Sorry, didn't mean to scare you. I just wanted to warn you." He clasped his hands behind his back, swaying forward and backward as his gaze skipped to the island before returning to focus on Alex. "You know, you are not very good at hiding your heritage, to be honest. Not many humans talk about hearing a song while out at sea, nor should it have been possible to escape the stretch of ocean where barely a wave crests when those creatures are awake, nonetheless the ones that would capsize the boat." Suzuhah grinned as Alex tried hard to keep his expression in check. "There was also your, well, I would normally say quite beautiful humming, but I digress. As much as you try to hide it, for someone paying attention, well, I simply made a guess. After all, we are heading to a demon refuge, but the only other people on this ship are two slaves, a demon hunter and a witch."

Alex swallowed heavily and took a step forward, glaring at him. Though he couldn't put too much heat in the look. Suzuhah was so certain, but Alex tried to dissuade him. "Couldn't I be following Milos to hunt them?"

"No." Suzuhah shook his head, as he walked to one side, his fingers grazing over the wood. "They talked about you as if you are not a demon hunter. All three of you respect each other as comrades-in-arms, true, but..." Suzuhah hummed, the same tune Alex used that morning, causing Alex to stiffen. Something in him told him to run, to bolt, but he held still, where would he run? "In truth, both of them keep an eye on you, almost like guardians, not the other way around. You seem to know each other well."

Alex turned, unsure what to say to that, mainly because it wasn't necessarily wrong.

Suzuhah peered at him, a strange expression on his face. "So, we'll be landing soon. What are you going to do?" He spread his arms as he turned. "After all, you mentioned it yourself this morning, you're suspicious of me. No matter how friendly you might act, that fact won't be erased."

"That's true," Alex spoke, unsure of how else to respond, getting a smirk from Suzuhah before he continued. "But I can still try. I want to get to know people so I'm not suspicious anymore. Why would I push you away or throw you off the ship, along with your sister, if that was the case?" He shook his head. "It's human nature to be suspicious of new people who come into their lives, but it's also human nature to want to get to know those people and push past the suspicion, isn't it?"

Suzuhah stilled, staring at Alex with an unreadable expression. His arms slowly dropped to his sides as he spoke, voice quiet. "Why do you have to make this so difficult?" A hoarseness slipped into his tone, startling Alex.

"Huh?" Alex blinked, confused. He pushed off the last bit of conversation, finding himself almost annoyed at the constant change in topic. "Um...I'm not trying to make this difficult or anything." Alex floundered for a moment before stepping forward. "How about this. Just because you've figured something out doesn't mean I'll just ditch you or, well, your sister. It's not like you acted on that knowledge." Alex's attention drifted to the day stones glimmering softly overhead, a gentle warm glow.

Silence fell over the boat. Alex heard a strange sound, almost like a muffled choke. Suzuhah held a hand to his face, a strange smile curling over his lips, just visible under his palm. "You know, I'm not sure whether to call you blunt, strange, or both."

Alex felt affronted by that, but didn't comment.

"I thought you would keep denying it. That, well..." He spread his arms to either side, the smile widening. "That you would find it terrible that someone like me, a complete stranger, knows you are a demon. That someone like my sister and I can just waltz into your little party like it's no problem. Yet, again and again, you and the others keep surprising me."

Before he could say more, the door to the map room swung open. Alex and Suzuhah glanced over in time for Rita and Milos to barge onto the deck. Well, more Rita, Alex acknowledged. Milos was a few steps behind, arm resting lightly on the sword hilt.

Suzuhah's expression shifted, a strange resolution and almost madness sparked in his gaze as he stepped in front of Alex, intercepting Rita's racing figure. Alex took a step back, startled. Suzuhah bowed, dipping low as he faced Rita.

"You know, it's been a pleasure working with you. It's been a long time since I've been able to speak with another like my mistress." Suzuhah's voice was soft, almost solemn and heartbroken.

Rita slid to a halt, a few steps in front of him, apparently confused. Alex tentatively stepped to the side, only to stop as a hand extended out from Suzuhah, as if to block the way forward.

"You know, it took me a while to decide what to do, how to respond to you, having one of *them* on your ship." His gaze shifted to Milos, who stiffened. "One of the ones for whom I longed to see die by my hand."

"What are you...?" Rita's words were cut off as Milos raced forward, fingers curled around the hilt of his sword.

Suzuhah sharply turned to Alex as golden wings snapped outward, almost eclipsing the entire left side of the ship. "Demons like you have no right to talk about what it's like to be human. You and all of your kind are better off dead."

Alex yelped, trying to backpedal, only for his back to slam into the railing. A grunt sounded from the other side of the figure, followed by a startled cry as burning gold eyes glared down at Alex from a furred face.

Something sharp curled around Alex's body as he tried to lunge to one side. He coughed as the breath rushed out of him. Gold wings beat down, lifting them clear into the sky, shooting high at a speed that made Alex's head spin. A pained cry echoed from the creature as their flight upward staggered. Fear pounded in Alex's veins as he struggled to break free from the creature he recognized carrying him.

"A Vulfulas?" he gasped out as the creature curved upward, aiming away from the ship, the mountain getting closer and closer to Alex's panic as blood dripped down one wing.

"You mean a demon like you didn't realize?" The voice that echoed from the creature was androgynous at best. A strange, faint laughter without warmth vibrated from the creature's chest as Alex struggled. Pain flared up one side, where the tips of the claw curled around his body, just barely shredding part of his tunic.

He heard a faint cry from below that sounded like Rita, screaming his name. His mind was dizzy from the sudden increase of height and the pain.

"Damn that demon hunter," the Vulfulas whispered, pained as they almost seemed to sway in the sky. "I wanted you to die in the sky. The place you water demons so fear." Alex's mind whirled at the words even as he scrabbled at the freaking *steel* holding him. The Vulfulas dipped, barely dodging past the ragged peaks of the mountain as it almost tumbled, its words starting to slur. "I'm barely keeping us aloft. I won't let you go. I won't let any of your kind go." There was a long pause, a disquieting silence. "I need to see you dead myself." Those words sounded wrong in Alex's ears, almost choked.

If that was the case, why hadn't the Vulfulas dropped him yet? Alex peered down, feeling a little dizzy at the height as they swooped to one side of the lone mountain splitting the island.

He could feel his demonic side responding, struggling to come forth. A sharp scream echoed from his mouth as his wings slid out, only to crumble against hard flesh and bone holding him, shoved harshly against his back at an angle he knew they shouldn't be. Alex growled, glaring up at the Vulfulas, feeling the horns heavy on his head. His own claws scrabbled at anything they could reach.

What was he going to do? Why was Suzuhah...no, this Vulfulas doing all of this?

"At least tell me why," Alex shouted, pain staining his voice.

He wondered if the words were lost to the wind, but it appeared the creature heard him as it tilted its snout down to him, hovering in the air with powerful wingbeats.

There was a strange expression on its furred face, a moment of hesitation before the thing growled, "Because water demons are liars, creatures of deceit. Your kind murdered my mistress... my sister in all but name."

Alex had nothing to say to that, feeling an ache in his chest that had nothing to do with the pain thrumming through his body.

The Vulfulas shook its head, tail thrashing back and forth, curling close to Alex for a moment before whipping away. He could feel the skin of whatever was holding him flex, as if unsure whether to crush him or release him. If he didn't do something soon, he was going to die and yet...

If the Vulfulas really wanted to kill him, wouldn't he already be dead?

"Why aren't you letting me go?" Alex asked. The flight stuttered for a moment as the Vulfulas curved in a semi-circle, the tail just touching Alex's cheek. The Vulfulas stared down at Alex as he peered back up at the furred face. Eyes so similar to Suzuhah's it was uncanny peered down at him with a strange mix of emotions. "If you really want to kill me, then why haven't you?"

"Shut up," Suzuhah shouted, the male voice piercing through the air as the creature curved upward sharply. "Shut up, shut up, shut up! I have to do this for my mistress, don't you get that? I have to avenge her death and if that means killing any demon like the one who killed her, then so be it."

"Do you really believe that?" Alex shouted, his mind screeching at him to stay silent. Why was he even saying all of this?

Silence was the only thing he heard as the creature curled its tail around them. A moment of silence pervaded the two of them.

"I have to..." was the pained whisper that slid from Suzuhah's throat before they suddenly swooped downward, the Vulfulas tightening its grip on him.

His mind howled as a sharp crack sounded from behind him. He let out a high-pitched note, feeling it more than hearing it in his haze of pain as it rang over the surrounding island.

The Vulfulas dipped down even more, just skimming the mountain edge, startled by the note. It gave Alex enough time to glance down.

He could faintly spot Milos and Rita desperately racing to stabilize the boat as waves thrashed at the wood, seen even at a distance. He let the note continue, cresting as some of the water formed up, easier than in his human form. The Vulfulas seemed to realize and dived toward the island, as if trying to put the mountain between it and the water.

Something in Alex wasn't going to let that happen. He cut the note off and, like a switch, something snapped.

A loud thrumming screech echoed through the air as a spear of water pierced the undamaged wing, shattering and falling in sheets over the pair. The Vulfulas let out a pained cry, their flight corkscrewing. Alex struggled to pull from the creature's grasp. Yet, in the creature's pained thralls, the claw grasped tighter, piercing his side as fur smothered his body, pulled tightly into the creature's chest. Wings flared outward, the downward spiral halting for only a moment.

They plunged face first into the tree line. Branches cracked and splintered as they fell through.

At the last moment, Alex felt a shift, his body swinging upward. His mind screeched, expecting the inevitable pain of landing face first with the creature on top of him. Instead, he found himself slamming into something soft before the claw around his waist opened and he slammed into the ground, landing and rolling harshly onto his wing.

A loud *snap* sounded and he let out a cry as his wing twisted at an angle he was positive it wasn't supposed to go. Coughs slipped from his lips, racking his whole body, as he curled into the ground, his fingers digging into the dirt as he did everything he could to stabilize his breathing, barely noting the faint flash of light not far from him. Snapped twigs and branches cut into his side as he struggled desperately to sit up. His side ached something fierce, but it was dull in comparison to his wings.

It was all he could do not to cry from the pain.

He focused all his energy on calming down, on getting his breathing under control. It took much longer than he would like to admit before he could finally observe where they exactly landed. To his chagrin, all he could tell was that it was a small forested clearing. On one side, only a few feet away, was Suzuhah, or at least, the human-like form the Vulfulas seemed to have taken.

Alex found himself scrambling away, his feet digging into the earth as he pushed himself backward, stopping a moment later as dizziness overcame him, and his hand darted to his side. Warmth coated his fingers almost immediately and, he noted, he was still in demon form.

Maybe it would help speed up the healing process? He could only hope. As his senses slowly came back to him, he mentally checked himself over, even while he kept part of his attention on the battered and bruised Suzuhah. With the way Suzuhah had been holding him, the claws must have dug into his skin piercing into his stomach. Thankfully, it didn't feel like they went too deep. He wasn't even going to think about his wings, still remembering the snapping sound as clear as day. He felt the wings twitch at the thought, and it was all he could do to stop himself from crying out, fingers accidentally digging into his injured side. *Okay, note to self, don't move my wings unless absolutely necessary.*

Other than those two things, he was surprised to find himself unscathed, considering the height at which they fell.

He glanced over to Suzuhah, who still hadn't moved.

He also knew, with how they were flying and remembering how he was distinctly *under* the Vulfulas, he should have landed face first right into the ground.

So, why was Suzuhah the more injured of the two of them, sporting what appeared to be a broken arm, numerous cuts on both arms, and a hefty bruise to his face?

Water dripped down Alex's face as he observed Suzuhah, noting he was still not sitting up. Suzuhah was drenched from head to toe in water and speckles of blood.

Alex growled, his demonic side aching to lunge forward at the being before him, at the thing that caused him so much pain. He felt his claws twitch as he watched the uneven gasps falling from the boy's lips. His eyes were squeezed shut, teeth almost grinding through his jaw.

Alex forced his hand down, just sitting there, pulling his thoughts back together. He didn't move forward, but he didn't run either.

He knew he had every right to run, to get away from this thing that tried to kill him, but...

He let out a long breath, thinking over the last few minutes. There were too many inconsistencies, too many questions. Alex knew he wasn't strong and had no means of catching himself even with his wings if Suzuhah had decided just to drop him, or throw him against the wall. Not to mention...he recalled the creature summoned lightning on the last island. It would have been so easy to have just electrocuted him.

"You cushioned my fall, didn't you?" he found himself asking as he stared at Suzuhah, remembering how the creature twisted at the last moment, how he landed into the soft underbelly of the creature before hitting the ground, instead of just plowing straight into the earth.

He heard a quiet groan and realized he needed to make up his mind and now. He didn't know how dangerous this place was or what to expect from it.

To his surprise, it wasn't as hard to decide as he thought, but he did find himself amazed at how easy it was to make a decision. A decision not influenced by anyone or anything else.

It was surreal, thinking about it later, but at the time, he didn't care.

He pulled himself over to Suzuhah's prone form, straining slightly as his muscles ached from the crash. He could mentally hear Rita yelling at him, screaming at him to go the other way, away from the person who just tried to kill him.

He was just tired of that. He ran when the Martinets attacked his home. He ran when Ame was dragged away for something he didn't want to think about. He ran, causing Rita's parents to die. He was always running.

Plus, if Suzuhah wanted to kill him, he would have. He was now certain of that.

What he wasn't certain of was *why* Suzuhah decided to spare him when there was obviously so much rage and hurt.

A faint smell of water and fresh wood met his nose as dirt clung to his skin. This island was as fertile as the last, though now he was certain that it was a hell of a lot bigger.

As he appraised Suzuhah, he realized the damage done to the wings ended up translating to Suzuhah's arms.

Maybe that's why Alex was still in his demon form. He wouldn't want to imagine what a broken wing would do to him in human form. Still, some of the wounds seemed pretty serious and Alex found himself wishing Rita was there, only to push the thought off. Knowing those two, they wouldn't be nearly as patient as he was being right now.

"What?" the boy choked out, eyes fluttering open in confusion and resignation.

"What am I doing?" Alex asked, pulling back so that Suzuhah had a clear view of him. He stared into Suzuhah's startled gaze. "Making sure you don't die. That's what I'm doing." He shrugged, examining Suzuhah closely in order to pick which of the larger wounds decorating the boy's arms to wrap with what little he had on hand. "Believe me, I'm still pissed as all hell that you tried to kill me." Alex glared down at Suzuhah, causing the boy to flinch. "But I'm not so heartless to leave someone to die if I can help it. Plus, once you feel better, I won't feel as bad giving you a piece of my mind at that spectacularly stupid stunt." He groused, pain flaring up his side. "Your claws hurt. I swear they were made of steel."

Whether he was talking at this point to Suzuhah or to himself, he wasn't quite sure. Suzuhah didn't seem to mind, just watching in silent wonder and wincing every so often as Alex worked.

Suzuhah blinked, faint tears disappearing as he chuckled, the sound throaty and miserable. "I thought this might happen."

"What, you trying to kill me, or me trying to save you?"

"Yes." Suzuhah smiled faintly, a soft and sad expression. "You have no reason to, after all. And, no, I didn't roll over for you. It just would have hurt landing on my claws, that's all."

Alex knew what Suzuhah said was a lie right away. Considering the way, they landed, it would have forced Suzuhah to hit the ground with his wings first. However, Alex didn't argue the fact, he just continued to work, "If you want to know, the main reason I'm doing this right now is because I can't stand the thought of someone dying in front of me." He shrugged.

"Even someone who tried to kill you?"

"You didn't do a very good job of it." Alex grinned, only to grimace as his thoughts flicked to Milos. Honestly? This felt almost familiar. "We need to figure out where we are. Rita and Milos are probably having a fit. Can you stand?"

"Can I stand?" Suzuhah's words were deadpan. "Yeah, just let me make sure my body isn't completely numb with pain after you and your demon hunter friend skewered my wings. You yourself somehow managed to scratch up my arms to ribbons and..."

"Okay, I get it." Alex sighed and squatted back down next to the startled Suzuhah, pulling an arm up, around his neck. Did Alex and Milos really do that much damage? His wings fluttered to remind him, quite painfully, that, yes, they had. At least in his case, they were only sprained, a lie, and he had enough energy to keep them out so they could heal. Obviously, Suzuhah wasn't able to. Suzuhah let out a yelp, before slumping against his side as Alex stumbled back to his feet.

Thankfully, Suzuhah was fairly light.

"Here," Suzuhah's voice was faint. Alex glanced over, only to almost drop Suzuhah when the body shifted, shrinking in the blink of an eye.

The little girl glanced up at him with a dull expression and Alex felt like he was stabbed. "So, you really have been..."

"I've been all three the whole time. It's a wonder none of you realized earlier." Her voice chimed faintly over the clearing as her arms draped around his neck. "Though, no, your friend Milos did figure it out, just a little too late."

Alex tentatively picked her up so she could sling her arms over his neck. Thankfully, she was even lighter in this form, so easy to carry in his arms. He would have put her on his back, but his wings didn't exactly allow that.

Milos figured it out? It made sense. The man was acting weird for the last little while. At least he now knew the man wasn't hurt or stressed in some way.

He felt a gentle touch and jerked, tilting his head just enough to spot as Suzuha reached up to touch one of the wings that fluttered closer to her fingers, examining his wings with a strange air of curiosity. "So, you aren't fully a water demon." Her gaze blinked blearily, on the verge of sleep. "I'm glad. Still, why are you so nice to a complete stranger? What are you?" Before Alex could respond, he felt the weight increase, Suzuha slumping over his shoulder, unconscious.

Alex stared for a moment before hefting her and picking a direction where faint humming sounded.

He would have called out, but his throat hurt and he had a feeling he would rather save his energy for now.

Hopefully, he would come across Rita or the others soon.

Chapter Nineteen

The only thoughts thrumming through Rita's mind were about Alex as she landed on the island. Milos was already a few steps ahead of her. The man was nursing a slight limp from having been thrown across the deck by the impact of Suzu...no, the Vulfulas' tail. Rita mentally cursed. How did she miss that? She was a *witch*. She should have been able to sense Suzuhah was a Vulfulas. How did she not see it? Did she simply delude herself?

She peered back up to the ship in time to spot the vague form of the Aqua Wraith. She looked haggard, almost stumbling as she leaned against the railing. She nodded down to Rita before disappearing through the floorboards.

The Vulfulas must have been draining magic. That's probably what happened to Ari and Leon. She wished she could do something for them, but honestly? The only thing she could do was let them rest.

No, her main priority was to find Alex and make sure he was okay.

Or, well, alive.

Milos must have noticed her train of thought as they hurried off the rocky coast and into a scraggly set of trees. Leaves crunched under her feet as he said, "He's still alive."

Rita glanced up, noting Milos' narrowed gaze, fingers curling tightly on the hilt of his sword, almost as white as her own skin. "I can sense the magic. He's still in his demonic form, so it's not nearly as hard to trace, even if it is hard to follow."

"Oh, thank Killah," Rita muttered, adjusting her satchel as she hurried forward, dodging around the scraggly trees. "Why is he still in demonic form?" She voiced the question out loud. Milos shook his head.

"Unfortunately, it feels like they crash-landed on the other side of the island. We don't have the manpower, the strength, or the time to bring the ship around. We'll have to cut through." He peered toward her. She noted his gaze was sharp. "We don't know what's on this island, so keep your voice low. We don't want to attract attention if we can help it."

Rita nodded, following his footsteps as they wove through the landscape. In some ways, the island faintly reminded her of the previous. While the last felt like a tropical paradise, this one...this one was a bit calmer. More reminiscent of the Underlands. Rocky hills pierced into the sky as scraggly trees started to grow thicker and heartier the deeper they moved through the island. Cliff faces cut out the view to the other sides of the island, making her wonder if there was even a place to land elsewhere. She could spot an animal or two scuttling through the undergrowth that coated the ground.

She stayed a few paces behind Milos, annoyed at the situation and at herself. Suzuhah showed signs of being a Vulfulas long before this incident. If only she paid closer attention. She was a witch. She should have known. How could she be so stupid?

"Wait." Milos extended a hand out, stopping her in her tracks and jerking her thoughts to a halt as he peered around.

She wanted to ask, but held her tongue. Milos was usually a very good judge when it came to situational awareness. She peered to either side of the little animal path they were traversing, hand drifting to her satchel. She had a couple bottles that held poisons she made from the last island, but she would rather not use them. Milos grasped her wrist and tugged sharply, leading her to one side of the path, out of sight. She wanted to protest, but froze when she heard footsteps.

She carefully peered around the tree, noting Milos watching from around the other side, hidden by the undergrowth.

The footsteps clanked louder and louder, confirming her thoughts. There were people on the island.

She just wasn't sure if they were demons or humans, or if they were even friendly.

She gulped, the noise sounding loud in her ears as three men and a woman, all dressed in furs and plantlike material, came around the bend. The woman held a bow while the men all held spears. A faint hint of something gleamed in the woman's ears, an earring? Rita watched them, staying low.

Wind whistled past her ear, freezing her in place, an arrow embedding itself within an inch of her foot. A startled squeal sounded a little to her right, a small animal she couldn't identify bursting out of cover and racing away.

The woman clicked her tongue. "I'm getting jumpy."

"Makes sense with flying demons landing on our island." One of the men spoke up, his voice gruff as he hefted his spear, stopping to turn to the lady.

Rita was still in shock as the woman dropped the bow to her side, fingers sitting lightly on the string. "Not what the Allegons would say."

"We're not Allegons, now let's get a move on. We need to find out how they got here, especially if they were injured." A third man spoke, his tone level and cold. He turned, continuing down the path. The others followed soon after.

Rita wasn't sure how long she sat there, holding her breath. It was when Milos shifted that she finally gulped down air, coughing slightly to catch her breath. "What?"

"Islanders. I should have expected," Milos cursed. "They are heading right to the boat."

"That's not good," Rita muttered, pushing herself to her feet. "Ari and Leon are still out for the count and..."

"We can only hope that the Aqua Wraith brought the boat out of sight. She probably knew about the islanders anyway. We need to find Alex and get ourselves out of here."

Rita nodded, hurrying after Milos as her thoughts whirled. They should be close to the demon's refuge, so why would there be humans, even here, who would want to kill them? Were they just simply afraid? Was it something else?

Rita didn't know, but it made her more worried about Alex's safety. She could only hope he was okay.

~ * ~

Alex stumbled to a stop by a small river, letting Suzuha off his back. He pulled himself over to the river, listening to its faint humming with relish as his tail curled around his leg. He wasn't sure if it was supporting him or merely from nerves. Now that they were out of the clearing and in a relatively safer area, he undid the belts and lifted up his tunic.

Maybe he shouldn't have walked with holes in his side, he noted as he cupped some water from the stream and splashed it over the wound to try to clean it.

To say it stung was an understatement. He hissed through his teeth as he let his hand dip into the water once more.

Thankfully, the water was helping to seal the wound, probably enhancing his demonic side or something. He wasn't about to begrudge a gift like that. Once he managed to wash most of the blood off, he turned his attention to Suzuha.

It was then when it finally hit him exactly what he'd done. Sure, he made decisions in the past, but many of them were more reasons for doing what he was doing than decisions.

This time, however, as he sat next to the river, thoughts focusing on the last few minutes, he realized the choice he made earlier was fully his. He tilted his head down, staring at his hands in shock. Usually, he left the difficult decisions up to others. Milos' strength and Rita's wit were some of the things that helped him to move forward, to come this far. Sure, he influenced them somewhat, but most of the decisions were made by other people.

He had no reason to save Suzuhah earlier, he could have just as easily decided to walk away and yet...as he thought back on it, he realized that his mind already decided for him.

He was grateful he hadn't been paralyzed by indecision, but it was mind-boggling how easy it was to decide something like that.

He tilted his head up, noting the way Suzuha was curled up on her side, shivering. He wondered if it was from shock. Suzuha's gaze drifted to him, wearily. "Ah...water, fitting." She chuckled that same guttural and miserable sound, unable to move more than her head, her arms damaged and twisted as they were. Alex knelt beside her, his tunic falling back into the place, covering the wounds.

To be honest, he felt almost relieved to be without the belts, though he didn't know why. "We need to get you cleaned up."

"I'll be fine." Suzuha paused before groaning. "Okay. That was a bald-faced lie."

Alex gave a weak smile before extending a hand. "Can you do it?"

"No." The girl sighed and took a deep breath. "Hold on, let me make this a little less awkward."

Alex stopped, watching in morbid fascination as her body lengthened, shifting and almost snapping into place, thankfully without said sound effects. Finally, Suzuhah lay before him, a quiet groan slipping from his lips. "God, that hurts."

"Well, you're talking, that's good." Alex helped him lay out next to the stream, grabbing a few nearby plants and moss to help support his head before pulling off the tunic and pants. Of course, Suzuhah's actions just raised more questions, but Alex decided to just push them to the side for now. He had bigger things to worry about. As he suspected, wounds marred the boy's arms and chest, considering he wasn't wincing, it seemed that his back hadn't gotten too badly affected, which was a bit of a surprise, considering how they landed. Alex cupped some water, gently cleaning the wounds with a corner from Suzuha's already blood-stained tunic, now that he had more time on his hands. There wasn't much point fixing it, so he might as well use what was still clean to...well, clean. Thankfully, as he brushed away the dirt, mud and blood, he was able to tell he had overreacted. The wounds weren't as bad as he thought. They definitely could have been much worse. They were not that great though, and he was really wishing Rita was around at that moment. He should have paid closer attention to her talks.

He delicately used his claws to rip the tunic into pieces, wrapping them securely around the boy's arms and chest before helping him back into his trousers.

"Sorry, I'm not exactly a medic, that's more Rita's area of expertise, but at least you won't be bleeding out anymore." Alex stood, heading a few paces away so he was right next to the stream, letting his claws graze into the water. His tail slowly swished back and forth behind him as his wings tried their best to stay in one place, failing at times. He winced as they fidgeted, resettling on his back. He would really have to get those checked out. He let out a yawn, feeling exhausted. He felt like he had been on an adrenaline rush for a couple hours now and being in demon form for this length of time, or more than a few minutes, was surprisingly tiring.

Now that he actually thought about it, why didn't he return to his human form? He reached his hand over to the belts, slapping them back into place before stretching out his claws. Thankfully, with some experimentation, he realized he could switch between them being sharp or dull, similar to deciding whether to use a finger or the fingernail, though he hadn't quite figured out how to get rid of them entirely. It was a weird concept, but at least he could touch things without fear of always cutting them. Next, he took a deep breath and tried to think of turning human. He didn't mind being in demon form, but he still, even now, felt more comfortable as a human. He took another deep breath, staring at the water as he focused inward.

He wasn't sure what happened. One moment, he was sitting near the edge of the water, the next, he was writhing on the ground. His mind screamed and cried and he wasn't sure which part he was doing out loud. Pure torture echoed through his body, loud and clear as he dug into whatever he could get his hands on.

"Return to demon form," a weak voice called, barely piercing through the haze. "You still have energy. Do it now." Alex wasn't sure if he heard it or not, his mind screaming at him that something was wrong. Very, very wrong.

He gripped at his demonic side, hearing the humming pierce upward before finally settling into an even tone. He let out a long breath, his tail curling so tightly around his waist he could barely breathe. His wings fluttered against his back as he opened his eyes, not even realizing he closed them to begin with. His arms were extended limply in front of him, and, a few paces away was Suzuhah, on his elbows, dragging himself forward. Suzuhah took one look at him and frowned. "You aren't used to changing forms, are you?"

"Why would I be?" Alex couldn't help but grunt out, tingles of agony still tracing up and down his spine. "What...?"

"Your demon form has been suppressing the pain neurons in order to focus on healing itself. All the parts injured are still intact, so it is able to communicate to the body what needs to be fixed." Suzuhah lay down, arms supporting his head, seeming tired from trying to drag himself over. "When you switched to your normal form, those same receptors were now gone. The body, unsure of what to do, but knowing it was still damaged, moved the damage to areas that were left, causing an increase in splintered neurons and, as a result, pain. To be honest, if I had the strength, I would be in my Vulfulas form right now." He winced. "Thankfully, I guess, I'm more used to dealing with that in all my forms."

How could you get used to that? Alex grimaced, firmly noting to himself never to do that again. He paused on that thought, frowning. "Wait, what do you mean you would be in your Vulfulas form? Why can't you switch to that form but have no problem switching between male and female?"

Suzuhah stayed still for a long moment, making Alex wonder if he fell unconscious, before responding, "My Vulfulas form takes a lot more of my energy, since it is bigger and a different shape altogether." Suzuhah turned his head slightly and Alex noted that the shaking seemed a bit worse. "Whereas my human forms are simple changes, nothing drastic, thus barely needing energy to sustain or commit to." He rested his head on his hands. "Truth be told, the pain you were just experiencing? I know it all too well, but there is nothing I can do about it with the energy I have now." His gaze turned away from Alex, attention drifting into the forest. "I need more energy, I need to eat, but that's not something I can do right now." He paused before laughing, the sound ringing off through the trees. "It's not something either of us can do right now, to be frank."

Alex sat in silence, watching as Suzuhah turned his gaze back on him. Alex furrowed his brow, leaning forward slightly. "So, the pain I felt earlier..."

"I'm feeling right now," Suzuhah spoke, the sound guttural and, now that Alex was listening for it, agonized.

Alex wasn't sure what to say to that, or even what to do. To think Suzuhah was able to talk and interact with pain at the level that he experienced just a few short moments ago was both astounding and disconcerting.

What did someone have to deal with to be able to handle that sort of pain?

Still, Alex supposed that Suzuhah didn't need to tell him this, nor did he need to try to help him by doing the equivalent of shouting the advice. He could have just left Alex thrashing and weakened and yet, once again, he didn't. It made Alex briefly recall the short conversation they held in the sky, the way Suzuhah was almost on the verge of crying even though Suzuhah appeared to have already made up his mind.

He decided to switch to a different thought. At least if he went from human to demon, he didn't have to worry, since he was adding. Going from Demon to Human? Just the thought sent a shiver down his spine as his wings, once more, reminded him of their damaged state. "So that's why..."

"That's why I can barely move two feet, even though all that was damaged, truthfully, were my wings." Suzuhah left out a breath as he supported his head on his crossed arms. "Which is why I was grateful when you carried me. I wouldn't have been moving at all and would definitely be dead unless I got incredibly lucky." Suzuhah smiled morosely. "Not that luck has ever been on my side, it seems."

Alex frowned, but didn't respond. He wasn't sure what to say to that. He let out a breath and glanced around the little clearing. He was exhausted just from the short walk and, truth be told, he was lost.

It wasn't a new feeling for him. He wished he could avoid it. He tried to relax, listening to the water as Suzuhah rested off to one side, appearing to have fallen asleep. How the boy could fall asleep so quickly and easily was beyond him, especially with what he just learned. However, he supposed Suzuhah desperately needed it, so it wasn't too far-fetched. He listened to the water, it was quiet and peaceful, flowing gently over the landscape. He couldn't quite tell what the source was, but it appeared to be funneling off the island and into the surrounding waters.

Was there a spring in the middle of the island or something? He almost wanted to follow it to the spring, but he figured the better option would be to head toward the ocean. He would have more of a chance of meeting up with the others at the beach.

Still, where did they land? He wasn't able to tell when they were free-falling and he was too panicked before that point to pay attention. He was regretting it now.

He heard the snap of twigs and stiffened, head snapping up as he listened quietly.

He noticed Suzuhah stiffen beside him, one eye peeling open in silence. Right, Suzuhah might know something about this island as well. Alex didn't know much about Vulfulas and Suzuhah didn't seem to be in the talking mood at the moment.

He slowly stood up, tail curling behind him as his wings fluttered. He held back a wince, keeping his attention on the surrounding environment.

He heard the snap of a twig and a soft gasp to his left. He whipped that way, crouching onto all fours in the same movement. Through the trees, he saw a young woman. She was incredibly pale and thin. She wore a simple dress without any ornaments and her attention was glued to Alex's horns. Her head slowly tilted down, watching him in horrified fascination.

He slowly sat up, noting that the woman was carrying a woven basket and not doing anything overtly suspicious.

"I'm sorry." She suddenly bowed her head, startling Alex. "I was unaware a Demon such as yourself was in our midst. Please forgive my rudeness."

Huh?

"Great. The Allegons," Suzuhah muttered with a hint of dismay, letting out a quiet breath. "At least I know where we are now."

Alex wanted to ask him the specifics, but the girl was now closer, her gaze flitting to Suzuhah. "Is that your prey?"

Alex stiffened and withheld a glare, though he was unable to control his tail and wings which whipped and fluttered in respective agitation. The woman seemed to realize and backed off, bowing her head once more. "My apologies. Come, my village is close. We will do all we can to aid you and your ilk."

Ilk? Alex decided not to ask, hesitantly moving closer to Suzuhah. It was better than walking around aimlessly, he supposed.

"I forgot about this," Suzuhah muttered drowsily. "Most aren't bad, but..."

"Oh, great," Alex muttered as he helped Suzuhah up. Strangely, this time, the boy didn't change into his child form. Alex would have asked, but decided not to bother as the woman came closer, tentatively helping to support Suzuhah from the other side.

Alex didn't, however, miss the way Suzuhah flinched in her grasp.

He watched hesitantly before following the woman's lead. She led them through the small forest, and this time, Alex actually got a chance to observe the environment. He was still hurt, sure, but he was at least going somewhere that was probably relatively safe.

He peered around in a hint of wonder. He saw a lot of lush wildlife and trees while on the previous island and, truth be told, he would have explored more, if not for Rita's and Milos' insistence. Of course, the whole Suzuhah and the Vulfulas affair cut the rest of their exploration short as well.

So, to now be able to immerse himself in wilderness he didn't know was possible in the Underlands. He couldn't stop staring.

"It's only a little farther, gentle Demon."

"Ah, my name's Alex, actually." Alex glanced over to the woman, peering around Suzuhah.

"My apologies, gentle Demon." The woman attempted to bow her head, only to stop, as if just remembering the person suspended between them. "It is dishonorable to be so informal around one of your stature."

Alex nodded reluctantly, not sure what to say to that. Why was she calling him "gentle Demon" anyway? The only demons he knew of, well...his thoughts flickered to his mother, the blood dripping from her claws, even though he hadn't known at the time it was her. He shook his head, shifting Suzuhah slightly.

That reminded him. He would have to thank Suzuhah later for

helping him when he transformed, though that was going to be more than a little awkward. He wasn't just *ignoring* the fact Suzuhah tried to kill him. In fact, he admitted to himself, he was still wary around the boy, even now. Yet he doubted he would have done anything differently. It wasn't necessarily in his nature to kill.

His gaze flicked to his wings. Whenever he was in demon form, the urge was not as easily suppressed. Every other time, his thoughts were narrowed, focused on one goal or idea, it was only after he was forced to change in the Martinet's base that he started being able to think a little more freely during his transformations. Either that or it could also be because he was no longer trying to push his demonic side away. He wasn't necessarily embracing it, he wasn't sure if he would ever really fully get used to it, but he could at least accept it. He heard a quiet trill of delight thrum through his veins and he pursed his lips. It wasn't a separate entity, nothing like that, no. It more felt like another part of him he'd never met before. A part that was more instinctually driven. He never noticed it before, but now, while he was forced to remain in his demon form to heal, he noticed his mind was much calmer, almost serene. It felt like he wasn't straining, or exhausting himself.

No. He felt like he was...normal? He felt his tail swish behind him before curling around his leg, his wings fluttered slightly, catching the other two's attention. He shook it off, turning to the woman. "How far are we going?"

"We're almost there, just a little farther down the river path," she spoke, gesturing ahead with her free hand.

Alex nodded, deciding to just focus on getting to a safer location. He was tired, even with the demonic side of him helping to keep him invigorated.

Thankfully, it wasn't much later when they came upon a set of gates. A stone wall, much to Alex's surprise, circled off into the tree line and two guards stood to either side of the simple wooden gate. The woman glanced at Alex briefly before pulling away and walking up to one of the guards, speaking quietly to him. Even for Alex, her tone was low, so she was probably aware of his sharper hearing.

Suzuhah grunted quietly, a hint of fear in his face. "Just try not to make too much of a racket." He kept his voice low. There was a tremor Alex wasn't used to in his words. Alex pursed his lips, unsure what to say to that. His demonic half was trilling that everything was all right, yet the more human side of him was uneasy and he wasn't sure why.

Chapter Twenty

Milos frowned, noting a waft of energy slipping through the trees. It was momentary at best before disappearing. Part of him wanted to head toward it, but another part told him to follow the path. They needed to know more about this island before they ended up running all over the place. He also briefly noted Rita seemed a bit tired. The day stones gleamed overhead, a wash of color over the surprisingly lush landscape. His thoughts briefly flickered to the ship and he frowned slightly. He wished he had some means of communication down here. It was more than a little frustrating how lacking the Underlands were in that regard.

"I'm worried about the others." Rita's voice caught Milos' attention as she peered over the landscape. "Ari and Leon are both incapacitated, Alex is nowhere to be found with a creature that tried to kill him and I'm stuck with you..."

"Yes, very comforting," he noted without even looking in her direction. "I know it's difficult to work with me, but..."

"Sorry." Her apology caused Milos to twist sharply, startled. "I really shouldn't lash out at you like that. I know you are worried as well," She trailed off.

A moment later, her brow furrowed and her gaze turned distant, she paused in her movement, arms still at her side as she slumped amongst the bushes.

Milos, recognizing the movement, stilled and waited. After only a few seconds of silence, she promptly shook her head and let out a breath of relief.

"What did you see this time?" Milos asked, noting the faint smile on her lips.

She turned to him, smile widening slightly. "I'm not sure, really,

240

but it was comforting. All of us were on our way back to the ship with Ari and Leon both awake. Suzuha was there as well." she paused. Her brow was furrowed. "The little girl, I think? Well, I'm not sure how comforting that is, but..."

Milos shook his head, unsurprised. "If Alex survived, Suzuhah probably did as well and you know, as well as I do, that Alex is too soft for his own good."

Rita nodded, before a faint frown graced her lips. "All of my other future visions...they've been omens of bad things, of something coming. To be honest, this one just seems too good to be true. So, then what could this one mean? What if I change it like I've done before? I don't think it's a vision that would happen soon so what if I screw it up somehow?" She trailed off, staring distantly into the trees as a heavy worry clouded her expression. "That's not a vision I want to screw up, but I also don't know how to obtain that vision. What if knowing about it, like all the others, makes me accidentally change it? Milos, what do you think?"

Milos found himself surprised as Rita turned to him with that final question, a strange worry and curiosity plaguing her features. "I don't know." Milos shrugged. "I don't know how seer's visions work. I only know that you've changed the previous ones by telling us about it. Whether that means this one will change by telling me or not, I cannot say."

Rita hesitated for the longest time, seeming deep in thought. However, after a few minutes she pumped her fist, puffing her cheeks out in a semblance of determination. "Well, whatever it means, I don't care. I'm going to make sure we get that future, no matter what, and you better help me." She pointed to Milos, who only raised an eyebrow in bemusement.

"Who said I wasn't going to?"

She opened her mouth, as if expecting an argument before snapping it shut with a huff. "Point."

They devolved into silence and, while Milos wouldn't admit it, he did feel somewhat comforted at the knowledge that there was a possible future of them getting off this island with everyone. Even if it was just a possibility, it was something to aim for in this mess of a situation. He briefly wondered whether the knowledge was actually helpful for Rita or not, having seen the full scene in detail instead of just being told like he was.

After all, seeing a future that might or might not come to pass based on your actions, when you didn't even know what actions are needed to be taken to cause said future, was more infuriating than anything. He found himself somewhat grateful that he didn't have such an ability. Sure, he could see the usefulness of it. He could also see where it would cause turmoil and second-guessing. What would lead to a good future, what would lead to a bad one? As much as he hated uncertainty, at least that was consistent.

He wasn't in the mood to think of the philosophical implications of such a thing. Truth be told, the other thing that worried him was...he wasn't sure the reasoning behind why Suzuhah would still be alive, or what actually occurred up above. From what he remembered, there were quite a few times he recalled the creature hovering in the air, a strange hesitancy seen even from so far away.

After a few more steps, Milos was tugged from his thoughts as he drew to a halt, finding himself at the edge of a small cliff. Water trailed over the edge, splashing down below where more trees filled the little valley.

"Is that a town?" Rita perked up, startled.

Milos didn't need to guess where her attention lay, already observing the quiet village. Through the trees, near the middle of the valley, was a bunch of houses, a small town in the northern reaches. Truthfully, even with having spotted the humans earlier, he thought it would be farfetched to find a location like this. Yet it seemed as if the Underlands, yet again, decided to prove him wrong.

They did that a little too much for his taste.

"It appears to be about a half hour away," he noted. There was a path off to the left, leading down the cliff and through the trees.

"Yeah. Would Alex, and Suzuhah, I guess, be there? Is it even safe?" Rita muttered, glancing over her shoulder. "Considering we followed the same path those four were on, I'm going to guess they came from the village. If that's the case, I wouldn't want to come across more of them."

Milos couldn't argue with that. He wasn't keen on the idea either, but that didn't mean much. "We don't have the means of searching such a large island by ourselves and we don't know if there is another village."

"Right. They used the term 'Allegons' or something?" Rita shook her head, hands on her hips. "Still, do you, of all people, really trust...?"

Milos gave her a sharp look. "It is nothing about trust. Only practicality." He stood, heading toward the path. "You still have your powders, if necessary, and I've already plotted a few ways out of the village if we can't get their help, or at least, some supplies."

He could hear Rita grumbling in distaste behind him as she followed. Truth be told, he would rather search the island alone. However, he had no doubt it would take too long. Either Suzuhah would have already killed Alex, which he was starting to doubt at this point, or both would succumb to their wounds.

If they were found by demon hunters like himself, or by someone else...either way, it could still cause issues, something he was not in the mood to deal with alone, or with only Rita at his side.

They descended the cliffside path, finding themselves in the little valley in almost no time at all. Milos peered around, wincing slightly. Being whipped by that creature's tail was worse than he expected. It certainly wasn't the first time, but he was getting a little tired of being batted into walls. He shook his head, grip on the hilt as he came to a stop. He could hear, of all things, music and chatter in the distance. Rita perked up, peering around him curiously. "It seems lively up ahead. Are we already at the village?"

Milos narrowed his eyes, creeping forward. He would let Rita come to her own conclusions as he peered through the undergrowth. At least this part felt similar to his training.

Through the trees, he could see a few houses, people wandered back and forth, a quiet chatter filling the air. To one side, he spotted a young man with a spear and clothes similar to the hunters from before. He seemed to be observing the forest. A guard.

Yet they didn't have a gate or fence or anything to keep people or animals out. Why? Being demon hunters, they should be more cautious than that, unless they hoped the natural surroundings would help?

Milos glanced upward, narrowing his eyes. Day stones gleamed down, definitely more like high noon if the faint growl from Rita and his own empty stomach was any indication.

"So, what now?" Rita muttered, gripping her satchel tightly with both hands as she watched the village. "Are we just going to walk in there? This looks like the same village that those people from before came from."

Milos nodded. "You are correct." He decided not to elaborate on which part of her answer she was actually correct on. "We need information. We could attempt to sneak around. However, I feel like that won't get us very far."

"Yet, it's not safe either. This is ridiculous." Rita muttered.

"If you have a suggestion, I would love to hear it." Milos' voice was low as his attention diverted from the village for a moment.

Rita opened her mouth before snapping it shut, indicating well enough that she didn't have anything.

Milos assumed as much, shifting a little closer to the village. He hesitated for a moment, lost in thought before once more turning to Rita. "Stay here for now. I want to take a look around myself."

"What?" Her voice came out strangled as she stiffened. "You are *not* leaving me here to twiddle my thumbs."

Milos scoffed. "I wasn't saying that." He adjusted the sheath slightly, the handle a little easier to grasp. "You are going to be a lookout. That is, unless you want to go in alone." His eyes narrowed. "Which I would not advise since you have no actual fighting ability in case of problems."

Rita's eye twitched, but she narrowed her lips in understanding. "Fine. I'll stay here. Just find out what's going on and *maybe* I'll save your butt if something happens."

Milos shook his head as she slunk back, hiding herself a little better in the undergrowth before he stood, wiping himself down. Truth be told, the other reason he figured it would be better if he went was due to his knowledge of demon hunters. If these were similar to the ones above, he would have an easier time talking to them than Rita or anyone else might.

He shifted out of hiding, heading purposefully to the town. The guard noticed him instantly, but didn't do anything, merely stiffened in quiet animosity.

Milos stepped up in front of him as the guard spoke. "I don't recognize you." He was definitely young, strange for a demon hunter. "You don't look like an Allegon."

"No, I have only arrived recently." He spoke firmly. "I wish for information about this island." Along with a chance to learn more about these Allegons, but he didn't feel the need to bring that up.

"From where?"

Milos stared for a moment. "The south."

The boy's breath caught before he nodded. "Oh, this way please." He bowed his head slightly before turning, walking through the village.

Milos followed after, earning a few looks from the residents as he passed. He highly doubted they got travelers through here often. Though he was still in slight disbelief that there was an entire village on an island in practically the middle of nowhere.

Off in the distance, he could see fields that seemed to be used for farming. He didn't think he would see something like this underground, but it was becoming more and more common as they headed north.

They wove through the village before stopping in front of a stone home, similar to many he saw in the southern reaches. It was two stories. The young guard rapped his fist against the door twice before pulling away. There was a clattering sound from within, followed by footsteps.

To Milos' surprise, the one to open the door was an older woman with a gentle, curious expression on her face.

"Elder, this is a traveler from the south." The young guard bowed before giving Milos a brief glance.

"Thank you, Ray, you are dismissed." The woman's voice was filled with an authority that made Milos straighten slightly. The young man briefly smiled before hurrying away. It was then when the older woman turned her attention on Milos, her gaze flickering to his signifier.

Her pure white hair was tied up in a high bun and she was slender, though slightly bent. Her blue-eyed gaze shifted to his face as a warm smile flitted on her own. "Welcome, Alertian, to our home." She bowed her head. "We have waited for one of your people to arrive for generations. It is good to see that one has finally overcome the seas to reach our humble home." She straightened. "However, did you not come with others?"

Milos tilted his head slightly, hiding the surprise of her words behind an impassive mask. "It is safer if I do not speak of such things at this time."

He observed the surroundings quietly. He couldn't deny the peaceful air around the village. It was strange. Usually, a group of demon hunters, or a village such as this, would be up in arms, especially with a new arrival.

The fact this woman knew who and what he was...yes, the signifier might have given it away, but that depended on how long she was in these parts of the land, considering the lack of communication.

"I understand your hesitation." She turned, walking inside the home.

From the doorway, Milos could see a small fireplace, gently lit by a fire stone. Tables and chairs decorated a sitting room and dining room area. Off to one side, he could see a stone staircase winding up to the second floor. She gestured to one of the chairs before taking a seat herself, after closing the door.

Milos took a seat, keeping himself forward in the chair. "I am mostly passing through. I just seek information."

"Of course." She nodded and let out a sigh. "First, introductions. I am the elder of this village, Teresa. You are?"

"Milos." Milos bowed his head slightly in acknowledgment.

"Milos. That name means pleasant in the ancient tongue." The woman chuckled.

Milos twitched slightly. He heard that before, but most demon hunters didn't really talk much regarding the ancient tongue, it was mostly used by demons. So why was this woman...? He shook his head, that was a question for another day.

The woman watched him quietly, as if waiting. Finally, she let out a breath. "This island that you have arrived on, it is a boundary island, the last island before the Straits of Cameron and the Demon refuge. That is why I knew an Alertian would someday come through, for it is the *only* way to come through."

Milos mentally hummed at that information, making sure to remember it for later. "So, I'm guessing you deal with demons and possibly travelers from both sides?"

The woman's smile widened. "You are correct. A few of our travelers are from the south, but just as many come from the north. Still, many a voyager has come to the north, either seeking riches and wealth, or freedom, but only a few can pass through unharmed." She bowed her head, her shoulders slumping. "This island is for those who decided they were done, that they were no longer interested in moving forward. In a way, it became a sort of refuge of its own, the last safe place of these waters."

"Yet, there are no other ways to pass." Milos leaned his elbows on his knees, his chainmail clinking.

"You are not wrong." She tapped her finger lightly on the seat as she leaned back. "Because of our close proximity to the refuge, we are a sort of gate island. As such, many of those on this island speak a variety of languages, including the ancient tongue."

A gate island. He didn't know such a thing was possible, but it wasn't far-fetched in this underground land.

The older woman stood, using her hands on her knees to help her up. "For many years, there has been a delicate balance on this island between those who hate the demons of the north, versus those who see those of the north as protectors, beings to be worshipped. Those, such as my village, are people who make sure no demons arrive that would disturb the balance, demon hunters similar to yourself. While most demons fleeing to the north are just in search of freedom, there are a few who have other desires."

Milos frowned, indecision trailing through him for all of a moment before he spoke. "If that is the case, then why are there no walls or fortifications? I would assume that you would be more willing to have such things in case of attack."

She only chuckled quietly. "I can see your confusion. The reason for our lack of barriers is because it is easier to flee the village if a demon were to arrive. The woods are our protection and everyone here knows how to fight. Lastly, there are ways in which we know when a boat arrives, if not always a demon. At least, not always one with wings." She sighed, turning fully to face him. "The reason I tell you, an Alertian, all of this is two-fold. We need your help or more specifically, the help of someone with your abilities. A year or so ago, a demon from the north, of all places, arrived on the island. We need you to find out the specifics about this demon and kill it."

Milos narrowed his eyes, a faint whiff of magic circled in the air briefly before vanishing, and for the life of him, he couldn't figure out what it meant. He watched the woman for a while, noting the way she just quietly observed him in return, a faint smile on her lips. It looked like he was going to have to ask a few more questions. The old woman's eyes sparkled.

He debated on bringing Rita in, since he had a feeling it was going to be a long night and he felt that those in the village, such as the elder before him, already knew she was around. However, he did still feel a sense of unease, so he kept quiet.

Usually, he wouldn't get himself involved in another person's struggles, but he was still a demon hunter at heart, he wasn't going to just let things slide if there was a demon on the loose. Still... "I want to make one request."

The woman blinked, surprised before she nodded. "That's only fair, since we are asking for a favor. What can I help you with?"

"A map of this island. I am looking for a friend of mine who got separated when we landed," he admitted, feeling it futile not to bring it up. He did need the help, after all. "If possible, I would like to know as much as you can tell me about the island."

The woman sat for a few minutes, deep in thought. She seemed almost hesitant, which Milos found strange, before she nodded. "We will see what we can do. Now, was there anything else?"

Milos shook his head and stood. "No, that is all for now. If you don't mind, I would like a chance to take a look at the village."

The woman quirked her lip up slightly, but nodded. Milos turned, heading for the door. Hopefully, Rita actually stayed put like he asked. Though he had a feeling that was probably not the case.

Chapter Twenty-one

Alex was led to a stone building off to one side of a stone-lined street. Actually, everything around here reminded him of the southern towns like where he first met Rita, just stone everywhere. It was strange to see, especially in a location like this one in the middle of a freaking ocean. Suzuhah was practically draped over his shoulder, barely maintaining consciousness. Admittedly, Alex was getting a bit worried for him. The woman didn't say anything, barely giving Suzuhah a glance. "Gentle Demon, I hope you don't mind, but I'm bringing you to our revitalization spring. After that, we may bandage you and your companion's wounds."

Alex pursed his lips, but didn't argue as his wing twitched in pain. Before he could say anything in response, they stopped in front of a short one-story building with two doors leading inside. The woman led them through the left-hand door and gestured inside. "I will need to get some bandages and such as well as the doctor. He'll be with you as soon as you get out." She bowed and hurried away. Alex wanted to thank her, but it seemed she was already long gone.

Well, he did want to actually get a chance to check on his wings more fully to see how he could speed up the healing process, so he guessed this would work. He was getting sick of not being able to revert back to human form. It was starting to drag on him.

The inside was warm and looked to be a higher-end location, if the detailing in the stone and workmanship of the furniture was any indication. Though, honestly, by this point, Alex just gave up trying to figure out how much something like this might cost. It would just give him a headache. Alex's thoughts flickered. It would be nice to have a warm bath, and the steam wafting through the doorway at the other end of the little sitting area was inviting. While swimming in the ocean was fun and helpful, there was nothing like warm water brushing over your skin and taking everything away. He shook his head, helping Suzuhah into the room. Steam filled the air and towels were already laid out on one side. He sighed and helped Suzuhah onto one of the benches.

As much as a hot bath sounded nice, he needed to talk with Suzuhah. The boy seemed to know something.

Suzuhah glanced toward him before chuckling weakly, seeming a little more awake now that he was resting. "I'm surprised you didn't just jump right in the water."

Alex glanced away. He wanted to. "Something doesn't feel right, especially with what you brought up and..."

Alex's thoughts flickered to when they were outside, walking through the town. The town was...lively? He wasn't sure that was the word for it. People moved about, but the chatter was dimmed, plus all eyes turned to him as soon as he stepped forward.

He was not used to being bowed at from all sides. That just felt weird and wrong on so many levels. He wanted to just tell everyone to stand up already and stop, but he doubted they would listen. He sighed at the memory.

"At least you aren't completely naive."

Alex would have been affronted by Suzuhah assuming he was naive, if not for the fact he technically proved it by helping someone who tried to kill him with only a little bit of hesitation. "So, mind telling me what's going on here?" Alex asked, carefully stretching out his wings and tilting his head to try to look at them.

"Let's get in the bath first," Suzuhah spoke up, as he began pulling off his clothes. Alex blinked.

"Huh? Wouldn't the bath be the *worst* place to talk?"

"No." Suzuhah's gaze flickered to Alex. "Plus, they won't wait long for us to bathe before the doctor arrives. Yes, she said they would wait till we got out but that's only if we're already inside."

Alex nodded, true. The woman was probably rushing to get the doctor. He groaned and, turning away from Suzuhah, pulled off his clothes. His tunic snagged slightly on his wings, but thanks to the earlier cuts he made in them, it wasn't as bad. Finally, towel around his waist, he headed into the bath area. Following Suzuhah's advice, since Suzuhah stepped in first, he brought his clothes with him.

Alex wasn't in the mood to try to argue with Suzuhah and that water was calling him at this point. He almost dived in, but stopped himself at the last minute. Placing his clothes off to one side, and making sure the makeshift bandages he had were pulled off, he let himself slip into the bath with a groan of pleasure. The warm water was definitely natural, a hot spring of some sort. He ducked his head underneath, ignoring the heat burning his face. Though his wings seemed to be trying to stay above water as best as they could. Weird.

He had a feeling his human side would be enjoying this a lot less.

He pulled himself back up and reached for one of his wings before glancing toward Suzuhah. "So, mind explaining?"

As Suzuhah got comfortable in the water, his own clothes and bandages off to one side, Alex cautiously felt over the wing, trying to figure out where the sprain actually was.

"This is the Allegon's village, a place that, as you gathered, worships demons." Suzuhah sighed. "When I was younger, I used to come and go from this island a lot with my mistress. I stopped coming after the mistress' death."

Suzuhah shook his head as Alex paused in his examination. Alex thought he should probably ask about that, and he decided he would, but for now, he needed to know more about where they were and Suzuhah was his best bet.

"I don't know much about the island. I mostly came to enjoy the hot springs and it's a good stopping point in regards to the Northern reaches, especially for flyers." He grinned. "After all, for flyers, they just go over the coming strait and boom, they are there, at the refuge. Too bad flyers are quite rare. Very few demons actually have wings, or the ability to do more than glide."

Really? Alex thought, as he felt over his wings. Was flight that rare in demons? He never thought about it, but thinking back on when they left the Martinet's guild, there were only a few who flew out of the building, most ran or slithered. As for the rest of what Suzuhah said...he mentioned the strait. What was it?

Before he could ask, Suzuhah continued, grimacing, "However, during the last few visits, there was talk of seeking a new ruler, at least amongst the Allegons. I don't know the specifics, but I remember my mistress being distraught by it, having foreseen something to come, and made me promise to never go back here again." Suzuhah let out a weak laugh. "I was hoping to get rid of you all before we arrived, or at least causing it so you wouldn't stop here." His voice trailed off as he dipped his chin under the water, curling inward. "Maybe at first, that was what I wanted. To get your witch friend Rita, away from the boat, away from here and someplace safe, but you all..."

Alex frowned, letting his wing go. Something about Suzuhah's words made him flash back to the frustrated and resigned expression on the Vulfulas' face as they flew over the island, the way Suzuhah cushioned his fall. "What changed?" Alex asked quietly.

Suzuhah curled inward, staying silent as his face dipped farther into the water, eyes shining a soft gold. Bubbles rose as he sat up, turning to Alex. "My thoughts." He shook his head. "That's all. Maybe just some memories of my mistress, I suppose."

Alex watched him for a while before returning to his wing. It seemed it was mostly just bruised, no actual breaks or sprains. "What happened to your mistress?" Alex pulled his other wing over, his gaze turning away from Suzuhah, feeling guilty as a distraught expression flashed across Suzuhah's face.

"I guess I left that subject open, didn't I?" Suzuhah's words were faint as he let out a breathless chuckle. Alex could hear movement and then the faint sound of bubbling before Suzuhah took a breath. "There's no point in *not* talking about it and this is probably the only time we'll be able to. I'll need help leaving the island, since my wings aren't going to heal at the same speed as yours."

Alex briefly glanced over to Suzuhah, pausing to see the boy was practically hidden in the water. He resumed feeling over his wing as Suzuhah spoke.

"I wasn't lying when I said it was six years ago when the 'Vulfulas' appeared." Suzuhah's voice was soft. "My mistress was a seer, a powerful one who lived in the northern reaches to escape something in the south. Whether it was something that already passed, or was going to come, I don't know. She created me as a companion, an ally." Suzuhah chuckled weakly, pulling his legs close to his chest, curling up on the stone seat surrounding the bath as water splashed gently. "Truth be told, I'm young for a Vulfulas. I was created around the time my mistress finished her seer's initiation, aided by another powerful seer that is now long gone, about thirty-five years ago."

Thirty-five? Alex stared, freezing. This person before him was thirty-five years old? What did he mean by created? Didn't he mean born? No, he specifically used "created." Rita did mention something about them being associated with seers. How was it possible to create someone like, well, Suzuhah?

Suzuhah's gaze flicked to Alex and he chuckled. "Vulfulas grow at a much slower rate because of the fact that they are created, not born."

Alex flinched even as his words confirmed his earlier assumption. "I would probably be around eighteen to twenty in human years. Though I don't remember much of those early years." Suzuhah shook his head. "I'm not here to talk about the biology of a Vulfulas, we don't have the time for that, so I'll skip ahead. About six years ago was when it happened. Around that time, some travelers from the south were passing through. They had a water demon companion who got quite attached to my mistress. At least, I'm almost positive it was a water demon, even if it did look fairly human. The ship stayed on the island, our island for some time. Similar to how you all stayed."

Right...the water serpents. They would have trapped other travelers there as well. Wait... our island? So, it was a witch's island, or, well, seers, he supposed was the better term.

"It was a few hours before they were supposed to depart. The water demon asked my mistress to go with them. The thing is, my mistress received a premonition the night before. She never told me about what it was, or what scared her so badly, but because of that premonition, she denied the request.

"I was away from my mistress at the time, collecting herbs for one of her potions. I returned in time to see the water demon dragging my mistress with him as the ship tried to depart a few hours early. I tried to help her, but the water demon had already dived below the waves, a place I can't touch."

Sharp fingers almost like the Vulfulas' claws dug into Suzuhah's skin as he trembled. Alex stared, curious on what he meant, but didn't ask, giving the boy time to continue as he slowly loosened his grip, a thin trickle of blood flowing into the water. "The boat ended up capsizing and I found my mistress' body a few hours later. She must have fought to escape. I don't think the water demon planned to kill her, just take her with them." Suzuhah glanced up at Alex, eyes narrowed. "After all, a water demon controls all water, which includes, if they are especially powerful, allowing those they deem worthy to breathe underwater for short periods of time."

Whoa. He could do that? No, Alex, focus.

"Mistress must not have let him. On top of that, I was never able to find him. Even though I searched in my Vulfulas form all those years..." His hands slowly clenched once more, though not as tight, the water rippling. "So, when you appeared, six years later, with just hints of that same thing, I wanted to know. I wanted to know if there was any relation between you and that demon." The way he spat demon made Alex cringe. "But, well..." His gaze flicked to Alex's wings, reminding Alex that he needed to finish his examination. "You weren't like that demon, almost the complete opposite." A faint tired smile flashed on his face, fast enough, Alex almost thought he missed it. "I didn't know demons could be that kind."

"You were someone in need of help. We weren't going to leave you there."

"I don't mean just with that." Suzuhah shook his head. "Don't worry about it now. Just know, if you ever meet that demon, be careful. You two are practically polar opposites and yet he is good at hiding that fact."

"I'll keep that in mind." Alex couldn't help the small smile from forming on his face. "Speaking of, how are your wounds holding up? Do you need me to do anything?"

Suzuhah blinked before letting out a laugh, uncurling from his position. "Geez. This is what I meant." His chuckles faded and a gentleness fell over his face. "You, that demon hunter, those two servants..." He winced slightly, almost apologetically. "Rita. You all accepted me and your friend, the witch? She reminded me a lot of my mistress."

Oh, so that's why—his thoughts were cut off as pain ripped through his wing. Ah...he found the sprain. Ack, no, that was very much a break, his mind supplied before his body actually caught up to the fact he was still holding it. He let out a tremor of agony as he leant forward, almost diving back into the water to escape the pain. His wing snapped out, as if to avoid the water as it splashed upward. Searing sharp heat hit his spine and trembled down his body as he let out a quiet whine, much to his chagrin.

Once the pain ebbed, he allowed himself to once more reach up to carefully feel over the break. He could feel the bone was bent at an angle it wasn't supposed to be. He hadn't visually noticed due to it only being a slight shift and right after the curve of the wing, but it was enough to cause the bones to keep shifting over the break. He gritted his teeth. Yeah, he had no idea what to do about this.

He heard movement and quiet splashing and glanced over in time to see Suzuhah step up beside him. He flinched back as the boy reached forward.

"Let me look at your wing." Suzuhah stayed still, eyes imploring. "We can wait for a doctor, but the doctors here..." Suzuhah grimaced. "They probably don't know how to fix wings. Not in the same way as us, as creatures with wings."

Alex hesitated, somewhat annoyed to be called a creature, before finally letting out a breath. He leaned forward enough for Suzuhah to be able to reach comfortably. The hot water felt soothing as Suzuhah's fingers almost danced over the break, barely touching it.

"I'm going to try to reset it." His voice was soft, almost gentle. "My mistress did this once for me before and explained how she did it so, if need be, I could do it myself. I will warn you. It is going to hurt." Suzuhah seemed to pause, deliberating on something, before speaking up. "Hold on."

Alex heard movement, the pattering of footsteps on stone and water dripping. A moment later, Suzuhah returned, with a piece of fabric. "Put this in your mouth so you don't accidentally hurt yourself. I would prefer something like wood, but this will have to do."

Alex hesitated, taking the cloth, which felt surprisingly soft to his touch, before nodding. Making sure it was secure so he wouldn't bite his lip or tongue, he clenched his fist.

"Are you ready?"

Alex let out a quiet hum, before letting some notes drift from his throat to calm himself. If the pain was anything like earlier when he transformed into a human, then he would appreciate the preparation.

He felt Suzuhah place one firm hand to the base of his wing. Oh God, that felt weird. "I'm going to talk a bit while I do this, it won't completely distract you, but..."

Alex glanced over his shoulder, wondering why he was saying that.

Suzuhah seemed startled by the movement, before realizing. "Huh? I guess you're wondering why I'm helping you." He didn't say anything for a moment, feeling over the wing carefully. "Truthfully, it's because of how my mistress created me, to bond to those around me and be helpful. Since your friend, Rita, was a witch similar to my mistress, it was quite easy, and I guess that just extended to the rest of you." He shrugged. "Enough of that, I don't have any good means to splint your wings, so we'll have to just use bandages." Suzuhah's gaze flickered to Alex. "Unless you want to wait on the doctor?"

Alex debated for a moment. While it was true a doctor would probably be better, to be honest, he trusted Suzuhah a tiny bit more than a strange doctor from a strange place such as this. Plus, Suzuhah did have a point in regards to someone with wings knowing better how to treat wings. Suzuhah didn't move, just watched him silently, for which Alex was grateful. After another moment Alex nodded, turning away to focus on something else.

There was a moment of surprise and relief, followed by a warm sound. "I'll try to work quickly, but do your best not to move your wing, understood?"

Alex nodded, let out a long humming breath and tried to relax, keeping his wing as straight as possible.

Two hands firmly gripped his wing...

White hot *agony* shredded down his spine as Suzuhah tugged, shifting the bone. Alex bit deeply into the cloth, his hum cutting off in a quiet shriek. His whole body shuddered as he tried to keep his wing still. Suzuhah worked quickly, grabbing ripped pieces of cloth and wrapping tightly. It took everything Alex had not to curl away from Suzuhah.

He heard splashes and felt hot water suddenly fall over the bandaged wing, and yet the hand at the base was still there, thumb pushed in such a way where he could feel his wing going numb, unable to move. He hissed, wanting to slash at whatever was causing the pain. He struggled to remind himself that it was Suzuhah. The boy wasn't doing anything else, just holding his wing.

The hand on his back trembled slightly as a faint stuttering of breath reminded Alex of how injured the boy was.

"It seems the water is binding it quickly." Suzuhah's breath was short and slightly pained. "I expected as much, but it is fascinating." There was a faint splash and Alex turned to see Suzuhah slumped in the water, head leaning back as he pulled in breath. "Still, it was a good thing we did that before you thought to dive underwater fully. Your bones seem to already be mending themselves with just that little bit of water, I wouldn't even want to imagine what they would do if you dived under. They probably would have mended themselves in a way where the doctor or myself would have had to rebreak it to set it properly. No wonder it was harder to do than I thought."

Alex reached a trembling hand up, noting that the pain was starting to ebb away as he pulled the cloth from his mouth. He gently dipped it in the water, washing it before handing it back. Suzuhah blinked in surprise before taking it.

"I'm not surprised," Alex trailed off, staring at his bandaged wing. "You are technically more hurt than me and yet..."

Suzuhah remained silent for a while, even as Alex turned his gaze back on the boy.

"Your wounds, as I said you are healing incredibly fast even for a water demon." His tone was soft as he stared at the water. "Even though water demons only need pure or clean water to help the healing process of their wounds, you are able to heal broken bones to an extent that many others wouldn't be able to...to a point where the bone is almost knitting itself back together." He glanced up solemnly. "I know you are part water demon, but do you have any idea what the other part of you is?"

Alex wasn't sure how to respond. That was one thing he hadn't figured out from the trip to the Martinet's guild or what his mother was.

Suzuhah, seemingly having realized Alex's uncertainty, pushed himself out of the water, startling Alex. He stumbled for a second before heading for the door. "I'm going to check to see if the doctor is here."

"Wait." Alex turned, pulling himself half out of the water, causing the boy to freeze. Alex sighed and sat back down, meeting his gaze. "I wanted to thank you for helping me with that even though your own injuries..."

"Save it, Alex." Suzuhah turned away. "Just make sure you're healed up."

"Oh...hey."

Suzuhah stopped at the doorway, causing Alex to let out a breath. "Would you happen to know...would it be possible to change back?"

Suzuhah stared at him for a while, curiosity shining on his face for a split second before he responded, "Not for a while longer. The wound is still healing, after all, even with that ridiculous healing speed. Give it at least a day before trying again." With that, he turned and grabbed up his clothes.

Alex turned away, allowing Suzuhah to get changed in peace before the sharp creak of the door indicated he was gone.

He let himself sink down into the water, watching the bubbles trail up onto the surface. This time, he felt his wings spread out, slipping into the water as well.

Guess his demonic side knew not to do anything with the water, just like with the change, he wondered what would have happened if he let his wings dip in the water before the break was fixed. He thought over what Suzuhah said and shivered. He wasn't sure he wanted to think about it. Though, the idea of being in his demonic form for a whole day...he found it more than a little unnerving to think about.

He let out a breath, seeing the water ripple out and away from him. After a few minutes, he got out to check on Suzuhah. He still wanted to stay in, but this was a foreign area and it felt worrying without someone else around. He grabbed his clothes, threw them on, not particularly caring if they got wet, and hurried into the entrance where a doctor in a white robe was checking over Suzuhah, who must have changed earlier. His arms and legs were already wrapped in fresh bandages. The doctor stiffened upon Alex's entrance and stood from his check-up.

"I was just checking over your companion. I assumed you did not want to be disturbed and your companion confirmed it."

Alex would definitely have to thank Suzuhah for that, even if the boy got tired of hearing his thanks. He wasn't sure how he would react if some stranger walked in on him. "It's fine. How is he?"

The doctor straightened. "He will need some rest, but he will be fine. What about you? May I check you?"

Alex felt a little uncomfortable, but he sighed and nodded. He wasn't sure why, but he felt uncomfortable around these strangers. He knew there was something wrong with that...with feeling more comfortable with the boy who tried to kill him over a village that seemed to revere him, but he couldn't help it. There was also the fact that his human and demon side were clashing with each other, his human side wanting to run and his demon side wanting to stay. It was confusing and tiring.

The doctor nodded and walked over. He checked the wing first, a strange furrow in his brow as he peered over it, adjusting some of the bandages before checking over the rest of his wounds, using an ointment that smelled similar to Rita's. His wing felt stiff as the man wrapped over Suzuhah's bandages, pulling the wing close to Alex so it was resting, closed, on his back. He could tell he wouldn't be moving it for a bit as the man finished wrapping it. How he had enough bandages for it, Alex wasn't sure he wanted to know. At the end, he used what looked almost like a sling to wrap around the wing and his chest, probably to help keep it in place.

Alex was suddenly grateful he had thrown his clothes back on. He could see Suzuhah watching the whole time with a narrowed gaze, though not specifically at Alex. Alex wondered why, but brushed it off. After checking him over briefly for any other damage, the doctor backed away, causing Alex to let out a breath of relief.

"I've bandaged your wounds, so for now, you both need to rest. The young lady who brought you here will lead you to our best inn." With that, he bowed once more before hurrying out the door.

"You'll have to tell me how this village is here," Alex muttered and Suzuhah sighed.

"I will, once we get to the inn. Just don't do anything rash." He paused and blinked before sighing again. "Right, I forgot who I'm talking to."

"That's Rita." Alex said blankly. He wasn't exactly the rash one in the group.

"I know."

Alex blinked, unsure how to respond to that before he spotted the door opening, revealing the woman from before, bowing almost completely at the waist. "Right this way."

Honestly, a lot of the people here reminded him a little too much of the slaves he was used to in the south, but why? He glanced in the windows as they passed, but there didn't seem to be slavery here and everyone's signifiers were, well, strange would be the best way to put it. Actually, how did the people here have signifiers? Were there Martinets on this island as well? Was it just a tradition at this point? Where did all these people come from anyway?

His thoughts swirled as he followed the young woman. Hopefully, Suzuhah would be able to answer these questions. He was willing to answer the previous ones earlier.

That reminded him. How did he feel about Suzuhah? The boy's words came back to him, that he saw Rita as a replacement for his mistress, how as a result Alex was seen as someone he needed to help. So then, why did the boy try to kill him? Was it just because of the type of demon he was? If so, was that why he hesitated, or was it something Alex said? He would have to clarify what Suzuhah meant when he next spoke to him. Hopefully, this time, they would have more time.

His thoughts flicked to Rita and Milos and he felt worry surge through him. Were they okay? Were they on their way to find him? All he could do was hope that they were all right and heal up. Maybe if he kept his head down, everything would be all right.

It's not like bad things could *keep* happening to him, right?

Chapter Twenty-two

Rita cautiously slipped forward through the trees. As much as Milos said she should stay put, she couldn't help it. It bugged her not to be doing something, mainly searching for Alex. How freaking big was this island anyway? This was just unnecessary at this point. She heard movement and glanced over. There was nothing there, or nothing visible anyway.

She let out a breath before she heard the sharp snap of wood and felt something press into her back.

"Who are you and why are you sneaking around the village like some snitch?" The voice was flat, a young man's voice. She stared ahead, hand over her satchel. She slowly moved her hand down, into the satchel, only to freeze as whatever was against her back moved a little closer. "Don't move."

"Geez," she muttered quietly, mostly to dispel the nerves racing through her system. She took a slow breath. "I'm just trying to find a friend."

There was silence for a moment before the thing against her back pulled away slightly. "Stand up and turn around."

Rita did as she was told, deciding there was no point in causing a racket right now. She recognized the boy instantly as the same guard who led Milos through the village. A spear sat in his hand, still aimed at her, but thankfully far enough away, she didn't have to worry about being poked clean through. Not a pleasant thought. She let a flicker of a frown pass over her face before she said, "I'm not lying." She hesitated before groaning. "My comrade and I are searching for a friend of mine who got separated from us. We didn't realize how big this island would be."

The boy examined her quizzically before shaking his head. "I'm going to assume you are with that blond-haired man. If that is the case, I apologize for my rudeness, but you were acting rather suspicious." He gestured. "I'll bring you to him and the elder."

Rita pursed her lips before nodding, only to stumble back as the boy jerked his spear forward, twisting it to one side at the last moment. She stiffened, her instincts screaming at her to grab one of her potions and pounce. Instead, she slowly moved forward. To her surprise, they didn't go through the village, instead circling around. A few people glanced their way, but didn't do much more than that. Finally, they came upon a large two-story home. The door opened just as she approached, revealing a startled Milos.

He quickly schooled his expression, but Rita smirked. It was so rare to see Milos taken aback. As uncomfortable as the situation was, she appreciated small mercies or opportunities. Milos gave her a sharp look, probably already noticing the spear wielder behind her.

An older woman stepped up to the doorway, pushing Milos promptly out of the doorway. "Thank you for bringing her."

Rita stiffened as Milos narrowed his eyes. The woman simply smiled. Rita could hear footsteps, but didn't let her gaze wander. "You're a witch," she spoke softly.

The woman's smile widened. "Not completely correct. I was a witch who became a psychic, but now I am neither."

Rita stiffened. It was almost unheard of for someone to switch allegiance, especially with the rivalry.

The woman chuckled and turned back inside. "Let's just say, I was fascinated in knowledge, knowledge I couldn't obtain through one medium or another." She peered over her shoulder. "Much like the seers of the past and their ability to foresee the future, a talent that's been slowly corroded over the years."

"So that's why..." Milos muttered as Rita glanced toward him for a moment before diverting her attention back to the woman in front of her.

"You knew we were coming."

Rita was almost certain of that now as she observed the woman quietly. The woman nodded before walking back inside. Despite herself, she found herself intrigued. Other than the initial interaction with the spearman, there wasn't anything hostile about the situation.

Sure, it was stupid to trust someone like this, but she didn't have much choice if she wanted to find Alex on this way too big island. It seemed Milos drew the same conclusion.

They both exchanged a look, though Milos' gaze was more questioning. Rita shrugged. "Let's just get this over with. She knew we were coming anyway. Maybe she would be willing to help us find Alex, since you can't seem to use your Alertian abilities to track worth crap."

Milos outright twitched at that, glaring at her. "Actually," he cut in with a quiet hiss. "I've been trying to. However, I keep getting random bursts of magic that makes my tracking all but useless. Plus, his signal seems to be blending with a few others."

"Then just track the group." Rita flung her arms up in exasperation, which earned a bemused expression from Milos.

"I would, except for they have similar energies spread out in a couple different locations. I can't be positive which is Alex's."

Rita's eye twitched. "Seriously? I thought you could tell them apart."

Milos grimaced. "Usually, but with the amount of water around these parts and with our friend being part..." Milos trailed off before shaking his head. "It makes it nigh impossible to distinguish him. Plus, if he is hurt, which I have no doubt he is, most of the energy will be sent inward more than outward, it would be harder to sense."

"Huh, that would make sense, actually," Rita muttered, hand to her lips.

Animals did have different actions to others depending on if they were healthy or not. Oh geez. She wanted to bang her head against the doorframe. She was thinking of Alex as an animal now. Thank Killah she didn't voice it out loud.

Milos shook his head before walking inside, reminding Rita exactly where they were. She blinked, peering wildly around before hurrying after him.

Right. She needed to be more observant sometimes. She couldn't believe she let herself lapse like that. These last few days at sea definitely seemed to have screwed with her head.

~ * ~

Alex tentatively took a seat in the surprisingly lavish hotel bedroom the doctor and lady provided. Suzuhah was off to one side, curled up on the bed and watching the door warily. His injuries were still not that great, but everything was bandaged up. He was at least doing a little better.

Alex shook his head and took another examination of the room. It was moderately sized with stone and a few pieces of wood furniture. Thick quilts sat on the two beds set to one side with a wide window peering out over the landscape. Which, speaking of, the landscape was surreal. He knew he hadn't gotten much of a chance to observe the island when he was being carried, well, throttled was probably the better term, but he hadn't thought the island to be this big or vast. Then again...his thoughts flicked to before they arrived, that wasn't actually true. The beach stretched either direction, a mass of land all its own.

He was reminded of that as he stared out the window over the surprisingly lush landscape. The village itself was set into the side of a hill, slowly sloping upward. The hotel they were in was a little up the slope, high enough to spot the gates they passed through only a little bit ago. He could see people wandering about through the stony streets. Houses, shorter than the building he was in, slanted downward toward the fence. To the left were some waterfalls, a few of them disappearing past the houses. On the right was a large swath of forest before it just ended, revealing the ocean beyond.

Forest stretched before him and he found himself staring. It was one thing to be amongst the trees, but to peer down on them. It was something else entirely. He knew it was nothing like the Overlands, a pale representation, but he found himself enamored nonetheless.

"So, what are you going to do now?"

He jumped, turning to face Suzuhah who tilted his head up tiredly. "What do you mean?"

Suzuhah shrugged. "Well? What do you think I mean? We are in a city that practically worships your kind. We're both injured and you still need a full night's rest before you can revert back to human form. If you know how to revert bits and pieces of your form that would help, but I doubt you do."

Alex stared. He could *do* that? Before he could think about the implications of what Suzuhah said, the boy continued, "Lastly, you probably want to check on those friends of yours, right?" A sadness seemed to cross his face as his attention drifted to the window. "It would be kind of nice to see her again."

Alex held no doubts on who he was talking about, though Rita would probably have the exact opposite reaction of seeing Suzuhah. He let out a long breath. "I guess I'm going to search for the others. They are probably on this island by now and I have no doubt they are worried sick. Though, I doubt they would show it." Alex chuckled slightly before he let the chuckles die. "I'm grateful these people helped heal us, but..." He trailed off, that familiar feeling from before welling up in his stomach. The split feeling called for him to relax and run at the same time. It was so disorienting.

Suzuhah sighed, stretching his legs out as he stared out the window as well. "I see..." He trailed off before swaying side to side. "I don't have many other options." His uncertainty was clear as he turned to Alex. "I mean, the only option I have is, well, it is to stay with you."

The last few words were said much quieter, almost nervously and Alex couldn't blame him. He found himself hesitating for a moment before shrugging.

"As I said earlier, you didn't kill me, you saved me from the fall. I'm not exactly one to hold a grudge. We can deal with that after we all are back on the ship and you can talk with the others." Alex smiled, letting a little warmth into the expression to help alleviate some of Suzuhah's concern. "For now, we're stuck in this situation together, and, as I said as well earlier, I trust you more than I trust the people here."

Suzuhah pursed his lips, staring at Alex for the longest time before finally just slumping. "I don't think I'll ever understand you."

Alex snorted, but didn't argue.

Suzuhah shifted, sitting cross-legged on the bed as his gaze drifted to the window. "Why don't I tell you what I know about this place and we can go from there. Sound good?"

Alex nodded and Suzuhah continued, "I don't know much, mind you, but I should be able to give you the gist of things. This village? It houses the Allegons, people descended from humans who fled from the south, namely, slaves."

Alex stiffened as Suzuhah's smile dropped. "They are the people who worship demons, in the belief that because they are so close to the refuge, that is what gives them their freedom. Now there is another village on the opposite side closer to where the boat would have arrived, the Veragon. Predominantly housing demon hunters, they are descended from those who got caught here, unable or unwilling to continue on. The two villages have never seen eye to eye, at least, not that I've heard of." Suzuhah leaned back with a groan. "I guess it's somewhat good that we landed on the side with the Allegons. Considering I know nothing of who their leader is or anything else that may have happened in the past few years, that could also be detrimental." He lifted his hand, pointing at Alex with a glare. "The reason I'm bringing this up is because I have no intentions of dying here."

"If they are former slaves..." Alex trailed off, peering down through the window.

Suzuhah shifted, his voice dropping into a soft monotone. "A slave is still a slave, even if their shackles are gone. After all, once the human spirit is broken, there is almost no means of bringing it back, and freedom has a different meaning for everyone. For these people? It means a life where they can do what they want in a given space, as long as they follow orders to the letter whenever they are given and that thought process extends just as much to their children."

Alex clenched his fists as he bit his lip. That's not what freedom was, though, right? "How is that freedom?" he muttered, turning back to face Suzuhah, who shook his head.

"I don't know. Remember, I'm just a creature. Someone created by a human master." Suzuhah's expression was distant, almost sad. "I wouldn't know how humans think, would I?" He grinned. "So, what knowledge would I have of the concept of freedom anyway?"

Alex stared at the boy, finding himself at a loss. "I don't believe you," he muttered quietly, startling Suzuhah. "At least, about how you don't know how humans think. After all, you called me out on it earlier."

"Ah...yeah, I apologize about that."

Alex waved it off before he continued, "What I'm trying to say is, if you truly didn't know how humans think, you wouldn't have been so undecided on whether to kill me or not, you would have followed your instinct, right?" When Suzuhah didn't respond, Alex leaned forward to try to catch his attention. "You obviously have some humanity in you, after all. If not, I think Milos would have probably attacked you much earlier and Rita might have noticed something as well."

"Not yourself?"

Alex hesitated for a moment before chuckling quietly. "Probably not." He lightly rapped knuckles on his head. "Considering two of the people I travel with have tried to kill me before, I don't think I have a right to say anything."

"Two?" Suzuhah uncurled from his seated position, curiosity clear on his face.

Alex winced. "Not really the point. The thing I was trying to say is that those two would have done something much sooner if you and your sist...well...other half, I suppose, were acting like a creature or animal like you say, so..." Alex trailed off. "I think you get what I'm trying to say, right?"

Suzuhah watched him for a bit before letting out a long and tired breath. "I suppose I do." He paused for a moment before flopping sideways onto the bed, startling Alex. "It is something to think about at least." His gaze flicked to Alex. "For now, though, it is getting late and we need some rest. They were at least kind enough to provide us a room, so let's use them while we can, all right?"

Alex hesitated for only a moment before laying down as well, only pulling his shoes off. They got new clothes at one point, courtesy of the young woman they met. Though Alex did have to tear some holes in them with his claws for them to fit slightly. Though, for his wings, especially the bound one, he had Suzuhah help him.

Suzuhah changed into the ones he received, his original clothes so tattered and ripped to be almost unsalvageable. Alex's weren't much better, so he also changed, though at least the clothes were similar enough to not be scratchy or uncomfortable.

Still, as he got comfortable, his mind wandered over what Suzuhah said, and found himself getting caught on the idea of Suzuhah being created. What exactly did Suzuhah mean by that? Rita mentioned that Vulfulas were created by seers, but how was that possible? How was Suzuhah still around if his creator was dead? What did it mean?

Part of him wanted to ask, but another part of him wanted to stay silent and just let Suzuhah sleep.

He heard a quiet shifting and tilted his head enough to see Suzuhah curled on his side, facing away from Alex. The way he was positioned obviously would have hurt.

"Suzuhah?"

Silence filled the air for a few moments as the day stones outside completely disappeared into their night time counterparts. As the meager light drifted through the window, Suzuhah finally stirred. "What?" His voice was soft and a little choked.

Alex went to open his mouth before snapping it shut. "Never mind. Sleep well." He rolled over, deciding not to ask the boy for now. He would ask when they were in a better position to talk. Mainly, back on the ship with everyone else.

He let out a yawn and grimaced. He was surprisingly tired. Much more tired than he would like to admit. Suzuhah was right, he needed rest, but...

He didn't feel comfortable. It was bad enough he needed to get in a bath with a practical stranger at this point, but to sleep in the same room in a strange place? He wasn't an idiot. He knew full well how dangerous this situation was, but though his mind said that, his body curled inward, another yawn ripping from his lips as his tail shifted around his waist, his wings settling against his back. He made sure the door was locked and even grabbed one of the two chairs set into the room before carefully shoving it under the handle. Suzuhah hadn't argued with the movement, assuring Alex that maybe his worry was sound.

Still, it wasn't much, but it was better than nothing. It didn't help that his demonic side was practically purring at the idea of sleep. He never thought he would use the term purr in any context regarding himself, but there he was.

He was way too tired for this.

He awoke with the night stones still coating the sky and a sharp knock on the door, feeling surprisingly drowsy. Suzuhah was still dead to the world, his breaths slow. Alex wondered if he was using the sleep to help recover a little, which would make sense. Of the two of them, ironically, Suzuhah was more injured overall. He pushed himself up, having slept, a little uncomfortably, on his stomach, and walked over to the doorway. He moved the chair out of the way before opening the door slightly. "Yes?" he asked, keeping his voice low so as not to wake Suzuhah.

To his surprise, it was the woman from before, a faint smile on her face. "Ah, you're awake. Did you get some rest?"

Alex frowned. "Yes, but..." His gaze flickered to a nearby window in the hallway. "Why are you here at this time?"

"My apologies, gentle demon." She bowed her head before standing straight back up. "I bring a message from our lord. He wishes to speak with you as soon as you are able."

"Your lord?" Alex pursed his lips, remembering what Suzuhah said before about someone being chosen as a king or something to rule these people.

The woman nodded, a strange smile on her lips. "Yes, our lord. He wishes to meet a gentle demon such as yourself." She trailed off, glancing over his shoulder. Alex shifted slightly, deciding to keep Suzuhah out of her sight, though he wasn't sure why he was so worried about such a thing.

"I would rather rest for tonight, if he doesn't mind." Alex kept his voice soft, feeling more than a little unsettled once more. Though that could have just been the shadows on the walls flickering as more night stones brightened through the window. "Speaking of, I don't think we ever received dinner. Could I have something small to eat?"

A frown flashed across her face before she bowed once more. "Of course, I apologize. It is late after all. I will see if I can scrounge anything up. If you need anything else, I will be right down the hall. Please let me know if you are in need of supplies or have some questions."

Alex nodded, watching her go before carefully closing the door, wondering at the strange exchange. He made sure the door was locked before promptly putting the chair back under the handle.

He peered at Suzuhah once more before sighing. It seemed the boy was too out of it. He took a seat in the other chair, waiting as his stomach twisted slightly in hunger. His eyes drooped as he found his head tilting downward with each passing moment. At this rate he was going to fall asleep in this wooden chair, which he was not inclined to do. He flopped back down onto the bed. His mind was sluggish from still being half-asleep. The exchange was somewhat worrying, but at least now he knew what his plans were for tomorrow morning. Plus, the woman would knock when she brought the food, right?

Maybe some more rest would do him some good. He hoped the others were okay.

Chapter Twenty-three

When he woke up this time, it was to Suzuhah hovering over him.

Alex blinked a few times and would have reacted accordingly, if his brain wasn't still trying to catch up with his body. Suzuhah stared down at him before sharply pulling away. "Didn't mean to wake you." He pointedly turned away, heading to the door. "Guess I wasn't thinking straight."

"Ah-huh," Alex muttered as he sat up, rubbing his eyes tiredly. "That's why you were hovering over my bed like a creep?"

Suzuhah stiffened before coughing slightly. "Ah, well...what can I say? I'm hungry."

Alex blinked a few times before his brain finally caught up with him enough where he deadpanned, tugging the covers up just a bit more, pulling his legs up toward his chest. "Hungry? What the heck were you planning on doing?"

"Nothing like *that*!" Suzuhah jerked, glaring at Alex, who relaxed slightly. "I—that is—Vulfulas..." He sighed. "We need lifeforce, okay?" He cut in, scowling at Alex. "I'm injured, so my body is using my own lifeforce to heal me. Vulfulas don't produce enough on a regular basis as it is, that's why we need to siphon it off other things. Well, remember yesterday when I was mentioning about being hungry, but unable to do anything about it?"

Alex paused, relaxing a bit more as he recalled the conversation. It was right after he transformed and he found out Suzuhah was actually in the same pain as him, just unable to do anything about it. He winced. "Oh."

"Exactly." Suzuhah grimaced, hand curled around the doorframe as he turned pointedly away from Alex. "Usually, I can get by with small animals or sometimes witch's herbs, but you and your friend did a lot of freaking damage to my wings, thus..."

"Thus, you're starving." Alex slowly dropped the quilt, anxiety shooting through his veins. Lifeforce. There were creatures that ate lifeforce. He didn't know that was possible and it creeped him the heck out.

Suzuhah's eye twitched. "Yeah, yeah, most people don't like it, but it's how we are made." He shook his head, grabbing the chair before pushing it out of the way. "Don't know why I bothered," Suzuhah muttered about to race out the door.

"Wait," Alex yelped, stumbling out of bed. "It doesn't kill them, right? When you eat?"

Disgust shone on Suzuhah's face as he jerked, turning to Alex. "No. Never. Even when starving, I can somewhat hold myself back from completely draining someone or something. Plus, lifeforce recovers over time. It just leaves the person or thing weak for a little while, that's all."

Alex hesitated for a moment, staring at Suzuhah. The boy pursed his lips, looking away. "Look, I overheard you talking last night. You are going to meet with the lord, correct? I'll go around town and grab some things so that if anything happens, we can just run, all right?"

With that, he stepped out the door, startling Alex, but before he could say anything, Suzuhah was gone.

Alex stared for a moment, finding his arm outstretched toward where Suzuhah disappeared. He let it drop with a huff. Alex wasn't sure what to think regarding what Suzuhah mentioned, but it might at least explain how out of it Ari and Leon had been lately, right? Alex wasn't sure how he felt about the situation either. He shook his head, pulled on his boots and decided to head out. He was awake now and he would rather meet this "lord" sooner rather than later. Though first, food sounded good. He wondered why the lady never came with any, but he supposed it was pretty late. Plus, Suzuhah did have a point at least: one of them should get supplies and Suzuhah knew this place better than he did.

Didn't stop him from being annoyed at Suzuhah's antics. He grumbled to himself as he left the room, shoving the door to their room closed behind him before peering left and right down the long hallway. He couldn't exactly blame Suzuhah too much if what the boy said was true. Alex knew how it was to be hungry. You do incredibly stupid things when hungry. He winced, remembering all too well when he first fled from home. He still could remember the stench from the garbage dump as he dug for anything halfway edible. Plus, Suzuhah knew how uneasy Alex was around him, for good reason.

On his way down the steps, he heard movement and paused.

"Gentle demon, I was unaware you were awake."

Alex jerked, glancing up the steps to find the woman from the night before, a simple dress tumbling down and drifting around her legs as she slowly descended, a light stone in hand. "Oh, sorry." He hesitated. "I didn't mean to wake you."

She shook her head, a strange smile on her lips. "It is fine. Here, why don't I lead you to ma-my lord's home?"

Alex didn't miss the slight slip, but he wasn't quite sure what she meant to say as she walked past him and down the steps. "Actually, I wanted to grab something to eat, I'm kind of hungry."

"It will only take but a moment and then I can lead you to one of our finest eateries, will that suffice, gentle demon?"

Alex hesitated before letting out a long sigh. If it only took a minute, he could deal. He'd gone longer without food than this before. Alex followed after her. He could tell the night stones were just starting to disappear and he pursed his lips at that. He'd been out of it all night; he wasn't sure if that was a good thing or not.

Speaking of...he glanced over at his wings, remembering them for what felt like the first time in a while as he kept his pace with the woman. He should probably get her name soon.

His wings were, for the most part, pressed against his back, both due to the binding and some inherent need to rest. No wonder he slept strangely last night, though at least he finally managed to find a comfortable position. It was the first time he had ever actually slept in his demon form.

Probably explained why he wasn't nearly as panicked to waking up with Suzuhah's face right above him. Something about this place relaxed his demon side, and it bothered him. His gaze flicked to the woman as they left the inn, climbing the steps toward the top of the hill. He wondered if he should ask her since, well, they worshipped demons. That meant they should know how to take care of them, right? Though he thought he had a feeling she wouldn't be able to give him much of an answer.

Not knowing what else to do, he let out a quiet groan, his tail curling around his arm, the texture so strange. He felt over it, as if to try to calm himself, as they walked up the crest of the hill, the homes thinning out as they went.

With it being still quite early in the morning, the streets were practically dead, almost no one walking around.

He pursed his lips, feeling a tugging in his chest as they continued forward. He hesitated. "I'm going to regret this, aren't I?" he muttered as he once more caught up to the woman who was waiting for him. His demon half crooned in delight as they grew closer.

It was a very *odd* feeling. Finally, the duo reached the top of the hill and the woman stopped, bowing. Alex followed her gesturing arm and froze. On the other side of the hill, to his surprise, was a sprawling pond and a small mansion. He hadn't seen it from where he was before, the mansion having been hidden by the buildings and hill, but now, as he stared down at it, he wondered at the size and intricacy. Stone pillars were placed evenly before a set of large double doors made of what seemed to be, from a distance, wrought iron. Flowers...the white flowers that bloomed all throughout the Underlands after the epidemic curved around the building, decorating the windows and walkways alike. Alex twitched slightly at that, frozen in place. He never was much of a fan of those flowers and this place had how many? He thought it was utter bullshit, but kept his mouth shut. He felt a gentle tap on his back and stumbled forward, staring back at the woman in surprise. The woman smiled just a little bit wider. Alex felt a shiver run down his spine as he began to walk down the slope. It took him more than a minute to realize that he hadn't actually decided to continue forward.

It took him another minute to realize he *couldn't* stop. Panic flared through his mind as he made his way down to the pond. The woman was no longer following, seemingly still at the crest of the hill.

As his feet brought him steadily forward, his demonic side preened.

His human side? His human side was cowering, trying desperately to run away, to stop this descent.

The two disparaging halves left him standing awkwardly in front of a placid-looking pond. The same one he saw earlier. What was he doing here? He had no reason to be here.

Oh, right, meeting the lord.

He wasn't sure he wanted to meet this lord any more. Not when it was causing his mind to literally split down the middle in indecision.

He shut his eyes before turning away, forcing his muscles to move back up the slope. Needless to say, his demonic half was not too keen on the idea, screeching at him to turn around. He felt his wings jerk as his tail squeezed his arm.

"You're leaving so soon?"

Alex stumbled to a halt, quieting both halves of his mind as he whipped around.

Standing before him, dressed in fine clothes, was an older man with a short brown hair cut. Gray eyes peered at him curiously with a sharp and jagged scar stretching down one side of his face. Alex belatedly wondered where the man came from. Was he that out of it?

He shook the thought from his head. Was this the lord? What was he doing up?

"So, you are a demon as well." The man spoke, humming in a strangely familiar way.

"As well?" Alex asked, voice weaker than he intended.

His demonic side was back up, curious and crooning? As if the man before him was familiar.

Alex never saw the man before in his life.

Amusement flashed over the man's face as he bowed his head. "I am the demon king. Ruler of this island and you must be the young demon my lovely servant found yesterday." His gaze flicked up the hill. "Thank you, my dear."

Alex heard a quiet giggle from behind, but didn't turn. His human side was yelling at him, telling him that something about this entire situation screamed danger.

He gulped harshly. "So, demon?" He wasn't sure what exactly he was asking, or why he felt so nervous.

The man nodded, turning to him. He shifted to his left leg and in the same movement...

Alex stilled. Standing before him was the same man, he knew that, but a bluish glow coated his skin, gill-like appendages at the side of his neck and a long tail, similar to Alex's own, swayed behind him.

Yet, one thing that caught Alex's attention was that the man didn't have any wings. It was strange, looking at the figure before him. Part of Alex felt like he should know him, or at least, recognize what he was. The other part was completely clueless and freaking out.

"I'm sorry if I startled you. It has been years since a demon such as yourself has landed on this island." He shook his head sadly, slightly pointed ears showing as his hair was swept to one side.

Alex found himself reaching up to his own ears, before promptly pushing his hand down harshly.

"We used to have demons come and go quite often, but recently, they haven't dared land here, probably in fear of the Veragons." The man walked over, stepping past Alex.

Alex managed to convince himself to turn, following the man's gait. The man turned to him. His hands were clasped behind his back as he appraised Alex quietly.

"As you can probably assume, I am of Nyx blood." He grinned. "A shape-shifted form, mind you. After all, you and I both know Nyx cannot be male."

Alex opened his mouth before snapping it shut as the man leaned forward just enough to cause Alex to shift uncomfortably. "But what are you?"

He stared up at Alex's horns in curiosity before his gaze drifted to his wings, fascination and another emotion Alex couldn't quite identify shown on his face. "I've never seen your type before."

Alex took a couple steps back, catching his breath before glaring. "Can you give me some breathing room at least?" He knew he shouldn't be talking to a king like that, but nothing this guy did gave off the vibe of someone, well...he pushed the thought away. "Why did you have someone wake me up in the middle of the night to talk with me? That wasn't necessary."

The man chuckled, pulling back to give him the desired space. "My apologies. I find myself fascinated by other demons. The idea of knowledge is especially appealing." He smiled apologetically. "As for your other question, I was just so excited at meeting another demon in these parts that has aspects of a water demon such as myself, I wanted to meet you." A faint smile flitted onto his lips as he turned slightly to face the pond, gaze no longer on Alex as Alex stiffened at his words. It took all his will not to ask how the man could tell what he was when even Milos had trouble upon meeting him.

"This place is beautiful, don't you think? Clear waters and fresh land. A place to call home in many ways."

Alex faced him, his attention drifting to the water, almost captured by the dazzling light it let out from the emerging day stones. "Especially this time of day, when the soul is closest to the earth."

Alex furrowed his brow, wanting to ask what he meant, but now, his demonic side felt more hesitant, as if starting to agree with his human side. Something about this situation, about that pond, felt off.

"You are a strange one like I assumed, only a select few..." The man shook his head, as he squatted down, fingers just grazing the water. "Come, you are probably hungry. Oh, where are my manners?" He stood, turned and bowed his head slightly toward Alex, peering up at him. "You may call me Ransel. You are?"

Alex hesitated for the longest time, unsure if he wanted to give his name, before he finally said, "Alex."

"Alex," he spoke the word as if tasting it. His smile slipped a little wider as a strange expression slid onto his face. "Well then, Alex, why don't we get you something to eat? I would be more than happy to show you around. We have many fine items and food here, enough to fill whatever your heart desires."

"I'm quite good actually." Alex finally spoke up, the words coming out hesitant. "I must be going."

"Nonsense. Come." The man gestured, as he wiped down his— those were robes, weren't they? When he first saw them, they seemed akin to high-end clothing, but now he could see the intricate designs on the sleeves and sides, almost symbolic in nature.

Alex found a foot sliding backward. "Actually, there are some people waiting for me. I said I would be meeting with them soon. I only wanted to say hi since she," he gestured behind him, half-expecting the woman to be there, "said you wanted to speak with me."

"Well, yes, that is true." He paused, slight confusion shining on his face. "I usually like to speak with any demon that enters this domain so they are aware of what to watch out for. You see, Alex, there are a lot of dangers on this island as of recently, not counting the steady increase in Veragons over the past few years."

"Right, well, I appreciate you warning me, but I must be go... ing..." Alex's tongue jammed to the top of his throat as a strange hum echoed from the man, his smile dropped enough to be eerie. His posture was stiff and almost menacing. Before Ransel could respond, Alex turned and darted up the slope.

As he fled, he mentally berated himself on his attitude and mannerisms. Usually, he was a lot calmer than that, but for some reason, the guy just freaked him the heck out.

He rushed past the startled woman, who tried to reach out to catch him. He dodged her, mind shrilling not to get caught.

That was it, he was finding Suzuhah and leaving this village, just as Suzuhah expected. Yeah, he was still injured, but he would rather be going around the island than stay in this place any longer than he needed to.

He jogged through the streets, keeping his ears open for any sound, anything to indicate where the Vulfulas could have gone or if he was being chased. The town was still eerie so early in the morning.

Now, he was used to quiet, that was the norm in the Underlands, but this quiet, in a village no less... He shook himself from the thought, noticing he was getting close to the gates. He paused, staring at the gates out of town for a moment from a couple streets away. Sure, he could probably just leave, Suzuhah already showed he could take care of himself, but... Alex sighed, observing the gates once more. The guards, to his surprise, were the same as the ones before, the ones he walked past the night before. Shouldn't they have changed guard duty? He frowned, observing them quietly. They were stiff and, as Alex watched, barely moved. He crept a little closer.

"I wouldn't get any closer if I were you."

Alex almost let out a startled scream, almost, if it wasn't for the fact that he'd been searching for the bearer of that voice. His gaze flicked to Suzuhah, feeling more than a little relieved. He wondered why Ransel or that woman hadn't caught up yet, but he wasn't going to question it.

He was glad that Suzuhah seemed to at least appear a little bit better, though Alex decided he *didn't* want to know the details of that. He did, however, note the small bag of items Suzuhah had in his hand, which he promptly tossed over to Alex. Alex fumbled for a moment with the grab, almost hissing as a few bits he touched were almost searing from heat, was it food? He hoped so because he was definitely hungry now. He shook it off and glanced toward Suzuhah. "Why do you say that we shouldn't get closer? How did you find me?"

Suzuhah flicked his gaze toward Alex with only a slight bit of irritation. "You are still in your demon form. Truth be told, you aren't very subtle. Even with your healing causing your aura to be a bit more hidden, you still have some that leaks out. Since we're in the same village, and I've been beside you the whole time, it stands out. Well, yours and a few others, but the rest are on the opposite side of town." Suzuhah shivered. "I have no inclination of going anywhere near that area."

Was he talking about the mansion? He pulled from that thought as he brought an arm up, hoping to figure out what Suzuhah meant about aura.

Suzuhah snorted softly before shaking his head. "I'm not a demon or anything. Truth be told, I just figured you would be near the gates and waited for you. I can't sense individual demons like your Alertian friend, but I can feel fluctuations in the air." He pursed his lips. "This island has only gotten worse since I last came here. It's easier to sense now that I'm no longer as hungry but it must be messing with things, considering your

Alertian friend hasn't found us yet."

Alex relaxed slightly, though his thoughts raged. That's right, Milos hadn't found them yet. Did something happen to him? Was something else going on, interfering with him? Alex wouldn't be surprised at this point. After all, this island was already needlessly huge with two freaking villages on it, plus Suzuhah's reaction as well as his in regard to the mansion and, more specifically for him, the lord. He groaned, massaging the bridge of his nose. He wouldn't be surprised if there was something else here causing problems with tracking. He shook his head and glanced back at Suzuhah, returning to their original topic. "What do you mean, we shouldn't get any closer?"

Suzuhah's eye twitched. "Can you seriously not sense it?"

Alex let his expression morph into a deadpan. "If I could, would I be asking?"

"Point." Suzuhah glanced back at the two guards. "I thought I sensed it when we came in, but I was still too weak at the time, now I definitely can. Close your eyes and concentrate on the two in front of us." Alex hesitated. "Don't worry, I'm not planning on doing anything."

Alex huffed, but complied. He closed his eyes, focusing on the two guards in front of them. After what felt like a few minutes, and finding himself thinking a little of what he saw Milos do, he was able to notice a faint silhouette of the two before him. It was strange. Energy twisted and coiled around them, seemingly locked in place, a tentative form overlaying what appeared to be humans. Why? What for?

What was that energy anyway? It felt familiar. "What?"

"Demons."

Alex stiffened, eyes snapping open in surprise as Suzuhah stood next to him, squatting down slightly to remain out of sight. "What?"

Suzuhah's gaze shifted to Alex for only a brief moment before returning to the two guards. "They are fairly weak, not sure what type, but they are definitely demon."

"They appear human, though." Alex fought weakly, as his brain reminded him that his mother looked human as well, and so did he.

Suzuhah shook his head. "They may look it, but that may also be because..." Suzuhah trailed off before pursing his lips. "They knew we were coming." He spoke matter-of-factly, startling Alex.

"What do you mean? Knew we were coming? How?" Alex tried to keep his voice low, but didn't succeed as it racketed up in pitch.

Suzuhah clicked his tongue, glancing behind him. "That woman we met, she probably was specifically sent out to find us and, being closer to this village than the other, she would have definitely found us first."

Alex remembered how the woman led him to the mansion, lightly pushing him down the hill and trying to catch his arm when he fled. "Why?" He wasn't sure if he was asking in regards to what Suzuhah said, or what he just thought. "I thought this place worships demons?"

Suzuhah didn't bother responding, and Alex didn't blame him as the day stones finally took over their night-time counterparts. Sound started to echo in the streets, as if the village was starting to come alive. Alex shivered at the thought.

"Well, we can't stay here," Suzuhah trailed off before letting out a long breath. "Give me a sec."

Alex glanced over in time for a faint flash to dazzle him before the younger girl stood before him. Suzuha glanced up at him with a surprisingly warm smile. "This should be enough to distract him, wouldn't you say?" Before Alex could respond, Suzuha waved cheekily. "Well then, wish me luck."

The little girl was already moving, humming quietly to herself as she practically skipped up to the guards. Alex let out a long breath, unsure what to feel as he watched Suzuha act even peppier than normal, which he hadn't thought was possible. Seriously, the sheer disparity between the young man he was just talking to and the little girl made his head spin. Still, he watched as the girl came to a halt in front of the two guards, talking about something or other and startling them slightly. With her smaller size the guards had to bend slightly to speak with her, which gave Alex a chance to cautiously walk forward, keeping his tail wrapped closely behind his back, half hidden by the belts. He missed his cloak, which he knew was still back on the ship, but there wasn't much he could do about it as he kept his wings close. He paused in his thoughts even as he continued forward, could he switch back? He did get a good night sleep at least. He felt his wing twitch and grimaced. He wasn't in the mood to check that right now. He might not be able to put away his wings, but... He closed his eyes, trying to pull back on his demonic side just a bit like Suzuhah mentioned earlier. He could feel a set of weights leave his head and almost let out a groan of relief. He didn't realize just how heavy the horns were until they were gone. Thankfully, sometime in the night, his claws disappeared, something he hadn't noticed until now. He probably would have found that strange, if he wasn't also getting used to them.

He was almost to the gate at that point, keeping to the overhanging shadow of the buildings and fences until he was almost right behind the guard. He waited for a split second more as Suzuha spread her arms out wide, just as a wide smile appeared on her face. One guard was kneeling on one knee while the other rolled his eyes.

Taking his cue, he bolted, racing right past the startled guard and disappearing into the undergrowth of the surrounding forest. He heard a high pitch laugh that could only be Suzuha before footsteps sounded behind him. She must have used his run past as her own distraction.

He heard a quiet roar behind him from the two guards, a sound that resonated with his demonic side, sending a thrill through his veins. His human side shrieked and decided not to stop.

That thought was reinforced when something shot through the woods. Alex glanced slightly over his shoulder and paled. Fire raced passed the trees and Alex was forced to duck as another flame blasted just over his head.

"What the heck?" Alex yelped as Suzuha scrambled up beside him. Her smaller stature gave her a lot more speed, it seemed, as she wound her way through the forest with an ease he was *almost* jealous of...almost.

"I guess they were a type of Djinn. Should have seen that coming." Suzuha dodged past a tree just as a blast of fire split the ground where she was running.

"Djinn?" Alex would have asked for specifics or why she called them Djinn instead of Demon, or was Djinn just a type of demon? His wing snapped up, sending him tumbling forward, just barely dodging another blast of fire. Okay, right, focus on running away instead of thinking.

"Well, it would explain why no one leaves," Suzuha muttered as she reached a hand down, helping him to his feet.

"That doesn't help right now," Alex hissed as he ducked behind a stone outcropping, catching his breath for a second before peeking around the corner. Through the trees, he could spot a creature, still in the guard uniform, almost floating through the trees. Wait, floating? He barely suppressed a yelp of panic as he remembered hearing that was possible, but he thought only a demon with wings like his would be able to do that. Good to know, he supposed.

Red glowing eyes searched, scanning over the environment. On the demons' wrists were shackles, something Alex hadn't noticed on the guards before. Did it not translate to their human form or something? He shook his head, he probably missed it since those signifiers were all too common.

"Any suggestions?" Alex kept his voice low and directed toward Suzuha, who was almost hidden in the undergrowth beside him.

She shook her head with a grimace. "I've never dealt with Djinn before or many demons, for that matter. I only know the water demon from..." She trailed off as Alex stiffened.

"Young master, please return with us to the village," a voice echoed, quite literally through the trees. It held almost a ghost-like quality. It was the only one he heard, was the other one elsewhere?

Young master? Alex held still as one of the Djinn came closer, unable to really catch any details from where he hid. The Djinn stopped a few feet away, staring out into the forest.

Alex noted the creature's skin, a reddish hue with what seemed to be a tail in place of legs, hovering just over the ground. Horns curled over its head, a deep red, making Alex wonder how similar or different they looked from his own. He never got a chance to visually see his full form. He mentally pushed away the thought as broken chains clanked on the demon's thick arms. It was a buff creature and not something Alex wanted to mess with at the moment, or ever, for that matter.

It opened its mouth and spoke again. "We have no intention of hurting you. It is not safe in these woods for you, young master. Please return with us."

Not safe? Alex wanted to snort. The Djinn tried to barbecue us. Alex would rather take his chances with the forest.

Silence reigned for a moment before the creature turned. "I will contact the master. He was looking forward to being with you." With that, he left.

Alex would have let out a breath, if not for the choice of words. He choked. Being? What did he mean by that? Alex would understand if they said speaking, but being? He shivered. He knew there was something wrong with the earlier exchange, but...Alex slowly shook his head. Okay, he was being paranoid. He probably just misheard. Alex finally let out the breath he was holding in. Thankfully, it seemed the Djinn could only go so far away from their post.

"Great," Suzuha groaned, slumping onto the ground with a tired huff. She peered up at him with a bit of worry clear on her face. "You okay?"

Alex nodded, staring back where they left from.

"I'm not sure I want to know who this master is if they have two Djinn under their employ as guards. It would definitely explain why no one leaves." She paused before raising an eyebrow. "What did he mean by being?"

Alex shivered. "I wish I knew."

Suzuha stared up at him before pursing her lips. "Being with you, why does that sound familiar?" she muttered before letting out a breath.

Alex's wings twitched, straining slightly against the bandages. "Yeah. Anyway, we should go and find the others. Maybe we can get off this island."

"Huh...you actually make sense for once."

Alex rolled his eyes, noticing as Suzuha smiled sheepishly.

Well, even though he still hadn't eaten, at least they were able to get a good night's rest before they started traipsing through the island again. He couldn't complain too much with that, he supposed.

~ * ~

After a night's rest, Milos was more than willing to move. The air of the island was saturated, almost choking him. As the day stones rose, he found himself jerking awake, hands going toward his throat as he forced himself to breathe. The air was thick. He never felt anything like this before. He cringed, a sharp pain piercing through his head, a sudden spike from a distant part of the island. He struggled to his feet, stepping outside in hopes to get some air. Thankfully, his room was right near the exit, so in no time, he was leaning against the wood siding outside, catching his breath as the day stones slowly began to glow. Finally, able to concentrate, he frowned, thoughts whirling as he tried to pinpoint what that feeling was.

It felt—

He froze. "A ritual?" he muttered, staring up at the day stones as they finally finished lighting and the feeling eased.

Once more, the island was filled with the sporadic bursts of energy he felt the day before but now, those sporadic bursts felt a hell of a lot more sinister.

He pushed away from the wall, brushing the sweat from his brow. What the elder said the night before came back to him as he focused on getting himself back together.

Rita, having been curious about someone who was both a seer and a psychic, sat them down and talked for a good while about the differences. While Milos found it fascinating, it was nothing new to him. After all, the two classes, before the war, were one and the same. While the seer's guild stayed uniform, the Psychics guild grew more into science, trying to mix science and their form of magic. It helped in some capacity, which allowed the guild to have fairly equal footing with its seer counterpart. The conversation, eventually, ended up switching for the reason behind why the elder desired Milos' help.

"A few years ago, a strange thing started occurring." The woman's eyes were tired, almost resigned as she spoke. Milos couldn't help but feel uneasy at the unusual expression. "This island has always been used by travelers. It's the nature of the island. Many from the north used to descend here through unknown paths to get away from the refuge every so often. However, about six years ago, a demon arrived on the island." The woman shook her head, trembling hands in her lap. "We don't actually know where he came from, we suspect from the north, but rumors also speak of him coming from the south. Within no time, he ended up becoming king of the Allegons." She let out a long breath, gaze drifting to the window. "That's when it started. Demons began to stop coming to the island. The Allegons, a people that usually doesn't interact with us much, stopped interacting at all and every morning, our most sensitive demon hunters are hit with a sense of nausea that passes once the day stones are fully up. We've tried to send scouts to figure out what's going on, and people to infiltrate the other village. But..." She shook her head, indicating well enough to Milos what probably happened to them.

Rita gulped loudly, horror on her face, as well as realization. "Milos?"

Milos tilted his head in acknowledgment before turning to the woman. "The Allegons, they live past the mountain, on the other side of this island, correct?"

The woman nodded. "Yes, while we have a surprising abundance of nature, they have a large amount of water and minerals. In the past, before these six years, as much as we disagreed with each other, we would often trade for goods and items. That dried up almost instantly after that demon became king. After all, just because we have opposing views doesn't mean we are constantly in battle. As long as neither side interferes with the other, there is no reason to."

"That's why you asked for my help," Milos deduced as his gaze drifted to the window, finally acknowledging Rita's thought. "You and your people can't interfere with what's going on with the Allegons, for fear that you will start a war you don't think you'll survive. Is that correct?"

"Yes." The woman smiled thinly. "You are correct. While we managed to recover the bodies of our brethren and hide the fact that they were there, we weren't able to obtain any information and doing anything more direct would just lead to the king declaring us no longer useful and slaughtering us." She shook her head. "Thankfully, you are not of our people: you're a foreigner, just happening to land on this island. Sending you would not signal to him that we have rebelled. Plus, you are a Demon hunter, an Alertian. You of all people should be able to take care of this. Of course..." she trailed off, a snarl crossing her face that twisted it into something horrific. "Personally, I wish for you to destroy that demon who calls himself king. This island may not have been peaceful and we may have needed to fight to make sure no demons or other creatures invaded the island, but anything is better than this. Then being unable to do anything as a creature rules over us...as a creature forces us to live under him, always wondering, who will be next."

"Wait, does this demon do anything?" Rita hesitantly asked. "I mean, does he force his rule? I haven't really seen anything like that here."

The Elder leaned back. Her hands finally stopped trembling. "The Allegons worship him, because they fear him. He is an unknown, something they don't understand, with an ability to ingratiate demons to him, or so we believe."

Rita jerked as Milos thrummed the hilt of his sword. To ingratiate a demon, a demon commanding another demon. He only knew of a few demons who could do that, however... "What about this village?"

The woman glanced away, knuckles white. "Every year, he asks for a sacrifice." She chuckled faintly as horror flashed on Rita's face. "Almost like those old storybook tales. One person is picked from the village and never returns. We, my people, they tried to fight it the first time, but while we might be good against one or two demons, he was powerful and well prepared."

Milos pursed his lips, but it was Rita who spoke, terror in her voice. "I'm guessing he also had help. A lot of help."

The Elder nodded, finally leaning back on the couch as the day stones waned. "We were forced to surrender. While he allowed us to continue to operate as we usually would, we have not had need to. We send out forces in order to intercept any boats or demons that might arrive, but demons disappear almost upon arrival and no one else has traveled here."

Milos frowned as Rita slumped backward, shock clear in her posture. "Shvite," she muttered.

For once, Milos didn't feel the need to argue. It seemed they were going to have to meet with this demon. "We'll do it."

The Elder's beaming and hopeful smile spoke volumes.

Now, as he was coming to terms with what she mentioned, the nausea others felt, he knew he would have helped anyway. He pulled his thoughts to the present, finally getting his wits about him. It wouldn't do to collapse like that. At least, now that he was aware of the feeling, he could be more prepared for it. Of course, what could cause it? The air was flooded, so he wasn't positive he could pinpoint it, but for a split second, he remembered thinking it was a wave, a tsunami crashing over the island, originating—his gaze snapped to the lone mountain, towering a few miles away, spiraling up to the ceiling. The feeling, he couldn't help but think, came from the middle of the island, from the only mountain on the whole island.

He heard footsteps before the creaking of a door alerted him to Rita's arrival. The girl let out a yawn, walking up to him with a stretch. "I thought I was antsy to find Alex."

She grinned before pausing, seemingly spotting something on his face. How that was possible, Milos didn't have a clue.

She watched him for a while before leaning on one leg, hands on her hips. "All right, so what are we doing now? Got anything figured out?"

"You suppose I do? What do you think has changed from last night?"

She rolled her eyes. "Maybe because you were staring off at the mountain and you look like you've tried one of my potions again."

Was he that obvious? Well, he did just get rid of the nausea; he supposed he wasn't fully recollected. "I suppose." He turned to her. "Something the woman said last night caught my attention. Why would this demon need a sacrifice? At least, a yearly? If this demon is powerful, it would just use the entire village, or have more frequent sacrifices."

"Wait, you think there's a *reason* that lunatic is doing this?" Rita waved her arms.

"Lunatic?" Milos glanced over as she let out a huff.

"Well, yeah? What else can I call him? Demon doesn't work because, well, that's just rude to Alex and I can't call him human because he's not, so lunatic."

Milos resisted the chuckle from leaving his lips, though they did quirk up in a faint smile. "It sounds like a child's logic."

"Oh, and you think you have something better?" She growled, sticking her finger toward his chest. "What would you call someone like that?"

"Dictator would be one word."

Milos moved away from her finger, heading toward the edge of village. He was originally planning on stocking up, but he was no longer willing to take anything from the people here, not at this time. If they hadn't been able to trade for six years and there were no attacks, they were definitely struggling to make ends meet.

"Well, that's true, but..." Rita paused before spotting where he was going and, yelping, chased after him. "Hey, wait."

Milos slowed his pace, but did not stop, earning a huff from Rita as she caught up with him, glaring. "Geez...still, that's not our business, right? We just have to find Alex and..."

Milos shook his head, startling Rita. "My job is to hunt demons." He grasped the hilt of his sword tightly as he moved forward, passing into the tree line so similar and yet different from home. "I was asked to hunt, so I will do my duty, that is all there is to it. Remember, I am here of my own free will, not from a desire to help you." His voice was cold, but his thoughts churned. "Though I suppose looking for Alex is important..." The last few words were more muttered than he would have preferred and, truth be told, he wasn't sure which part of the sentence was a lie.

Rita slowed for a moment, startled, before racing past him. She peered up at him for a split second before a wide smile shone on her face. "Ah-ha! You are worried about him."

She placed her hands behind her head, shifting her hat slightly as Milos stiffened. "You are just trying to hide it with that Alertian bull-shvite that you usually come up with. You are such a lout, you know that?"

"You believe that?" Milos tried to keep a straight face, but the widening grin on Rita's made him finally relinquish with a sigh. "Fine, yes, I am worried about him." He straightened himself, and caught, just in time, Rita stumbling forward from surprise. At least it was worth seeing that.

She turned to him, a gleam in her expression. "I thought so. I was wondering why you stayed with us, and I doubted the shvite you gave Alex about just going to the refuge. You actually care for us."

Milos' fingers twitched toward his blade. "Let us move, and stop talking, or we will never catch up with them." With that he strided purposefully forward, forcing her to yelp and stumble to catch up. He didn't slow his pace at all.

"Okay, okay. Will you slow down you lout?" Rita panted after a few minutes of the harsh pace. "How are we going to fight a demon who seems to be able to control other demons? Hm?"

Milos' gaze flicked to the mountains as he slowed his pace enough for her to catch up. It took a moment for her to catch her breath before he responded, "We're going to figure out how he does that."

Rita's response was silence, as her arms dropped to her sides before following his gaze. She groaned. "Ugh, I guess that makes sense. At least this pace is a bit more reasonable." She didn't say more, for which Milos was grateful.

He felt a little grateful that she was staying with him instead of going off on her own to search for Alex. He would question the whys of that when he *didn't* have a pounding headache from both the surroundings and her words.

Chapter Twenty-four

Alex cleared the tree line much earlier than he would have liked. The light bit of dirt disappeared into rocky outcroppings. He slid to a halt, staring up at the lone mountain he and Suzuhah almost crashed into earlier. He was steadily moving toward it, his good wing flickering for a moment in indecision.

"We should probably go around," Suzuha, the little girl, admitted as she took a seat on a nearby slab of stone, pulling out a bag.

Alex briefly wondered why she was still in female form, but figured it was just easier to move around that way.

To Alex's relief, she pulled out some food, tossing it over to him. He had been ignoring it, but he was very hungry after almost a full *twenty-four* hours without food. Even though it was just basic bread and cheese, it at least hit the spot for a quick ration. Though it didn't stop the shudder from passing through him at the thought of climbing the mountain at his back. The only thing was... "That would be great, but I don't see a path."

Suzuha's response was a quiet hum as she slung the bag back over her shoulder before she sighed. "Yeah, true."

"Too bad neither of us could fly," Alex muttered, wings fluttering at the half-hearted jab.

Suzuha's response was to stick out her tongue. "Well, if someone hadn't thrown a water spear through my wing."

Alex felt his eye twitch, but he resisted the urge to respond, slumping onto another seat beside her. They had been walking for a while now and he needed to rest for a moment. Suzuha flopped onto her back, arms spread wide. Alex paused, peering over her. Bandages crisscrossed over her arms and peeked out from under clothes, one or two showing speckles of red.

"You still don't have enough energy to change form to heal?" he asked hesitantly, catching her attention.

She pushed herself up, lost in thought before she shook her head.

"It's not as easy for me to change into that bigger form as it is for you. I think I mentioned this earlier. Although it was a blur, so if I did, I'll apologize." She leaned forward slightly, gesturing toward her back. "While my winged form is my base form, it also uses up the most energy. While it would help in my recovery, it isn't exactly subtle. Plus, I just simply don't have the means to change. While I'm not exactly starving anymore, I'll be lucky if I can continue changing back and forth between my male and female forms."

Alex leaned forward, finding himself curious. "How were you able to change when you were first injured?"

She pursed her lips, attention drifting to the rocks coating the ground. "People's life force, for me, is similar to food. Each person is different with different advantages and flavors." Alex shivered at the thought, but let her continue. "You, and those on your ship...they held a lot of life, the idea of possibility, but the people here?" She shook her head. "The people's life force here is subdued. So, while I'm getting full, it's a full that's the equivalent of just eating bread all day, no nutritional value. I'm not sure why my mistress made me this way, or why I'm still alive." She leaned against a nearby rock, smile wan. "I sometimes wonder if I was supposed to be this way. A Vulfulas should only obey one master, the one who created them. I've searched for information, trying to find out more about Vulfulas, if this is normal, if I'm normal." She shrugged, returning her sharp gaze to him, startling him. "To answer your question. It was because the life force I retrieved before arriving was still strong, but as my body focused on healing, it dwindled. That's why I didn't transform back at the village until the last minute, amongst other things, and it's why I'm not transforming now into my male form."

Alex found himself observing the ground, trying to avoid connecting with Suzuha. It was weird to think that a creature could live like that, but Suzuha spoke about it so casually and a part of Alex believed her.

Strangely, he didn't feel frightened. He knew he should. Technically, he was food for her too, but she wasn't approaching him, wasn't doing anything besides sitting there, soaking up the light of the day stones. At this point, was there any reason for him to feel afraid of her?

He would have asked more questions if she didn't decide to hop down, the sound of her feet thudding onto the earth, startling him. He jerked upright as she waved to one side. "Well? We should go."

Alex pushed himself to his feet, trailing after her as she headed down a path that he hadn't noticed earlier, one she obviously spotted.

So, if she spotted it, why didn't she take it? Did she just want to rest? To talk? He chuckled faintly as he caught up with her. The two walked for a while in silence, clamoring over small portions of stone and sliding down into lower paths. He could feel his tail swaying behind him, as if curious. The tugging feeling from before ebbed as the day progressed. Their walk was hampered, but he felt like they were making good time. After a few more hours, they drew to a stop once more to rest. Water hummed quietly, flowing down from a brook that seemed to lead up the mountain and down toward the sea. The surroundings were slightly covered with a rocky overhang. They didn't have much for food, besides what little Suzuha had scrounged up from the village. Realizing this, Suzuha rolled up her sleeve and dove into hunting for prey as Alex found himself waiting in a rocky alcove. It wasn't long until she returned, carrying the carcass of something. Alex grimaced, but let her work, watching as she cleaned and gutted the thing with a knife strapped to her waist, having been hidden under the long tunic.

"Wait, when did you have that?"

She barely glanced up as she cut through the food. "This whole time. It's conducive to hunting, but I wasn't about to stick it in your gut. That's too painless, or at least, I thought it was."

"Joy," Alex muttered, finding himself chuckling. She glared at him, but didn't respond. "That just proves my earlier point though."

"About me not killing you? Yeah, I get it."

Suzuha let out a breath as she finished up, washing up in the stream before heading over. She peered at him, staring at the wings for a moment before returning her attention to the strips of meat.

That's when they realized the other problem. They had no means of cooking it.

"You wouldn't happen to know how to start a fire, right?" Alex tapped the stone beside him as his stomach growled. The rations certainly helped, but the idea of eating meat was just a little too enticing.

"If I could switch forms for a moment, yeah, but..." She let out a sigh, slumping to the ground.

Alex stared. Either he ate that raw, and threatened to get sick or... "If you have energy, would you be able to cook it and possibly get us out of here?"

Her gaze flicked up to him, a wary expression on her face. "Animal life force is a good supplement, sure, but as injured as I am..."

"So fleeing is a no go?" He quirked his lips up in order to make the disappointment in his voice sound less harsh. She caught it anyway.

"Even if I had more than that, I could only transform for a short time. It would speed up the process, sure, but I wouldn't be able to lift more than my own body weight. I certainly wouldn't be able to fly," she supplied delicately.

Alex stared down at the stream, thoughts churning a mile a minute. Truth be told, while Suzuha put on a brave face, he could see her stumbling forward, barely keeping up with him. Blood still seeped from the wounds, he noticed, staining the bandages, and a grimace was practically etched on her face by this point.

As much as it might have been easier to leave her behind someplace safe and go find the others, he couldn't convince himself to.

However, that meant their progress was a lot slower than he would have liked. He just wondered why no one managed to catch up to them, or knew where they were.

He brought a hand to his face. If he went through with the crazy idea that just popped into his mind, he could solve two birds with one stone. However, was he willing to put himself in such a situation? At such a risk?

He let out a groan. How was this new idea any different from usual? He was used to pulling off stupid things anyway.

"How about mine?"

Suzuha stilled, entire body seeming to lock up where she stood, organizing the strips. "What?"

"How about my life force?" He let out a breath. "I might not be any better, but..."

Suzuha shook her head and turned to him, actual fear shining on her face for a moment, startling him into stopping, teeth clacking shut.

"No. You, Rita, even that demon hunter friend of yours. It's been hard *not* doing anything."

"Huh?" Alex shifted slightly as Suzuha's attention drifted to her hands, tightly grasping the meat.

"Remember how I said each life force is different? Well, the three of you...it's been a long time since I've seen and felt life force that strong, that hopeful, that proud. For me? It's the equivalent of..." She trailed off as Alex lifted his arm, confused on what she meant. Sure, Milos talked before about tracing him through the magic and all, but was that the same as the life force she mentioned?

"And, that would mean?"

She winced, curling in slightly. "It's tantalizing and I'm not sure if I would be able to *stop*."

Alex froze as her words met his ears and he shivered before pulling a sharp breath in through his nose. "How would you need to eat?"

Suzuha jerked, staring up at him in shock. He waved, letting out a tired, "I'm not an idiot, I'm well aware of what I'm saying, but I also know we both need to be at, if not full strength, at least heading that way." He gestured to the water. "I do have a bit of water demon in me, like you guessed, I'm getting a lot of energy just by resting here. Plus, if you get too greedy..." He grinned, crossing his legs and placing his hands on his knees, leaning forward slightly. "I still owe you for trying to kill me earlier."

She stared before letting out a snort. "You three are so strange," she muttered before sighing. "Extend your arm out."

Alex blinked, doing as she said. She tentatively came forward, gently twisting his arm so his wrist faced upward. "This doesn't work as well as being right next to a main vein, like your neck, but it should do."

With that, she leaned forward and Alex had to withhold a grimace, hand flinching in her grasp.

It was the strangest feeling. He could see her gulping, as if drinking something, but the only thing touching his wrist was the tip of her nose. Her mouth was slightly open.

He shivered at the sight, quickly facing away. It felt so weird. He could feel himself tiring slightly as she ate and it almost felt like there was something biting into his skin, though he knew nothing was actually touching except the hands and nose. To anyone watching, it would seem like she was sniffing his wrist.

When he began to feel dizzy, he turned back, lightly pulling his wrist away. Her grip tightened as the feeling of teeth dug in harder. He tugged harder and she let out a sound, much like a growl, muffled slightly.

Well, he did warn her. He uncurled and brought one leg up. With enough strength to shove but not injure, he pushed into her side. She resisted for only a moment before he pushed harder, back to the stone for leverage, causing her to yelp and stumble back. She let go of his wrist as she rubbed her side, blinking wildly. "Huh?"

She stared down at herself before turning to him as he brought his arm back, shaking it out with a grimace. "That just feels wrong."

"You..."

"Did that help?" he asked as he stood, stepping over to the water, dipping his arm in. The liquid soothed the slight burn he felt racing through his veins. He kept half his attention on the girl, watching as she stared at him.

"I expected you to slug me, not just push me away with your foot."

"Believe me, I was tempted," he mumbled as a faint smile trailed onto her lips.

She giggled slightly before a faint flash caught his attention.

Where she stood, now stood the Vulfulas he saw before. The wings curled onto either side of the body, wrapped and bloody as the long tail curled around the creature's feet. The furred face stared at him. Its golden eyes were gleaming.

Yet he didn't feel scared. He wasn't sure why that was, considering he wouldn't necessarily be able to fight back right now, but...

The Vulfulas jerked, head tilting upward as it shifted defensively.

To his surprise, the creature darted forward, grabbing him up by the scuff of his neck, tossing him over its shoulder. He yelped and scrambled to grab hold of the fur just as it jerked forward, leaping over the stream and away from their campsite. Away from the food he knew he needed.

Just in time, Alex noted with horror as ice, honest to goodness *ice* pierced up where the Vulfulas was standing. Within moments, the entire area where they just were, was coated in ice, interlocking pieces weaving together to create a sort of cage.

"Holy," he breathed as he clung to the creature's back.

"I almost didn't sense it in time." The Vulfulas spoke, barely opening its mouth as it darted over the terrain. While its wings were weak, its movements were still fluid, as if it was just as used to the land as it was the air, bounding through the sparse trees with ease.

"Where?" he asked weakly, peering over his shoulder.

The Vulfulas shook its head. Ice pierced out, trying to catch them as they dodged. That's when Alex noticed her.

Out of the corner of his eye, floating over the ground, racing forward was a woman. She had long black hair, face hidden and she was wearing a long, ragged robe. He jerked, turning to face her just as she tilted her head up.

For a split second, he spotted pale skin, blue lips and a black gaze. Then, she was gone.

A shiver raced up his spine as the Vulfulas dodged to the left, a ring of ice curling around where the Vulfulas had been.

"A Yuki-onna? What is one of those doing here?" The Vulfulas cursed, wings fluttering.

"Yuki-what?" Alex choked out.

"A type of demon. They control ice and snow and are often, if not always, women, unlike Djinn, which are always male." The Vulfulas ducked around a pillar of rock, ice splashing over the side as if it was water, curling around. They were gone by the time it enclosed around it.

"It's strange. I've never seen the two near each other."

Alex gulped tightly, wings fluttering in panic. His demonic side was twisting, desperate, a thrill of fear trailing down his spine, along with that consistent familiarity. He knew that demon, somehow, but from where? He leaned forward, trying to create as little wind resistance as possible, his entire body flush against the soft fur under him. He wasn't sure how long they moved, or where they went. Whenever he thought they got away from the demon, he would spot her out of the corner of his periphery and Suzuha would dodge away.

It was as they were getting close to a cliff edge, water crying out to him, he shot up. "Jump down," he called.

Suzuha started, but seemed to follow with his words, leaping off the edge as ice crisscrossed where she'd been.

Water sat below, wide enough for the both of them. He closed his eyes tightly just as they splashed down, diving underneath.

It felt completely different being under the water, finding he had no problem seeing underneath the waves. He kept his grip on Suzuha as the creature shifted, grasping onto him tightly in human form, panic clear on her face. He held her tightly close to him as, contrary to every part of his human thoughts, he dived down.

None too soon as ice coated the water, shredding over the surface and quickly moving downward.

He listened to his demonic instinct, swerving around a pillar of stone, realizing his good wing was boosting him as much as his legs. The water curved around him, helping him move faster. Up ahead was a crevice that he hoped led into the mountain.

He slipped through and lunged up, almost leaping out of the water with a gasping breath, scrambling up onto a side ledge, pulling a shivering Suzuha with him just as the ice finished freezing everything inches from his feet. The girl was curled onto her side, panic running through her. Water dripped down them as they stared at the firmly frozen pond, watching to see if the ice would spread any more.

Silence filled the little cavern as they caught their breath. Nothing moved, no sound besides their panting reached back to them.

Finally, he let out a long breath and turned to Suzuha, checking her over. She was breathing, but he could tell their dive into the water had, well, terrified her.

"You can't handle water," he whispered, shock thrumming through his veins as he reached down. Suzuha grasped his hand like a vice, almost curling around it. His breath caught in his throat, but she didn't do anything else, just hung on, water dripping from her hair and coating the ground around them. He reached another arm forward, slowly rubbing her back, much like he remembered his mom doing oh so long ago.

Slowly, so slowly, Alex was beginning to worry anew, she uncurled from her prone position, breath returning to normal. She let go of his arm and leaned back against the rock, staring at the slowly dissolving ice in a quiet horror.

Alex couldn't blame her. That was terrifying, looking back on it. He wasn't sure they were safe now. Did that woman know of this place? He hadn't noticed while they were running, adrenaline racing through his veins, but now?

"Well..." he trailed off, not sure what he was going to say.

Suzuha shook her head, wringing out her clothes as her hair hid her face.

"Thanks," she mumbled.

"I think that extends both ways," he pointed out with a faint grin. "You were the one who noticed her there."

Suzuha stayed silent for a long time before she let out a sigh. Alex took that as a weary agreement as he returned his attention to the ice that was slowly starting to thin out. "We probably shouldn't stay here, just in case she notices." He paused, turning back toward Suzuha. "Still, what was she after? Who was she?"

"Probably the woman who found us in the forest earlier. Her signature felt familiar." Alex jerked, noting how Suzuha's head was bowed. "I hadn't noticed too much at the time. I only had vague feelings and thoughts, considering how weak I was, but she felt like she had a similar energy to the Djinn. I have a feeling she was sent to either kill or capture us."

"Why?" Alex muttered, briefly remembering what the Djinn said earlier. Being with...he shivered. "Why are there so many demons? I get that place was to worship demons, but..."

Suzuha shook her head, slowly pushing herself into a sitting position. "Your guess is as good as mine. I haven't been here in years. I don't know what has changed. However, what I find strange is that, from what I've learned, Yuki-onna usually work alone. They aren't a demon who tends to work with others, nor do they tend to obey anyone except those they deem worthy."

Alex pursed his lips at that thought before letting out a long sigh. "Well, sitting here isn't getting us any answers." He groaned, stomach growling. He wished he hadn't lost his lunch, but at least he wasn't starving. The dive into the water helped a little, thank the heavens for his demonic side in that regard, and Suzuha was probably fine as well in the hunger department. Alex was still feeling slightly dizzy from her earlier feast. He pushed himself to his feet, extending an arm down to a surprised Suzuha. Suzuha hesitantly took it, hoisting herself to her feet. "Do you at least feel better?"

Suzuha blinked before relaxing slightly, a faint smile on her face. "Oddly? Yes."

"Good." He turned to the only other exit he could see out of the little cavern, an entrance that the dim light of the surrounding light stones was doing almost nothing to break through. "Because it looks like we have a ways to go."

"Oh, goodie," Suzuha muttered, but followed after him as he moved forward.

It was going to be a *long* day.

Chapter Twenty-five

Milos winced, stumbling slightly. Rita stared at him worriedly as he righted himself, a chill running down his spine.

"Hey, you okay there?" she called for what felt like the fifth time in the last ten minutes.

Milos was no longer able to tell her otherwise. He let out a grunt, getting his feet under him. The nausea was long gone, but for the last few minutes, he felt as if he was hammered with energy, powerful magic that no demon should be capable of. At least, none except the most powerful. He hadn't expected the feeling. After all, such a feeling was detrimental for a demon hunter, but this entire island was messed up, so why not everything else? Milos shook his head as he slid down another slope, the light stone hanging around his neck offering enough illumination in the darkness of the cave. They had been traveling for a while, only stopping to eat before heading out again.

The cold feeling finally subsided and he was better able to pinpoint it. It was a ways away, almost the exact opposite of where they walked as if it was the far side of the mountain

"So, what was it this time?"

Milos shook his head as Rita came to a stop beside him, brushing down her skort before hurrying to his side. "Not sure," he admitted as they continued forward. "This island is messing with my senses. It's as if it's intentionally making it difficult for me to figure out anything."

"Lovely," Rita groused as she moved ahead, her own light stone jostling slightly as she lifted it from her chest, highlighting the next corridor. "We've been stuck down here for an hour already, I think. I didn't think I would *ever* say this, but I'm getting sick of being stuck underground."

Milos snorted, unable to suppress the sound at the irony of her words.

"Ha-ha, laugh it up," she said. "An Underlander getting sick of being underground, but this isn't the same and you know it."

"True, but this is more of what I expected when I first descended into the Underlands."

Rita didn't respond to that, stopping in her tracks. She turned to the wall, staring at it with a heavy frown. Milos trailed to a halt, not saying anything. He recognized that expression and decided it was best not to distract her. It wasn't the first time it happened since they descended into the cave.

"Again," she muttered. There was irritation laced into her words. "Another witch's incantation." She traced her fingers over an area of stone that honestly seemed no different to Milos.

Rita stopped, her fingers pausing to one side before she scoffed. "Whoever is putting these up is an amateur." She reached for the pen she put near her ear after the second time she spotted one of these and reached up, scratching some lines over the stone.

The difference was subtle, but still noticeable. The air cleared slightly. A faint sound, like a cry, echoed from within, one Rita didn't seem to notice.

Milos sometimes wished his senses weren't so sharp. He was starting to get perturbed as they descended, her scratching out whatever she was seeing as they went. He hadn't thought the need to mention it, but now he was starting to wonder if he should.

He shook his head as she placed the quill back near her ear and turned toward where they were heading. "All right, let's get moving." She marched forward with determined steps as Milos followed behind, fingering the hilt of his sword as they went. Their footsteps rang over the stone, echoing up and down the path with a clarity Milos was *not* appreciating.

"Hopefully, we won't have to go too much farther." Rita watched the walls as she spoke, hand occasionally grazing over the stone. "Most of those were meant to waylay travelers, both in and out. The path itself is pretty straightforward. It's possible this is where they brought the sacrifices." She shivered at the word, stumbling slightly before righting herself. "But why would they still be alive if they were sacrifices?"

Milos had no answer to that, nor was he sure he wanted to know the answer as they descended farther and farther downward. He heard another cry, sounding so strange to his ears. He extended an arm out, startling Rita into stopping. Her gaze flitted to him, but something on his face must have answered her unasked question. She moved back, as Milos slunk forward, grip tight on his sword. He carefully covered the light stone he made sure to bring with him, using only the bare minimum to move forward before peering around the corner of the next bend. Light filtered in through a hole that led into what he could only assume was a cavern. He couldn't see much from his angle, but it seemed like he was staring more at what he thought was a psychics lab, or the lab he saw in the Martinet's guild. It wasn't something he thought he would find out here, so far north. He could hear quiet sobs from within as he slowly gestured Rita forward.

The girl was silent as she moved to step beside him, squatting down and covering her own light stone. She stiffened, spotting something he probably didn't see before her lips curled up in disgust.

"Another one," she quietly spat as she slunk forward, moving around the corner, but staying out of sight of the light. She stopped a few inches away from him, just across the path as her fingers grazed over the stone. "A sound suppressant and a cage for those within the barrier. This one isn't even to keep anyone out anymore." She gripped her quill tightly and reached up, slashing a few choice lines.

Milos wished she didn't as the faint cries he heard up until this point shot up into almost animalistic howling. Rita stumbled back, scrambling to catch the quill before it landed on the ground, though she needn't have bothered. The sounds of screams and cries, of the humming of machinery and the loud pounding of water over stone enveloped the hallway, smashing into him with the force of a physical object. He was still doing better than Rita, who was holding her ears tightly, almost curled up on the ground as he grabbed her, dragging her out of sight of the exit.

He should have warned her, but he hadn't thought it was going to be that bad. He only realized when she mentioned sound suppressant. If he was still hearing the cries over a witch's spell, it was only that warning that prepared him when it all came crashing down.

Rita wasn't able to completely avoid it, curling in on herself as she stared at the wall.

Milos turned away. These sounds, they were all too similar to the sounds from the Martinet's guild. From the slaves who still had willpower left in them, those that were still fighting, along with those on the verge of giving up, all twisted in some way he couldn't quite distinguish. Sounding more animalistic than they had any right to be.

It was a sound he didn't want to hear again and never thought he would hear this far north.

"Why?" Rita vocalized the words, horror seeping through every part of her. "I mean, I knew to expect something when I heard of sacrifices, but we're away from the Martinet's guild, away from..."

She trailed off and Milos had to wonder what exactly was going through her mind at that moment. He knew enough about what caused her to flee to feel; it might have something to do with that, but he couldn't be certain. He turned his attention back to the corner.

"Would they be able to tell you messed with the spell?"

"N-No," she whispered. "It... I set it up so it only affects this corridor. Anywhere else, the spell is still holding."

"Good." Milos stood, moving around the corner, only to withhold a yelp as Rita latched onto to his arm.

"Good?" she squeaked. "How is any of this *good*?"

Milos turned to her with a sharp look. "It's good, because it means they, whoever is in there, probably haven't noticed us yet."

Rita opened and closed her mouth, but didn't respond, slowly letting go of his sleeve as anger took over. "Those..." her words faltered, but her determined steps as she moved in front of him spoke volumes.

Milos let her, watching her back as they moved closer to the entrance, preparing himself for what he would find within.

~ * ~

Julie Boglisch

Rita's ears were still ringing, her mind going round and round.

Though she needn't have worried: the thoughts and her own footsteps slammed to a halt as soon as they stepped into the light.

Before her was a large cavern. They stood on an upper ring of a two-story place, stone rails circling the room with a set of stairs leading down to a first floor on the left and right. The first floor held a set of cages off to one side, hard to see from where they stood. On the opposite side was a wall of metal and wires, a strange contraption connected to glass tubes filled the whole wall. A few people in strange tunics and hoods hurried around.

She almost let out a yelp when she felt an arm forcefully push her down. She struggled for only a moment before she realized who it was. Milos was squatted down beside her, gaze firmly on the surroundings or, more specifically as she followed his line of sight, a few of the hooded people at the opposite end of the cavern who were working on the strange metal console.

Her breath caught in her throat as she noticed one of the tubes she spotted earlier was filled. A young woman was curled up in a fetal position, hair floating as much as she was. She was surrounded in a strangely blueish green water. Her skin was patchy and scarred and her eyes were open, staring blankly ahead. They glowed softly in the light of the light stones, an eerie blue. No, not by the light of the light stones. "Her eyes, they're..." Rita trailed off, her voice so low as to be nonexistent. Milos heard it anyway, nodding.

"I sense a lot of demonic presence," he spoke quietly, voice seemingly carefully blank. "Thankfully, it doesn't seem they've noticed us yet."

It was true, she sighed at the thought, their path brought them to a part of the upper lip away from the stairs, almost like a side entrance. She shivered.

"It's been a while since I've seen a psychic's lab." Milos peered off to one side and Rita followed his gaze, noticing the large winding pipes crisscrossing off to the right. "After being down here for so long, it's strange to see technology at this level."

"Technology? Right, science," Rita muttered, reorganizing her thoughts.

She honestly forgot that bit. Unlike seers like herself, psychics held up the past as their example of the proper way to live. They often researched into the occult and technology of the eras long before the Human-Demon War, dating back to even some old documents she once read, stating about some great technological kingdom lost centuries ago. But that research, especially lately, was always confidential, so she hadn't thought about it.

What was that research doing here? *What* were they researching?

Her answer was given a moment later when a guttural scream crashed over her, emanating from the woman in the tube. She suddenly uncurled, thrashing and scratching at the tube as something flashed over her skin. For a split second, Rita thought she saw the woman's hair turn a deep black, before returning to the brown it already was. Her skin flaked, almost falling off as she scrabbled bloodstained fingers against the tube. All the while, she screamed at the top of her lungs as the 'scientists' worked, A moment later, she stilled, slumping over as a red light flashed above her tube, a fire stone, Rita noted vacantly.

The tube drained and she collapsed to the bottom, out of sight from their perch.

Rita couldn't help but continue to watch, seeing the woman dragged away and thrown in one of the cages, a few of the hooded figures shaking their heads before moving to another cage, pulling out a middle-aged man with blueish skin and claw-tipped fingers. Chains bound his arms as he was dragged over and placed into the tube, much like the woman.

At that, Rita finally turned away, rushing back into the tunnel. Milos didn't stop her and she was grateful as she heaved, leaning heavily against the wall. She heard quiet footsteps and managed to shoot a shaky glare toward Milos, only to pause. If she didn't know the man the way she did, she would have thought he was impassive to what they just saw, but no, she knew the man well after the last few weeks. He was pale, hand slightly shaking as he gripped the hilt of his sword, his brow pinched just enough to show he was trying hard not to follow her own example.

She wiped her mouth, shivering.

"That was not pleasant," he admitted, turning to peer back down the tunnel from where they came, the light still shining through.

"What were they...?"

Milos didn't respond for the longest time, his knuckles a pure white. Finally, he relaxed his hand, crossing his arms over his chest as he leaned against the wall. She moved away from her position, sitting a few inches away as she recentered her thoughts.

"Do you remember when I mentioned the information we managed to gather about Alex?"

Rita listened, nodding enough for him to continue.

"One piece of information we found, that I didn't mention and it seems neither did he, is that we found out a bit more about his father." Rita perked up, staring up in shock as Milos leaned one foot back against the wall, as if trying to hold it up himself. "I'd never heard of it happening before, but supposedly, part of the psychics' guild conducted experiments to mix demon DNA into humans. The experiments didn't go as planned, from what I could assume. Alex's father was one of those experiments. Remember when I said Alex seemed like a water demon? That's from his father's side."

"So that's why, but what...?" Rita suddenly cut herself off as she followed Milos' gaze, directed toward the light. "Those are—that's a psychics lab and experiments. They are trying to create human-demon hybrids."

"Exactly." Milos' voice was quiet, almost tired. "Yet it seems it isn't going well. Makes sense, considering it's hard enough to create a natural birth mix."

"What reason would they have to do that so far north? In an area that's supposed to be so close to a refuge?"

Milos winced, pushing away from the wall. "Can't say. It would explain the weird fluctuations I've been feeling since we arrived, though."

Rita pursed her lips at the thought, debating. They knew, but what could they do about it? "We wouldn't be able to rescue them, right?"

Milos stayed silent, his expression grave.

"Would they want to be rescued?" she finally muttered, thoughts flicking to the dead gaze of the woman, the slumped-over figure of the man.

Neither of them had an answer to that.

~ * ~

Alex peered around another corner, before letting out a quiet groan of relief, dropping a piece of light stone that managed to stay lit after he broke it off. It was starting to fade, so he was grateful they finally happened across a stretch of tunnel that was gently lit with a soft blue glow. Suzuha's young frame leaned forward, peeking around the corner before she slipped forward, walking quickly down the path. Alex followed at a more sedate pace, listening quietly to the surroundings. They had been walking for a little while, with only the quiet drip of distant water and their own footsteps ringing back to them. Light was sparing, and he was forced to break off a new light stone whenever the one they were using finally faded. He missed his own, but it was with his cloak, which was back on the ship.

Alex's tail curled around him as his wings rustled against his back, the bandage feeling constricting at this point. At least it didn't hurt as much.

The tunnel they were walking down began to widen out into a small cavern. Stalactites and stalagmites curled around the entire room, water dripping down and pooling at the edge of the floor. Light stones gleamed as they scanned the area. To Alex's annoyance, there were a few different paths they could take and he wasn't sure he could sense which one to follow. Rita or Milos would know, but he wasn't as good. Though, now that he thought about it, Milos did get lost for around a month when he first arrived, so that was probably a moot point.

"Gah, this place is way too big," Suzuha groused, plopping onto the ground with a huff. She crossed her arms as she peered into each of the options.

Alex couldn't argue, his wings fluttering as soft humming filled his ears. "Doesn't help we basically came in through a back entrance, in a way." He stepped over to one of the tunnels, peeking in, hoping to find some clue. Not finding much of anything, he pulled back with a sigh. "I'm glad we didn't get trapped in that place. It could have just been an alcove instead of leading into the mountain."

"True," Suzuha admitted, swaying side to side. "Still makes me wonder what that Yuki-Onna was after. She didn't keep the ice up for very long at all and more often than not, it seemed like she was trying to create cages instead of kill us."

"That's a pleasant thought." Alex stepped away, returning to Suzuha's side. "I met the demon king. He was a bit..." Alex trailed off, unsure how to really describe the man. Weird was one thing, but he also felt strangely familiar and Alex had no idea why.

"You met him?" Suzuha perked up, tilting her head toward him.

"Yeah. He said he was a..." Alex furrowed his brow.

He said he was a Nyx, that's a type of water demon, the same type of creature that Suzuha mentioned killed her mistress. Did he want to bring that up right now when he needed Suzuha to remain calm? He wasn't in the mood to try to deal with a pissed-off Suzuha, not by himself in a place he wasn't even sure they could escape. He shook his head. "A shape-shifter, taking on a male form." Alex shrugged, letting out a breath of mild relief when Suzuha only nodded at that. "He mentioned shapeshifting into that form, though I'm not sure why."

Suzuha shrugged. "I'm not sure about shapeshifters, but I know a lot of times, I like shifting form on a whim. Sometimes, I just prefer to be in this form, like right now when speed and stealth is of the essence. Other times I prefer my male form, which is taken more seriously and has a bit more strength to it, so I wouldn't be surprised if they were the same way. Probably what threw me off for you, considering you can't shape-shift yourself, though you are part water demon."

"Yeah, no, I don't know how to use my demon side at all." Alex glared at his wings as they slid closer to his back, almost cowering. He wanted, so badly, to put them away, but he could tell they were still in the healing phase and his mind was letting him know it would be a bad idea.

"Speaking of, since you can't use it, have you tried switching back to your human form?" Suzuha tilted her head slightly, expression neutral. "It might still hurt, but your wing is almost recovered." She paused as Alex furrowed his brow unsure how to answer. She chuckled and continued, "Is it because you feel stronger in that form? Maybe it's comforting in a place like this with water all around and only me as a bodyguard."

"Bodyguard? I wouldn't really call you that," Alex responded without thinking, his attention on her earlier words. "I guess it makes sense, though there is a lot of water still lingering and, I guess, even with my injured wing there is a feeling of power that my human form doesn't have." He frowned. "Sure, my human form feels safe, but right now, I feel like instinct is a better option to have, especially in a place as dangerous as this."

Suzuha nodded, humming the same tune from before, which felt almost calming. "Makes sense. Each of our forms have their own purpose and reason for existence, though we might not always know what that reason is." She glanced at her hand. "Might as well use the benefits when we need them, right?"

Alex peered toward the dripping water, watching it slowly trail down the stalactite. "Makes sense." He returned his attention to Suzuha. "Still, what now? Now that we know changing forms would probably not be wise right now, what do we do? I mean, me meeting the demon king isn't going to be much help getting us out of here."

"No, but at least we somewhat know to avoid him and any other demon around," Suzuha pointed out, easily following along with his change of subject, hopping off the rock she sat on. "Speaking of, I would try something myself, but my energy level is still low, even with the food you gave me, so we'll have to make do."

"Try something? Do I want to know?" Alex asked as Suzuha picked a direction and started walking.

"Probably not."

She hummed as Alex huffed, hurrying after her.

Their footsteps sounded loud as the light slowly faded behind them. Alex almost wished he actually took the time to sit down and rest for a moment, much like Suzuha had, but there wasn't anything he could do about it now. If anything, he just wanted to get out of these tunnels. Of course, that made him think of the others. Were Rita and Milos all right? What about Ari and Leon? What about the Aqua Wraith? What happened to the ship? There was so much he didn't know, and he hated that. It felt like there was always something he didn't know.

He knew it was impossible to know everything, but sometimes he wished he did.

He let out a long breath, only to hear a yelp and stop, his wings— or more specifically, the unbound wing—snapping out as if to drag him to a halt. Pain seared up his back and he hissed.

Suzuha stumbled back, slamming into him harshly. He winced, barely catching them before steadying himself.

"That was..." Suzuha's voice was hesitant as she peered ahead at something Alex couldn't see.

He could definitely feel something though. Not just the burn from his wings snapping out and wrenching at his back. He rubbed his shoulder for a moment before peering down the hallway.

"Whatever it was, my demonic side *definitely* didn't want to go any farther forward."

Suzuha nodded, pulling away and patting herself down, as if to recenter her thoughts. "It's no surprise. I only sensed it at the last minute as well. Plus, you said, you're not used to your demonic side. Maybe try focusing on that? It might help you sense it."

Alex hesitated for only a moment before he let himself focus, similar to how he would focus when using or sensing water.

That's when he felt it. A few paces ahead was a strange surge of magic, swirling past in a constant stream, as if piercing through the tunnel. It wasn't a barrier, because Alex could sense there was a path around it from above or below, but the stream of magic was still powerful.

Though, Alex noted, it seemed to be waning. As he stood there, it was easy to tell it was growing weaker. "What is it?" he finally asked.

"Wish I knew, it seems familiar, but I can't quite place why." Suzuha shrugged, leaning on one leg as she contemplated the tunnel. "I do believe, however, that we should try to avoid it. Especially you."

"Ugh...me again?" Alex groused, earning a quiet chuckle from Suzuha.

"What, does this happen a lot?"

"More often than I would like to admit," Alex admitted.

Whatever it was wove up and down, almost crisscrossing through the tunnel. He stepped forward, carefully moving through the path. He could hear footsteps behind him that sounded like Suzuha, who had a much easier time with her smaller frame. Within no time, they were through and chatter reached Alex's ears. He perked up slightly, waiting as Suzuha stepped up beside him before continuing forward. They stayed silent, listening as the quiet talking grew, the sound having been suppressed somehow before that. The distant sound of water was slowly fading as they moved and Alex felt uncomfortable at the thought. He could sense something ahead, but it wasn't the same: it was almost dead. His wings rustled, agitated. He had a feeling he wouldn't be nearly as uncomfortable in human form, but at this point, he was almost too scared to return to human form. Though, he kept expecting to suddenly shift back like before, he was honestly surprised he hadn't at this point. They slowed their movements, creeping around a bend and, to Alex's surprise, they came across a door. A wooden door, carved into the stone, that seemed surprisingly new, compared to everything else in here.

He frowned, slowly stepping up, fingers tracing over the carved wood. It was so strange to see.

"A random door? How nice," Suzuha grunted, a tendril of worry slipping into her words.

Alex couldn't argue, leaning his ear against it to listen on the other side.

He could hear conversation from the other side, but it was muffled through the door.

Noting a handle on one side, he carefully turned and pushed forward just a little bit to take a peek inside.

Light and warmth pushed its way out through the opening. The room wasn't large by any stretch of the imagination, but light stones glittered over the ceiling, a few fire stones placed at careful intervals around a pool of placid water. Water very similar to the pond above and feeling very off. Strange scrawl was placed around the outer edge with a few open circles every few feet, interjecting with the patterns.

"A ritual. An old one at that." Suzuha's voice was quiet as she peered around Alex, almost leaning on his shoulder.

Alex, not spotting anyone, slipped inside with Suzuha right behind. Within moments, Suzuha was next to the scrawl, kneeling on one leg to give it a closer examination. Alex carefully walked over.

"What's it for?" Alex asked hesitantly, as he wondered where the prior voices went.

"Don't know." Suzuha's gaze drifted around the cavern. "I can make a few guesses, but, well, I don't want to deal with it right now and the guesses I do have are not pleasant. Let's just keep going."

Alex followed her example, noting another doorway on the far end, opposite of where they came in.

That one was metal.

Alex felt a bit unnerved at that. He moved around the pond, feeling a tug toward it, but was able to ignore it a bit easier this time. He had a feeling it was because his demonic side was weakening, the longer he stayed in it.

He stepped up to the door and listened in. This time, he could clearly hear words.

"...Found their ship?"

"No, ma'am, we have been unable to locate it due to—"

"All I asked is if you found it."

A strong sigh echoed through the doorway as quiet footsteps rang behind him. Alex barely noted as Suzuha stepped close, listening as well. "Master is going to be displeased. Though, I can't deny that he already is."

"Mistress, were you really..."

"They slipped away from me into the caverns. I came here to check on the status of the sacrifices and the humans. That is all."

A flip of fabric and a quiet whoosh filled the air, followed by a grunt from the second speaker. "Just because you have a higher position doesn't mean squat. From the sounds of it, your position is going to be null and void anyway, stupid b..."

Alex pulled away, grimacing. At least he knew Ari and Leon were probably safe, but he doubted Milos and Rita stayed on the ship. So, where were they?

He ducked to the side, Suzuha taking her place across from him when footsteps sounded past the door and it opened with a bang.

A creature stepped through, and...

Alex pursed his lips, trying not to gag. A strong smell met his nose as the short squat creature shuffled through the door and toward the inscriptions on the floor. "Don't know why it's always my job to get the ritual ready so early. Sure, it takes all night and all, but seriously," the creature muttered, face hidden by a hood.

Alex had a feeling he was grateful for that when he spotted a clawed hand reaching out with a stick of chalk, the hand covered in blotches.

Alex glanced over in time to see Suzuha slip through the still open doorway. Alex scrambled after her. The next room was surprisingly nice, almost like a waiting room, a few doors adorned the edges, though Alex wasn't sure he wanted to check, and one opening led further into the mountain, no doorway there.

"None of this was here when my mistress and I last came. This is new." Suzuha peered around, hesitant as they moved away from the door and toward the open tunnel. "That other one who spoke, that was the Yuki-onna, wasn't it?"

Alex nodded, recognizing the voice, now that he thought about it. So that meant the creature working with the chalk—what was that again, a ritual? —was a demon as well. What did he mean by position? Alex shook his head. There wasn't enough to go on.

"So, do we follow her?" Suzuha piped up, head tilted slightly to the side with a smirk.

Alex sighed. Truth be told, they didn't have any other options. He nodded, heading for the tunnel. He winced as pain shot through his head, he stumbled, catching himself on the wall as a low hum filled the air.

What was going on?

Chapter Twenty-six

Milos peered over the railing of the upper floor, staring down at the lab in distaste. He was getting sick of seeing labs filled with demons. First the Martinet's guild and now here. He didn't necessarily feel sorry for demons, but people who were once human? He was disgusted at the idea. No human should ever be forced to become a demon, or have demon blood. If they were like Alex, and lived with it, fine, but...he pulled away from the thought, returning to what he was doing.

They had been debating what to do, mostly in silence, for the last few minutes. Curious to get a better layout of the surroundings, Milos convinced himself to return to his earlier place. The scene hadn't changed much, but he was certainly glad Rita had decided to stay back. He wasn't interested in another heaving event. He could see the people at work, wires slipping into the man's skin as he hung, suspended, in the tube. Lights flickered on and off on the console.

He had seen similar technology at home—and, now that he was recalling it, at the Martinet's guild as well. He never found much interest in it, considering no one knew how it worked. Only a select few knew when it was created or why the knowledge was lost to begin with. Now he was somewhat regretting his ignorance.

He heard a faint sound and, at the back of his mind, a distant feeling of familiarity. He paused and mentally cursed. He gripped the hilt of his sword tightly, pushing himself to the ground just as a strong demonic energy slid over his skin, a door opening to the left not a moment later. The demon, what he quickly identified as a Yuki-onna, glided over to the tubes. The workers stopped, bowing as she approached.

"What is the status?" Her voice held a tinge of frost, the air cooling enough to see one's breath.

The humans below shivered before one stepped forward.

"I am sorry, my lady. The latest subjects are rejecting the DNA and the previous are starting to deteriorate. If we don't get more soon..."

"Even with *his* DNA?"

"My lady, we've..." the spokesperson gulped as the air froze slightly. "We've tried, but his DNA completely molded with his human half in a way we can't figure out. We're doing our best with what knowledge we have, but we would need some data from the original."

"That should not be necessary." The woman swirled to one side, moving toward the tube. The man within stared straight ahead. She appraised him for a moment before turning to the workers. "I will be checking on the ritual site before I meet with Master. He's already in a bad mood, so if you don't want to end up on the other end of that tube, you will provide results, understand?"

"Y-yes."

The Yuki-onna didn't seemed to bother nodding, she just simply turned, floating up the stairs before pausing. Milos had no doubts to what she was sensing, and only hoped she had no interest.

While he could certainly fight her, it was more prudent to avoid powerful demons when having a tagalong and, while he knew Rita could hold her own, she wasn't an Alertian, or a run-of-the-mill demon slayer.

He wasn't about to try to explain to Alex that he failed to keep Rita safe.

The Yuki-onna peered in their direction for the longest time before shaking her head and disappearing down the hallway.

"Did she notice us?" Rita asked hesitantly, attention locked on the hallway in question.

"It's possible." Milos stood, stepping close to the wall so he was still out of sight, but able to get a better view of the surroundings. "She might have sensed us, but believed it to be something else, similar to the fluctuations I've been receiving."

Rita nodded, peering over the edge, straight down. Thankfully, the workers didn't seem to notice, too busy trying to find the data she was seeking. "What did she mean by DNA from *him*? Who's him? Why would this DNA or whatever be important?"

Milos could only shake his head, arms crossed over his chest. "Either way, what are you planning on doing?"

"Well, stopping this, of course," Rita pointed out, digging into her satchel. "Strike while the fire stones are hot and all. They are in a panicked state because of that demon's words." He could tell she stumbled a bit, not sure if the term was correct before continuing, "Now would be the perfect time to catch them off guard and release their captives."

Milos hesitated before pushing away from the wall. "I'll simply follow your lead."

Rita paused, giving him a half-annoyed look before shrugging and hurrying to the right. She stopped near the top of the stairwell, judging the distance before pulling out a bag from her satchel. The powder was familiar, the same sleeping agent she had tried to use on him when he was still chasing Alex.

He gripped the sword as she snuck down the steps, keeping to the shadows. It wasn't long until she reached the bottom floor, and it was only a second later when she darted forward, powder already coating the air.

It was instantaneous, the panic. The hooded figures darted away, scrabbling at their faces and holding their breath.

Milos hesitated for only a moment before practically gliding down the steps and, with quick movements, swung forward with the flat of his blade.

The figures toppled dead to the world, but very much still alive.

Rita would have his head otherwise.

"Hey, I had that," Rita pouted, as she dug into her satchel for what he could only presume was an acid to melt the chains and locks.

"Of course, and you hadn't thought of the fact they may be wearing masks?" He kicked one over, showcasing a thin bit of white over the man's mouth and nose.

Rita blushed slightly, slightly fumbling with the vial she pulled out before dripping it on the lock. "Like you haven't made mistakes like that before."

Milos didn't bother responding, simply stepping up to the tube, sword still in hand. He peered over the console, debating on what to do before he sighed. He slid the sword back into its sheath and peered over the buttons until he found one labeled, release.

He certainly could have cut through the glass, but they were trying to make as little noise as possible. He wasn't about to test to see if the Yuki-onna or some other demon would be able to hear the shattering glass, or anything that might happen after.

The mechanism worked the same as with the woman, dropping the man to the floor of the tube where a sliver opened at the bottom to drag the man out.

Milos was about to move forward, only to spin around as a spike of energy fluctuated behind him.

Rita jumped back from the newly opened cage, just barely holding back a scream as a young man leapt through, teeth bared as he landed on all fours like some deformed cat. Much like the others, his skin was flaking and gray. Patches of fur covered parts of his body with a set of deformed gills on his neck. He hissed before leaping forward.

His extended claws met Milos' sword, inches away from Rita's startled and now much more panicked face.

"Rita, I would advise for you to run." Milos spoke simply as he spun, flinging the man to the opposite side of the room with his sword. In the same movement, he turned, catching another clawed hand, this time from the woman they saw earlier, her wild blue eyes were desperate, but animalistic. "It seems that, whatever those workers were doing, it's forced them to rely on instinct."

"Right," Rita stumbled over her words, ducking just as the man Milos released lumbered over, a guttural roar ringing through the room.

To Milos' dismay, it seemed that Rita actually managed to open all the cages before the first encounter, which meant he was now up against possibly six different creatures that were neither fully demon...nor fully human.

This was proven only half-right when an older woman who seemed to have been here for quite some time, even longer than some of the creatures around him, stumbled out of the cage, searching around wildly before noticing Milos.

Milos only spared her a moment before rolling out of the way of the first woman's attack. A short-panicked scream echoed from the older woman before a breathy sound filtered out.

Milos wasn't completely prepared when she scrambled forward, grabbing his arm tightly and outright bawling.

Milos winced as he flicked his sword, just barely managing to catch the lumbering man in the side, knocking him back. "Rita!"

He could hear babbling at his side that sounded like the older woman clinging to his arm, but he couldn't make heads or tails of her words, only that they very weakly resembled what was probably supposed to be the demonic dialect.

He ducked a lunge, pulling the woman down with him just as Rita slid beside him, already tugging at the woman's arm.

The movement gave Milos enough of an opening to pull himself free and flip around, just barely catching a clawed hand from the first man he'd thrown inches from where his back had been. "Find if there is anyone else who HASN'T gone insane."

"On it," Rita called, though Milos was unable to check to see what exactly she was doing.

Much to his dismay, he was surrounded, a fourth person or more creature, he supposed, joined into the mix. A short stout man with a long whip-like tail.

Milos peered around. He could tell they were human, or at least, they once were. While he could sense demonic energy from each of them, he also felt they held a similarity to Alex. That the demonic part didn't make up their whole being. However, where Alex was naturally the way he was, and thus was mostly able to retain his humanity, these people...

"You've lost your humanity, haven't you?" Milos found himself whispering, posture low as he held his sword out, just barely taking note as Rita helped two people up the stairs, the last of the sacrifices.

The four still around him paused, tilting their heads slightly as if they realized he was talking to them.

The thought unnerved him, but he continued, "Demons are creatures of instinct. It is how they live and thrive." His glance flitted to each, never fully losing track of the others in the process. "I'd hoped that truth was wrong, but I suppose it isn't." He smiled slightly. "I guess that does make some things easier. This means I don't have to hold back. After all, you aren't Alex. You aren't truly human anymore, are you?"

Those last few words seemed to spark something in the four. Milos tightened his grip in an instant on his sword as the four howled, anger reverberating around the room before they lunged.

Milos weaved and dodged, spinning and dancing in the area that was once a clean lab. Blood splattered over the ground as he sliced through an arm, a scream reverberated off the walls as he cut through bone and sinew. He flipped back, the sword hilt slamming down between one creature's eyes, its skull shattering upon impact and dead before it was on the ground. Time lost meaning as Milos moved, fluid and concise.

"You...you can stop now," Rita's voice hesitantly called down, causing Milos to still. Silence filled the air, only broken by the occasional dripping sound. Milos glanced down to see the blood-stained sword. He twisted, flinging to one side with a practiced movement. It released a good chunk of blood and whatever else stuck. He slid it into its sheath, noting to himself he would have to clean it later, before turning to Rita.

"Milos? What the...?" Rita's voice was a mix of angry and horrified. Milos couldn't quite figure out why.

After all, all he did was slaughter the demons attacking him. It was his job. He shrugged it off, weaving around the dismembered corpses and unconscious workers that littered the floor. He moved up the steps and noticed how the two behind Rita shrunk back. Demonic attributes evident on their skin and around them. Eyes glowed in fear as they observed him. Right, he was supposed to take care of all the demons. Alex really was the only exception. He reached for his sword once more, only to pause when Rita suddenly stood, arms spread out and a glare on her face. "Stop. That's enough."

"Rita. Move." His voice was even as he noticed the sound was still there, the sporadic dripping.

Rita shook her head. "You took care of the ones who fully turned. These two are still human."

Milos paused, once more glancing at the two figures. The demonic energy wafted off them, escalated by their fear, but...he paused, frowning slightly. This mentality, he hadn't been in this mentality for a long time. Not since...he relaxed his stance, letting go of his sword. He noticed them relax only slightly.

Rita smiled weakly before saying, "Why don't we get you cleaned up?"

"I'm not injured," Milos spoke.

"I know. That's not what I meant." Rita cut in, gesturing.

That's when Milos really took notice of what she meant.

The blood dripping down his face and arms, splattered onto his tunic and some sticking to the chainmail. He hadn't noticed, having been focused on the task at hand, but now...

He let out a breath, slumping down. "Right. My apologies," he spoke as Rita dug out her medical supplies.

She dabbed water onto one of the clothes and, much to his surprise, instead of handing it over, she reached up and brushed over his face, startling him.

"Oh, good, you are still human." She grinned weakly as she wiped away the blood.

Milos paused at that and sighed. "I'm an Alertian, what did you expect?"

"I guess I didn't," she admitted, checking his hands over as she continued. "I didn't realize how much you were really holding back, and those weren't full demons." Her gaze drifted up to his and Milos stilled. "If this is what you would do to those turned, what would you do to a full demon?"

Milos had no answer to that, at least, none that he knew she would accept.

She seemed to realize and let out a breath.

Milos jerked, glancing over toward the opposite wall, where the Yuki-onna entered before. A flare of demonic energy resonated from somewhere down the way she came, a powerful feeling he didn't recognize.

The two behind Rita cringed back, as if children, curling up on themselves. Milos didn't blame them. He held no doubts they sensed it as well.

Chapter Twenty-seven

Rita swallowed thickly, noticing a strange tension in the air. Though, maybe it was not that strange, considering the fact what blood she wasn't able to clean still stuck to Milos' clothes, not even quantifying the sight to her right and down a set of steps. The mangled bodies were seared into her mind and the nonchalant, almost casual air in which Milos moved was eerie at best.

Yet, she could tell it was Milos, how he was somewhat apologetic. Still, her question stood. What would he do to a full demon? What would he do to the people at the refuge? Why was she asking herself this when she not only knew the answer, but knew that there was no way any of them would abandon him? She noticed the way he stiffened as she went to wipe at a bit of blood on his face and could feel the two she had rescued clasp onto her blouse, holding tightly with quiet whimpers.

The two behind her were strange. She could tell they weren't going to attack like the others. They seemed almost child-like in their behavior, even though one was an older woman and one a man around Milos' age. She wanted to know how they ended up like this through the experiments, but now wasn't the time.

Her gaze flicked to the doorway as Milos pulled away, slinking forward with a tight grip on his sword. Rita hoped he wouldn't pull it out, she wasn't sure if she could handle another sight like that again unless it was against the guy who would allow such things to occur. She wasn't sure how she would feel, but she definitely wouldn't feel horror. Maybe gratification?

Pushing the thought aside, she returned her focus on Milos as he carefully opened the door, peering into the passage that, undoubtedly, led beyond.

"Odd." He spoke faintly, pulling back with a frown. "I know I sensed it."

"Sensed what?" Rita was getting annoyed at her inability to sense the same things as Alex and Milos. She understood the reasoning, sure, but it still bugged her.

"A demonic signature." Milos shook his head and relaxed his stance, turning back to her. "About those two, you do realize we can't bring them with us, right?"

"I know," Rita admitted, glancing back at them. "I just don't know what to do or how to convey to them how to get back to the village."

Milos stared for a moment, deep in thought, before he stepped forward. The two froze, not moving a muscle as he knelt on one knee before them. Rita could tell his movements unnerved the two, but she stayed silent. After a bit, they seemed to relax, the younger man tilting his head in curiosity.

That was when Milos spoke. "It's not safe." His words were short and clipped, but surprisingly warm, at least for Milos, of all people. Rita wondered what he was thinking. "That path?" He pointed toward where they entered the building and the two followed his finger. "That way is safe." He kept his tone at a base level, almost gentle, though Rita would never use the term to describe the man.

The two exchanged glances before hesitantly standing up. They headed toward the tunnel, stopped and turned. When neither Rita nor Milos moved, genuine smiles crossed their faces and they took off.

Rita watched them go, relieved. She was glad she was able to help some of them, but... "What's going to happen to them once they reach the village?"

Milos stood, shaking his head. "If they have family left, they should be fine, if not..." Milos turned to the doorway he just peered into earlier and headed through.

Rita scrambled after him, startled at his words dropping off the way they did. "If not, what?"

"I figured you would connect the dots." Milos barely spared her a glance as they stepped into the dimly lit hallway. "They are partially demon, with only a bit of humanity left, going into a village that hunts demons."

Rita suddenly felt queasy. In a way, she thought about it, but it didn't click how BAD of an idea that was. "So, you just..."

"Sent them to their death? That is unclear. Like I said, if they have family, they should be fine and as long as they don't attack people like those who completely succumbed, they might just be able to recover. It is a better chance than staying here, and less of a burden than having them come with us."

"That's..."

"Harsh?" Milos' gaze drifted to hers and she snapped her jaw shut in realization. "You know as well as I do that our options are limited right now. Sure, we could follow them back out, now that one of our main prerogatives is accomplished, but that means less likelihood of finding Alex or the Demon King. I'm not willing to risk that."

Rita bit her lip before letting out a huff, hands on her hips. "Jeez, you better hope we find Alex this way or I'm going to make sure you can't sleep for a week." She slumped her shoulders slightly. "If we can get off this island any time soon. I hope the ship is okay and I'm hoping that vision actually comes true. Though I'm not sure if it is even possible at this point."

Milos hesitated at that. "Ah, true."

Silence fell over the two as they practically marched down the hallway, taking a turn here and there.

Quiet chatter and footsteps sounded ahead of them, off to the left, and they paused, glancing toward the tunnel they were passing.

Milos stilled before the faintest of relieved smiles crossed his face.

Rita didn't even need a second to analyze that before the sound of voices got closer. She took off down the path before she really thought about it.

She heard the chatter stop as she rounded the corner, caught sight of Alex and promptly threw herself at him in a tight gripping hug. He yelped, one wing flaring in and out as he stumbled back. "You

DINGBAT! DO YOU KNOW HOW WORRIED I WAS FOR YOU?" She was doing her level best not to scream, but the words still came out somewhat tremulous as she pulled back, glancing him over. Her practiced eye instantly took in the various wounds and the fact that he was in demon form, his tired, but amused eyes and the bandage around his wing.

"Hey, Rita." He chuckled as she pulled back, somewhat gratified that, at least he was on the mend. Someone had healed him.

She heard footsteps as Milos rounded the corner behind her and, at the same time, she took notice of Suzuha.

The little girl stiffened, practically hiding behind Alex. Alex didn't say a word at that, only a hint of bemusement and honest worry on his face.

"You," Rita's voice dropped as she stared at the girl. Suzuha winced as Milos joined the group.

He was leaning on one leg, grip light, but obviously on his sword. He sent a quick smile to Alex before returning his attention to Suzuha.

Silence very quickly enveloped the group before Alex, of all people, sighed. "All right, I know we have a lot of explaining to do, but can we just get out of here first?" he asked, voice hesitant. "It's been a heck of a day already."

"Tell me about it." Rita shot Milos a sidelong glance, causing the man to shrug.

"As long as it doesn't attack anyone, I'll worry about it later." Milos' words were slightly cold. The fact he turned his back and began walking back down the passage they came from was indication enough he wasn't going to recklessly attack the girl before them.

A small relieved expression flitted across Alex's face before he turned toward Rita. "Well? Shall we?"

"We'll discuss this later," she conceded, sparing Suzuha a searing glance before stepping to Alex's other side, following after Milos. "Still, how did you end up here?"

"I would like to know that myself," Milos spoke, peering over his shoulder. "We were sent to rescue some sacrifices and defeat a demon king."

"You say that so casually." Alex blinked before chuckling quietly. "Ah, man, I missed this."

He shook his head, his chuckles subsiding as he stumbled slightly. Rita shifted, arms reaching forward as Alex halted. For a brief moment, he seemed to stare at the far wall before something—snapped.

With a whoosh, his wings disappeared as he crumbled. Suzuha yelped, catching him at the same time as Rita, causing both of them to stumble.

"Alex?" Rita called as Suzuha grunted, struggling to hold him up.

Footsteps sounded beside her as Milos knelt on one knee, reaching forward to tip Alex's face up. After a moment of inspection, he let out a breath of relief. "He's just resting." He pulled away, turning to Rita. "My guess is that he felt relieved to see us and that sense of safety caused him to relax." He stood. "His demonic side, no longer needing to keep him safe, allowed him to return to his human form."

"You figured that all out from a quick examination?" Rita scoffed as she shifted, trying to pull Alex up.

Milos glared sharply. "It seems reasonable enough. After all, you are quite relieved to see him as well, aren't you?"

Rita quickly looked away. She heard movement along with a quiet slapping and glanced over to see Suzuha lightly hitting Alex's cheek, a hint of worry on her face. "Either way, staying here is not a good idea." She glanced to them before shrinking away slightly. "We should at least wake him and go."

Milos stared for a bit before nodding. "That's reasonable."

"Ugh, really, Alex?" Rita muttered, following Suzuha's idea.

It didn't take more than a minute or so before a quiet groan echoed from Alex's throat. A hand pulled away from Suzuha's shoulder and reached for his head. "What happened?"

"You collapsed again, Dingbat." Rita spoke, unable to suppress the faint smile on her lips. "You scared us, you know."

He winced, smiling sheepishly. "Ah, sorry." He pushed himself up onto his feet, wavering slightly. "I've been in my demon form for *way* too long."

"I figured." Milos waved, other hand lightly gripping his sword hilt. "For now, we should get moving and find our way out of here before anyone else collapses."

Alex huffed, but nodded, glancing sidelong at Suzuha. "Come on, we should go."

Suzuha nodded, gripping onto his hand for a moment before letting go as Rita crossed her arms, trailing beside them as they started moving.

"Anyway, I was going to tell you guys what happened on our side." Alex spoke up after a few steps. "The short version is that Suzuha and I ended up in the demon-worshipping village. I met the demon king..."

Rita did a double-take, along with Milos—she was going to immortalize that look if it killed her—earning a scoff from Alex. "...whom I guess you've heard about, considering you mentioned you were sent to defeat him." He shook his head. "We fled the village, chased by two Djinn and a Yuki-onna, and wound up in here."

"Geez," Rita muttered. "I thought we were having a busy day."

Milos shook his head, seeming amused. "So, what can you tell me about this demon king?"

Alex hesitated, a strange expression on his face as he stared at Milos, as if confused, before shaking his head. His gaze flickered to Suzuha for a moment, who seemed to notice with a furrowed brow. "Ah, right." He paused, took a bit of a breath before saying, "He was a Nyx..."

Everyone stilled at that, causing Alex to stumble. Considering Suzuha's grip on his waist, Rita held no doubt why that was.

"You never mentioned that." Suzuha spoke up. Her voice was faint, but anger surged through. "You said he was a shapeshifter."

"Really?" he asked in a hesitant voice, almost as if he was aware of that fact, purposefully not looking toward Suzuha. He frowned warily before letting out a breath. "Sorry, I guess I didn't want you to worry about it at the time." He glanced toward Milos. "He said he was in his male form, since he preferred it. However, I've never seen a Nyx before. He still appeared fairly human, but I figured that was just a part of being a shape-shifter."

Silence enveloped the space. Rita could tell, both Suzuha and

Milos were deep in thought about his words. She returned her attention back to Alex. "So then, how did you get away?"

Alex smiled. "We were still in the village. I guess he couldn't do anything outwardly to keep his reputation as king, so I was able to flee. It was once we got *out* of the city that we had to watch our backs."

"He came after you?" Milos glanced over, brow furrowed. "You mentioned he seemed fairly human still, correct? What exactly did he look like in his shape-shifted form?"

Alex blinked, startled, before saying, "He had a blueish glow to his skin with gill-like appendages at the side of his neck and a long tail, similar to mine. I remember he was wearing a strange robe and, I think, he had brown hair."

A quiet gasp sounded from behind Alex as Rita and Milos exchanged horrified expressions, or at least, Rita did as her mind flashed to images of the experiments, their gills and tails more specifically.

Milos seemed suddenly much calmer, a placid, dangerous mask. "I see," was the only thing he said.

Rita went to say something, trying to rationalize what she was hearing, compared to the experiments she saw earlier, when Suzuha spoke up. Her voice was carefully quiet, almost eerily so. "That's how you describe him?" All attention drifted to her as she pulled back from Alex, watching him carefully. "Did this man...was he wearing fine clothes to begin with and then robes later? Did he have gray, narrowed eyes, or a scar tracing down the right side of his cheek?"

Alex jerked, startled. "Huh? Uh, now that I think about it, yeah." He frowned before he suddenly jolted. "Wait..."

"That..." Anger suddenly erupted from Suzuha as a growl, much like a Vulfulas. No, Rita noted, stunned, as the girl shifted into the older male form in a flash. "That deceitful, villainous, rotten, no-good piece of Nyx's blood snake."

Suzuhah stomped past both a startled Milos and an admittedly unnerved Rita. He stopped in front of Milos. His gaze strictly pointed his direction so Rita couldn't see Suzuhah's expression. Though Rita was glad she couldn't, from the way Milos' seemed to shift eerily into his earlier mannerism after a moment of surprise.

Suzuhah continued, voice calm as ice. "Milos. I am aware you have no desire to help me, nor any desire to work with me. However, I asked you a few days ago if you would help me kill a certain demon. I want to make a slight amendment to that."

His body seemed to shake and Rita did *not* think it was anything besides fury.

"I have a desire to at least have a moment of time with that creature who calls himself king. It can either be before or after you defeat him, but I will get my pound of flesh. Is that clear?"

Milos stared at him as Rita shifted away.

It was Alex who responded. "Suzuhah?" His voice was soft and filled with worry. "You know this man, is he...?"

"The same one. The same one who killed my mistress all those years ago. I could never mistake that appearance."

This time, Rita shivered, Suzuhah's burning gaze boring through both of them. She hadn't heard about this, but she was *not* going to ask at the moment.

Alex's expression shifted to one of understanding before he gave a sharp nod. He turned to Milos. Before he could even open his mouth, Milos waved it off. "I'll find out the details about the why later, once we're out of here. All I need to know is that he is on our side against this king and, considering the other atrocities the king's done, I'm more than willing to let things slide for now. Plus, I did agree to help him regarding this situation."

Alex nodded, snapping his mouth shut as Rita let out a breath, relieved as the tension abated just a little bit. She turned to Suzuhah, causing the boy to start and curl inward, almost as if he wanted to switch back to his girl form. Rita wasn't going to ask why. "I'm still pissed at you. You tried to kill my..." she hesitated at her words, before continuing, still feeling like they weren't right on her tongue. "Best friend." She shook her head, hands on her hips. "He might be all right with you now. We might have a common goal to get rid of this scum douche, but that doesn't mean I'm happy to be working with you, or that I forgive you for trying to kill him."

Suzuhah winced and nodded, meeker than earlier.

Silence reigned for a moment before Alex sighed. "You know, he didn't really..."

"Alex, it's fine," Suzuhah muttered quietly, causing Alex to glance his way.

After a moment, Alex shook his head and spoke. "Well, now that we've cleared that up. Where are we going?"

Everyone blinked and exchanged bemused looks.

"Now that you mention it," Rita paused. "Milos?"

Milos shook his head. "I was able to sense Alex because he was so close, but this place is still a mess. As much as I might want to, I still can't sense any other demons, just random fluctuations."

Rita huffed. She crossed her arms over her chest. "How nice." She didn't even try to hide her annoyance.

Milos seemed unamused.

Alex faintly chuckled before continuing down the path Rita and Milos came from. "Well, you guys came from that direction and there aren't any places behind us. So, let's go back down this path and go on from there?"

After a moment's hesitation, the other three followed, with Rita only a pace behind Alex. She hadn't missed the bandages, now loosely hanging over Alex's shoulder where his wings were only a few minutes before.

Alex must have noticed her watching because he peered back. "Rita?"

"What happened? How did you get hurt and why were you still in demon form?"

Alex grimaced. "That's..."

"My guess is because, not only was it probably helping you deal with what was going on, but your demon form was aiding in the healing process?" Milos pointed out, startling Rita and getting a surprised blink from Alex. "Demons are well known to have better healing abilities than humans. It's a wonder we survived the Human-Demon War all those years ago."

"Oh yeah, you would know that." Alex nodded, before turning back to Rita. "What he said. Basically, it was helping me heal and, honestly, I would rather not be in a position where I'm a bit more on the fragile side in a place like this, though I guess that doesn't mean much now, since I switched back."

"I wonder if a willing switch back would have kept you conscious or if you were going to collapse either way from the long period of time in that form," Milos muttered, brow furrowed slightly in contemplation.

Alex seemed to have no answer to that, nor did anyone else.

Rita sighed, parsing through what items she had available to her. She did need to have more things to fight and help in instances where Alex or someone else collapsed. It was happening way too often for her taste. Sure, she was good with powders along with one or two poisons. That didn't mean much, though, and she hadn't gotten much of a chance to train with Milos on dodging. Though what little she did do helped.

She would have to worry about it at another time.

Chapter Twenty-eight

Alex peered over his shoulder, feeling hesitant for multiple reasons. He didn't miss the bits of blood still decorating Milos' frame or Rita's tense shoulders and half-there smile. Of course, there was also Suzuhah, who was able to figure out that the demon king...was the demon king actually the same Nyx that killed his mistress? Was it just Suzuhah's imagination, making him believe it was the same? Alex doubted that, but the chances of Suzuhah meeting the same demon who killed his mistress from six years ago seemed strange.

Though, with their luck, Alex shouldn't be surprised.

He finally drew to a split and waited for the others to catch up, pointedly avoiding meeting their gazes, feeling strangely uncomfortable. Milos slipped past him, his movements seeming more fluid than usual, which was probably where Alex's uncomfortable feeling was coming from. They seemed less conscious and a heck of a lot more dangerous than he could recall seeing Milos in quite some time.

He followed, turning to Rita. "So, what about you? How did you guys get here?"

Rita pulled her attention from her satchel. "Oh, right, we hadn't mentioned that yet. Well, long story short, Milos and I left the ship to search for you, leaving the Aqua Wraith, Ari and Leon to keep an eye on the ship. We arrived in a demon hunting village that asked us to kill the Demon King. Milos led us into this mountain where we came across a lab and managed to rescue, well, two of the people taken captive." She trailed off, seeming uncomfortable.

Alex decided not to press, sensing she would probably tell him later.

Honestly, he had a feeling there was a lot they needed to say to each other, once they were no longer in the middle of such a dangerous situation.

He shook his head. He still felt tired from his earlier collapse. To be honest, it frustrated him. He let his guard down, relaxed because both Rita and Milos were there, and found himself reverting back. He was still coping and it was all he could not to stumble over his feet.

"Alex?" Rita's face was inches away from his when he opened his eyes.

He jerked and smiled shakily. "Ah, sorry."

Milos watched warily, his expression showing his concern, no matter how hard he was trying to hide it.

Alex waved it off. "I'm fine, just stumbled for a second. The sooner we are out of here, the better."

After a moment, Rita sighed and shrugged. "Well, I can't argue with that." She glanced down the path, deep in thought. "Still, what exactly are we going to do? We have to defeat a demon king, find the ship and get off this island."

"Do we have to?" Alex muttered quietly, a deep frown on his face at the thought of meeting that creepy guy again.

All three turned to him with a mixed reaction. While Rita seemed startled and Milos speculative, Suzuhah appeared pissed.

"Of course, we do," Suzuhah snarled, glaring down one of the paths. "Now that I know where he is, I can take him down."

"That's the thing, we don't know where he is," Alex pointed out. "Sure, he could be back in the town, but how do we get there from here? Not only that, but all of us are tired, as you can see." He gestured toward his back where his wings were clearly missing. "This place isn't safe to stay in and other demons could be around. I don't know about you, but I'm not in the mood to fight off a Yuki-onna and a Djinn at the same time."

Suzuhah snapped his mouth shut, a faint hiss slipping through his lips.

Alex turned to Rita and Milos. Rita seemed hesitant, unsure as Milos just leaned on one foot, gesturing. "That is understandable. From the look of things, neither of you..." he glanced toward Suzuhah with narrowed eyes, "...seem capable of fighting at the moment, if the wounds and bandages on both of you are any indication. Plus, I am not inclined to fight in these constrained corridors. Retreating at this time might be our best option."

"Ugh. I never thought I would agree with you," Rita muttered, shifting her satchel. "I don't like this island and, as much as I hate that creature, I don't think any of us are prepared to take on a being called the demon king."

Alex didn't miss the way Milos flinched, but ignored it as Suzuhah shifted, fists clenching tightly. He could see the boy about to say something and turned to him, his voice low and gentle. "Milos and Rita are right, you know." Suzuhah peered at him as he continued, "I know you want to charge in. Believe me, I understand and so do many of us here." His gaze flickered briefly to Rita before returning to Suzuhah. "But now is not a good time. and I doubt I'm the only one about to collapse."

Suzuhah pursed his lips, fists shaking as he continued to peer down the corridor before slowly uncurling and letting out a long breath. "Right, fine. We can rest and attack another time."

Alex smiled, nodding before gesturing. "Let's move."

He regretted those words a few minutes later when he came upon a room that appeared to have been painted in red on one side.

A hand slapped to his mouth as he froze in the doorway, Rita and Milos a few steps ahead of him. Rita was pointedly looking away and now Alex knew why.

Scattered across the ground was the remains of...of what, Alex wasn't even sure. Suzuhah stood beside him, shock clear on his face as Alex forced himself to turn away, following Rita.

"Come on, it's this way." She spoke firmly, eyes blazing.

Milos followed her at the back, keeping half an eye on their surroundings.

Alex paused at the same time as Milos, glancing to one side of the cave. They had been traveling for a little while down a rocky passageway when something caught Alex's attention. Movement shifted through the rock before Alex almost found himself thrown off his feet as a sudden crash sounded nearby, the stones shaking from whatever impact must have hit it.

"What was that?" Rita yelped, stumbling forward as a resounding *crack* echoed through the path.

"Something or someone is trying to collapse the tunnel," Milos shouted, his gaze up ahead, catching Alex's attention.

He jerked, peering forward in time to see that same movement disappear up the passage as another resounding *creak* sounded through the air.

Milos grabbed Alex as he took off running. Suzuhah seemed to have grabbed Rita, startling the girl, but not stopping her as they darted forward, scrambling toward the exit.

"It's hard to sense." Milos spoke up over the sound of another *slam* echoing past. "I believe there is a demon causing this, but I can't tell where it's from."

"Well, you're helpful," Rita shouted, pulling herself away from Suzuhah as she dashed ahead.

"Damn Witch. Try sensing a particular type of magic when it's all around you. You're lucky I can even sense it at all."

"Less bickering and more running," Suzuhah called sharply, which Alex couldn't argue with as something crashed down right where his foot had been.

"Hurrying," he yelped. He felt a sharp tug as Milos pulled him almost into his side as something stabbed upward where Alex had been, similar to a cage he'd seen the Yuki-onna try to make.

Milos grunted, hair falling out of his ponytail as he pushed Alex forward. "Keep moving."

Alex didn't argue, dodging as the tunnel continued to rumble and quake, the roof cracking as dust shuddered over them. He could see Suzuhah and Rita ahead, pulling themselves out of the tunnel with Milos only a few paces behind him. He spotted movement once more and felt as Milos pushed him forward. Another rock crashed down where he stood, shaking the floor. He heard a hiss of pain as he scrambled out, glancing back to see Milos stumble back slightly, shaking his head as a little blood trickled down from a slash on his arm, a rock mere centimeters from his foot. He seemed dazed for a moment as something moved in the rock to his right. Milos must have noticed, head whipping to one side. Not even a second later he rolled forward, barely avoiding as something pierced out like a javelin, slamming into the wall. The ground shook once more, causing Alex to stumble back, almost hitting into Suzuhah, who caught him with a grunt as dust filled the air and a harsh slamming sounded from the cave. Milos glanced over his shoulder for a brief moment before diving forward, practically sliding out of the cave just as the rock crumbled, collapsing in sheets behind him with resounding booms and thuds.

Rocks pelted down, rolling over where he'd been only a moment before as he pushed himself to his feet gesturing for them to move as he rushed past. Alex didn't think twice, racing after him.

A few minutes later, they finally slowed down, Alex barely catching his breath as he peered over his shoulder.

"Holy hell in a hand basket. What happened back there?" Suzuhah sputtered out, breath heaving in and out of his chest. "The tunnel just started collapsing out of nowhere."

"Oh, good, I'm not alone in wondering that." Rita slumped to the ground, barely catching her own breath.

The only one who didn't look that badly worse for wear was Milos, though he did lightly touch his arm in distaste at the bit of blood decorating the skin.

"I saw something." Alex found himself speaking as he pushed himself up, catching his breath. "It was in the passage, but..."

"It was a demon." Milos spoke up, turning to them. "I can only guess at the type, but I would say a stone demon. From what I know, they aren't as intelligent as many of the other demons, but their instincts are much stronger. Though that one seemed determined to capture rather than kill." Milos paused, gaze flickering to Alex for a brief moment before turning away. "We should be safe here for the time being. Stone demons don't typically leave the area where they make their home, which is fortuitous in a land such as this which is almost all rock and stone."

"No kidding," Rita huffed out as she pushed herself to her feet. "Well, I wasn't expecting that when I woke up this morning."

"Whoever is?" Alex muttered, getting a slightly breathy chuckle from Suzuhah, who shifted to stand beside him. "We should keep moving. Obviously, the demon knew where we were, so I have no doubt others know as well."

Milos nodded as Rita groaned. "That's just great, can't we go to an island that *isn't* trying to kill us?"

Suzuhah smiled weakly, glancing away awkwardly.

"Well, either way, I'm hungry and tired. I just want to get back to the ship and check on the others." Alex waved, unable to suppress the yawn from leaving his lips. "Let's get moving."

Rita nodded, before pausing. "Though, the only way I know how to get back to the ship is through the village." She glanced toward Milos, who shrugged. "I for one, don't want to try to take a shortcut and end up lost on this island."

"We can go around the village if need be." Milos turned, heading down a path Alex supposed they traversed earlier. "You are correct, that is probably the best way to go to leave this island quickly. Plus, if we do end up meeting some villagers, it's only right to let them know we didn't accomplish what they asked of us." Milos winced as he said that, getting a sympathetic momentary glance from Rita before she turned to Alex.

"Yeah. I want to check something as well. That's only if we have no other choice. I would rather avoid it all together, but..." She furrowed her brow as she peered toward the distant, now buried, entrance. "There is something that has been bothering me for a little while that I want to check out." Her gaze flickered to Milos as a sly grin slithered onto her face. "I'll lead the way to the village so we don't have to worry about anyone getting lost."

Alex could almost feel how hard Milos rolled his eyes. He wasn't touching that bait. Alex chuckled as Milos shook his head, trudging after her, Alex a few steps behind him and Suzuhah a few steps in front of him. The boy seemed wary, glancing between Milos and Rita hesitantly as he continued forward. Alex felt a little bad, but...

"Milos?" Alex's voice caused Milos to slow his pace slightly in order to match his. Alex smiled gratefully before continuing, "Once we're out of here, what do you plan on doing to Suzuhah?"

Milos hesitated for a moment. "Why do you ask?" he spoke, tilting his head slightly. "You do know you can't trust people who try to kill you."

Alex wanted to roll his eyes, but resisted. "I've trusted you."

Milos faced forward. "I know you have. My words still stand though."

Alex stayed silent for a little while, unsure how to respond to that. After a few moments of thought, he shrugged and said, "I don't agree." Milos jerked toward him, probably spotting the smile Alex was unable to hide from his face. "I mean, I'll trust you either way. I know you are an Alertian, and I'm not dumb enough to believe you're doing all this or following us for some selfless reason. If anything, it probably has to do with the refuge, but..." He shook his head. "That's not my business and you've been here to help since we've met, so of course I trust you."

Milos pursed his lips, peering ahead once more. "You are..."

"Naïve?" Alex chuckled. "Maybe a little, but I like to think of it as trying to be optimistic. I mean, heck, look at Suzuhah." He gestured ahead to point out the slight bounce in Suzuhah's step. "He's trying to stay optimistic, though he knows both you and Rita probably hate him and want to skewer him. After all, being pessimistic doesn't help much. It didn't help when I was fleeing from home, nor when I was trying to get back to you guys. Though, I suppose I'm not the pessimistic sort to begin with."

"No, I suppose not."

Alex stepped ahead slightly, tilting his head to face Milos. "Still, going back to the original topic. I want to make sure you and Rita are aware I trust Suzuhah, just like I trusted you all those weeks ago."

Milos watched him for a bit, before he let out a long and tired sigh. "We will decide when we get back to the ship. I believe Ari and Leon should have a say as well."

Alex winced. "Are they all right?"

"They should be fine."

Alex nodded, hesitance in his step for a bit before he spoke up, voice a little quieter. "What about when we get to the refuge? You're not going to attack them like the demons back there, right?"

"They attacked first." Alex glared, causing Milos to wave it off. "However, I promise I'll try to hold off doing anything outright."

"I guess that's the best I'm going to get, isn't it?"

"It is."

Alex sighed, shaking his head. "I suppose I shouldn't be surprised." He grinned. "I'm really glad you two came for me. I guess I'm grateful I met you two in the first place."

"Aw, that's sweet of you, Alex," Rita chirped. He felt a warmth envelope his face and promptly turned a sharp glare onto Rita.

"That's not what I meant and you know it," he snapped. "How much were you listening anyway?"

"Enough." Her gaze flickered to Suzuhah, who was a few paces ahead, watching them curiously. "I'll agree with Milos for now. We'll deal with it when we get back to the ship."

Alex nodded, frowning slightly. "Still, I am glad you came, to have friends at all."

Rita's smile widened as she trailed a few steps ahead, showing off a bit by walking backward, hands behind her head. "I know that's what you meant. I think it's the first time you've outright mentioned it to all of us."

Alex glanced away. "I think you're thinking of Milos there."

Milos promptly stared ahead. "I have no clue what you are talking about." His pace seemed to increase slightly when Alex and Rita exchanged amused glances before turning to him once more. "Anyway, we should hurry."

With that, their pace increased once more, silence enveloping the group as they focused on making their way to the village.

Alex let out a long sigh. Rita and Milos were lightly bickering as usual and Suzuhah was watching quietly. He seemed unsure and Alex didn't blame him. He still needed to worry about Rita's and Milos' judgement and no matter how optimistic he portrayed himself, the other two probably only saw the same person who tried to kill Alex.

Alex shook his head as the smell of cooking food caught his attention. His stomach growled as Milos smirked, obviously noticing. Alex blushed before glancing toward where the smell came from. Off to one side was the village. So far, they avoided it, but the smell was amazing and he was hungry.

He heard a yelp and glanced over as Rita stumbled, holding her head. Suzuhah stopped a few paces farther, turning to them. He blinked and his eyes widened. "A vision?"

"What?" Alex jerked, turning to Suzuhah who continued to watch Rita.

"I recognize that, the sudden onset of what could be construed as a headache. My mistress got it occasionally. But why now?" he muttered quietly.

Milos, who stopped to, surprisingly, help steady Rita, shrugged. "She needs to choose more opportune times."

"Funny," Rita groaned, shaking her head as she peered into the distance. "Let's get going."

"Not going to tell us?"

"Not unless it's relevant, you lout," she responded distractedly.

Alex exchanged worried glances with Milos as the man let her go. Suzuhah tilted his head, but stayed silent as the trio of boys followed her. They were most of the way around the village when Alex spotted a strange sight. There were two people dressed almost in rags with wounds and cuts all over them, not doing anything to hide the demonic attributes.

Rita let out a sigh of relief as she spotted them as well. "Good, they are still all right." She frowned, gritting her teeth. "So, that really..." She clicked her tongue and Alex held no doubts she was talking about her vision. He didn't ask.

Before they could continue forward, the two demon-like people glanced up. They spotted Milos, momentarily shrinking away, and Rita, who they smiled toward, before turning to Alex with curious expressions on their faces.

At least for a moment, before bright smiles caught Alex off-guard. The two hopped to their feet in the same movement and hurried over. Alex yelped as they got right in his face, offering some bowls that seemed to be steaming soup, babbling something that felt familiar.

He leaned back, confused as hell. Just so they would move away, he took one of the bowls that was practically shoved into his hands. They pulled back, watching him intently. The woman seemed to clasp her hands as if in prayer, watching him earnestly as the young man tilted his head in expectation.

"Well, they seem to like you," Rita joked, curiosity shining on her face before she frowned. "Though, I feel like I've seen this before."

Milos frowned slightly. "Strange. You would think they would be wary."

"True. You're around, after all."

"Not going to argue that point," Milos responded, receiving a sigh from Rita.

Alex ignored it, tentatively taking a sip of the soup. That seemed to be what the duo was waiting for, because while the young man moved back to what seemed to be a small unused hut, gesturing for them to follow, the older woman lightly took his elbow and tugged him to follow. Alex hesitated before shrugging, spooning down another bit of soup along the way.

"Ah, now I remember." Rita muttered as they found themselves moving into the village proper. "This same thing happened when we met the boatman a couple days ago. Why are *you* the only one who ever gets food? I would like some soup too, you know." She huffed, though he could tell it was only half-hearted, a faint smirk on her face.

He shook his head, taking another mouthful as Rita and Milos examined the village. While Milos seemed confused, Rita's somewhat forced cheerfulness drifted to a resigned acceptance. So, the village did have something to do with her vision.

Alex wasn't even sure if this was a village. It was so quiet, just like the other village during the early morning hours. It was almost eerie. Still, there must have been someone there because the soup was still warm and he highly doubted the two before him could make it, considering they kept reminding him of children in their mannerisms.

"I don't know why you are always so chill about these things," Suzuhah pointed out, utterly baffled as Alex shrugged.

"I doubt the food's poisoned or anything. Besides Rita's here, I'll be fine."

"Dingbat. That's not how it works," she grumbled half-heartedly as they stepped into the hut. The two demons pulled away and sat on either side of an older woman as she stirred at a cauldron similar to what Alex saw Rita work on before when she was still aiming for her witch's grade.

"Ah, Elder." Rita leaned forward, eye twitching. "I didn't expect to see you here." The way she said that sounded odd to Alex's ears. Suzuhah stiffened, as if sensing it, or something else, too.

The elder smiled, pulling away from the cauldron, nodding, before glancing toward Alex. "So, you must be the young man these two were looking for."

"Did we mention that?" Rita muttered quietly as Milos minutely shrugged.

Suzuhah stayed back, hesitant.

"So, what brings you back here?"

"We were passing through to recover a little and..." Rita trailed off, shrugging.

The woman continued to smile and Alex began to feel a little uneasy, or, at least, he finally recognized the feeling. He could see Milos and Suzuhah shift, the latter seeming more uncomfortable than before.

"We best be going then." Milos nodded and turned to the doorway.

"Did you take care of the task I asked you for?"

The way she said it was nonchalant, but something about it sent a shiver down Alex's spine.

"Still working on it." Rita frowned, tapping her satchel in a strange way.

So, it wasn't just his imagination.

The woman nodded, giving a quick stir to the cauldron. "Yes, well, don't worry too much about it. We will figure our own way out of it."

"Because you are still demon hunters." Milos hesitated, fingers lightly tapping on his sword hilt in much the same way as Rita.

"That is part of the reason, for sure." Another twirl of the spoon as a faint smoke began to lift from the cauldron. "By the by, thank you for rescuing the survivors. I haven't brought them to their families yet since they came to me first, but I will."

Why did they go to her? He found his thoughts drifting. Something smelled quite good. Alex blinked before taking a step back. "I'm, just, going to go outside for a bit." He promptly turned and walked out, hearing a faint cry from the two demons and a relieved breath from Rita. Strange, but he wasn't going to question it.

Once outside, it was a bit easier to breathe, the day stones casting a weak afternoon light over the landscape. He leaned against the wall, arms crossed, as he stared into the surroundings. Something about this whole thing irked him, and he knew he wasn't alone. He heard movement and glanced over as Milos walked through the doorway, shaking his head with Suzuhah only a step behind.

"Rita not with you?"

Milos' attention flickered to Alex as he pushed away from the wall. "No, I think whatever is going on is related with the vision she received earlier. Last I knew, she was asking the woman about the potion she was concocting."

Alex pursed his lips, but didn't have a response to that. He peered back at the doorway with a faint frown.

The village was as silent as the cavern. Only the faint sound of talking and skittering echoed through the area.

"Geez, is this a ghost town like what my mistress liked to read about?" Suzuhah muttered, rubbing his arm as he peered around. "I wish we could just keep going like we planned. I don't like sticking around like this."

Alex shrugged. "Not much we can do. I'm not exactly leaving Rita behind, which leaves us sitting and waiting." He reached over toward Milos, handing the other half of his soup over. Milos hesitated, staring at it for a bit. Alex shoved it closer, voice impassive as he said, "You're hungry, you're our fighter and I prefer stew over soup. Eat."

Milos seemed on the verge of rolling his eyes, but with considerable willpower that even Alex could recognize, he held off. He took the bowl and ignored the spoon all together, sipping from the edge of the bowl.

"Boo," Suzuhah leapt forward, hands waving. Milos simply

pulled one hand away as he continued to eat and smacked Suzuhah upside the head, causing the boy to let out a faint "ow."

Alex shook his head, amused and feeling a little better. "Smart." He chuckled as Suzuhah shrugged.

"The silence of this place is getting to me. A village shouldn't be this silent and I know it was lively when I was here over six years ago."

Alex pursed his lips at that, curious, but held off. He watched Milos finishing up what was left of the soup. True, Alex probably could have eaten more, but what he said was true as well.

Plus, with him still being mostly exhausted, Milos and Suzuhah were the only ones they had for protection. Rita could fend for herself, as evidenced, but...

His thoughts were cut off when the door wrenched open and Rita darted out. She spotted the three of them and grabbed Milos' and Alex's arms as she passed, hauling her way toward the tree line. Milos barely missed a step, throwing the bowl backward. Whether he was aiming or not, Alex didn't know. Though he didn't miss the howl and crash that rang up behind them.

"Mind explaining our sudden race?" Milos pulled his arm away, but kept easy pace as Suzuhah flipped to her more agile female form and darted ahead.

"You'll see," Rita muttered, "three...two...one..."

Alex almost stumbled as a pulse vibrated out from the house's direction, followed by an angered scream, heard even as they flung themselves into the forest proper. "What was that?"

"Me messing up a seer's level potion that would have, if she got the chance to pour it on the ground, created a mass sleeper spell, knocking out anyone who wasn't a demon."

"That's what you saw?" Alex yelped at that, dodging around a tree as he tried to keep pace.

"Honestly? That's the simplified version. The vision mostly just confirmed some things I was already suspecting. I knew something was up when we got there, we all did. I wish I saw it earlier, the first time Milos and I arrived." She shook her head. "The last time I met her, I was so focused on finding you and checking out the island, I didn't think of paying attention to her."

She gritted her teeth as she took a sharp inclined turn, heading up a cliffside path. "I should have realized, what with those seer-level, if amateur, incantations on the wall, it should have been obvious that a demon would have no way of creating one of those."

"Uh, you're done explaining your reasoning, right? Cause it looks like we have some company," Suzuha cried out, stumbling back as Rita slid to a halt at the top of the path, Milos and Alex a step behind. In a semi-circle was a group of men and woman, bows taut at their sides.

"Oh, you have *got* to be kidding me," Rita groused.

"Hand over the young demon and you will be free to go." A woman stepped forward, bringing her bow up, directing it toward Rita. "If not, we will fire."

"Yeah...no." Rita shook her head, a faint smile without mirth on her lips. "One other thing I forgot to mention, the reason those demons we rescued went to the elder? She was the one who took care of them. At least, my vision showed me that."

"I'm sorry. What?" Alex blinked, feeling more than a little lost with the situation and why was Rita being so calm with an arrow in her face?

Milos clicked his tongue, already in a defensive stance, hand hovering over his blade as Rita continued, staring down the shaft of the arrow, "What I mean is that, for the last six years, that seer has actually been *helping* that man, the demon king, sending sacrifices for her own gain, or maybe to protect the village, as she said, but I doubt that."

Silence invaded the air as the people stilled. Rita walked a few paces forward, moving around the arrow so she was parallel with the stunned woman, continuing, "I'd wondered while we were entering the mountain where the seer's spells came from. That was reinforced when I saw the demons relaxing outside her home and *not* looking for their family. However, it was confirmed when I met with her just now. She wasn't surprised to see us and she knew well enough already that the Demon King wasn't dead, yet she didn't particularly seem to care, more focused on her seer's brew. A seer's brew that would have knocked us out. All of us."

"Blasphemous," the woman snarled as she swung, arrow knocked and pointed at Rita, who glared back at her.

"Right. She is still your elder, after all." Rita leaned back with a furrowed brow. "An elder who betrayed the trust of her people. I would rather not stay in a place such as that."

"Well then, let's vacate the premises, shall we?" Milos spoke up.

Suzuha clapped her hands. "I have a bit of energy left and I'm still a little hungry."

Alex shivered at that, but let out a breath. Not many options. "So, we're fighting our way through?" Alex was at least grateful that the other two kept their voices low so the only ones who heard were the woman and their small group.

"To put it bluntly?" Rita smirked, hand in her satchel and staring the woman dead in the eye. "Yes." With that, she dodged to one side as Milos cut into the woman. Rita turned, flinging powder through the air as the others brought their bows up. Suzuha and Alex, having anticipated that, covered their mouths and darted after her as some of the hunters, caught off-guard, hacked. Milos stayed back, helping to deal with some of the more experienced that seemed to have gathered what was going on and went on the offensives, dodging the powders.

It was hectic for a few minutes as Alex wove and dodged, just avoiding another cloud of powders. The slice of a sword, and he spotted Suzuha pulling one person down into the foliage, out of sight. After a few minutes of dodging and trying to find a path through the hunters, he managed, racing into the tree line with the others close on his heels. Rita hurried to the front, guiding them through the trees, the tassels of her hat just visible through the thinning landscape.

It bothered him. How they were basically leaving the situation unfinished, demons on their tail and a demon king out there somewhere.

"So, you know the way to the ship?" Milos hummed as Rita nodded, before pausing.

"Er, well, it was in this direction."

"The Aqua Wraith probably moved the ship," Alex pointed out, earning a harsh glare.

Suzuha chuckled. "Do you want me to look above? I can't fly for long." Her gaze flickered to Alex. "I have a little bit more energy left from when I last ate, but..."

After some hesitation, and as they slowed down a few paces from an all-out race to just a speedy walk, Rita nodded. "Better than nothing."

Suzuha did a cheeky little salute before shifting forms and flying up through the trees a few paces away, circling high above. Honestly, her Vulfulas form was such a strange sight to see, the gold reflecting the day stones brilliantly as her long tail whipped around her almost like a protective barrier. Her long wings allowed her to hover above, gliding through the air. She flipped once before turning sharply to the right. She dived down, flipping in the air before disappearing in a flash. A moment or two later, the young girl struggled through the trees and pointed to the left, finger to her lips.

That was all the sign the three of them needed, hurrying quietly over the landscape after Suzuha. Milos twitched occasionally, probably hearing something they couldn't, though Alex did occasionally catch the faint sound of howls and cries echo from the other direction.

He peered to Suzuha, who spared him a sidelong glance and whispered, "Thank you for the food earlier, I don't have a lot of energy left and what little bit I just got helped."

Alex nodded, but didn't respond, finding himself still feeling exhausted from trekking all day and possibly all night. He wasn't sure.

Thankfully for his aching limbs, it wasn't long before they made it to the coastline.

To his slight surprise, the boat was nowhere in sight.

"Suzuha?" he asked, tilting his head toward her.

"It's coming." She grinned, hands behind her head as she swayed side to side.

"There." Rita pointed off to the left where the familiar boat wove around a rocky wall, wind stones at a low whistle as it glided over the water.

Alex was more than a little relieved to see it, hurrying after the others as they raced down the coastline. He noted briefly as Rita peered over her shoulder, a moment of shock on her face, followed by joy. Considering Milos held a similarly impressed expression, Alex would have to ask later.

A few lines were flipped over the side and, Alex grinned, it seemed Ari and Leon were doing fine. The two slaves were busy tying the lines securely. Leon used his good arm, tugging at the rope Rita grabbed, hauling her up at a fast clip. Suzuha took the other.

"It's good to see they are all right." Alex smiled.

"It seems like—" Milos suddenly cut off his words, gaze snapping to the tree line. "Alex, get on board."

Alex blinked, glancing back at him to argue, but slammed his jaw shut. He winced in realization; they were followed, weren't they? Was it one of the demons? Someone from the village? The rope Rita used smacked back down in the cresting waves and sand, pulling him out of his thoughts. He darted over, tugging himself up. His arms shook, but thankfully with Rita, Suzuha, Ari and Leon's combined strength, he was on deck in no time. After doing a quick perusal of the two slaves, Ari giving him a faint smile while Leon just nodded, he was relieved to find they seemed to be much better. He turned to the coastline.

Good thing too, as water leapt upward, curving around the place he was only a moment before, crashing against the ship. Ari barely managed to catch herself before turning and racing to the cabin, probably heading to the engine room as Leon hurried over to the wheel. The boat rocked as another wave crested on the other side, as if to knock it over.

Alex stumbled slightly. When he turned his gaze back onto where Milos stood, the man's sword was drawn and a figure was walking out of the tree line. Alex gulped, recognizing the figure right away as a sharp intake of breath sounded by his side.

The scar down one side of his face, the blue gills decorating his neck and the thin, whip-like tail glittered in the darkening day stones' light. The figure, Ransel, Alex remembered, stopped a few feet away from Milos, his gaze drifting from the man toward the ship with a curious expression.

After a moment, he turned back to Milos and spoke. "An Alertian, all the way out here? How peculiar."

Alex heard a faint crack and glanced sidelong to see Suzuha gripping the wood of the railing tightly, golden eyes piercing forward toward the creature before them, a snarl curling her lips up into a contorted grimace.

"Maybe. I assume you are the Demon King?" Milos spoke, and Alex didn't miss the slight waver as Milos' posture shifted into a ready stance. "You seem plenty powerful."

The man smiled, gaze drifting up toward Alex once more, locking eyes with him. "You, Alex, who was your father?"

"If you say you, I'm going to gag," Rita muttered under her breath and, while Alex wanted to chuckle, a part of him found himself shaken by the intensity of Ransel's gaze.

"Why?"

"Because you remind me of someone. As I stare up at you, I can't help but remember *him*." The man took a few steps forward, only stopping as a blade slid to his throat, Milos at his side and blade still.

"You will step no farther." Milos' words were cold, and yet the man didn't even turn to him.

"Him?" Alex gripped the railing tightly, confusion making way for uncertainty. "What are you talking about?" His gaze flicked to the others, part of him wishing Milos would just get on so they could flee. He'd only met this man once before, and found himself more than a little freaked out.

The man spread his arms, tail lazily moving through the air. "You're a smart boy, evading my demons this whole time. Surely you can figure it out, what with our *many* similarities." He brought one hand to his chest. "I sense the water demon in you, just as you sense it in me, and yet you are very much human, as am I. Only a few obtain such power and ability, and only a few survive."

"You are speaking in riddles," Milos spoke firmly, blade pressing deeper into his throat. Alex wondered why Milos wasn't just killing him. He knew the man could do just that and, while he wasn't keen on the idea, he could feel how dangerous Ransel was. As Ransel's gaze pierced his, his human side screamed to run as his demon side curled forward toward the familiar feeling.

"Why aren't you killing him?" Rita shouted, her grasp on the railing beside Alex startling the boy. "You stupid lout. Kill him and get on the ship."

It was then Alex noticed the sweat beading on Milos' brow, the gritted teeth as he realized. The blade wasn't moving and a thin layer of ice coated over his fingers and onto the blade, swirling around his boots, barely visible in the dwindling day stones light.

"The Yuki-onna," Suzuha shouted. "Damnit. Get away!" With that, she dove off the side, twisting into her Vulfulas form as a familiar woman shifted from the trees, ice piercing upward to surround Milos.

Milos gritted his teeth, sweat pouring as he managed to wrench himself free, one boot almost coming loose as he tumbled backward, barely dodging away from the interweaving cage that sprouted up where he stood.

"Verona, please, focus your attention on our dear friend." Ransel glanced over his shoulder briefly before turning toward Alex, who found himself taking a step back, guarded and partially wishing his demon form was out at the moment. "After all, dear boy, as I continue to observe you, I know for certain. You are Alfred's son, are you not?" He once more spread his arms out, reaching forward. "How I've longed to meet another like me, one who escaped slavery and those brutal experiments. You look much like your father, and yet it took me so long to recognize you."

As these words echoed through the air, Suzuha let out a cry, corkscrewing to one side as something launched itself past her wing, crashing into the sand and waves, feet from where she flew. Milos spun to the side, bringing up his sword just as a spear of ice jutted forward to catch his leg to pin him.

Alex's gaze snapped to the ensuing battle, barely able to process everything that was going on. Ransel's words, the demon's attacks, they were almost overwhelming after the long day.

"Come with me, dear boy, Alex. I will treat you well, as a companion, as a comrade, to have by my side as an equal." A hand reached forward and Alex found himself taking another step back as Rita shifted in front of him.

However, it was Suzuha who let out a screech, voice mingling between male and female, "You said the same thing to my mistress, then you killed her. Murdered her. How dare you say this now." She spun in the air as a boulder flung upward and she dived down, claws digging into Milos' shoulders as the man rolled to one side, unable to fully get onto his feet from the barrage. She lifted off, Milos' expression startled and hesitant.

Sadness, a despair Alex had only witnessed a few times, shown over Ransel's face as his hands shook, grasping toward his heart. "I didn't want to. I wanted to protect her, keep her safe. She was to be my lifelong companion, my love, someone who could understand me. Yet she ran and drowned, deciding to choose death over me. I could have been everything for her. Even for a creature like you. I didn't care." His words, his voice, now seemed to break slightly from the calm he was portraying before, a wave of emotions passing over his face before he turned to Alex once more. "Please. All I seek is companionship. If I meant you or yours harm, they would be dead. You know that." He reached a hand forward, palm up. "Dear boy, come back with me. As one of similar blood and being, you can understand."

Suzuha swerved upward as the rocks and ice stopped moving. On Ransel's left hovered the Yuki-onna and on his right was that familiar creature Alex saw in the ritual-like room, his hood forward and features as gnarled as he remembered.

Milos, who had been surprisingly quiet up until that point, spoke. "Alex."

Alex's gaze darted over to Milos as he was set down by Suzuha, who curled her wings up, tail shifting around Alex almost protectively. "Do you remember what we need to do?"

Alex opened his mouth, unsure how to respond before he blinked. Right, his mother. He was here for his mother. They were all on the ship. He felt a sharp pain as the sea churned. He heard the yelps and movement as the ship swelled, cresting, but never quite descending downward. He glanced to one side and froze as a spear of water hovered to either side of the ship.

"I don't like the idea, I don't want to hurt your companions, but I am not going to lose another, not again." Ransel's voice echoed over the water and, though Alex couldn't see him anymore with the swell, he felt a chill down his spine. He gripped his tunic tightly before turning to

Milos as Ransal's voice echoed over the waves. "Not to such a weak Alertian, not to a freak creature of my lost love's creation, not to anyone."

A moment of hesitation trembled over Milos' posture before his gaze snapped toward Alex with anger. "Well?"

All Alex could do was nod. "Please..." he found his voice somewhat choked. "Get us out of here."

A faint smile, a hint of uncertainty that Alex almost missed, and a confident turn was all Alex caught until Milos walked over to the pipes and said, "Wind stones, forward, now."

There was a pause, a moment of stillness before a sharp humming rev echoed from below. With a burst of wind, and a shout of "Hold on," from who knew where, Alex found himself being jerked backward as the ship raced forward, shooting off the swell and crashing into the waves, which practically split behind them.

A large scream echoed over the landscape as Alex felt a surge of power, a closer surge. His gaze flickered to the Aqua Wraith as she swirled onto the deck, her voice echoing over the wood and waves.

He could feel Ransel now, the clawing magic as water churned, trying to pull at them, tug them back.

Alex didn't hesitate, he found himself joining in with the Aqua Wraith as the ship rocketed forward, almost leaping over the waves.

He could see Suzuha, in her Vulfulas form, wings sheltering him, Rita, and Milos hanging onto the railings for dear life as Leon fought with the wheel. He could feel hints of his demonic power, humming in his veins, but never truly coming out. He felt a gentle hum as the feeling of anguish subsided and only one other familiar presence swirled beside him. He felt a heavy weight flutter over him as he swayed.

Hopefully, that would be enough.

Chapter Twenty-nine

Milos peered back as the island grew smaller and smaller behind them, ice and stone rocketing forward and plummeting a good distance behind; waves reached forward before crashing behind them like grasping hands, just out of reach. He pushed away from the railing he found himself slammed against, turning in time to see Rita race over, catching Alex as he collapsed, once more unconscious. The Aqua Wraith herself stared off into the distance, a strange expression on her face.

Suzuha stood off to one side, peering back at the shore, her wings fluttering as her tail curled through the air. The creature turned and, in the same movement, shifted to her smaller, more feminine form as her gaze locked with the Aqua Wraith. "It's you." Suzuha's voice echoed over the ship.

"Greetings, young one," The Aqua Wraith swirled to face her. "You did well back there, especially against creatures such as them. Thank you for protecting my charges." She bowed, and, to Milos' faint surprise and Rita's definite, she stayed bowed, head low as if waiting for something.

"You hid from me, this whole time. You knew he was still alive and yet..."

"I was not aware of the extent of his degradation. I was only set to guide him to his chosen path, just like all others which I have taken." The Aqua Wraith turned to Milos. "I am simply a guide on these waters."

Milos stared for a bit, but it was Rita who spoke, still supporting Alex in her lap. Milos would have to tease her about that later, after he got his own thoughts in order.

"I think you're a bit more than a guide. You came back for us, after all." She grinned quietly. Her expression was surprisingly soft.

"You hid the boat though, right? You protected Ari and Leon." The Aqua Wraith stayed silent, as Rita continued, "You helped us escape, guided Alex on what to do and were there for me when..." She paused.

Milos shook his head, he could see this was going to get confusing and more than a little dramatic, which he was not inclined to deal with right now. He glanced around and noted that Ari was missing. He moved over toward Leon. "Where is Ari?"

"Down below, in the engine room."

Milos nodded, cutting Leon off before asking, "Are you all right?"

Leon hesitated for a moment, eyeing him worriedly. "Yes, Master."

"It's Milos." Milos shook his head, feeling a little sick to his stomach. The man's words, as much as he detested them, rang through his mind. He felt his hand twitch near his sword, the useless thing already back in place at his side. "Just Milos."

Leon blinked and chuckled. "Master Milos it is." Milos snorted, but didn't argue.

He could hear the semi-joking tone of voice and knew Leon would very much drop the master if he thought it necessary. That, in a way, made him feel more relieved than seeing the island disappear into the distance as he checked the slave over. "Well, for now, swap with Ari, I want to make sure she is all right."

"Of course." He bowed and hurried away, descending down into the ship.

It wasn't long until Ari appeared, her thin frame lighting up slightly upon seeing him. The barest hint of a smile forming on her normally stoic face. "Master Milos, you are all right."

He resisted the urge to stop her calling him master and nodded. "As are you, it seems. It is good to know." He glanced forward. "Well, then, if you are ready, let's get out of here as fast as possible. You probably saw the Nyx before heading below, correct."

"Yes, I did." She frowned slightly, worry shining for a brief moment.

"As long as we get moving, we should be fine. Even so, a pseudo-demon like that is going to follow us in no time." He withheld the wince as his thoughts flickered to what little he could do. It was thanks to Suzuha he had made it to the ship. The Yuki-onna had caught him off guard, which could have easily been a fatal mistake.

"Master Milos, is something the matter?"

"No, it is nothing." He turned away. "For now, just focus on getting us moving, all right?"

He could tell himself it was nothing, he could receive nods of affirmation up and down the ship, but he had been scared. He couldn't deny that feeling. It was so foreign, strange, but he knew what it was. He felt it painfully clearly as he tried and failed to move to his feet. He couldn't even touch the Nyx, never mind the demons at his side. He was out of his league and the demon's words at the end...

He pulled his long hair over his shoulder, staring at it quietly, lost. He was weak? Part of him knew that wasn't the case. Another part knew it was, and that part was becoming stronger as he thought over his own actions. He was an Alertian. He came down here to prove that, to finish his initiation and...

He trailed off in his thoughts, tightening his grip on the long strands. It was in his blood, he was an Alertian through and through. Yet he was consorting with demons, not killing them on sight like he was supposed to, like his lineage, his whole life, pointed to. What was he thinking? Why was he ignoring his life's purpose?

Was it really his life's purpose? He'd always wanted to prove himself, he still did, but...

He shook the thought away as he heard Ari telling Leon to up the power. Milos tossed the hair back over his shoulder, resolving to retie it later as he heard the engine rev and the wind stones produce more air once more at a steadier rhythm. He moved back to where the show was taking place. He could see Suzuha off to one side and hesitated. He hadn't thought of it much at the time, but he recalled letting the Vulfulas help him onto the ship. What was strange was he didn't feel any malice or hatred from the creature. In a strange way, he felt the creature did want to help him. It threw him off balance, making him wonder what indication he was given to assume such a thing. The only thing he could think of, off the top of his head, was that Suzuha had only been helpful since they met her with Alex. She scouted ahead, helped Alex when he collapsed and, back there, she pulled him away from being skewered. He shook his head, returning his focus onto what was happening. It seemed he'd missed a bit, but it wasn't hard to miss the increased tension in the air. The Aqua Wraith hovered to one side, watching Suzuha carefully. Suzuha, on the other hand, held an impassive expression on her face.

An impassive expression that was rapidly falling away to reveal anger.

Rita sat a bit away, running her hand through Alex's hair in a way Milos could tell was subconscious. She met his gaze and shook her head, confused.

So, he hadn't really missed much if Rita was confused as well.

He decided to remain silent, leaning against the wall of the cabin, arms crossed. He wasn't about to go downstairs in case the Nyx caught up with them, as he knew it was likely.

"Young one..." the Aqua Wraith tried to begin.

"Save it." Suzuha sighed, seeming to slump where she stood, shaking her head. "All those years ago, six years now, you were only following through with your oath to guide those bastards to our island, to make sure they died and yet, not only did you guide *him* right to us, you also failed to kill him when you deemed it necessary. I know you were only following your oath, your duty, but it doesn't hurt any less."

The Aqua Wraith shifted slightly, her watery hair curling around her as a soft frown graced her face. "I did not intend for that to happen and when I realized I tried to correct my mistake." She shook her head. "I truly thought he was on board."

"He wasn't." Suzuha's gaze flickered to anger once more. "He never was. You slaughtered that whole ship and failed to kill the one responsible. You killed innocents and left the guilty alive."

The Aqua Wraith hesitated. Her movements were somber. "I did what needed to be done. The only thing I could do at the time. I know you have every right to be angry at me, but now is not the time. If I disappear, if my oath is broken, then we will all perish."

Milos frowned. What did the Aqua Wraith mean by that? Rita

seemed to have the same question because she perked up. "Wait, what? What do you mean?"

Suzuha and the Aqua Wraith turned to Rita, both suddenly hesitant. The Aqua Wraith let out a breathy hum, the water singing around them for a moment. "My oath, my duty, is not only as a guide, but also as a test." She glanced toward Milos for a moment before continuing, "If you recall, the gatekeeper sends those with free demons through the underground passage for safety. However, not all of those who go through the passage deserve to make it to the refuge." Her gaze drifted to the open water. "Six years ago, there was another band of travelers, much like yourselves, with a water demon on board of mixed blood. I sensed his turmoil and anguish. His grief was so strong, but his loneliness..." she shook her head. "In hopes to save his soul, something I cannot do for myself, I wished for him to meet with someone kind, who might be able to help him." She turned to the group. "After all, my duty is to take different courses of action on where I see fit to guide those like you. If I felt you were genuine or with a good heart, I would try to warn you of the dangers, however..."

"If not, we would have died long before making it here," Rita summarized, slight horror on her face as her gaze flitted to Milos, who did everything he could not to look away, though every part of his being wanted to. "That's also why your warnings were vague, because you were still testing us."

"That, and it has been many a year since I have graced these waters. I am but a spirit, my memory is only so long. Some islands, I can only faintly recall, while others..." She turned to Suzuha. "Other islands, I thought creatures, such as your friend, would have left after their mistress' death."

"But I didn't. I couldn't. That was my mistress' home."

"Yet you came with us," Milos pointed out, finding himself getting involved in the conversation, though he knew he shouldn't.

Suzuha nodded, a faint smile on her lips. "Yeah, that was an impulse decision for sure, but I don't really regret it."

"Even now? When you still need to face both Rita and myself for what you tried to do?"

"Nope." Suzuha chuckled, clapping her hands. "Still don't regret it, because I know the same thing the Aqua Wraith realized." She hummed, but stopped before she said anything else.

Realizing, Milos turned to the Aqua Wraith to explain. The Aqua Wraith actually giggled at that before she moved, swirling through the wood and back out the other side around Milos. "She's talking about what I've come to learn about the five of you since we began." She shook her head, hair curling around, not quite settling back like it should. "As I said earlier, six years ago, I learned of that man's desires, of his wish for companionship, and so I helped lead them to Suzuha and her mistress' island in hopes that it would soothe his soul and allow the others safe passage. However, his desires were much greater than I realized, for he tried to take Suzuha's mistress by force and ended up killing her instead. I wished to drown him, but he convinced his crew-mates to help him escape, and so when they fled into the only momentarily dormant field of water serpents—"

"You let them drown." Rita's eyes widened in shock, glancing at the floorboards below her feet.

"How is this ship still functioning?" Milos asked, staying still.

The Aqua Wraith swirled to the other side of Milos, head poking over his shoulder. "The ship is a part of me, just like a sword is a part of an Alertian. No matter how much you may try to dull it, it will always come back sharp as steel." Her gaze flickered to Milos as he stiffened.

Right. She was a spirit, not a demon. So, did she know? Know what he'd been struggling with this whole time?

She turned away and floated over to Rita, moving down to pat Alex's head gently. "I'm bound to these waters, to this ship. I can capsize this boat at will, turn it to nothing, scrap and let it wash back to my friend, the gatekeeper. I can make it sturdy, and help guide it through the toughest waters as is necessary at times. It's not perfect. Just because I can make it sturdier, doesn't mean it won't still capsize if you're not careful or if a monster attacks it." She pulled away, turning to Suzuha. "I'm sorry I didn't appear earlier. I was frightened. I knew of your anger, felt it through the very boards of this ship. I knew if I appeared before you..."

"I would have killed you. I almost did kill you." Suzuha grimaced. "I was desperately searching for your oath the entire time. That vial you showed my mistress all those years ago which she reinforced." Suzuha slumped. "I guess it was a good thing I never found it. At least, not until we were almost at the island." Suzuha's gaze drifted to the cabin. "Right next to the diary. Heh, should have expected as much. Still, I guess I'm glad I held off, I wouldn't want to see anyone on this ship be taken down with you," Suzuha said as she stared up at the dwindling day stones. "I knew that, but...yeah, it was probably a good idea not to show yourself."

Silence fell over the group and Milos sighed. "So, just to get it out of the way, can we rely on you to help us get the rest of the way?"

The Aqua Wraith smiled. "I would not have waited for you if I thought otherwise."

"Good, so what little can you tell us of this part of the ocean? The straits we're approaching?" Milos peered past, deciding to put the whole conversation behind him for good reason, in his opinion. The others promptly agreed when they followed his gaze.

"Holy," Rita gulped, probably just having spotted what Milos had been watching for the last little bit without really having thought much of it.

Mainly because it was hard to think such a massive structure could exist down here. Towering ever closer, spearing into the sky and practically meeting the ceiling above were great pillars of stone. Water swirled around them, whirlpools of massive size curled around the edges as a light mist coated everything, farther in he could just barely see massive cliff-faces of stone that boggled the mind. Even at a distance, a good hour away, it was terrifying to behold. "Plus, we are going in at night." Milos shook his head with a sigh. "We are going to need a miracle."

"We can rest our anchor here for now," the Aqua Wraith spoke. "We made good time and even if that man were to follow, we gave ourselves enough of a buffer he won't be able to ascertain our actual spot until much later." She peered up as the last of the day stones fell away, the night completely taking over. "He won't want to search at night. This area is treacherous even in the brightness of the day."

"Then let's rest." Milos pushed away from the wall as the Aqua Wraith nodded, swirling away. After a few minutes, he heard a faint thump of the anchor as the wind stones began to die down.

"Sounds good, but first..." Rita turned to Suzuha, who stiffened. "We need to talk."

Suzuha winced, fiddling with her fingers as she shifted from foot to foot. "I..."

Milos walked over, fingers dancing on the hilt, though he didn't look straight at the girl. "It's not the first time one of us has tried to kill him." He glanced sidelong at Rita, who stilled in her ministrations.

After a long time, she let out a breath. "You're right, and Suzuha has helped us, plus Alex trusts her more than I would like him to."

"So..."

Rita snapped up, glaring and causing Suzuha's jaw to snap shut. Though Milos didn't miss the almost playful gleam in her gaze that Suzuha obviously did. "Oh, no, you aren't getting out without punishment." She spoke up, her voice lilting slightly and Milos almost snorted. Yeah, now she was just playing with Suzuha. He doubted the girl was really still that pissed at Suzuha after everything they just went through, but she had an appearance to keep, it seemed. "You were the reason we got into this whole mess in the first place. We wouldn't have needed to worry about that island at all if you hadn't decided it would be a good place to try to drag Alex to his death. We didn't even need to stop on the island after stopping on your mistress'."

Suzuha winced, her posture as small as she could seem to make it while still standing. Milos left this to Rita. While he was certainly annoyed, his thoughts were on other things, on the Aqua Wraith's words, how his sword never fully dulled. On the Demon King, how he had called Milos weak, how a *demon* of all things was unimpressed. His mental switch in which he noticed nothing except the demons which he needed to kill.

He was returning to his Alertian roots, returning and failing. That alone somewhat scared him.

It didn't help that he knew how pissed off he was at Alex's mother for abandoning her son or how his desire to prove himself never really disappeared. In fact, he was now certain it had grown after this last escapade, especially after having gotten batted into a wall or railing for the second time since coming down here.

That desire was definitely still there, no longer just an inkling in the back of his mind. He saw what desire could do to a person, but he also knew *why* it could do that to someone, how strong it was.

His fingers tightened on his sword hilt as he forced himself back to focusing on Rita's words.

"Hey, lout, did you hear me?"

Milos blinked and turned to Rita, who was staring up at him in annoyance. He carefully plastered a neutral expression on his face, which seemed to cause Rita to stiffen slightly, before responding, "I did not. You were talking too much."

Her brow twitched, but she didn't do more than that, only letting out a sigh. "Why do I bother?" She turned back to Suzuha. "Well, I'll just say this." She lifted her fingers, showing three of them. "I have three rules for you to follow, and you will follow them to the *letter* or else."

Suzuha winced as Rita curled one finger down. "One, you are not allowed to attack or hurt any of us unless we explicitly say so."

She put another finger down as Milos watched, feeling slightly bemused as he noticed Suzuha glance away, the young girl completely missing the growing smirk on Rita's face. "You are to answer any of our questions truthfully and as much as you can." Last finger. "Lastly...you're on cleaning and cooking duty for the next month, both on this ship and wherever else we might end up when we get to the refuge."

Milos resisted the urge to chuckle as Suzuha's head snapped back up to face them, finally noticing the grin on Rita's face. "Pretty relaxed punishments there." Milos hummed.

"Oh, I don't know. Your talking irks me as much as I bet it does her but she can't retaliate."

Milos felt his eye twitch. "That feeling is quite mutual, I assure you."

Rita grinned at that as she went to stand up. "Well, first order of business, bring Alex to bed."

"Your priorities are skewed." Milos shook his head, but walked over to help her pick up the exhausted boy.

"How are they skewed?" Rita blinked, annoyed. "He's not going to be able to do much else—"

"If he doesn't eat first." Milos glanced at Rita, who paused and sighed.

"Fair point. Suzuha, get dinner started." With that, Milos helped her get Alex to wake up and on his feet.

"Why?"

Milos didn't turn, but Rita did, a faint smile on her lips. "We're not the grudge-holding types. Well, Milos might be, but he doesn't have an excuse to blame you for this one since he did try to kill Alex in the past."

Milos didn't need to look to feel the stare on his neck as Alex blinked awake, lifting an arm to rub his eyes tiredly.

"Plus, keeping food for these guys and a clean place is a chore in itself. So, get going."

"R-Right." Suzuha's voice held a surprisingly chipper tone to it as she raced through the doorway and out of sight.

Alex let out a yawn as he leaned against Milos for support. "We good?" he muttered.

"We're good." Milos nodded, earning a cheeky smile from Alex.

Rita patted Alex's back as the two of them helped him through the doorway and downstairs into the cozy warmth of the ship. Milos trusted Ari and Leon to take care of themselves and he knew the Aqua Wraith would hold to her promise. He felt surprisingly relieved at all of that.

They still needed to tackle the straits tomorrow. The last leg of their journey. It was strange to think about, but he was quite content to just enjoy being around people he saw as part of his own...comrades, he supposed, though he wasn't sure if that was the correct word either anymore.

All he knew was that his mind calmed a little as he listened to Rita's conversation to a half-asleep Alex. As much as he might not want to admit it, he appreciated being on their way for more than just the fact that he was so close to his goal.

Actually, at this point, he wasn't even sure what his goal was.

Chapter Thirty

Rita chuckled as she helped Alex take a seat in the warmth of the kitchen, briefly noting the drying pans off to one side. It seemed that Ari and Leon already ate. Milos sat beside Alex who appeared confused as some bread was put down in front of him by an apron-clad young man, Suzuhah. The boy must have shifted forms to make it easier to cook and he seemed to be doing it with gusto, humming a surprisingly jaunty tune, some of it reminiscent of Alex's songs. Rita chuckled at that before speaking, "Suzuhah?"

Suzuhah glanced back as he continued to cook, expression curious. "Yes, miss?"

"Oh, don't use that." She gagged, waving her arm. "I'm not Milos." She felt the glare there and purposefully ignored it. "Just call me Rita as usual. Anyway, my question is what can you tell me about you? Who was your mistress? What can you do as a Vulfulas?"

The boy stilled for a moment before letting out a breath. "Some of that is rather long..."

"Tell us the shortened version." Milos spoke up, tapping his finger lightly on the table.

Suzuhah huffed, shaking his head, but spoke a moment later, "Right, forgot who I was speaking to." He turned the flame down and shifted toward them. "Short version is this. I don't know much of what I can do as a Vulfulas. My mistress, a seer of high class, never gave me any instructions. The only thing she ever said was to live. I've read before and I think she was treating me as a son or daughter, depending on what mood I was in that day. Nothing more than that." He let out a breath. "I guess, she was seeking companionship too, which was why I was created without one of those binding oaths most Vulfulas have." He paused, as if to think it over. "No, the only oath I have bound to me is the order to live."

He chuckled morosely, placing a hand to his chest. "I'm getting ahead of myself. I'm young for Vulfulas standards since we grow much slower than humans and sometimes demons." His gaze flickered to something only he could see as a faint smile crossed his lips. "My mistress was a kind and gentle soul. Whenever someone arrived on the island, she would care for them and, occasionally, the two of us would travel to the few inhabited islands in these seas and the refuge. I guess she must have sensed the demon king, as he calls himself, was going to change the island. She warned me never to return to that island, even though we would continue to go to the others. Of course, now I know why." He sighed, turning back to his cooking, stirring what was probably meat and vegetables, a stew? "Six years ago, that man and a group of other sailors arrived on our island. I told this story to Alex, so he can tell you more, but..." Suzuhah trailed off.

"That man got attached to Suzuhah's mistress." Alex spoke up, taking over the story, Rita turned to him, startled, as he continued to watch Suzuhah. "The man, Ransel, by the way, became infatuated with Suzuhah's mistress and tried to court her, to ask her to come with him. Suzuhah's mistress must have seen something in her visions, much like you did, Rita, and tried to get out of the situation peacefully." Alex shook his head.

"That didn't occur." Milos spoke up, causing Alex to nod.

"Ransel attacked her and dragged her under the waves."

"Ah, right." Milos grimaced. "Powerful water demons can keep their victims alive under the water for hours, if not days or weeks."

"Except for if the victim fights back and catches the demon off guard." Alex winced. "It sounds like that's what happened because Suzuhah found her body a while later."

Rita shuddered. She was getting sick of death.

"So that's why you hated water demons," Milos muttered quietly. "It's why you attacked Alex even though he's only part. You were blinded by hatred."

"As part of it, yes," Suzuhah finally spoke up, passing out the food. "You asked another question as well. I can give you some answers, but I'm as tired as you all are, so..."

After a moment of hesitation, or none from Alex who dove right in, they started eating. Rita took a bite and blinked. "This is actually pretty good."

Suzuhah smiled. "Well, my mistress was a terrible cook, so I needed to learn quickly. Glad you like it."

"Right, mistress." She paused, thoughts awhirl before she perked up. "Is that why you're attached to us? Because I remind you of her?"

"More or less, though I can tell you two are distinctly different from each other." Suzuhah grimaced. "For one, you are a bit more...never mind."

"Oh, I want to hear this, continue." Milos' lips twitched into a barely there grin, earning a sharp glare from Rita.

"No. Thank. You," she growled before turning back to Suzuhah, who chuckled nervously. "Anyway, abilities."

"Right, those." He took a seat as the group ate. "Alex knows most of them, but I guess I'll start off with how I've managed to live this long with minimal amounts of food. I'd rather get this one out of the way anyway, since you did want me to be truthful and all."

Rita nodded as she chowed into the meat, so tender. No, focus.

"I, well, I like people food, it does give me some nutrients, but..." He trailed off, appearing incredibly hesitant.

A quiet clatter caught Rita's attention as Alex put his spoon down. "You're hungry now, aren't you?"

Suzuhah winced, nodding sheepishly and Alex sighed. "You know what? Might as well just show them."

"Um, are you sure?" Suzuhah blinked up at him, surprised.

Alex shrugged, letting out a yawn. "It's not like it's going to do any harm. You didn't hurt me last time and we're in the safety of the ship now. I see no problem with it and it should help these two understand anyway." He waved at Rita and Milos. Milos narrowed his eyes as Rita huffed.

"Wait, you not only know what he's talking about, but you also *fed* him? Are you kidding? Alex, you're so..."

"We needed food at the time, it's because I fed him that we were able to escape from the Yuki-onna and he stopped as soon as I pushed him away anyway." Alex grinned. "Though it was probably more of a punt than a push. Felt fitting either way."

"Yeah, and it still stings a little," Suzuhah mumbled, rubbing his side.

"You..." Rita strangled the air for a moment before slumping. "Fine, whatever. I'm surprised Milos isn't arguing."

"You're doing a wonderful job as it is, and I think Alex understands the dangers better than us anyway, no matter how stupid the actions may be."

"Gee. Thanks," Alex muttered, earning a faint smirk from Milos.

"You three are so weird," Suzuhah said under his breath, loud enough for Rita to hear. "Anyway..."

Alex took another bite before placing his spoon down once more and extending his arm out to Suzuhah, wrist upward. Suzuhah peered hesitantly between Milos and Rita, seemingly really uncomfortable.

Why? What was it that Suzuhah ate that would... oh.

Rita flushed as Suzuhah bent down, taking Alex's wrist gently and...

"So that's why you were hesitant." Milos' voice was stiff as the boy's hair covered a large part of his face, lips inches from Alex's bare wrist. Rita twitched in her seat, wanting to tug Suzuhah away, but held still. Alex seemed relaxed, just kind of watching.

Admittedly, she wasn't sure what she was watching.

"You're eating his life force," Milos whispered, shock quickly transitioned to slight anger. "Which you also did to Ari and Leon." Suzuhah glanced up past his bangs, but didn't move.

Alex, however, was the one who responded. "That's right. Suzuhah doesn't necessarily need it and it doesn't hurt, it just feels strange." Alex shrugged with one shoulder, keeping the other steady, though a slight glare did sit on his face. "He's learned his lesson from then. Still, just examine Ari and Leon, they are back on their feet and seeming as healthy as ever."

Milos pursed his lips, watching Alex as Suzuhah suddenly

yanked himself away, wiping his mouth. Alex waved his hand out before pulling back and returning to eating as if nothing happened.

"That...what?" Rita finally voiced out weakly.

"As Milos said, my preferred form of nutrition and food in general is life force. It's what allows me to shift forms and fight. I don't need a lot, especially from someone like Alex who usually has an abundance of it. Though, right now it is a bit low, so I didn't eat that much." He tilted his head toward Milos questioningly. "How could you tell what I was eating?"

Milos scrutinized Suzuhah with a quiet attention. "I've been wondering for a while and I recalled Ari's and Leon's states, plus you were right on a vein, but there was no blood drawn. Lastly, I felt a shift in the air which allowed me to deduce what it was."

Suzuhah nodded, appearing impressed. "That's correct." He shook his head. "As you can tell, it doesn't hurt unless I overeat." He winced. "I do have to apologize to Ari and Leon when I get the chance. When I came on this ship, I was nearing starvation and I might have, well, overdone it a bit when I finally got the chance to eat. Starvation does that to you," He meekly glanced up. "That's one of the distinctions between a Vulfulas and most other creatures. We have the ability to shape-shift, but only when we have life force, and if I'm in my Vulfulas form, I can create lightning, though it does cause damage to my human form." At that, he reached up to a burn mark at his neck and Rita's eyes widened.

"So that's why," she murmured, briefly recalling the lightning when they were on the island and the strange burn marks on both forms of Suzuhah.

Suzuhah nodded, letting out a slight yawn. "Thankfully, it's not extensive, and some of the older ones do disappear over time." Another yawn. "I'm full now and kind of tired, as I'm guessing you all are?"

Alex nodded, placing his food down. "I'm not in the mood to collapse a third time, thank you." He sighed.

"Yeah, that wouldn't be good." Rita grinned, earning her a glare. "Still, though, doesn't someone need to stay up to make sure that man doesn't come?"

Silence filled the air as Milos, of all people, hesitated.

A faint sound of running water echoed through the room before all attention drifted to the Aqua Wraith as she entered through the flooring. "Sleep for tonight." She hummed, a bemused smile on her face. "I shall keep watch and warn you of any aberrations. You all will need whatever strength you can acquire for the coming leg."

After some hesitation, Rita shrugged. "Works for me." She stood up, bowing slightly to the Aqua Wraith. "Thanks."

"Of course."

With that, it seemed everything was settled. Milos and Alex departed to the men's room as Suzuhah shifted forms to follow Rita to the girl's room, a slight happy pep in Suzuha's step.

Rita peered down at her, more than a little amused. "So, you're not going to randomly switch to your male form in the middle of the night, right?"

Suzuha stared up at Rita with a deadpan, "Only if it's a funny prank and won't get me shanked and thrown all the way back to the Capital."

Rita snorted, but didn't argue, slipping inside. She could tell Ari was already asleep in the hammock, appearing much healthier compared to the last time Rita was able to get a good look at her. She wondered if Leon was in the same boat, pun only slightly intended, within the men's room.

Rita shrugged at the thought, quickly getting herself situated and to bed. She peered over to Suzuha, watching the girl crawl into the hammock with another yawn.

"So, life force?"

Suzuha paused mid-yawn and sighed. "Yeah, I don't know why my mistress made me this way, or if she had a choice in the matter." Suzuha smiled weakly, expression morose. "I've never met another of my kind, so I don't know if I'm unique or this is just what being a Vulfulas is like."

Rita stared for a bit, unsure how to respond. "You must have been lonely." The words left her lips before she thought about it, memories of her parents flashing in her mind.

Suzuha paused. "I don't know. Is that what I was feeling?"

Rita didn't have a response to that. She laid down and listened to the quiet creak of the ship as it swayed back and forth over calm waves.

Chapter Thirty-one

Alex awoke the next morning with a start, breath escaping his lungs as coldness suddenly gripped at his chest. The moment of panic quickly dissipated to the point where he wondered whether it was just the remnants of a forgotten nightmare, or something else. He glanced around the room, trying to control what panic was left. Milos shifted beside him, still somewhat asleep, or at least until Alex peered down. Milos' eyes slowly opened with a grogginess Alex wasn't used to seeing with the other.

Milos' gaze flicked to him and a carefully bemused mask flipped onto his face. "This is rare." His voice was faint as he seemed to hold back a yawn and failed.

Alex chuckled, swinging his legs out of bed. "I haven't slept that well in a while." Even as he said that, concern filled his mind at both the strangeness of waking so suddenly and the fact he woke up before Milos of all people, who was barely reacting.

"It's only been a few days."

"So?" Alex smirked before shifting his gaze to the window with a frown.

The morning light was just starting to seep down from the day stones, and yet, while that feeling when he first awoke was gone now, he wondered what it meant.

"Do you sense something?" A faint ruffling of clothes and sheets, followed by the clomp of boots met Alex's ears. He nodded, unsure how to explain it.

Milos sighed. "If that is the case, then we should get moving. There should be enough light now."

Alex glanced toward Milos as the man retied up his hair, the signifier glinting in the light, blood red.

Alex shivered, recalling the morbid scenes from yesterday, how Milos could observe all that death, yet nonetheless do that without a moment's hesitation, without a seeming thought. It unnerved Alex more than he would like to admit.

Yet, it was still Milos, still his friend. He spotted Milos watching him curiously and stood up, quickly getting ready to head upstairs. It seemed Leon was already up. Considering the man was in bed before either of them, Alex wasn't surprised.

What surprised him was the man hadn't managed to wake Milos. Milos must have been more tired than he wanted to admit. It worried Alex a little more, but he decided not to ask. The duo hurried into the kitchen where Suzuhah was already working away, muttering under his breath. Rita was sitting down, yawning and pausing mid-yawn as soon as she spotted Alex.

"Oh, not again," she moaned, plopping her head on the table before shifting to face him. "Is there something we need to watch out for already?"

Alex smiled sheepishly, but didn't respond, unsure if he had just imagined things or not, which seemed to confirm her thoughts.

"Suzuhah, hurry on that breakfast, seems like the day's already starting."

"I noticed." He glanced over to Alex. "I thought Milos was the one with the sharper senses."

"Water demon." Rita pointed, never lifting her head. "Water." She pointed outside and shrugged. "As you know, he's pretty good at sensing the incoming dangers when it is water-based and the Aqua Wraith is probably too busy making sure the ship is ready and able to go instead of focusing on any threats. Though, threats for her would probably have to be major for her to sense them, due to being a spirit and all."

Suzuhah nodded, flipping something that appeared to be pancakes onto three plates before placing them down.

"We had flour?" Alex asked, blinking. "I just thought the bread was already..."

Rita shrugged, chowing down. Alex decided to follow her example with a sigh, enjoying the fruit Suzuhah sprinkled on top of each of theirs. He hadn't eaten good, old-fashioned pancakes in ages.

Thankfully, it wasn't long before they were hurrying upstairs. Alex was more than happy to be outside once more, the waves surrounding him as the day stones glimmered above. Especially as a headache slowly formed at the back of his skull, dragging at his thoughts.

What he wasn't prepared for were the massive pillars of stone he only briefly spotted last night. They appeared larger in the dawning light. The wind stones hummed as the anchor splashed back onto the deck. He jerked, glancing over as the Aqua Wraith swirled to their side, peering ahead. "Welcome to the Straits of Cameron. I have not traversed these waters in..." She trailed off, seemingly lost.

"A long time, got it," Rita said, peering up at the massive monoliths.

Giant waterfalls crested over the sides, splashing down with enough force to coat the surroundings in mist.

Alex stared. There wasn't anything else he could do. "How are we supposed to get through that?" he finally asked.

Considering his question, the silence he received was telling.

The Aqua Wraith swirled in front of him, floating at a slight angle. "Contrary to appearance, the path ahead that thou must follow is a short one. Should no problems arise, we can expect to emerge within half of a day's travel."

"Problems usually arise around us in general and around that place, no doubt, so..." Rita shrugged. "Seems like we're going to have to expect many problems."

"This is why I'm glad I can fly," Suzuhah said, peering forward. "It's quite easy to go above with flight, but through...even fliers like myself avoid flying through here." He paused before glancing over. "Of course, I could probably fly above, it would be so much easier, but I'm in no mood to abandon you all, so I guess I'm stuck going through either way."

"So, no flying through. Got it," Alex said, letting out a breath. "Though it doesn't make much of a difference. I can't exactly fly, period, so that's a moot point."

Rita chuckled and he sent a half-hearted glare her way before grinning. "So, are we diving in?"

"Is that a question?" Rita raised her eyebrow as Milos shook his head with bemusement.

"Nah, not really." Alex chuckled.

With those words, the group split. Alex and Milos stayed on deck. Rita went below to help man the engine. Suzuhah decided to flit between the two groups, helping wherever he was needed.

Alex still wasn't sure what he sensed so suddenly this morning. Now, the inkling that faded so quickly was coming back and it worried him. He couldn't quite pinpoint what it was, or where it was coming from.

The engine started up with a low, billowing thrum and pushed them gently forward into the roiling sea. The feeling intensified, but that meant almost nothing as the pounding of thousands of gallons of water met his ears, a harmonious chorus of sounds and music.

"The path ahead should not be too arduous." The Aqua Wraith's words reverberated over the ship, catching Alex's attention. "Thou is more worried about the pass itself."

"How so?" Milos asked, twisting the wheel slightly as they curved around one of the pillars, avoiding a whirlpool hidden under the faint mist, gaze flitting from the compass to Alex to the Aqua Wraith.

"Thin rapids maneuver through the pass. If caught between, thou and thy ship shall be torn asunder," the Aqua Wraith said. "However, we need not worry until we reach the sheer cliffs themselves. Time is our ally here. There, one should only hope one arrives where one needs to be. Once through, we need not worry about the rapids, nor any dangers, for it is a straight path through to our destination."

Milos nodded as Alex groaned in dismay. That did not sound like fun in the slightest. He paused, feeling a strange note ringing through the air. The sudden feeling from this morning returned with a thrumming cry, pounding into his skull. The Aqua Wraith jerked as Alex stumbled, palms slamming into his ears as a wave slammed into the side of the ship, pushing them toward one of the swirling whirlpools.

"That feeling this morning, I should have realized. He found us."
Alex winced, wondering why it took so long and how he could have
missed anything but Ransel's arrival. Was the man that powerful? He
could almost feel the battle between the Aqua Wraith and Ransel. Waves
crashed into the ship as it swerved, cresting one of them before sliding
down, almost plunging into the surf.

Alex could spot Milos struggling with the wheel as Suzuhah
stumbled outside, holding onto the door frame tightly. "What the...?"
Suzuhah snapped his mouth shut, shock and horror slamming onto his
face. Alex whipped around and stared.

"Shit..." was all he could say as he quelled, gaze locked on the
twin walls of water cresting up on either side of them. Now he understood
why it took so long. He didn't even know someone could amass so much
water that quickly. Sheets of a solid mass of ocean rammed past the stone
pillars, some crumbling under the force, crashing to the roiling ocean far
below.

The wind stones felt feeble, compared to the might of what was
around them.

"Alex, can you split the water in front of us to get us into the
strait?" Milos spoke with a forced calmness that Alex could sense.

Alex jerked, spotting what he was talking about. The massive
cliff faces that were steadily getting closer were intimidating, even with
the ocean ready to sink them on either side.

"I don't have much choice," he called back, kneeling down on
one knee to stabilize himself as he closed his eyes, singing and listening
not paying attention to what he was saying. He could feel the boat jump,
shooting forward as the duel waves crested above, metric tons of water
ready to crash over them with a roar.

The sky darkened. The day stones were blotted out by the cold
water. Alex could feel it, the power singing through the waves, a separate
being from what he could grasp and something he had no hope of
contesting in his human form.

He didn't need to. He opened his eyes, staring ahead as the wind
stones roared with one final boost, the water practically parting before
them in a chorus of cries and calls.

The roaring ocean sang out in a wordless orchestra, crying for him to both stay put and run. His fingers clenched as the water below their boat sang out a single note.

Silence filled the air for a split second as darkness completely eclipsed the ship.

A howl from the wind stones cut through the silence, as water fell over them in heavy rain, soaking them to the bone as the waves heaved downward.

Light.

The light of the day stones shone out as the ship shot into the strait.

The great waves finally slammed down, an earthquake that sent Alex tumbling head over heels as the ship heaved. The stone walls caught the brunt, but a torrent flooded into the passage behind them.

Alex could feel the Aqua Wraith trying to control the ship in such a way as to catch it and ride it. Alex helped as best he could, grasping tightly onto the railing, legs and arms tangled with the wood as clashing sounds met his ears. The ship spun to the right, almost slamming into the wall before Alex wrenched the water back, turning them forward once more.

It was touch and go for longer than Alex would have liked. The walls were eerily close for his comfort as the initial wave pushed them down through the passage. With one final shove, he felt the strange song dissipate, the water free from outside influence.

Ransel must have given up.

The relief was short-lived as they scrambled to center the ship on the clashing water.

Finally, as the water began to dissipate, Alex let out a breath, slumping onto his back. The wind stones were now a dull thrum as a chorus of groans echoed over the ship. A faint creaking rang from below as the ship swayed—a normal sway, much to Alex's relief, and not the capsizing kind. Somehow, in the madness, they had managed to land their ship on the correct side of the passage, heading north. He could feel the battling currents, but they weren't anything he needed to worry about, the notes in sync with each other. At least he didn't have to deal with the ship slipping into the contrasting current, or the wall.

The sky was still hard to see, a thin strip high above with light stones cluttering the sides to help light the passage. The song of the water was once more wild and free, singing a calming and happy tune. He never thought he would feel so happy about that.

"Let's not do that again, please?" he couldn't help but whine.

"I concur," Milos said, his tone and voice exhausted.

Alex held no doubt he was barely keeping himself from copying Alex's pose, flat on the deck. He heard a sound from the doorway and tilted his head slightly to find Suzuhah holding the doorframe, having collapsed to his knees.

"Everything's still spinning," he complained, seeming to sway side to side more than the ship.

Milos grunted as a sound caught Alex's attention, something that must have been the voice pipe. "Rita, Ari, are you two all right?"

"Could be better." Rita's voice sounded just as drained, but a hint of amusement filled her voice. "So, what were we racing from this time? A monster?"

"Two waves that could drown the capital in seconds, separately."

Silence echoed from the other end.

"Shvite," she muttered, just barely heard through the pipes.

"Believe me, it was much worse up here." Milos shook his head, squeezing some water out of his clothes. Alex figured he should do the same, but was too exhausted at the moment to think about it. "Ari?"

"I'm fine, Master Milos. A little bruised and battered from the last bit, but otherwise all right. I'm going to check on Leon. He was in the storage room."

"Do that, then let me know of his status."

Alex pushed himself up into a sitting position, following Milos' example, his hair sticking to his skin from the sudden downpour felt strange. The salt on his lips, he could have done without. His throat was a little sore, but he felt a hint of pride. "That was something. I can't believe we made it."

Milos nodded, pausing slightly as he squeezed out his long hair, gazing at it with an odd expression before flipping it over his shoulder and glancing at the compass. "Seems like we're on track. Suzuhah, take over for now."

Suzuhah groaned, but didn't argue, seemingly having avoided the worst of the downpour. He hopped up to the wheel as Milos walked toward Alex. "You feeling all right?"

"I'm going to need to sleep for a week when we finally get there, but I'm fine." Alex pushed himself against the railing and winced as bruises protested at the movement. "I'll probably be bruised all over for just as long, but there's nothing broken."

Milos smirked in amusement before his smile dulled. "So, that was really him?"

Alex nodded, grimacing. "I felt it right before I saw the waves. I've never felt such a surge of power before, or such a harsh song. He wasn't holding anything back."

"He knew you would survive, due to what type of demon you are. Smart, and a little too dangerous for my liking." Milos shook his head.

"At least he won't follow us anymore, right?" Alex perked up, hoping Milos would agree. "I mean, I sensed his power fading near the end so he must have given up, right?"

The man stayed silent for a long time before finally shrugging. "I won't completely count him out, not when he still has all those demons at his beck and call. With that expenditure of power, he probably won't be in any shape to chase us farther. I don't think we'll have to worry about him any time soon."

Alex let out a long breath. "Thank gosh." He let his head rest on the railing as he peered out over the water. "I could do without meeting him again...ever."

Milos chuckled faintly at that, his footsteps moving away from Alex. "I cannot argue with that idea. I hope for our sakes you are right."

"Way to be an optimist."

"I'm being realistic." Milos shrugged.

Alex chuckled. "Yeah, I know." He pushed himself to his feet, peering around. "Still, this place is actually quite beautiful."

"Didn't know you were one for aesthetics."

"Not really." Alex shrugged, spotting some blue light stones glowing off to the left, sparkling over the water. "I can appreciate something like this after a pseudo near-death experience, that's all."

Milos paused, following his line of sight before nodding. "I guess, I can't argue. I always thought the Underlands held their own beauty. Of course, I never expected such a vast amount of land or sea down here." He peered up to the ceiling far above, a strange expression on his face. "It makes me wonder how the Overlands are supported with such a large expanse of the Underlands completely open like the ocean."

Alex opened his mouth to respond before realizing he wasn't sure what the actual answer was. He never thought about it. It was just a natural course of things. The Underlands and Overlands were intertwined, so of course they could coexist. It made sense in his head, but thinking it over and reminded of how fragile the earth was, how those waves knocked over great pillars of stone like they were nothing, it did make him wonder how it was possible.

His mind flitted to weeks ago when they were journeying to the capital. They fled through the mountains, water collapsing into the passages and cutting off the routes. Why didn't that happen above?

Alex followed Milos' gaze, the day stones gleaming brilliantly down at them. "I don't know. I figured it was because the earth was strong enough to support it, but there isn't much gap between the ceiling and the Overlands, is there?"

Milos shook his head, facing Alex. "No. When I came down here, I recall watching the descent. The earth wasn't as thick as I thought it would be."

Alex sat there for a while, unsure how to respond before letting out a sigh. "Well, that's something I don't want to think about right now. I'm still struggling to comprehend everything that's happened over the past few days. I could do without any more existential crises at the moment."

Milos chuckled, nodding. "All right, we won't worry about that." He turned his gaze down the winding passage, seemingly lost in thought. "After all, we're almost to our destination."

Alex nodded. They were, and he wasn't sure how he felt about it. Was he excited to finally make it and find his mother? Was he angry?

Hurt? What was he feeling? He shook his head. He had a feeling he would know when he got there.

He heard movement and glanced over toward the doorway to see Ari stepping out. One arm was bandaged, but she seemed otherwise unharmed. "Master Milos."

Milos inspected her for a moment before nodding. "Good. Rita treated you and Leon?"

"He is all right. He sprained his wrist a little, but is otherwise fit."

"Good, if Rita hasn't bandaged him up, have her. If she already has or after she checks on him, have him figure out what needs to be repaired and let me know. He is not to move or repair anything himself."

Ari bowed before heading inside.

Alex smiled faintly. "You do care for them, and us, for that matter."

Milos stared after the doorway before facing Alex. "I never said otherwise."

"No, but you never struck me as the type to show it." Alex smiled warmly. "Now you show it almost all the time. It's nice to see that side of you a bit, you know?"

"Yeah, I can't argue there." Suzuhah piped up from the wheel, leaning over slightly. "If you were any other demon hunter, or more like an Alertian, for that matter, you would have skewered me where I stood, no matter what Alex here said. I'm grateful you didn't."

Milos twitched slightly at those words before speaking. "I wondered if it would be worth it."

Suzuhah snorted. "Harsh, but true." He then grinned. "Hey, there's no harm in lightening up a little bit. Heck, if you were still a full demon hunter like most of those idiots, everyone here would have been dead. After all, the Aqua Wraith is no joke when it comes to those things, especially since she was killed by one."

"How did you hear of that?" Alex blinked.

Suzuhah shrugged. "You really should read more of that diary you found when you get the chance, it did a terrible job portraying me, or my ancestor, but for the most part, it's fairly accurate."

Alex frowned, trying to recall what he was talking about, before snapping his fingers, remembering the little diary he and Rita found earlier in the map room. "I completely forgot about that."

"Figured." Suzuhah moved back to adjust the wheel once more. "Yeah, simple answer is that long ago, she was killed by a demon hunter and so isn't too fond of them. The fact that she's helping you all, with an Alertian on board, says a lot." He smiled brightly as he glanced to Milos. "Good thing you're able to rein in that side of you. Could be a lot worse if you were full Alertian all the time."

Milos twitched again, his hair slipping over his shoulder as he bent his head downward.

"Right." Milos turned, moving away. "Well, I'll be checking on the status of the rest of the ship. Let me know when we are close to the refuge."

Alex watched him go, frowning slightly before shaking his head. Milos was probably fine, just a little tired after everything that happened lately.

"Hm..." Suzuhah hummed quietly, staring after him. "I wonder if that was the right thing to say."

Alex shrugged. "Who knows? It's Milos. He'll be fine." Alex's thoughts drifted to Ari's words from long ago, to watch Milos. Alex knew Milos was struggling with his Alertian status, but he figured the man decided to give up his demon hunting.

However, thinking back on it, Milos never said he would. He didn't answer when Alex asked what he would do when they arrived at the refugee camp and he was growing more distracted, the closer they got.

He hoped, for all of their sakes, that Milos wouldn't make a rash decision.

Chapter Thirty-two

Milos slammed his fist into the table, gritting his teeth as he tried to reconcile his swirling emotions. He knew Suzuhah hadn't meant any harm in his words. He knew they were intended to console him. After all, they were still alive because he wasn't what they expected him to be, wasn't some hunter who killed on sight, like most of his kind.

What was he supposed to do with that? The thin strands of blond hair, tangled with his signifier, caught his gaze and he stared. He was an Alertian, he was *supposed* to be an Alertian. It was in his blood, his very being. He didn't have a choice in the matter.

So why did it hurt so much?

When he stared up at the walls of water, unable to do a thing, when he needed Suzuha's help to escape the Yuki-onna and the demon king—who he shouldn't have been running from in the first place—when he was injured by a simple parasitic plant...Alex himself. Everything that had happened over the past few weeks, or months, he supposed, finally hit him. Sure, he'd dealt with the half-demons in the lab, but that didn't mean much in the long run. They were weak. Experiments, basically already dead. He ignored it earlier, thinking he was content with the situation, but as a demon hunter, he was a disgrace. What demon hunter didn't kill demons? What *Alertian* didn't track down and kill demons? No matter whether they were half-demon experiments or not.

He pushed away from the table, stumbling to the stairwell and downstairs, away from Alex and Suzuhah. He knew Rita was still in the engine room, probably with the Aqua Wraith and he could hear both Leon and Ari in the storage room, fixing it up.

Which meant he had time to himself. He headed to the men's room and took a seat on the bed, door firmly closed shut. His gaze drifted toward the window as water lapped outside, glowing faintly with the gleam of the light stones.

The refuge would be his final chance. His chance to prove to himself that he was an Alertian through and through. Yet, what could he do? He was no match for Ransel, as Alex called him, or the Yuki-onna. He was dulled, a weakened blade, one that could only cut through already damaged half-demons.

Much like if Leon were in another's hands, especially with his only wrist sprained, he would be dead. As an Alertian, being weak was a death sentence.

He couldn't stand the thought. It hadn't hit him till now, but he had changed since coming down here. These lands had changed him and he wasn't sure if it was actually for the better. He couldn't be weak. He couldn't be seen as something other than an Alertian. He couldn't be seen the way Suzuhah and Alex saw him.

He let his head fall into the palms of his hands, his body shaking with indecision. He didn't know what to do, where to go or even what he was supposed to be feeling.

He was so close, and yet so incredibly far away. He could feel desperation clawing through his veins, a hopeless battle.

Was this how Ransel felt? This uncertainty? A desperation that made people do things they never thought they would do?

Was he going to be like Ransel?

How could he not? He didn't have a choice. He never had a choice to begin with. His thoughts stilled.

Right. That was right. He was an Alertian. He was a being created to kill demons, nothing more. His goal was to obtain the head of the child of Satan. The demons in the refuge would be bound to have those answers, and if not, all their heads would suffice.

As the Aqua Wraith said, an Alertian was always an Alertian; their blade always came back sharp as steel.

He had to remember that. He was nothing more than a weapon.

A weapon to kill a creature like Alex...like his mother.

Nothing more, and nothing less.

He heard a faint sigh. "Child, that was not what I meant so long ago. Nor what I wished," a quiet whisper echoed over the room before the gentle sound of water disappeared. What did that matter?

The Aqua Wraith wouldn't do anything now, couldn't. She was dead and gone. He was a fool for having thought she could figure out who he was.

No, he found himself worrying little for the Aqua Wraith's departure.

No matter how much his mind demanded otherwise.

A while later, movement echoed from above and cries of delight met Milos' ears. He straightened his clothes, retying his hair and adjusting his blade before standing up and heading out the door. He moved toward the staircase, spotting Rita as she faced him.

She recoiled, hesitant. "Hey, Milos? Are you all right?"

Milos tilted his head slightly, reminding himself that it would be prudent if the others didn't realize what needed to be done. "I am fine, Rita." He turned, heading up the stairs.

"Oh, hell no, you lout. You are *not*."

Milos stopped on the stairwell, his mind arguing before he peered over his shoulder, a faint smile on his lips that he tried to make as genuine as possible. Considering the way Rita paused, he must have succeeded. "Really, I'm not lying. I think you need to get your ears checked."

As soon as Rita was no longer in his line of sight, his smile disappeared in a flash as he continued up the stairs. He felt calm, his thoughts no longer swirling in his head. After all, he was an Alertian; he had no reason to get involved if he could avoid it. It was what he was always taught. How could he forget? How could he let himself forget?

He just needed to do his job and be done with it.

He stepped out the doorway, Rita a few steps behind. She glanced at him briefly before peering ahead. Suzuhah was still at the wheel, shielding his gaze just as the ship broke out of the pass. Ari and Leon were on either side of the ship, watching in awe. Alex was at the front, leaning over the bow. "There it is!" His words echoed with the warmth of a smile.

Demon...

Milos stayed his hand. No, the one before him was human, not demon. He moved his gaze past Alex as they broke out of the massive fortress of stone.

A large expanse of land met their gaze, a brilliant and beautiful kaleidoscope of colors. White sands and intertwining pieces of decorative stone and coral glittered in the day stones' light. A faint wisp of air filtered through, indicating they were near a vent as light gleamed over the land and water. A distance away from the sands and up a shallow cliffside were the first few intricate and beautifully designed homes that put most of the Underland homes to shame.

A stone staircase wove to a set of open gates, an arc beckoning them closer.

A pseudo-paradise, as most would call it.

One he had to destroy. It was his duty, as an Alertian and as someone who needed to recover from his failures.

"We're here." Rita's voice was breathy with wonder as Suzuhah smiled.

"Yeah, this place is amazing every time I come. The last remains of the demonic culture."

"Where my mom is..." Alex's voice reached them as he pulled back from the bow, a bit more subdued. "We made it."

Milos peered past him as the wind stones slowly decelerated with the Aqua Wraith's will. They were aiming for a set of docks set up to one side.

Milos stared at them without emotion. He couldn't have emotion. He wouldn't let himself have emotion.

He couldn't be dulled. Not now.

He would prove himself. He would complete his duty or die trying.

That was all he was for, after all.

He had no choice in the matter...no freedom to decide.

"We're here," Alex spoke quietly. "We're finally safe." He smiled back, warm and bright. "It took a lot to get to this point, I didn't expect it to take this long, or for these oceans to be this wide, but we finally arrived." His expression was determined as he returned his attention onto the horizon. "Now I'm going to meet my mom and find out the truth. I know she's here. I can feel it."

Milos didn't doubt he could. After all, the abundance of magic and *life* in this place was jaw-dropping.

He only wished he didn't have to.

He closed his eyes. His mind and heart screamed at him.

With one final shove, he cut them off, letting his body relax and mind rest.

They had finished one journey...they had made it to their destination.

Yet, he still had work to do. No matter what emotions kept popping up, he just needed to eliminate them. He couldn't let them hold him back now, not when he was so close to completing his objective, his duty.

He felt that wave of calm wash over him once more. The instinct he had felt only twice before.

The first time he had tried to kill Alex.

And the second time he *did* kill those half-demons.

This time, however, he wasn't going to let his emotions sway him. He wouldn't let Alex or Rita stop him. He couldn't.

Not until he was free...free of having to choose when he didn't have a choice.

Free from this hell he now found himself in as the demonic energy swirled around him, edging him forward, his blood singing.

He smiled thinly as his grip tightened on his sword hilt, pushing it down slightly. "We certainly made it."

Alex's light chuckle, filled with warmth, Rita's bemused hum, Suzuhah's jaunty tune. It all hung in the air around him. The slaves held a certain awe and happiness to them.

Yet, he was detached from it. Distant.

He wished, so desperately, that he could return to that, join them in their delight.

That thought was just as roughly squashed down.

After all, why should a weapon have the freedom to desire? The freedom to laugh?

He tilted his head up as the ship gently moved closer to the shore, closer to their final destination as a spark of power glimmered on the horizon.

Why should he—a failure of an Alertian—have any freedom at all? This wasn't his world, this peace and laughter, this warmth. He couldn't have it, no matter how much he wished for it.

So, he would get rid of it, finally cut it off. This was the end.

No matter how much his heart screamed otherwise...

Alex's emotions were a jumbled mess and he could admit it, but foremost, the emotion he felt was relief, closely followed by joy. They finally made it and, now, he could sense...

Wait...

He froze, a gentle feeling flitting through his veins. His demonic side cried out, a plaintive call, but why?

He spotted something shooting into the air from the island, a black dot on the horizon.

He took a startled step back as his veins sang in joy, though his mind was confused.

He heard the chink of a blade and glanced back to see Milos in an offensive stance, hilt in hand. Rita was near her satchel, watching the same thing with a tense silence.

"What is that?" she choked out.

Alex shook his head as he turned toward the approaching figure. Its form was familiar and he wasn't sure why.

With a sudden burst of air which he could feel from the deck of the ship, the figure soared past, leathery wings and whipping tail flicking past the ship's side before curving up into the sky to hover above.

Alex froze. It was that demon. The same one from home. He opened and closed his mouth, staring into the eyes of the creature before him. The creature flapped its wings once, shock flitting onto its face.

Alex found himself taking a step forward, words leaving his lips before he thought about what he was saying, "Is that you? Is that really you?"

The figure hovered, as if hesitant. He heard a shink and jerked. "Milos," he called, spotting his friend, sword almost completely out of its sheath. Milos hesitated, a strange expression on his face as Rita jerked, startled. "Don't! This is..."

Milos stared at Alex for a moment before he turned. Alex reached out to stop him, but needn't have bothered as Rita grasped Milos' upper arm, almost spinning him around with a furrowed brow. She whispered something he didn't catch before glancing back at Alex. She wore a broad but sad smile. Ari, who shifted closer to Milos, had a warm smile on her own face, not large, but gentle. Leon just seemed slightly amused, a slight quirk of the lip. Even Suzuhah was watching in a quiet awe.

Milos...Alex wasn't sure what to make of Milos, whose expression was now guarded and unreadable. He would have to talk to him later, if he could. While he was worried about his friend, he turned back toward the figure, somewhat surprised it was still there. Actually, no, he wasn't that surprised. "It is you."

The creature flapped once more, claws curling in and out as if in indecision. A moment later, a faint smile crossed the creature's lips as it swooped forward and dropped.

Alex took a startled step back, watching in awe as the wings disappeared. Long black hair billowed over thin shoulders and, with a softness that completely contradicted the earlier plummet, a familiar woman landed on the deck, her green dress settling around her petite frame.

Warm brown eyes met his and then he found himself in a familiar embrace, though who embraced whom, he wasn't sure about.

"Mother? It really is you."

"Alex, my little angel. I'm so sorry." He could feel his mother trembling in his arms as she held him close. "I wanted so badly to see you again, but..." She took a deep breath and pulled away, leaving her hands resting on his shoulders, that familiar soft smile clear on her face. "I'm so glad to see you alive. I'm so proud of you."

"So, that demon..."

Alex wasn't sure what to say, what to feel, it was the first words to come from his lips. His mother shook her head, pulling him close once more, one hand wrapping around his head and the other around his back.

"We have a lot to talk about, but first, let me just hold you for a minute, okay?"

Alex stiffened at the tight hold before relaxing. He did have a lot of questions, but right now, being in his mother's embrace, he could hold off asking for a little while longer.

For a brief moment, he wondered what the others thought. He peered over his mother's shoulder to see that not much had changed, Rita must have let go of Milos at some point, a contemplative, but content expression curling over her face. Milos was leaning against the doorway, arms crossed and still just as hard to read. Alex tightened his grip for a moment on his mother as a feeling of worry trilled through his veins at the sight of Milos, before forcing himself to relax.

It was Milos. That's just how he was. They were safe now, they had made it. To be honest, as tumultuous as his thoughts were, it was good to finally find his mother again and see she was alive and well. It was good to see all of them were there and safe. He missed this.

"I missed you." The words came out as he closed his eyes, resting against her shoulder blade.

She hummed quietly, a soft and gentle tune. "I know, my little angel. I'm sorry."

Alex decided to leave it at that for now. He would worry about what to do or say later. For this moment, he would relish in the peace and quiet of the situation and be grateful no one was interrupting.

It was good to finally be back with his mother again in a place that was safe and free.

He definitely had a lot of explaining to do, on both sides of things.

He could only hope his mother would accept Milos, Rita and the others...and that Milos wouldn't hurt his mother.

That was for future Alex to worry about. Right now, in this moment, he was just that lost little boy who had finally found what he was looking for. He would relish this for as long as he was able to.

About the Author

Julie Boglisch is a thrice-published twenty-seven-year-old who thoroughly enjoys a good book, a good cup of tea and a good video game to play in her spare time. A graduate of Gordon College, she double majored in Communication Arts and Music. Working the odd job to maintain her livelihood, she knows a lot about rolling with the punches and is not afraid of stepping forward into the unknown.

Demon's Song
Requiem of Stone Book One

Alex always wished to see the Overlands, a place of sunshine and freedom. However, as a slave in the far corners of the Underlands, it was all but a dream. That is, until he's framed for murder and is forced to flee during a demon attack.

Searching for the answers to why he was framed and seeking a chance at the fleeting freedom he's always dreamed about, he journeys to the capital, meeting friend and foe along the way. But the Underlands are both beautiful and dangerous. Having a demon hunter on his tail and a witch whose sole desire is to become the high Seer around him, he's in for quite the journey.

Chapter One

Alex stared out over the crystal-clear water. Thin streams cascaded from the rocks to one side, falling into the pool that shone with the light from the moss. The rock felt scratchy against his bare feet and his hands were bruised from scrabbling up the steep slope that led to this little cave, but it was worth it. He breathed in the smell of the water and knelt down, delicately dipping one hand. He pulled his hand up, watching the water flow between his fingers.

Water such as this was such a rare thing to find in the Underlands, so pure and untainted. Of course, the rivers were clean, but this, this gentle sparkle and warm glow was just something else. He turned his head up to the ceiling where the moss glowed softly. He wondered if there was water like this in the Overlands? That mythical place of sunlight... Would he have a chance to go there someday? No...he knew. With every fiber of his being, he knew it was impossible. After all, he couldn't leave these lands...

Even so, he reached his hand up, touching the cool moss as his thoughts wavered. He wanted to see it, to see what it was like above the stone. Sunlight, blue skies, meadows...

Alex's hand dropped to his side as he toed the cold water with one foot. He loved the feel of the water on his skin, how it just flowed over in gentle waves, just like he imagined an ocean would. It helped calm his thoughts.

He sighed. For some reason today, it only made him feel a bit depressed. He shook his head before turning away from the spring. He glanced out the cave entrance and quietly cursed. The day stones were starting to wane. He needed to get home soon or his mother would have his hide. He peered down the steep slope, trying to find a safe path down. After all, this was only his third or fourth time here. He never used the same path so he didn't know the best way down. The cave was high up, hidden by the curve of the ceiling. He could clearly see one of the day stones, its brilliant yellow white light, beaming down, even as it slowly faded into the blue of the night stone right next to it. If he reached up, he could touch the top of the ceiling. That didn't mean much though, considering the ceiling curved downward, dipping starkly toward his spot.

It made sense. It was near the edge of the Underlands, after all, buried deep underground beneath the stone and earth. He shook his head and focused on finding a path safely down. To his relief, he managed to find the path he used to get up this time and scurried down, just barely avoiding sharp rocks. His skin was already scratched from the climb up and was only made worse as he barreled down the hill. In the distance, he could see his home, the owner of which was the Grand Duke of Liliay. Past that, he could see a road, which stretched to a town in the distance. Off to the other side was a river, the only indication of it being water, being the thin blue band seen against the stark gray.

The slope eased up until he was once more on flat land. He raced ahead, dodging through the tall rocky outgrowths that resembled a forest, something that existed on either side of the house, blocking it from intruders on all sides except from the town.

At least, that was what his mother called the rocky outgrowths, but she was told that by her mother so who knows?

He took a sharp corner around one particularly big outcropping and came upon a large, but squat home, being only about two stories. The dirt path stood on his right, weaving out of sight. He could almost see the set of gates, blocking the way in. He turned toward the home, hurrying up to the delicate entranceway. It held a front porch with wood double doors and wide windows, set with weak light stones. He could see Riviera working on the house, repairing parts of it that had rotted away and replacing what he couldn't fix with stone. He was standing on a stone ladder, the duel sides stopping it from pushing into the rotting wood. Alex slowed down, wincing as the pain from his sore feet was made known to him now that he was stopped.

"Yo, Alex. Good to see you back!" Riviera called down, as he continued hammering the board into place, his signifying wrist chain jangling with a steady clacking sound. It was thick and looked heavy.

"Watch what you're doing," Alex called up right as Riviera yelped, barely avoiding smashing the hammer into his hand.

He grinned sheepishly. "Well, yes... Anyway, better get inside. It's late."

"I know." Alex waved him off as he stepped up to the doorway, ignoring the white flowers decorating either side of the entrance, the only other form of life and the only flower that somehow managed to survive in the Underlands. He pushed the door open as slow as possible, peering around the doorframe.

The inside was quiet, barely a light on in the house. He opened the door more and almost cried out as the Grand Duke of Liliay stepped from the shadow of the doorway with a 'boo.'

"Duke..."

The Duke frowned and Alex quickly adjusted his wording. "Grandpa!"

Alex placed a hand on his chest to catch his breath as the Grand Du...Grandpa gave a hearty laugh with great booming chuckles. He was fit for his age, but the wrinkles and liver spots were quite visible on his skin. Wispy white hair was partially slicked back and a wide smile with surprising white teeth shone as brightly as the pale skin of an Underlander. His signifier, a delicately made earring shaped in the form of a pair of wings, swung gently from his right ear as he turned and flicked on the lights. It was pretty, the signifier his grandfather had. It was carved of the finest metals, completely unlike the clunky signifier of a slave like Riviera and himself. After all, the duke's signifier was part of the upper class, a sign he was of a higher caliber then those bound by wrist or sometimes neck chains made of cold harsh metal. He looked down at his wrists. He heard his grandfather step down the hallway and turned his head up.

Alex watched as the stones heated up like the rising of the day stones, slow yet sure, until they were glowing with a soft ruby color.

"Lad, that's what you get for worrying an old man and your poor mother. Don't you know what time it is?" he asked, quieting his chuckles into a knowing look as he turned to face Alex. Alex gave a sheepish grin as he shrugged, toeing the rug.

Grandpa sighed and shook his head before gesturing. "Well come on, son, come inside. Your mother's making dinner as we speak."

Alex groaned.

"Oh, don't be like that! You know she tries her best. Plus, if you got home before all the day stones died for the day, you would have had a chance to make something yourself," Grandpa chided, his tone lighthearted. Alex sighed, mentally agreeing with the assessment. It was partially his fault for staying out so late. "Now hurry on into the kitchen, I will see you two when dinner's ready."

Alex nodded as Grandpa walked off. Alex watched him go. The foyer was now lit bright enough to showcase the splendid items of porcelain and jewels. A picture frame sat over a mantelpiece, front and center.

He recalled his mom and, vaguely, his dad both eyeing it oddly when he was growing up. He personally didn't mind the picture. It showed a knight holding the head of a grotesque creature in the sign of victory, sword gleaming in what Alex could only deduce was sunlight. Green could be seen as far as the eye could see in the picture and Alex always wondered if that was mostly what the Overlands consisted of, sunlight and green. What an amazing sight it must be...

He shook himself from his thoughts, trying to convince himself, as usual, that there was no way he would be able to go there, no matter how much he dreamed of it. He hurried to the left toward one of the two hallways. Traversing the long halls, he finally arrived in a room where the distinctive smell of burning came from. He winced before he opened the door and stepped inside.

Close to the stove was his mother, running around in a frenzy. Her frazzled expression was only amplified when smoke billowed out of the stove when she opened it.

Alex shook his head as his mother gave a quiet whine. He grabbed the nearby extinguisher and liberally spread the gunk that came out of it onto the fire. Slowly, it died and he stopped, letting the last of it dribble to the floor as he sent his mom an exasperated look.

"Oh, hey, honey..." she said somewhat sheepishly, though confusion still sat on her face. "I could have sworn I set it right this time. Four hours and fifty minutes at one hundred and twenty-five degrees."

"Mom, did you check to see which was time and which was temperature?" Alex deadpanned.

His mother looked at him like he had multiple heads before she picked up a surprisingly unscathed box and looked at it. She pointed and said, "Yeah. It says right... here..."

She stopped before glancing guiltily at Alex. Alex resisted sighing as he gave his mother another deadpan expression. "Let me guess, you were supposed to set it at four hundred and fifty degrees for one hour and twenty five minutes."

"Well, that's all in the past. I made some sandwiches earlier, and I only nicked myself a few times this time."

"Why...Mother...are you in the kitchen again?"

"Because Agatha called in sick and you know how my lor..." She stopped before shaking her head and continuing, "Callen likes to make sure his people are okay. She's on bed rest until she feels better and the others have other priorities."

Alex shook his head, wondering about that. The others would have come running to stop his mother from entering the kitchen. Alex stepped over to the cold storage. An ice stone sat in the corner, cooling the small cubby considerably. He looked around at the shelves before spotting the plate of sandwiches. He grabbed one after pulling off the paper wrapping and stepped out. He bit into it.

Damn. How was it she was so bad at the directions, but could make something taste so good?

"Hey, Alex, honey?"

"Hm?" He asked around a mouthful of sandwich.

He swallowed as he turned to his mother, who was already cleaning up the place.

Her black hair fell in sheets around her thin shoulders. The green dress she wore almost every day showed a petite figure. She had long fingers and wide brown eyes that seemed to look at everything with a type of naivete.

He knew his mother was nowhere near naive though, even as she turned, exposing the scar on her neck and the thin chains around her wrists. He shivered as he remembered one story she told him about her childhood, when she talked about it.

It happened long ago, before Alex was even born. Supposedly, she was seen as a rare specimen. Alex didn't ask why. Mother never explained, but that made it so she was often feared. In this particular instance, she'd just gotten through a...beating, she phrased it.

Alex had a sinking suspicion she meant something else, but didn't interrupt as she continued to explain. It was around that time she met Father, they fell in love at first sight, but...fate was cruel. Father was promptly sold, punished for grabbing her affection and she was secluded, unable to even leave her room.

Thankfully, after that, the duke, who managed to buy Father not long after that initial exchange, found her and bought her off her original owner.

Still, all the things she left out...it sent chills up his spine. After, she insisted he knew how lucky they were to end up working here, under the Grand Duke. Alex glanced toward her wrists, watching the chains shift against her skin, scars crisscrossing thinly across her flesh, just like it did around her neck.

In comparison, his skin was practically unblemished. He knew, from the conversations with the others, he was qualified as a slave, property of the duke. All he could recall was the duke caring for him like a parent would.

He pulled himself from his thoughts as his mother huffed and put her hands on her hips. "You weren't listening to me again, were you?"

"That depends," Alex replied, looking toward the stove.

His mother let out a long sigh and dropped her hands. "Alex..." She shook her head and looked him in the eye. "I heard that the Martinets are coming through soon, so please stay in the house, okay? You don't wear your signifying wrist chains anymore."

Alex glanced at his wrist, vaguely remembering the cold bite of the chains. He couldn't remember when they came off, but he knew he was still very young. It was only thanks to the Duke he got them off, and his mother. For some reason his mother fought with a vicious tenacity to have him no longer wear them, even though he was given them by the Martinets of the time.

Once the Martinets left, the duke conceded very quickly, supposedly having wanted to do that anyway. Still, it meant he had to avoid Martinets like the plague.

Why did his mother insist on his being removed again? Part of him didn't mind, considering how harsh, clunky and overbearing they were. Still, he vaguely wondered where they were now.

His thoughts were quickly returned to the present when his mother continued, "Both the duke and you could end up in trouble. So, don't make it hard on him. The Capitol is already giving him a hard time for not trading in his old slaves for new ones. We don't want to make it worse."

Alex hesitated. He was one of the only ones that worked for the duke that didn't have the signifiers. For some reason, everyone else was so used to it, they felt weird without them. Alex couldn't fathom why.

Still, she took his silence as acceptance, relief clear in her voice as she thanked him. "Now get to bed, it's late."

"Yeah, yeah." Alex waved, muttering under his breath as he walked toward the doorway.

"And sorry about not having dinner ready for you. I need to bring what I can to the others."

Alex nodded, knowing how busy his mother was. Even with her botched cooking, she did have to feed the duke and the other slaves. He also knew the duke planned to meet them at dinner, but Alex doubted there would be enough food if he went, so he stuck with the sandwich. His mother sent him a kiss, which he promptly looked away from, before calling another good night. Alex let the door swing shut and climbed up the stairs, chewing on the last of his sandwich.

He would have to watch out for those Martinets. From the stories he heard from the older slaves, it wasn't pretty to be caught by them. In all honesty, he would be seen as free bait, considering he no longer held a chain tag.

Maybe he should stay in the house the next few days...

He shook his head and stepped into his bedroom. It wasn't big by any stretch of the imagination, but it was cozy. A bed was set off against a small window with a stand next to it made of stone. On top of the stone side table was a simple, yet elegantly designed light stone. He wasn't sure what the history was behind the stone, since he never was able to go into school or anything. From what he'd gathered from the books in his grandfather's library, they were leftovers from the age of the demons, a race very similar to humans, long since thought to be extinct.

Alex gently touched the light stone, feeling it pulse slightly under his fingers. To him, they felt almost alive in a way that was different from the normal everyday stone that surrounded him and everyone else in the Underlands. He closed his eyes, feeling the slight pulsing of the light stone. He wondered what it was like above. What did a sky look like? The sea? He wasn't even sure he could even imagine, what with being confined to the manor his whole life.

He knew he was luckier than many people. He couldn't deny the fact. Even so, it felt like he was just there, another person to live his life and die.

He didn't want that.

He opened his eyes and pulled his hand away from the light stone and turned to his bed. He fell onto it and curled into himself. It was a pipe dream, he knew. There was no escaping the Underlands, even more so for those seen as slaves.

Yes, he didn't have the mark, or the chains like he once did, but that didn't make a difference down here. Unless you were known, unless you were part of a family, an elite, then you were nothing more than a piece of property. His hand slammed into the bed, feeling the mattress give under his hit. After all, a signifier, the only indication of where you lay, was created upon birth. The only signifier he ever had were chains with no meaning, something his mother threw away for him years ago, almost to the point where he couldn't even remember what they were. Yet he couldn't get a new set, even if he wanted to, after all, the census had him qualified as a slave, even now.

Why was he even thinking this? These thoughts never got him anywhere and only ever made him more upset.

Still, even though he knew how hopeless it was, he couldn't seem to give up, he would see the Overlands, just once. He let out a sigh and uncurled his fists. He would think on this tomorrow. He needed to get some sleep tonight, especially if the Martinets were coming. He'd need all the rest he could get.

Other books by Julie Boglisch
at
Rogue Phoenix Press

Epidemic
The Elifer Chronicles Book One

It has been forty years since America closed its borders and separated from the world following the Vietnam War. In the ensuing years, the country has developed in incredible ways, or at least, that is what Maxwell and Karina, a set of twins from a community deep in the forests of New England, have been told all their lives. In a town surrounded by larger than life trees and crags, they didn't have a reason to believe otherwise.

That belief is put to the test when they find their house ransacked, their mother missing, and their only chance to live is outside of the barriers they've grown used to. Barriers... that they never realized existed.

Retrieval
The Elifer Chronicles Book Two

Maxwell and Karina, twins who are the cure to a disease which is ravaging the country, find themselves journeying to the distant locale of Collern City in search of their missing mother. Meeting strange allies and dealing with dangerous enemies, they must learn to navigate the treacherous streets and discover more about what is going on behind the scenes in both the gated community and outside of it.

Meanwhile, their guardian and friend, Lex, struggles to deal with his family's desires. He finds himself caught between his own wish to flee his home, never to return. and the wish of his brother, Caym, who desperately wants him to stay.

FOR THE FULL INVENTORY
OF QUALITY BOOKS:
http://www.roguephoenixpress.com

Rogue Phoenix Press
Representing Excellence in Publishing

**Quality trade paperbacks and downloads
in multiple formats,
in genres ranging from historical to contemporary romance, mystery and
science fiction.
Visit the website then bookmark it.
We add new titles each month!**

www.ingramcontent.com/pod-product-compliance
Lightning Source LLC
Chambersburg PA
CBHW051058030726
47504CB00006B/1680